THRAXAS

MARTIN SCOTT

THRAXAS

Thraxas copyright © 1999 by Martin Scott. *Thraxas and the Warrior Monks* © 1999 by Martin Scott.

A Baen Book

Baen Publishing Enterprises
P.O. Box 1403
Riverdale, NY 10471
www.baen.com

ISBN: 0-7434-7152-0

Cover art by Monte Moore

First U.S printing, September 2003

Distributed by Simon & Schuster
1230 Avenue of the Americas
New York, NY 10020

Typeset by Bell Road Press, Sherwood, OR
Production by Windhaven Press, Auburn, NH
Printed in the United States of America

AXE ME NO QUESTIONS

I strap on my sword. Makri wears both her swords, more or less hidden under her cloak, and slips a long knife into each of her boots. As usual, she is not entirely comfortable without her axe, but it's too conspicuous. She tends to get stopped and questioned, which is inconvenient when we're on a case.

She's still grumbling as we depart. "You never know when you'll need your axe. Once, in the slave pits, I was fighting four Orcs and my first sword broke, my other sword got stuck in the second Orc, and when I stabbed the last one, my knife blade broke. So, right then, when I didn't have a weapon, they threw in this enormous Troll carrying a club the size of a Human. So that just goes to show."

"Goes to show what?" I ask.

"That you should never be without your axe."

"We'll just have to hope we don't meet a giant Troll. Did you kill the Troll with your bare hands?"

"No. I vaulted up the wall to the Orc Lord's gallery. His chief bodyguard ran in front of me so I took his sword off him, stabbed him with it, and leaped back into the arena. The Troll was confused and I was able to hack him to pieces. Then the Orc Lord's bodyguards leaped down into the arena, all eight of them. It was a pretty close thing for a while, but I managed to pick up another sword and once I had one in each hand, I just mowed them down. The crowd went berserk. I had the longest standing ovation ever granted to a gladiator."

"Is that story true? Or are you just practising for your speech at the rhetoric class?"

"Of course it's true. You think I can't defeat thirteen Orcs and a Troll? Now you mention it, though, it would make a good speech."

"What subject are you meant to be talking about?"

"Living peacefully in a violent world."

Contents

THRAXAS

Chapter One

Turai is a magical city. From the docks at Twelve Seas to Moon Eclipse Park, from the stinking slums to the Imperial Palace, a visitor can find all manner of amazing persons, astonishing items and unique services. You can get drunk and swap tales with Barbarian mercenaries in the dockside taverns, watch musicians, tumblers and jugglers in the streets, dally with whores in Kushni, transact business with visiting Elves in Golden Crescent, consult a Sorcerer in Truth is Beauty Lane, gamble on chariots and gladiators at the Stadium Superbius, hire an Assassin, eat, drink, be merry and consult an apothecary for your hangover. If you find a translator you can talk to the dolphins in the bay. If you're still in need of fresh experiences after all that, you could go and see the new dragon in the King's zoo.

If you have a problem, and you don't have much money, you can even hire me. My name is Thraxas. I've done all of the things mentioned above. Apart from

the King's new dragon. I haven't seen that. I don't feel
the urge. I saw enough dragons in the last Orc Wars.

I am forty-three, overweight, without ambition, and
prone to prolonged bouts of drinking. The sign on my
door mentions the word Sorcerer but my powers are
of the lowest grade, mere tricks compared to the skills
of Turai's greatest. I am in fact a Private Investigator.
Cheapest Sorcerous Investigator in the whole magical
city of Turai.

When the situation is bad and the Civil Guard won't
help, you can come to me. When what you really need
is a powerful Sorcerer but if you can't afford to hire
one, come to me. When an Assassin is on your tail and
you want someone to serve as cannon fodder, come to
me. If the city Consul isn't interested in your case and
you've been ejected from the offices of the high-class
Investigators uptown, I'm your man. Whatever people's
problems are, when they've exhausted all other avenues
and can't afford anything better, they come to me.
Sometimes I'm able to help them. Sometimes not.
Either way my finances never improve.

I used to work at the Imperial Palace. I was a Senior
Investigator with Palace Security but I drank myself
out of the job. That was a long time ago. No one there
is much pleased to see me these days.

I live in two rooms above the Avenging Axe, a
dockside tavern run by Gurd, an ageing northern
Barbarian who used to fight for Turai as a mercenary. He was a good fighter. So was I. We fought
alongside each other on many occasions, but we were
a lot younger then. It's a lousy place to live but I
can't afford anything better. There are no women in
my life, unless you count Makri, who works as a
barmaid downstairs and sometimes acts as my assis-
tant. Makri, a strange bastard mix of Human, Elf and
Orc, is a handy woman with a sword, and even the

drunken lechers who frequent Gurd's tavern know better than to abuse her.

As far as I know, Makri has no romantic attachments, though I've caught her a few times looking wistfully at some of the tall handsome Elves who occasionally pass through here on their way from the docks to Golden Crescent. No chance with them however. Makri's mongrel breeding makes her a social outcast practically everywhere. A pure-bred Elf wouldn't look at her twice, for all her youth and beauty.

I have no desire for any personal involvements, not since my wife ran off to the Fairy Glade with a Sorcerer's Apprentice half my age. Enough to put any man off. I wouldn't mind a client though. Funds are low and Gurd the Barbarian never likes it when his rent is late.

The Palace should hire me to find the missing Red Elvish Cloth. That's a big story in Turai just now, though they tried to keep it quiet. Red Elvish Cloth is more valuable than gold. I'd be in for a big reward if I found it. Unfortunately no one wants me. Palace Security and the Civil Guard are both on the case, and express every confidence that they'll locate it soon. I have every confidence they won't. Whoever was smart enough to hijack a load of heavily guarded Red Elvish Cloth on its way to the city is smart enough to hide it from the Guard.

Chapter Two

———◆———

Early spring in Turai is temperate and pleasant, but brief. The long summer and autumn are unbearably hot. Every winter it rains continually for thirty days and thirty nights. After that it freezes so cold that beggars die in the streets. Which is enough about the climate for now.

The brief spring has ended and the temperature is starting to rise. Already I'm feeling uncomfortable, and I'm wondering if it's too early for my first beer of the day. Probably. I'm broke anyway. I haven't had a client in weeks. You might think that the crime rate in the city has dropped, except that crime in Turai never drops. Too many criminals, too much poverty, too many rich businessmen waiting to be robbed, or waiting to make an illegal profit. None of this money is coming my way however. The last time I worked I was successful, finding a magic amulet that old Gorsius Starfinder the Sorcerer mislaid during a drunken spree in a brothel. I recovered it and managed to keep the whole affair fairly quiet. His reputation at the Palace might suffer if his fondness for young prostitutes was too widely known.

Gorsius Starfinder promised to put a little business my way in return, but nothing has come of it. You can't really depend on a Palace Sorcerer to repay a favour. Too busy social climbing, drawing up horoscopes for young Princesses and that sort of thing.

I've just decided that there is really no alternative to going downstairs and having a beer, early or not, when there's a knock at my outside door. I have two rooms and use the outer one as an office. A staircase comes right up from the street for anyone who wishes to consult me without walking through the tavern.

"Come in."

My rooms are very messy. I regret this. I never do anything about it.

The young woman who walks in looks like she might wrinkle her nose at anything less than a suite of rooms at the Palace. She pulls back her hood to reveal long golden hair, deep blue eyes and perfect features. Pretty as a picture, as we Investigators say.

"Thraxas, Private Investigator?"

I nod, and invite her to sit down, which she does after clearing some junk off a chair. We look at each other from opposite sides of the table over the remains of dinner from yesterday, or maybe the day before.

"I have a problem. Gorsius Starfinder told me that you may be able to help. He also told me you were discreet."

"I am. But I think you might already have earned some attention coming down to Twelve Seas."

I'm not referring to her beauty. I gave up complimenting young women on their beauty a long time ago. Around the time that my waistband expanded too much to make it worthwhile. But she is strikingly dressed, way too expensively for this miserable part of town. She's wearing a light black cloak trimmed with fur and under this she has a long blue velvet toga more suitable for dancing with courtiers in a ballroom than picking your way over the rotting fish heads in the street outside.

"My servant drove me here in a small cart. Covered. I don't think anyone saw me coming up the stairs. I wasn't quite prepared for—"

She waves her hand in a motion which covers both the state of my room and the street outside.

"Fine. How can I help?"

When an obviously wealthy young lady visits me, which is very seldom, I expect some reticence on her part. This is not unnatural, because such a person would only consult me if she's in some tight situation that she absolutely does not want any of her peers to know about, something so potentially embarrassing that she doesn't even want to risk going to a high-society Investigator up in Thamlin in case word leaks out. This young lady however is far from reticent and wastes no time getting to the point.

"I need you to recover a box for me. A small jewelled casket."

"Someone steal it?"

"Not exactly."

"What's in it?"

She hesitates. "Do you need to know?"

I nod.

"Letters."

"What sort of letters?" I ask.

"Love letters. From me. To a young attaché at the Niojan Embassy."

"And you are?"

She pauses briefly, slightly surprised. "I'm Princess Du-Akai. Don't you recognise me?"

"I don't get out much in high society these days."

I suppose I should have recognised her from my work at the Palace, but the last time I saw her she was ten years old. I wasn't expecting the third in line to the Imperial Throne to waltz into my office. Imagine that. If King Reeth-Akan, Prince Frisen-Akan, and Prince Dees-Akan were all to die in an accident right this minute, I'd be sitting here talking to the new ruler of the city-state of Turai. Over a plate of three-day-old stew. Perhaps I should tidy my place more often.

"I take it your family would not be pleased to learn that you've been writing love letters to a young Niojan attaché?"

She nods.

"How many letters?"

"Six. He keeps them in a small jewelled box I gave him."

"Why can't you just ask for it back?"

"Attilan—that's his name—refuses. Since I broke off our relationship he's been angry. But I had to. God knows what my father would have said if he'd learned of it. You understand this is very awkward. I can't ask Palace Security for help. The Royal Family has occasionally used Private Investigators for—other matters— but I can't take the risk of going anywhere I'll be known."

I study her. She seems very calm, which surprises me. Young Princesses are not meant to write love letters. And not to Niojan diplomats of all people. Although there has been peace for a while now, Turai and our northern neighbour Nioj are historical enemies. Nioj is very strong and very aggressive and our King spends half his time desperately keeping the peace with them. To make things worse, the Niojans are a deeply puritanical race, and their Church is particularly caustic about the state of the True Religion in Turai, always criticising something or other. Niojans are not the most popular of people in Turai.

If word of the affair leaked out there would be a terrible scandal. The public in this city loves a scandal. I still know enough about Palace politics to guess at what some of the factions would make of it. Senator Lodius, leader of the opposition party, the Populares, would exploit it as a means of discrediting the King. So I wonder a little about the Princess's apparent serenity. Perhaps our Royal Family are bred to control their emotions.

I take some details. I bump up my daily fee but even then I can tell she's shocked at how little I charge. Should have asked for more.

"I don't imagine it'll be too difficult, Princess. You mind spending a little money to get them back? I expect that's what he's after."

She doesn't mind.

She asks me not to read the letters. I promise not to. She covers her head with her hood and departs.

My mood finally lightens. An easy enough case, in all likelihood, and I now have some money. It's lunchtime. I go downstairs for a beer. No reason not to. Perfectly respectable thing for a man to do after a hard morning's work.

Chapter Three

The bar is full of dock workers and Barbarian mercenaries. The dockers drink here every lunchtime and the Barbarians are stopping off on their way to enlist in the army. All the tension between Turai and Nioj has led to heavy recruitment recently. There's trouble in the south as well, on the border with Mattesh. Some dispute about the silver mines. Turai belongs to a league of city-states with Mattesh and others, to defend us from the larger powers, but it's falling apart. Damned politicians. If they lead us into another war I'll be on the first horse out of town.

Gurd frowns at me. I give him some rent money. He smiles. He's a man of simple emotions, Gurd. I look round for Makri to see if she'll join me for a beer but she's too busy with the lunchtime trade, hurrying round the tables with her tray, collecting tankards and taking orders. Makri wears a tiny chainmail bikini at work, in keeping with the general "Early Barbarian" decor that adorns Gurd's place, and as she has a particularly fine figure and the bikini exposes almost all of it she generally does well for tips.

Makri is a highly skilled swordswoman and if she was actually fighting you would never catch her in a chainmail bikini. She'd be dressed in full leather and steel body armour with a sword in one hand and an axe in the other and she'd have your head off your shoulders before you noticed whether she had a nice figure or not, but the bikini keeps the customers happy. Her long black hair hangs down over her dark, slightly reddish shoulders, her unusual skin colour the product of her Orc, Elf and Human parentage.

It's actually regarded as virtually impossible to carry the blood of all three races. The extremely few people who do so are considered freaks and outcasts from society. In the smarter areas of Turai Makri would not even be allowed into a tavern. Makri gets a lot of abuse about her parentage. On the streets children taunt her with "half-breed," "triple-breed," "Orc bastard" and much worse.

I notice her slipping some bread from behind the bar to Palax and Kaby, a young pair of travelling musicians who've recently moved to the neighbourhood. They're good musicians, but busking brings in little money in a poor place like this, and they're looking hungry.

"Never like to see a man drinking alone," says Partulax, joining me.

I nod. I have no objection to drinking on my own but I'm happy enough to have Partulax's company. He's a big red-haired man who used to drive wagons between the docks and the warehouses up in Koota Street. Now he's a paid official in the Transport Guild. I've worked for him once or twice on small matters.

"How's work?" I ask him.

"Okay. Better than rowing a slave galley."

"How's things with the Guild?"

"Trade's good, wagons are full but we're having a hard time keeping the Brotherhood at bay."

I nod. The Brotherhood, the main criminal fraternity in the south of the city, is always trying to make inroads on the labour guilds. Probably the craftsmen's guilds as well. Maybe even the Honourable Association of Merchants for all I know. The Brotherhood seems to be all-pervasive these days. More troublesome too. There have been numerous gang fights and killings involving them and the Society of Friends, the criminal organisation operating in the north of Turai. Most of the disputes revolve around control of the dwa trade. Dwa is a powerful and popular drug and there's a lot of money to be made out of it. The Brotherhood and the Society of Friends are not the only organisations angling for their share. Plenty of otherwise respectable people make a good living from dwa, even though it's illegal. The Civil Guard doesn't seem to do anything about it. Bribery works well in Turai.

"You hear about the new dragon?" says Partulax.

I nod. It was in the news-sheets.

"I hauled it up to the Palace."

"How do you transport a dragon?"

"Carefully," replies Partulax, and guffaws. "It was asleep most of the time. The Orcs sent a keeper who drugged it."

I frown. The dragon story is a bit weird when you think about it. The King has one dragon in his zoo and the Orcs have now lent him another one to mate with it. Very kind of them. Except Orcs don't perform acts of kindness for Humans. They hate us just as much as we hate them, even if we are technically at peace right now. Partulax, another veteran of the last war, doesn't know what to make of it either.

"You can't trust an Orc."

I nod. You can't actually trust most Humans either, and the Elves aren't a hell of a lot better when it comes right down to it, but we old soldiers like to air our prejudices.

The bar empties as the dockers in their red bandannas make their way back to their afternoon shifts in the cargo holds, casting not a few backward glances at Makri's bikini-clad figure. Makri, ignoring their stares and comments, comes over to my table.

"Any progress?" she asks.

"Yes," I reply. "Got a case. Paid Gurd the rent."

She frowns. "That's not what I mean."

I know it's not what she means, but what she means is a difficult proposition. Makri wishes to study at the Imperial University and she wants me to help her. This, as I have pointed out on numerous occasions, is impossible. The Imperial University is a deeply conservative body and does not accept female students. Even if it did, it would not accept a student with Orcish blood in her veins. Completely out of the question. The aristocrats and rich merchants who send their sons there would be up in arms. Questions would be asked in the Senate. The Turai news-sheets would create a scandal. Apart from all this Makri doesn't even have the basic academic qualifications necessary for entry.

Makri scoffs at these objections. She claims that it's well known that any student can get into the University, no matter how sparse their qualifications, providing they have a rich father to pay their fees or wield influence at the Palace.

"And anyway, I'm going to philosophy night classes at the Revered Federation of Guilds College. I'll get the qualifications."

"The University doesn't teach women."

"Neither did the College till I insisted. And don't go on about my parentage, I've had enough of that today from the customers. You promised you'd ask Astrath Triple Moon to help me."

"I was drunk when I promised," I protest. "Anyway, Astrath couldn't help."

"He's a Sorcerer. He must know people."

"He's a Sorcerer in disgrace. None of his old friends would do him any favours."

"Well, it would be a start," says Makri with the look of a woman who is not going to stop harassing me until I give in. I give in.

"Okay, Makri. I'll talk to him."

"You promise?"

"I promise."

"Well you'd better then, or I'll be down on you like a bad spell."

I ask Makri if she wants a drink but she still has a load of tables to clean so I take a beer upstairs and finish it off while I'm getting dressed to go out. I put on my best black tunic, which is patched, but quite professionally, and my best boots, which are a mess. One of the heels is about to come off. Not very impressive for visiting a Niojan diplomat. Staring in the bronze mirror I have to admit that I'm looking a little shabby these days. Altogether not too impressive. My hair is fine, still dark and long, and my moustache is as impressive as ever, but I've put on weight recently. In addition to my expanding waistline I seem to be getting a double chin. I sigh. Middle age.

I tie my hair back in a braid and hunt around for my sword. I remember I pawned it last week to buy food. What sort of Private Investigator pawns his sword, for God's sake? Turai's cheapest, that's what sort.

I consider looking into the kuriya pool, but decide against it. The ability to use kuriya is one of my few claims to sorcerous power. It involves entering a trance and staring into a small pool of kuriya, a rare dark liquid, wherein may appear mystical insights. In a saucer full of kuriya I have occasionally been able to find the solution to an investigation—a missing husband, a thieving nephew, a lying business partner. Very convenient. Solve a mystery in the comfort of your own room. Unfortunately it rarely works. Using magic to draw a picture of the past is extremely difficult. Even Sorcerers with a great deal more power than myself are only sometimes successful. It requires precise calculations of the phases of the three moons and suchlike, and entering the required trance is no easy feat. The Investigating Sorcerers of the Civil Guard will generally only attempt it in the most important criminal matters, and fortunately for Turai's criminals they often get it wrong.

Another problem is the price of kuriya. The black liquid comes from the far west and the one merchant who imports it keeps his prices high. He claims it's dragon's blood, but he's a liar.

I place the sleep spell in my memory. I can only put one spell in at a time these days, and even that takes a lot of effort. Major spells don't stay in the memory after you've used them, so you have to learn them all over again. If I'm out on a case and think I may need a little outside help I usually memorise the sleep spell, but I find the whole process pretty tiring these days. I'm not much of a Sorcerer. No wonder I have to work for a living. A good Sorcerer can carry two major spells at once. A truly great one can walk around all day with three or even four spells safely tucked up in his memory, just waiting to come out. I should have studied more when I was an apprentice.

I step through the outside door and get to work. I mutter my standard locking incantation over the door, this being a minor spell which I'm able to use at will. Quite a number of people can use these minor spells. They don't require much studying.

"That's not going to help you much if you don't pay Yubaxas what you owe him," comes a rasping voice from the bottom of the stairs.

I glower down at the large man who's waiting there for me. He's very tall, very broad, and a virulent sword scar runs from his temple to his collar bone. With his shaved head he's an ugly brute by anyone's standards, and one I'd rather not have hanging around to see me. I go down the stairs and stop on the third from the ground so that our eyes are level.

"What do you want, Karlox?" I demand.

"Passing on a message from Yubaxas. Money's due in five days."

As if I needed reminding. Yubaxas is the local Brotherhood boss. I owe him five hundred gurans, a gambling debt after some very unwise speculations at the chariot races.

"He'll get his money," I grunt. "I don't need gorillas like you to remind me."

"You better come up with it, Thraxas, or we'll be down on you like a bad spell."

I push my way past. Karlox laughs. He acts as an enforcer for the Brotherhood and he's a violent and unpleasant man. He's also dumb as an Orc. No doubt he enjoys his work. I leave him without a backward glance. The gambling debt is worrying me, but I'm not going to let an ox like Karlox see that.

The air stinks of rotting fish. It's hotter than Orcish hell out here. I redeem my sword at Priso's pawn shop. I'd like a new pair of boots but I can't afford it. Nor can I afford to redeem my illuminated staff or my spell protection charm. I get depressed about my poverty. I shouldn't gamble. I should have stayed at the Palace, riding around in official horse carts and raking in bribes. I was a fool to leave. Or rather I was a fool to get so drunk at the wedding of the Head of Palace Security that I tried to make a move on his bride. No one at the Palace could ever remember an Investigator being dismissed from his post quite so abruptly, not even proven spies and traitors. Damn that Deputy Consul Rittius. He always hated me.

I buy some bread at Minarixa's bakery. Minarixa greets me in a friendly manner as I am a very frequent customer. Outside I notice she's put up a wall poster asking for donations to the Association of Gentlewomen. Quite a bold move on her part; many people disapprove of the Association of Gentlewomen, an unofficial organisation, deeply frowned on by the King, the Palace, the Senate, the Church, the guilds and practically every man in the city.

"A sinful thing," says a voice beside me.

It's Derlex, the local Pontifex, or priest of the True Church.

I greet him politely, if slightly dubiously. I always feel nervous around Derlex. I get the impression he disapproves of me.

"You don't sympathise with their aims, Pontifex Derlex?"

He doesn't. A women's organisation is anathema to the True Church. The young Pontifex seems quite upset by it. Not only does he dislike the poster, he doesn't seem to approve of Minarixa's bakery.

"Women should not run businesses," he states.

As Minarixa runs the only decent bakery in the whole of Twelve Seas I can't agree with this at all, but I keep my silence. I don't want to argue with the Church, it's too powerful to offend.

"I haven't seen you at church recently," says Derlex, taking me by surprise.

"Pressure of work," I reply, foolishly, which gets me a lecture about putting my work before the Church.

"I'll certainly make every effort to attend this week," I say as convincingly as I can, and make my escape. I can't say I enjoyed the conversation. The Pontifex isn't all that bad, provided he leaves you alone, but it's not going to be much fun if he suddenly starts worrying about my soul.

Chapter Four

I step over three young dwa addicts lying unconscious in an alleyway. I sigh. The opening up of the southern trade route through Mattesh was proclaimed by our King as a triumph of diplomacy. Commerce has started to flow but unfortunately the main import has been dwa. Use of the powerful narcotic is now rife throughout the city and the effect on its population has been dramatic. Beggars, sailors, youthful apprentices, whores, itinerants, rich and idle young fashionables—all manner of people, once content to alleviate their sufferings with ale and occasional doses of the much milder drug Thazis, now spend their days lost in the powerful dream brought on by the ingestion of dwa. Unfortunately dwa is both expensive and addictive. Once you've taken your dose you're as happy as an Elf in a tree, but when you come down you feel dreadful. Those regular users who spend part of their lives lost in its pleasant grip are obliged to spend the other part raising money to buy their next day's supply. Since dwa swept Turai crime of all sorts has mushroomed. In many parts of the city it's not safe to walk the streets at night for fear of violent robbery. The houses of the rich are ringed by walls and guarded by hired members of the Securitus Guild. Gangs of youths in the slums who used to steal the occasional piece of fruit from market stalls now use knives for street robberies and kill people for a few gurans.

Turai is rotting. The poor are despairing and the rich are decadent. One day King Lamachus of Nioj will come down from the north and sweep us away.

I feel better when I've got my sword tucked snugly in my belt and I'm riding in a horse cab, or landus, up Moon and Stars Boulevard, the main street running north to south, up from Twelve Seas docks through Pashish, a poor though generally peaceful area, eventually turning on to Royal Way, which runs west through the upper-class suburb of Thamlin to the Imperial Palace. Attilan, our Royal Princess's erstwhile lover, lives here on a quiet street popular with young men about town.

I'm prepared to dislike him. Niojans are never friendly to Private Investigators. Private Investigators are in fact illegal in Nioj. Most things are illegal in Nioj. It's a grim place. Thamlin isn't. Our well-off citizens make their surroundings very comfortable—yellow and green tiled pavements and large white houses with fountains in well-tended gardens. Civil Guardsmen patrol the streets, keeping them safe from undesirables. It's a peaceful place. I used to live here. Some time ago. My old house is now occupied by the Queen's Royal Astrologer. He's a dwa addict, but he keeps it quiet.

A young Pontifex greets me politely as I turn into

Attilan's private pathway. He's carrying a bag marked with the sign of the True Church. Busy gathering contributions from our wealthier citizens I expect. A servant answers the door. Attilan is not home and is not expected back in the near future. The servant shuts the door. I never enjoy having doors slammed in my face. I walk round the back. No one interrupts me as I stroll through the small garden, ending up in a patio at the back with a small statue of Saint Quatinius and various well-tended bushes. The back door is solid enough, and locked. I mutter the opening incantation, another minor spell which I can use at will, and it flies open. I walk in. I can guess the layout of the house. They're all much the same, with a central courtyard containing an altar and private rooms at the back. If, as I suspect, Attilan only has one or two servants, and they're lounging in their quarters while he's away, I may be able to carry out some uninterrupted investigating.

Attilan's office is neat, everything in its proper place. I check the letter rack. No sign of the Princess's letters. A safe behind a painting almost resists my opening spell, but eventually creaks open reluctantly. I might have made a fine burglar, although anyone with anything really valuable to hide gets their safe locked tight with a good spell from a competent Sorcerer. Inside the safe I find a jewelled box with the Princess's royal insignia on it. Very good. Things are going well.

I am about to place it in my bag when my curiosity overwhelms me. The Princess specifically requested that I did not open the box and read her letters. Which gives me an irresistible urge to open the box and read her letters. Sometimes I just can't help myself.

It doesn't appear to contain any letters. Just a parchment with a spell written on it. I frown. This is definitely the box the Princess asked me to retrieve; it carries her royal insignia. The spell is an unfamiliar one, not native to Turai. When I read it through I'm more puzzled than ever. It seems to be a spell for putting a dragon to sleep. Why would the Princess want to do that? I slip it into my bag, and hurry out the back way. It should be an easy getaway but as I plunge through the bushes I trip over something and cry out in surprise.

"Who's there?" demands a servant, appearing at a run. He stares in horror at me. Or rather, at what's at my feet, which is a dead body.

"Attilan!" he screams.

The case just took a bad turn. The servant obviously regards me as the man responsible for sticking a knife in his employer. So do the Civil Guards, who appear in less than thirty seconds. Not unreasonable, I suppose, as I decline to offer any explanation for my presence. They drag me off. As I'm being hauled through the garden I sense the faintest aura of something unusual but it's too fleeting to identify and I don't have a chance to think about it. I'm dumped in a wagon and driven smartly up to the prison. As the Guards fling me in a cell, I reflect that, of all my reversals of fortune, this is surely one of the quickest.

Chapter Five

The city is divided into ten administrative units, each one overseen by a Prefect, who, among other things, oversees the Civil Guard in his area. Prefect Galwinius, in charge of Thamlin, is a large, tough individual who wastes no time in informing me I'm in serious trouble.

"We got no time for Private Investigators round here," he snarls at me, again. "Why did you kill Attilan?"

"I didn't kill him."

"Then why were you there?"

"Just taking a short cut."

I'm flung back in my cell. It's stiflingly hot and stinks like a sewer. Out of curiosity I try my standard opening incantation on the door, but nothing happens. This is to be expected. All cell doors are regularly serviced by the Civil Guard Sorcerers using powerful locking spells.

Hours pass. I hear the Crier calling Sabap, the time for afternoon prayer. At this all faithful members of

the True Church—in theory the whole population of
the city—are supposed to get down on their knees and
pray. Pray for the second time, as all true devotees will
also have prayed at Sabam, the start of the day. I
missed the morning prayers. Didn't wake up in time.
I haven't done in years. I decide to pass on the afternoon session as well.

The door rattles and Captain Rallee strides in.

"Don't you know all citizens are legally obliged to
pray during Sabap?" he says.

"I don't see you on your knees."

"I'm excepted for official business."

"What business?"

"Coming down to order you to stop being such a
fool and tell the Prefect what he wants to know."

It's some relief to see Captain Rallee, though not
much. We've known each other a long time; we even
fought in the same battalion during one of the Orc
Wars. We were fairly friendly once, but since I left the
Palace and set up on my own we've grown apart. He
knows I'm not a fool but he doesn't owe me any
favours.

"Look, Thraxas, we don't want to keep you here.
We've got better things to do. No one thinks you
personally stuck a knife in Attilan."

"Prefect Galwinius does."

Captain Rallee makes a face indicating he doesn't
think too much of the Prefect.

"We ran a test on the knife. Our Sorcerer reports
that your aura isn't on it. Of course some Sorcerers
could remove their aura, but you aren't good enough
to do that."

"Absolutely, Captain. I'm strictly small time."

"But he picked up your aura in the house. What
were you doing there?"

I continue staring at the ceiling.

"You know how serious this is, Thraxas? Attilan was a Niojan diplomat. Their Ambassador is raising hell. The Palace is raising hell. The Consul himself's been down here asking questions."

I'm impressed. The Consul is Turai's highest official, answerable to no one except the King. Captain Rallee stares at me. I stare at him. He's weathered his middle age better than I have. With his long blond hair and broad shoulders he's still a handsome man. Probably still a hit with the ladies, in his smart black tunic and cloak. No fool, though. Sharp as an Elf's ear in comparison to some of the blunderers they've got in the Civil Guard.

"So what's going on?"

I remain silent.

"I don't reckon you killed Attilan," says the Captain. "But I reckon you might have been involved in a little robbery."

"Don't be stupid."

"Stupid? Maybe. Maybe not. I've never known you rob anyone before, but then again, I've never known you owe the Brotherhood five hundred gurans before."

He sees my look of surprise.

"You're in big trouble, Thraxas. Yubaxas will have your head if you don't pay. You need money badly, which naturally makes us suspicious when you're found in rich people's houses where you haven't been invited. So why don't you tell me what's going on?"

"I don't discuss my business with the Civil Guard. Or anyone else. If I did, I'd soon be out of clients."

"Who's your client?"

"I don't have one."

"In that case, Thraxas, you'd better reconsider your attitude to prayer. Unless you tell us what we want to know it's going to take divine intervention to get you out of this cell."

He departs. I remain. Languishing, I believe would be the correct term.

Later I bribe a jailer to let me have a news-sheet. *The Renowned and Truthful Chronicle of All the World's Events* is one of the various rags published each day in Turai. It's neither renowned nor truthful, being given more to hinting at scandalous relationships between Senators' daughters and officers of the Palace Guard, but it's entertaining. It's a single sheet, poorly printed, and often contains nothing but gossip, but today it has the sensational news of Attilan's death, about which the Niojan Ambassador is indeed raising hell. He has protested to the King about this gross breach of diplomatic privilege. He has a point. You can't have your diplomatic privilege violated much more than being murdered. For our King, always keen to appease the Niojans, it's a tricky situation, and the Palace needs the murder cleared up quickly. Quickly enough to pin it on me, quite possibly.

Thinking it over in my cell, I can't make much sense of the affair. I've no idea who killed Attilan. Or why the Princess sent me to recover some love letters which turned out to be a spell for putting a dragon to sleep. Who needs to do that? There are no dragons around, apart from the King's pet in his zoo, and the new one from the Orcs. I muse about this. It's an interesting tale. This dragon, newly arrived at the King's zoo, was on loan. The Orcish nation of Gzak sent it to King Reeth-Akan last week to mate with the King's dragon as a token of friendship. There is, of course, no friendship whatsoever between Turai and Gzak, or any Human and Orcish nation, peace treaties notwithstanding. Why exactly the Orcs have sent it I'm not sure. I doubt very much that they are overly concerned that King Reeth-Akan's dragon might be feeling lonely.

Maybe it's just to fool people into thinking they aren't planning another war as soon as they can get their armies up to strength after the last beating we gave them. Gzak is one of the richest Orcish nations and has its own gold and diamond mines. It won't take them too many years to build up their strength again.

Why, however, Princess Du-Akai might want to put this or any other dragon to sleep is a mystery.

I glance at the rest of the news-sheet. Usual round of Palace intrigue and scandal, and a story about a killer called Sarin the Merciless who's apparently carried out a string of murders and robberies in the southern nations, making her the most wanted criminal in the west. This makes me laugh. I tangled with Sarin the Merciless a long time ago. Ran her out of town, if the truth be known. Just another small-time crook. The news-sheets always like to build up these petty criminals into something they're not. I hope she comes back to Turai. I could do with some reward money.

Under this is a piece about Senator Lodius, the leader of the opposition, who is haranguing the Consul for the outbreak of lawlessness in Turai. Killings and robberies are on the rise, and there's still no sign of the Red Elvish Cloth, for which the Treasury will have to pay the Elves, even though we haven't got it.

What makes this cloth so rare and valuable is its ability to form a total shield against magic. It's the only substance in the world no sorcery can penetrate. Very handy in a world full of enemy Sorcerers. But it's presumably far away from the city by now. If it had been brought to Turai by the hijackers, our government Sorcerers would have traced it by now. In its finished state, the cloth is undetectable, but Elves aren't dumb. Any time they despatch some, they brand it with a temporary sorcerous mark only they can remove. Once

the Cloth reaches our King, an Elvish Sorcerer removes
it. So someone has spirited the stuff away from the city.
It's well known the Orcs have been after Red Elvish
Cloth for years. If they've finally acquired some, it's
bad news for us.

My musings are interrupted as the cell door bangs
open and the jailer ushers in a young woman. She
introduces herself as Jaisleti and flashes an official seal
at me.

"I'm Princess Du-Akai's handmaiden."

"Whisper. You never know who's listening."

Jaisleti whispers, "The Princess is worried."

"It's okay. I hid the box before I was arrested. I've
kept her name out of it."

Jaisleti looks relieved. "When can she get the letters back?"

"As soon as I get out of here."

"We'll see what we can do. But you mustn't mention her name. Now Attilan's been murdered it would
be an even worse scandal if the relationship were to
be discovered."

"Don't worry. Stubborn silence is one of my strongest points."

She departs, sticking to the pretence about love
letters. No mention of dragons at all.

Chapter Six

The call for Sabav, evening prayers, rings out through the jail. Sabam, Sabap, Sabav. Three prayer calls a day. Gets me down. Still, we get off lightly in Turai. In Nioj they have six. I kneel down to pray in case some jailer is spying on me; there's no sense in giving the authorities another excuse to hold me here. Perhaps it isn't such a bad idea, because I'm released shortly afterwards. God may now be on my side. More likely the Princess pulled some strings. Captain Rallee is most displeased. He can't understand how a guy like me can still have any influence in this town.

"Who you working for, the Royal Family?" he grumbles, as a Sorcerer mutters the spell to let me out the front gates. "You watch yourself, Thraxas. The Prefect's got his eye on you. You try putting anything over on him and he'll be down on you like a bad spell."

I smile graciously in reply, and climb into a landus heading for Twelve Seas. I stop off at the public baths, wash off the stink of prison, grab a beer and food at the Avenging Axe and head off out.

"Where have you been?" asks Makri as I'm leaving.

"In prison."

"Oh," says Makri. "I thought maybe you were hiding from the Brotherhood."

I glare at her. "And why did you think that?"

"Because you can't pay your gambling debts."

I am outraged to learn that Makri knows about this too.

"Does everyone in Twelve Seas have to stick their noses into my personal affairs? It's high time people around here started minding their own damned business."

With which I storm out into the street. A beggar sticks a withered hand in my direction.

"Get a job," I bark at him. It makes me feel slightly better.

It's dark by the time I reach Attilan's house. It's risky returning so soon but it has to be done. In the time between my discovery in the garden and my arrest, I threw the box under a bush and I need it back. No one seems to be around, apart from a young Pontifex hurrying home after a hard day's praying. I wish I could make myself invisible but the invisibility spell is way too complicated for me. Trusting to luck, I haul myself over the fence, scramble through the garden and dive beneath the bush. The box isn't there. Someone beat me to it. Two minutes later I'm back over the fence and hurrying south, not pleased at the way things are going.

Horse traffic is banned in the city after dark. The night is still hot and it's a tiring walk. When I reach Pashish I decide to drop in on Astrath Triple Moon. I've promised Makri I'll ask him if he can help her. More to the point, I need a beer.

Pashish, just north of Twelve Seas, is another poor suburb, though relatively crime-free. Its narrow tenemented streets comprise mainly the dwellings of harbour workers and other manual labourers. It's an unlikely place to find a Sorcerer, but Astrath Triple Moon is somewhat of an outcast among his kind, thanks to certain allegations a few years back when he was the official Sorcerer at the Stadium Superbius, with responsibility for ensuring that all chariot races and suchlike were run fairly, without outside sorcerous interference. Certain powerful Senators felt that their chariots weren't getting a fair deal, leading to a Praetor's investigation accusing Astrath Triple Moon of taking bribes.

Astrath employed me to dig up evidence on his behalf. He was, in fact, as guilty as hell but I managed to cloud the issue enough for him to escape prosecution or expulsion from the Sorcerers Guild. This allowed him to remain in the city—no Sorcerer expelled from the Guild is allowed to practise here—but the stigma attached to his name thereafter forced him to leave his high-class practice in Truth is Beauty Lane. He ended up in straitened circumstances with a small practice in Pashish ministering to the humble needs of the local population.

Astrath is still a powerful Sorcerer. As always he is pleased to see me. Not many men of my learning and culture visit him these days. He pours me a beer and I down it in one. He pours me another.

"Hot as Orcish hell out there," I say, emptying the glass.

He pours me a third. He's not a bad guy for a Sorcerer. I dump my cloak and bag on the floor among the astrolabes, charts, test tubes, herbs, potions and books that form the standard paraphernalia of a working Sorcerer.

I ask him about the spell, describing it as best as I can remember.

"That's a rare item," says Astrath Triple Moon, stroking his beard. "As far as I know, no Human Sorcerer has ever concocted a successful spell for putting a dragon to sleep. The best we've come up with is some temporary distraction."

He's right. I know from painful experience. My platoon faced a dragon in the last Orc Wars, and I tried my sleep spell, full strength. I had more power in my spells then but the dragon hardly blinked. Still, we killed it in the end.

"Do the Orcs have a spell like that?"

"They might," replies Astrath Triple Moon. "After all, they have more experience with dragons than us. And their Sorcerers work on a different system. Weaker in some ways, stronger in others. It wouldn't surprise me if they've mastered dragoncraft enough to put one to sleep. I wouldn't have thought they'd let a spell like that out of their hands though. There's always Horm, of course."

"Horm the Dead?"

I suppress a shudder. You can forget to include me in anything involving Horm the Dead. He's not the only mad renegade Sorcerer in the world but he's one of the most powerful and, by all accounts, by far the most frightening.

"You ever have any dealings with him?"

Astrath strokes his beard.

"Not really. But a few members of the Sorcerers Guild have encountered him in the course of their travels and they told me stories about him. That was back when I could still go to Sorcerers Guild meetings of course. Takes dwa and flies, apparently."

"So do a lot of people."

"No, he really can fly. So they say anyway. And rides dragons."

"I thought only Orcs could ride dragons."

"Horm is half Orc," says Astrath. "And he spends his time in the Wastelands working out ways to combine Orc and Human magic. Last we heard he was working on a spell to send a whole city mad. The Eight-Mile Terror, he called it. So we were told anyway. Of course, you can't trust informants from the Wastelands, but it worried the Guild enough to start work on some counterspell. Horm the Dead doesn't much care for Humans."

"I can't see why he'd have any involvement in this spell the Princess had though."

"Neither can I," admits Astrath Triple Moon. "And from what you can remember of the spell, it doesn't really sound like his work. More likely it was stolen from an Orcish Sorcerer. Or maybe their Ambassadors brought it here just in case the dragon decided to go mad and start burning the city."

I should hurry home and work this one out. After another beer, a little klee, and a portion of beef from Astrath's servant, I do just that. I sit in my shabby room and mull it over. What would a Niojan diplomat be doing with an Orcish spell? Trying to sell it perhaps? A valuable item, certainly, which any government would pay well for, but how did he get it? How did the Princess learn of it and why did she want it? And where is it now? Who removed it from Attilan's garden?

Faced with so many questions, I go downstairs for a beer. Makri comes over to my table and I tell her about the case. She's a sensible woman, often good for talking things over with, providing she's not haranguing me about helping her get into the Imperial University.

"I don't think Attilan was ever on diplomatic duty in the Orcish lands, but its possible he's come across the Orcish diplomats at our Palace. They don't show

themselves in public but they must meet other
Ambassadors sometimes."

"Maybe he didn't steal it," suggests Makri. "Maybe
they gave it to him."

"Seems unlikely, Makri. Niojans are all swines, but
they don't like Orcs any more than we do. And even
if he was working with them, what was he doing with
that spell? And why is the Princess involved? She sent
me to find it. How did she know he had it? And what
did she want it for?"

"Maybe the dragons in the King's zoo make her
nervous."

"Could be. Dragons would upset anyone."

"I fought one once," says Makri.

"What?"

"I fought one. In the Orcish slave arena."

"On your own?"

"No, there were ten of us. Big fight to entertain the
Orc Lords. We beat it, though I was the only one left
alive at the end. Tough skin. My sword wouldn't go
through it. I had to stab it in the eyes."

I stare at her. I'm not sure if she's telling the truth
or not. When the twenty-year-old Makri arrived in Turai
a year ago after escaping from the Orcish gladiator slave
pits, she was a hardened fighter but unused to the ways
of civilisation. That is to say, she didn't tell lies. After
a year in the Avenging Axe, surrounded by notable
embroiderers of the truth like Gurd and myself, she's
learned the art.

"I fought a dragon too, back in the Orc Wars," I say,
which is true, though rather beside the point. I just
don't like Makri to think she's the only one round here
who's done any serious fighting.

Some customers call for beer. Makri ignores them.

"I hope you're not going to get Princess Du-Akai
into trouble," she says.

"Why?"

"Because if you do a good job for the Princess she'll be grateful and you could ask her to use her influence to get me into the University."

The standard degree course at the Imperial University features rhetoric, philosophy, logic, mathematics, architecture, religion and literature. Why the hell Makri wants to learn all that is beyond me.

"Also," adds the young Barbarian, "I heard that Du-Akai is sympathetic to the Association of Gentlewomen."

"Where did you hear that?"

"At a meeting."

I stare at her. I'd no idea Makri was going to Association of Gentlewomen meetings.

"Don't come crying to me if you all get arrested for illegal gatherings."

"I won't."

I consider consulting the kuriya pool for some answers but decide against it. I don't know enough exact dates and places for the things I'd like to know, so a good connection with the past would be almost impossible. Anyway I've hardly any of the black liquid left and I can't afford any more. Sorcerous Investigator. Big joke. I can't even afford the basics.

"Get a job," says Makri.

"Very funny. You want to play some niarit after your shift?"

Makri nods. She tells me she saw some Elves today, travelling up from the docks on horseback with an escort of Civil Guardsmen.

"Probably some deputation from the Elf Lord who sent the Red Elvish Cloth. I don't imagine they're very happy it's gone missing."

Makri grunts. The whole subject of Elves is troubling to her. Basically, her Orcish blood appals them.

Makri pretends not to care, but really she does. She won't admit it, but I've seen her looking almost longingly at some of the young Elves who pass through Twelve Seas.

She adjusts her bikini and gets back to work, taking orders from thirsty late-night drinkers. This includes me and it's around two in the morning by the time I stumble upstairs.

Sitting on my grubby couch is Princess Du-Akai.

"I let myself in," she says. "I didn't want to come into the tavern."

"Feel free to visit any time," I grunt, with less politeness than would be normal towards the third in line to the throne. I'm not particularly pleased to find anyone, even a Royal Princess, in my rooms uninvited. It gives me the strong suspicion she might have been searching them.

"Did you get the box?"

I shake my head. "I went back for it. Someone must have seen me hide it. It's gone."

"I must have those letters!"

I stare at the Princess. For the first time she looks uncomfortable. Good. I decide to give it to her straight.

"There weren't any letters, Princess. Your box was there in Attilan's safe all right. Nice box. Very fine inlay. No letters though. Just an Orc spell for putting a dragon to sleep."

"How dare you examine the contents!"

"Welcome to the real world. And how dare you send me on a case with false information. Thanks to you, Princess, I'm up to my neck in the murder of a Niojan diplomat. Sure, you used your influence to get me out of prison but that's not going to prevent the Consul pinning the murder on me if no one better comes along. So I'd suggest you start telling me the truth."

We stare at each other for a while. Princess Du-Akai shows no inclination to start telling the truth.

"Do you know who killed Attilan?" I demand.

"No."

"Did you?"

She's shocked. She denies it.

"Why did you want me to get that spell? Where did it come from? And why was it in your box?"

The Princess clams up. She makes to leave. I'm mad as hell. Anytime I'm thrown in a cell I at least like to know the reason. I say a few less than complimentary things to her. She tosses a small purse on the table and tells me our business relationship is ended.

"Don't slam the door when you leave."

She slams the door. I count the money. Thirty gurans. Three days' pay. Not bad. Another four hundred and seventy and the Brotherhood will be off my back. I wish I knew what it had all been about. I drink some more beer. It feels too hot to go to bed. I fall asleep on my couch.

Chapter Seven

I'm woken about three thirty in the morning by Makri.

"Makri, how many times do I have to tell you not to barge into my rooms? I might be doing something personal."

She laughs at the thought.

"I'm going to start putting a closing spell on that door."

"Your closing spell wouldn't hold out for fifteen seconds against me, Thraxas."

I expect it wouldn't. Makri started fighting in the slave pits when she was thirteen. Seven years as an Orcish gladiator does give a person a tendency to be forceful. I struggle to rise as Makri clears some space on an old box to set up my niarit board.

"What's the matter with you?" she asks. "You're looking sadder than a Niojan whore."

I tell her what happened with the Princess. "I got three days' pay but I was hoping for a lot more. I guess she won't hire me again after this. And I wouldn't count on her help getting into the University."

"You mean you insulted her?"

I admit it, but point out it was justified.

Makri takes out a couple of thazis sticks.

"This'll cheer you up."

"If Gurd catches you taking them from the bar you'll be out on your ear."

She shrugs. I light my thazis stick.

"How's your studies at the Guild College?" I ask.

"Okay. Better than rowing a slave galley."

"You don't sound too happy about it."

"It would be fine if the other students weren't on my back all the time. I heard someone whispering "Orc" when I was coming out of my rhetoric lecture. I'd have chopped his head off except then they'd throw me out. Also they don't let me take my axe into class."

Makri lights up another thazis stick and sets up the opposing forces on the board, the front rank being, from left to right, Foot Soldiers of the Hoplite variety, Archers, then Trolls. The back rank comprises Elephants, Heavy Mounted Knights and Light Mounted Lancers. Each player has in their side a Siege Tower, a Healer, a Harper, a Sorcerer, a Hero and a Plague Carrier. At the very back of the board is the Castle, the object of the game being to defend your own Castle and storm your opponent's.

"Kerk was hanging around outside your door earlier," Makri tells me.

Kerk is an informant of mine. Fairly useless generally, and a hopeless dwa addict.

"Must have some information for me. He wouldn't come in if he heard I was with a client. I'll look him up tomorrow."

I open a bottle of beer, pour us out a little klee, draw deeply on my thazis and make my standard opening, sending my Foot Soldiers up the flanks. Makri responds, as she generally does, by sending out her Mounted Lancers to harry them but I notice that she is also surreptitiously preparing to bring her Plague Carrier up the board early. I advance my Archers to support my Foot Soldiers and make sure my Sorcerer and my Healer are ready to react.

Makri, generally an impetuous player, tries to force an early engagement by suddenly sending out the rest of her Heavy Cavalry, followed by her Elephants. I withdraw slightly and, in a new variation, send my Harper, protected by my Hero, to play to the Elephants. The Harper's music has the power of entrancement and it sends Makri's Elephants to sleep. She can only watch in frustration as my Trolls advance among the immobile beasts and finish them off.

My solid phalanx of Hoplites and Archers is meanwhile holding off her cavalry and I start to send my Siege Tower lumbering up the board. Makri's cavalry are causing casualties among my Hoplites but I've already got my Healer on hand to alleviate the situation. My Sorcerer is meanwhile holding her Hero at bay.

Due to her imprudent attack Makri's Sorcerer is out of position and when battle is thickest in the centre I am able to send my Hero up the right flank with a horde of Elephants and I start to break through. My forces have an awkward moment when Makri suddenly and unexpectedly backtracks with her Plague Carrier and I lose a few Elephants to the plague before my Hero engages the Plague Carrier and puts him to flight. Meanwhile my own Plague Carrier is sneaking up the left flank, weakening Makri's forces. Suddenly I break through on both sides. My Trolls and Heavy Mounted Knights surround and kill her Sorcerer and her Hero. My Hoplites break her cavalry in two and march up the board, followed by my Siege Tower. She tries to muster her forces but her last resistance is broken when my Plague Carrier kills her Harper before getting in amongst her Trolls and decimating them. Soon I'm swarming over her forces and I move my Siege Tower right up to her Castle.

In niarit it's possible to come back from a poor position but not when playing against a master like me. Makri's remaining forces are hemmed in and gradually whittled down as I prepare my final assault. My Hero leads a horde of infantry up the Siege Tower and into her Castle. Victory to Thraxas.

"Damn," says Makri, and looks extremely annoyed. She's not a good loser. Neither am I. Fortunately I always win.

"I'll beat you next time," states Makri.

"No way. I'm still number one chariot around here."

Makri grins, drinks the rest of her klee in a gulp and departs to her room along the corridor. I struggle into my bedroom, blow out the candle and settle down to sleep. My slumbers are badly interrupted when Hanama, deadliest member of the extremely deadly Assassins Guild, pricks my throat with her dagger. It's a poor way for a man to be woken up after a hard day's work.

Chapter Eight

A night candle casts the merest glimmer of light in my room. Barely enough to illuminate the knife at my throat, or the figure of the Assassin looming over me. I'm pinned to my bed, unable to move. A bad awakening indeed. I've encountered Hanama before. She's number three in the Assassins Guild, a ruthless killer. And yet, as my senses clear, I realise I'm not about to be immediately assassinated. If I was I'd be dead already. The Assassins don't worry about formalities like waking up their victims.

"Where is it?" she hisses.

"What?" I croak in reply.

"The Red Elvish Cloth," says Hanama, plunging me into further confusion.

"What are you talking about?"

She presses the knife a fraction further.

"Hand it over or die," says Hanama, her eyes as cold as an Orc's heart.

The door to the next room swings open. Light from a lantern floods in. There stands Makri, sword in hand.

"Let him go," she snarls.

Hanama laughs, a thin, humourless Assassin's laugh.

"Nice bikini," she says, mockingly, and in one swift movement draws a short sword and drops into a fighting crouch. Hanama's small, thin figure is exaggerated by her featureless black clothes, making her appear almost childlike. I wonder if Makri realises how deadly she is. I ready myself to spring to her aid. Suddenly the outside door crashes open. Men pound into the office and on into my inner room. Makri and Hanama whirl round to face the intruders. I leap from the bed and grab my sword. There's no time to think and little room to move as a horde of savage sword-wielding thugs threaten to sweep us away by sheer force of numbers. A massive man waves an equally massive scimitar at me. I avoid it nimbly and stick my knife into his heart. My next assailant slams a hatchet towards my head. I dodge the blow, kick him in the knee and slash my knife through his throat. I'm good at this sort of thing. So are Makri and Hanama. We drive our attackers back into the next room, then Makri leaps after them impetuously, followed by Hanama and me.

In the larger space of my office we find ourselves at a disadvantage. More attackers are pouring in from outside and they start to encircle us. There's little time to think, though I get a brief glimpse of Makri scything two men down with one blow and flying over a low slash aimed by another to smash her boot into his face. I parry another blow but before I can counter-thrust my senses start going haywire. I detect magic, powerful magic, very close. I gain an impression of a large, cloaked figure in the doorway, one arm raised, before there's a violent flash and I'm thrown back against the wall along with Makri and Hanama. The three of us lie there, gasping and bleeding. I don't know what the spell was but it was pretty effective.

"Kill them," says the Sorcerer, entering the room.

Suddenly Gurd, roused by the commotion, hurtles into the office with his axe above his head. Two men fall dead before they can scream. I drag myself to my feet as Gurd disappears into a maelstrom of blades and bodies. The interruption allows Makri and Hanama the few seconds they need to recover. A knife flashes out of Hanama's palm, transfixing one man, while she deftly stabs another in the back. Makri hacks her way through to Gurd. I do likewise. Our savage attack begins to carry the day and our attackers start to crumble. One more push should do it. My senses go haywire again and I realise we're in for another sorcerous attack. Damn all Sorcerers.

It's interrupted by the shrill screech of whistles in the alley below. The Civil Guard has arrived. There's confusion as our attackers fight their way down the stairs to make their escape. I don't bother to pursue them. I can hardly stand upright. The exertion of the battle and the effects of the spell have really drained me. Also, I have a hangover.

"What was that about?" demands Gurd, as Civil Guards pile into the room.

I shake my head numbly. I don't know. I look round to check on my companions. Makri is fine, calmly wiping blood from her swords on to the clothes of one of our many dead opponents. Of Hanama there is no sign. She's slipped out in the confusion.

"What was that about?" echoes Captain Rallee.

"No idea," I pant. "But I'm sure pleased to see you."

"We had them beat anyway," says Makri, dismissively.

Makri fights with a sword in each hand, or a sword in one and an axe in the other. It's an unusual technique, almost unknown in Turai, and her mastery of the skill makes her pretty much invulnerable against your run-of-the-mill street fighter.

"Look, Captain," cries one of the Guardsmen, holding up the arm of one of the bodies and pointing to a tattoo. The Captain crosses over to examine it. Two clasped hands.

"Society of Friends," he says. "What have you done to offend them, Thraxas? You owe them money as well?"

I shake my head. I had no idea I'd offended the Society of Friends. I try to avoid offending large criminal organisations.

Considering there are nine dead bodies in my room the Civil Guards make surprisingly little fuss. The attackers' tattoos confirm them all as members of the Society of Friends, and the Society cuts little ice down here in Brotherhood territory. The Civil Guard isn't going to waste too much time on the matter, especially as I'm a Private Investigator. Captain Rallee observes that, whatever the reason for the attack, I probably deserved it.

Gurd is distressed at the damage to the room, but reasonably jovial about the whole affair. He hasn't had a good fight for a long time.

"Who was that woman?"

"Hanama. A high-up member of the Assassins Guild."

Makri's eyes widen. "There's an Assassins Guild? I never knew they were so organised."

"Well it's not an official guild. They don't go to meetings with other guilds or send representatives to the Senate. But they exist all right. And a bunch of very deadly killers they are too. They're behind most of the political murders here, and they'll work for anyone who pays them."

"But she wasn't trying to assassinate you, was she?"

I shake my head. "She seemed to think I had some Red Elvish Cloth."

"Huh?"

I shake my head. I can't make it out either. "The consignment that went missing on its way to Turai," I explain. "But what it's got to do with the Assassins, or why Hanama thinks I've got it, is a mystery."

A municipal cart rolls up outside and some government workers start carrying the bodies out. Tholius, Prefect in charge of Twelve Seas, doesn't spend a lot of the King's money on keeping the place tidy but he does at least provide a service for mopping up corpses.

"What is this Cloth?" asks Makri, as I pour myself a beer to calm myself after the fight.

"The most valuable substance in the west. Worth more than gold or dwa because it's completely impenetrable to sorcery. It's extremely rare and the Elves guard it pretty closely. They make it from the roots of some bush which only flowers every ten years. Or maybe twenty. I can't exactly remember, but it's rare. It's illegal for anyone but the King to own it here. He's got a room lined with it at the Palace where he discusses state secrets with his advisers. Because it forms a total magic-proof barrier it's the only place that's completely safe from prying Sorcerers, so he can be sure that enemy Orcish Sorcerers aren't eavesdropping in wartime for instance. The Orcs don't have any of this stuff, which gives us an advantage. Plenty of people would like to get their hands on some."

"Were the Society of Friends after the same thing?"

"It's possible. I can't think why else they'd be here. How did word get around that I've got the Red Elvish Cloth? It's got nothing to do with me. It's not even in the city."

"How do you know?"

"Because the Elves mark all their cloth when it's in

transit. A sort of magical signal, so any Sorcerer can locate it. After it reaches our King, an Elvish Sorcerer removes the mark, making it undetectable, but before that's done, Palace Sorcerers could locate it with their searching spells, and I know they've been scanning the city."

"Maybe whoever stole it removed the mark," suggests Makri.

"Unlikely. Elvish magic markings are practically impossible to erase. Usually one of their own Sorcerers does it for the King. I wish I knew how I'd become involved in all this. I'd better learn a more powerful locking spell for my door. It didn't take Hanama long to get through it."

"I like her," says Makri.

"What d'you mean, you like her? She was holding a knife at my throat."

"Well, apart from that. But she was a good fighter. I always like good fighters."

"You'll be a fine philosopher, Makri."

I sleep soundly for what's left of the night. Crisis or no crisis, I'm a man who needs his sleep.

Chapter Nine

I look suspiciously at the coin in my hand. An Elvish double unicorn. Very rare. Very valuable.

"We will pay you another one if you find it."

I look suspiciously at my visitors. Elves are very well regarded in Turai—fine upstanding race, good warriors, excellent poets, beautiful singers, kind to trees, at one with nature and so on—but I have my reservations. In my line of trade I've seen some evidence of Elvish misbehaviour that most people haven't. Okay, I've never come across an Elf who was a vicious killer like some Humans I've known but I've certainly encountered a few with distinctly criminal tendencies. What's more, in my business a visit from an Elf usually means trouble, because if they have any sort of minor problem then their Ambassador sorts it out for them, with plenty of help from our authorities, who always like to keep on their good side.

Yet here are two young Elves, green-clad, tall, fair

and golden-eyed, and they want to hire me. Hire me to find the Red Elvish Cloth. The substance is plaguing me. I've already explained my involvement in the whole affair is accidental.

"If you heard a rumour I have it, it's just that, a rumour. I don't know how it got started but I've no idea where the Cloth is."

"We have heard no such rumours," states Callis-ar-Del, the older of the two. "We have come here because our cousin, Vas-ar-Methet, loyal adviser to Lord Kalith-ar-Yil, who sent the Cloth, recommended you to us as a clever and trustworthy man."

I enjoy being called a clever and trustworthy man. I look on the young Elves with more sympathy. More importantly, the name of Vas-ar-Methet takes me back. One of the very few Elves I've ever been really friendly with, he came up from the Southern Islands with an Elvish battalion in the last Orc Wars. After the western forces took a beating we ended up sharing a ditch together along with Gurd, ingloriously if prudently hiding from a large Orcish dragon patrol scouting the area. We hid for three days before fighting our way back to safety. Sneaking back to safety might be more accurate actually, but we did have to cut our way through a band of Orcish warriors before we reached the city. It's one of our favourite wartime stories. I relate it at least once a week in the bar downstairs.

"How is Vas these days?"

"He is well. His tree of life grows strong with the sky."

I don't exactly know what that means but decide not to pursue it.

"Before we left the Islands he instructed us to come to you if we found ourselves unable to make progress."

The Elves have been sent from the Southern Islands by their Elf Lord to locate the missing Cloth but they

have made no progress. So here they are. They've been
to their Ambassador, seen our Consul, been to Palace
Security, consulted the Civil Guard and asked around
at various Investigating Sorcerers uptown, all to no
effect. Which brings them to Twelve Seas—rotting fish
heads, stinking sewers, cheap detective. Welcome to
the big city.

I shrug. Since I'm already involved in this affair,
someone might as well pay me now I've been sacked
by the Princess. I agree to take the case. The Elves,
Callis and his companion Jaris-ar-Miat, tell me what they
know, which isn't much. Their Elf Lord, Kalith-ar-Yil,
sent up the Cloth on a ship bound for Turai, but it had
to put in south of Mattesh because of storm damage.
Rather than wait for repairs to be completed the Cloth
was loaded on to a wagon train and sent up to the city.
Somewhere along the way the escort was murdered and
the Cloth disappeared. And that's about it. Callis and
Jaris don't seem to have learned anything since being
sent to investigate, but then they're not professionals.

I stare again at the double unicorn in my hand.
Very valuable indeed. And another one to follow if
I locate the Red Elvish Cloth. That would go a long
way towards paying off the Brotherhood. Then there's
the reward for the Cloth offered by the Consul.
Things might be looking up. I might even earn
enough to get out of Twelve Seas. The Elves prepare
to leave. A very well-mannered pair. They haven't
wrinkled their noses at the state of my rooms.

Makri appears, failing to knock as usual. She is taken
aback and gawps dumbly at the Elves, who stare back
at her. Their manners let them down. They can sense
her Orcish blood and it requires little insight to see
they don't like it at all. They edge away from her
uncomfortably. A look of annoyance flickers over
Makri's face.

"Well?" she demands, aggressively.

The Elves nod to me and hurry out. I ask Makri what she wants.

"Nothing. I've got work to do," she says with what she probably imagines is dignity, and storms out, banging the door behind her.

I'm annoyed. I don't like to see Makri upset, but before I can pursue her Pontifex Derlex appears at my door. I try to look like a man who woke up in time for morning prayers. The Pontifex expresses concern for the attack last night.

"I'm fine," I assure him. "Me and Makri fought them off."

Derlex suppresses a grunt. His concern for my welfare doesn't extend to Makri. With her Orcish blood, chainmail bikini and sword-wielding abilities, Makri is about one step up from a demon from the underworld in the eyes of the Church.

"I am gravely concerned at the increase in crime in the Twelve Seas," says the Pontifex, fingering his sacred beads. "As is Bishop Gzekius."

I grunt. "I doubt Bishop Gzekius will lose much sleep over me, Pontifex."

Derlex looks pained. "The Bishop is concerned with the welfare of every one of his flock," he says. He keeps a straight face, which is more than most people could do when attributing Bishop Gzekius with any sort of charitable feelings. The good Bishop Gzekius, whose pastoral responsibilities include Twelve Seas and the rest of Turai's miserable dockland slums, is an ambitious schemer with his eyes on the Archbishopric. He's far too busy striving for power and influence among the city's aristocracy to worry about the poor of Twelve Seas, or anywhere else.

"Why did the gang attack you?"

I profess not to know, and usher Derlex out after

again promising to attend his church. I'm finding this concern for my health a little hard to take, particularly before breakfast.

My breakfast is a cheerless affair, eaten under the frosty gaze of Makri who is currently as angry as an Orc with a toothache. She slams my plate down on my table and refuses to speak.

"Don't you think you're being a bit over-sensitive?" I venture, as she passes with a mop in her hands.

"I don't know what you're talking about," she snaps, brandishing the mop in a quite dangerous manner. "I'm as happy as an Elf in a tree."

She mops under a chair, knocks it over, and stamps on the remains.

Customers arrive for an early drink, ending our discussion. I curse the delicate sensitivities of my axe-wielding friend and prepare for a day's investigating. I go down to the local Civil Guard station to see if Guardsman Jevox can throw any light on things. I once used my influence to protect Jevox's father from the Brotherhood when they were threatening his livelihood as a bookmaker at the Stadium Superbius, which makes Jevox rather more helpful to me than your average Civil Guardsman.

"Any leads on the theft of the Red Elvish Cloth?"

Jevox is surprised at my question. "You working on that?"

I look vacant and he doesn't press the point. Jevox has heard about the fight at my house with the Society of Friends, but he can't throw any light on why they or anybody else should have thought I had the Cloth. He does tell me that the Society is rumoured to have been connected to the hijacking, though there's nothing definite.

"Are you saying they don't have it any more?"

"Possibly."

I ask him to let me know if the Guard makes any progress, particularly on the name of the Sorcerer who might be working with the Society, and Jevox agrees. He asks me how I got mixed up in it.

Naturally I decline to explain. "What's the reward?"

"Just went up to five hundred gurans."

A nice figure to a man in urgent need of money. Tholius, Prefect of Twelve Seas, arrives unexpectedly and throws me out. Tholius doesn't like me. Prefects never do. Any time I solve something it makes them feel inadequate.

Outside the Civil Guard station some young kid from the Koolu Kings, the local street gang, shouts a disparaging remark about fat men who always gamble on the wrong chariots. I scoop up a stone and hurl it at him in one smooth movement. It hits him on the nose and he bursts into tears.

"Never mock a trained soldier, brat."

Palax and Kaby are busking beside the harbour. Both are dressed in their usual bizarre assortment of shabby but colourful clothes. They augment their outfits with many strings of beads and great numbers of earrings. Each of them wears a metal stud piercing their left eyebrow (among other parts of their anatomies) and they dye their hair in colours bright enough to get any normal citizen attacked in the street, though as travelling entertainers they have some licence in this sort of thing. Their horse-drawn caravan is parked on a patch of waste ground behind Gurd's tavern. I was shocked the first time I saw them, and recommended that Gurd ran them off the land, but I'm used to them now. They're actually a nice young couple and we're quite friendly. It's beyond me why they have to look so strange though. I mean, pierced noses and eyebrows? Ridiculous. I listen to them play for a minute, and drop a coin into their cup.

It's time to visit the Mermaid, one of Twelve Seas" least pleasant taverns, which is saying something. More youths from the Koolu Kings jeer at me as I pass. Everyone in Twelve Seas knows me, but I wouldn't claim to be popular. The prostitutes and dwa dealers ignore me as I pick my way over the filth strewn over the street.

Kerk can usually be found around here. As a dwa dealer he often learns interesting facts in the way of his business. Unfortunately for him, he consumes rather too much of his own product, and is therefore generally in need of money. I find him outside the tavern, leaning unsteadily against the wall. He's tall and dark but his once handsome features are sunken and undernourished and his large eyes are dull and vacant. From his eyes I think he may have a trace of Elvish blood, which wouldn't be so strange. Elvish visitors to our city are not above dallying with our whores, whatever their professions of moral superiority.

I ask him if he knows anything about the Cloth.

"Choirs of Angels," he mutters, staring at the floor. I don't know what that means. I presume he's in the grip of some powerful hallucination. Kerk's been getting worse recently. I'm surprised he manages to keep his business going.

"Red Elvish Cloth," I repeat.

He focuses on me with some difficulty.

"Thraxas. You're in trouble."

"I know that already. I just don't know why."

"You robbed Attilan."

"No I didn't."

"That's what people say."

"Well what about it?" I demand.

"Attilan was trying to get his hands on the Elvish Cloth for Nioj. Some people think he already had it when you killed him."

"I didn't kill him. Or rob him. Anyway, how could Attilan have had the Cloth? It isn't in the city."

Kerk shrugs. "Don't know. Maybe Glixius Dragon Killer's behind it all."

"Who the hell is Glixius Dragon Killer?" I demand.

Kerk looks at me. "Don't you know anything? You're not much of an Investigator, Thraxas. Surprised you've stayed alive so long. Glixius Dragon Killer is the rogue Sorcerer who hijacked the stuff in the first place. He's been working with the Society."

Kerk holds out his hand. I press a coin into it.

"Choirs of Angels," he mumbles again. He dribbles, slides down the wall and passes out. I must find some informers who are not the scum of the earth. At least I now know why my name became connected with the Cloth. Attilan was after it and I had the misfortune to be arrested for his murder. No wonder people thought I'd robbed him.

I stare with distaste at Kerk's unconscious figure. I doubt I'm the only person he sells information to. If he's been spreading what he knows it's no surprise that various other people might think I have the cloth.

It's hot. I want to go home and drink beer. However, with the Assassins Guild and the Society of Friends both out to get me, and two Elves waiting to pay me handsomely, I have an incentive to start work. I need to talk to Captain Rallee but it takes a while to find him. He had a cushy desk job at the Abode of Justice up till last year, which he didn't mind at all, but then he fell out of favour when the wheels of internal Palace politics moved against him. Deputy Consul Rittius replaced him with his own man, and the Captain is therefore once more pounding the streets. Which does at least give me something in common with the good Captain, because Deputy Consul Rittius, the second most important government official in Turai, hates me as well.

I find the Captain staring morosely at a few dead bodies on the outskirts of Kushni.

"What happened?"

"Same as usual," he grunts in reply. "Brotherhood and Society fighting over territory for the dwa trade. It's getting out of hand, Thraxas. Half the city's caught up in it."

We watch as city employees load corpses into wagons and drive them off. I don't bother asking the Captain if he's planning to arrest anyone. The drug barons of the Society of Friends and the Brotherhood have too much protection in this city for the Civil Guard to touch them. As for their lesser minions, there's so many of them it hardly makes any difference how many he throws in jail.

"Just trying to keep the lid on things till I retire," sighs the Captain. "And now the elections are about to start. More chaos."

He shakes his head, and asks me what I want. I explain my situation to him, without mentioning the Elves. He nods.

"We heard a rumour that Nioj was interested in the Cloth. The Elves don't like selling to them. They get annoyed when the fundamentalist Niojan clerics denounce them as demons from hell. Don't think the Niojans were involved in the hijacking though. We've obtained information as to who was responsible."

"Yeah, I know, Glixius Dragon Killer," I say, disappointing the Captain. "I've met him already. Any leads on where the stuff is?"

"No," replies the Captain. "But I reckon it's long gone. Probably never reached Turai at all."

I ask him if the Guards are any closer to finding Attilan's killer.

Captain Rallee sneers. "We reckon you make a pretty good suspect, Thraxas."

"Come on, you know I didn't kill him."

"Maybe. But that might not stop us charging you anyway. If no one better comes along. Rittius would be delighted to see you in a prison galley. And he's going to have to charge someone. The Niojan Ambassador is raising hell."

"Don't you have any real leads?" I ask him.

"You expect a lot, Thraxas. Information from me, but you won't say what your involvement is. Why should I help you?"

"I once pulled you out from under the wheels of an Orc chariot?"

"That was a long time ago. I've done you enough favours since then. You got yourself mixed up in this, and now the Society's on your tail. Tough. Come clean with us, Thraxas, and I might be able to help you. Otherwise you're on your own."

That's as much as I get from the Captain, though he does tell me that an even more powerful form of dwa has appeared in the city, going by the name of Choirs of Angels. No one knows where it's coming from.

"Kerk seems to like it. Well, Captain, if you refuse to help me, I'll just have to find the Cloth myself. I could do with a fat reward."

"Well, if we find you were mixed up in its theft, you won't get out of prison to spend your reward. Still, Thraxas, maybe you should look for it. If the Society of Friends think you've got it, your life isn't worth much anyway. Not that it's going to be worth anything at all in two days' time if you don't hand over five hundred gurans to Yubaxas."

I sneer at him.

"No doubt the Civil Guard will provide me with constant protection if a criminal organisation such as the Brotherhood is out to harm me?"

"Yeah right, Thraxas. Sure we will. Best thing you could do is leave town. Except you can't, because you're still a suspect for Attilan's murder. Looks like you're in a difficult position."

"Thanks a lot, Captain."

The heat is becoming oppressive. The sun's rays are trapped between the six-storey slums that line the streets. It's illegal to build above four storeys in Turai. Too dangerous. The property developers bribe the Prefects and the Prefects pass on some money to the Praetors" officials and then no one minds that it's dangerous any more. Stals, the small black birds which infest parts of the city, sit miserably on the rooftops, lacking the energy to scavenge for scraps. I'm sweating like a pig, the whores look tired and the streets stink. It's a bad day. I might as well visit the Assassins.

Chapter Ten

Kushni is the most disreputable area of a city which has more than its fair share of disreputable quarters. The narrow, filthy streets are comprised of brothels, gambling dens, dwa joints and dubious taverns. The streets are full of pimps, prostitutes, derelicts, junkies and thieves. It is perverse of the Assassins to have their headquarters there. Not that they're in any danger of being robbed or assaulted by any of Kushni's low-life habitués. No one would be so stupid.

"I'm surprised at you visiting us," says the black-hooded woman sitting opposite me. "Our informants didn't say you were possessed of great intelligence, but neither did they tell us you were a fool."

I'm sitting in a plain room without decoration of any sort talking to Hanama, Master Assassin, and I can't say I'm enjoying it. Hanama is number three in the Assassins' chain of command, or so I believe. They don't publish details of their ranks. She's around thirty,

I think, though she looks younger, but it's hard to tell as her head and part of her face are generally covered by a black hood. She is small, very pale-skinned, and rather softly spoken.

"It was easy to break the locking spell on your door," she murmurs. "I doubt if your protection spell would hold out against me for long."

Little does she know I'm not carrying a protection spell. I put the sleep spell into my subconscious before I came out, and I can't manage two spells these days. Could I utter the sleep spell before she made it across the table to kill me? Possibly. Possibly not. I've no intention of finding out.

"I don't expect to need protection. After all, you're mistaken in thinking I have the Red Elvish Cloth. Why did you think I had it?"

No reply.

"Why do the Assassins want it?"

"What makes you think I would answer questions from you?"

"I'm just doing my job. And protecting myself. If you, the Society of Friends and God knows who else believe I've got the Cloth, my life isn't going to be worth much. The best I can expect is a long stay in the King's dungeon. Or rowing one of his triremes."

She gazes at me silently. This annoys me.

"Perhaps I should report last night's events to the Civil Guard," I say. "The Consul and the Praetors tolerate the Assassins because they find them useful. But they wouldn't be very pleased to hear you were trying to get your hands on Red Elvish Cloth reserved for the King."

"We would not appreciate anyone spreading false rumours about us," says Hanama, threateningly.

"I'd hate to do anything the Assassins would not

appreciate. You know anything about the theft of the Cloth?"

"The Assassins do not indulge in illegal activities."

"You kill people."

"No charges have ever been brought against us," says Hanama, coolly.

"Yeah, sure, I know. Because you're always hired by people rich and important enough to avoid the law. Why are you looking for the Cloth?"

"We aren't."

"No doubt you're aware the Cloth is valued at thirty thousand gurans?"

Hanama maintains her cool indifference. I get more annoyed.

"You cold-blooded murderers make me sick. Stay well away from me, Hanama. Bother me again and I'll be down on you like a bad spell."

Hanama rises gracefully to her feet.

"Our interview is over," she says, slightly less coolly.

I've succeeded in riling her. Good. Just goes to show what a reckless old fool I've become, riling an Assassin in her own den.

"Just one last question. How do you Assassins all keep your skin so pale? Is it make-up, or special training, or what?"

Hanama pulls a bell-rope. Two junior Assassins enter the room and escort me along a corridor to the front door.

"You should brighten the place up a bit," I suggest. "Get a few pot plants."

They refuse to reply. Practising being grim-faced, I expect. Outside, in the dusty road, I shudder. Assassins. Give me the creeps.

Chapter Eleven

Walking through the busy outskirts of Twelve Seas I take my usual short cut through Saint Rominius's Way, a narrow alley. Round the first corner I'm confronted by three men with swords at the ready.

"Well?" I demand, drawing my own sword.

They take a few steps towards me.

"Where's the Cloth, Thraxas?" demands one of them.

"No idea."

They move to encircle me. I bark out the sleep spell. My three assailants instantly fall to the ground. Very satisfying. I'm most pleased. Every time I do that it gives me a warm glow. Makes me feel like my life has not been entirely wasted.

The sleep spell usually lasts for around ten minutes so I have time for a little investigating before I quit the scene. Delving into their pockets, I find nothing of interest, but they're all tattooed with the clasped hands of the Society of Friends.

Behind me someone speaks. I wheel around, and realise I've made somewhat of a blunder in hanging around. The words belong to one of the arcane languages known only to us Sorcerers, and they formed a common countermanding spell. Which means any spell currently used in the area is no longer operational. Which means that three angry members of the Society of Friends are at this moment coming back to consciousness.

I glare at the Sorcerer with disgust. There's no point in me going to all the trouble of learning, storing and using a sleep spell if he's just going to come along and countermand it. Whilst glaring, I notice that, for a Sorcerer, he's pretty damned big. Carries a sharp-looking blade as well. "You must be the Glixius Dragon Killer everyone's talking about." He doesn't reply. The three Friends start climbing to their feet, groping for their swords. I run like hell along Saint Rominius's Way.

I'm worried. Not so much by the blades of the three men—I'll take my chances at swordplay against most inhabitants of Turai—but by the Sorcerer. Something in the way he chanted his counterspell makes me feel that he's a powerful man, skilful enough to be carrying one or two more spells. If one of those is a heart attack spell I'm done for. Even a sleep spell would give them the opportunity to finish me off. I was a fool to pawn my spell protection charm. I must have badly needed a beer.

For a man in poor condition I'm making good time, but as I round the next corner I see three more thugs coming towards me. Six armed men and the Sorcerer. I certainly have offended the Society of Friends.

In front of me I spy a wooden manhole cover. The sewerage system of Turai is one of the wonders of the world, so they say, with a tunnel leading all the way from the Palace to the sea. Not for the first time in my crime-fighting career, I find myself in a position to admire it. I whip off the cover and plunge into the tunnels.

The stench is unbearable. Rats scatter in all directions as I stumble my way through the blackness in front of me. I bitterly regret pawning my illuminated staff along with my protection charm. This is a grim, hellish place to be in the dark. Still, having been here before, I know this sewer leads to the harbour, and just before it discharges into the sea there's another manhole cover through which I can make my escape.

Unsure of whether I'm still being pursued or not I halt and listen.

"Try further down," comes a voice.

Somewhere behind me is a greenish light. The Sorcerer's illuminated staff. I worry again about how many spells he might be carrying. Rogue criminal Sorcerers are rare in Turai, thanks to the Sorcerers Guild, but when they appear I've no real protection against them. I wade on through the filth, ignoring the stink and the squeaking rats, feeling along the wall for the ladder which will tell me when I'm under the exit. I hope there aren't any alligators down here. Rumours abound of alligators living in the city sewers. I don't think I believe them. Even they must have somewhere better to go. There's a whole sandy bay outside, unless the dolphins chase them in here, I suppose. Dolphins aren't fond of alligators, apparently.

I pick up the pace a little, but this is a mistake because almost immediately a man somewhere behind shouts that he can hear me and this cry is followed by the sound of feet splashing quickly through the water. I curse and hurry on but the splashing footsteps draw nearer.

Round the next bend I pause and turn with my sword and dagger at the ready. An ignominious death,

I reflect, succumbing to a heart attack spell in the city sewers. Everyone will think I fell in drunk.

The sewer is around four feet wide and just tall enough for me to stand up in. Not a lot of room for fighting. The faintest of glows appear round the corner, followed by the first of my pursuers, groping his way round, a dagger stretched out in front of him. He's dead before he even sees me, his throat cut by my blade with the sort of well-measured stroke I learned in the Army when I was a confident young soldier and we drove the Niojans back from our walls and the Orcs out of our country.

After this it's not so easy. The next two advance more slowly. A little more light now shows, allowing them to see me more clearly. I use my sword and dagger to parry their dual attack and retreat slightly, aware that this is risky. Who knows what I might trip over down here. The combat is grim and silent. The two Society men drive me steadily back, offering no opening for attack. Behind them I can just make out the dim outlines of their companions, and further back is the largely shadowy outline of the Sorcerer, his staff casting an eerie green light over us all.

My assailants are not top-class fighters—gang members rarely are—but in the confined space of the sewer I find it hard to bring my superior sword fighting skills into play. The sewage comes up to my knees, preventing me from manoeuvring, and all the time I'm worried that the Sorcerer will unleash a deadly spell in my direction, although this depends on what he's carrying. Some aggressive spells are hard to direct. In this tunnel he'd be quite likely to hit his own men too.

The fighter on my right grows impatient and makes a sudden lunge, but he's careless and leaves a gap low down in his defence through which I plant the tip of my sword into his thigh. He groans and stumbles backwards. Another man is about to step into his place when the Sorcerer pulls him back.

"Leave him to me," he commands, and his staff glows brighter.

I've only a fraction of a second in which to act. I draw back my dagger, preparing to hurl it at the Sorcerer's face, and hope that he's not carrying a personal protection spell. Before I can release the weapon, or he can utter his spell, a horrifying shape erupts out of the water. The swordsman closest to me screams and leaps backwards in fear and the Sorcerer's spell is choked off in mid sentence. Attracted by his light, an alligator surfaces from the mire and grips the Sorcerer's leg in its monstrous jaws.

I look on, frozen with horror. The beast is huge and the grip of its jaws must be terrible. I'm sure it's death for the Sorcerer, but he's not a man who is prepared to surrender his life easily. Mere seconds away from being dragged under the stinking water he shouts out a spell and immediately the alligator starts to writhe dementedly, shaking its huge body around in wild agony, all the while holding on to the leg of the unfortunate Sorcerer.

I turn and flee. He must have used a heart attack spell, or something similar. What this will do to an alligator I'm not certain. Kill it eventually, I'm sure, but maybe not before it killed you. Whether the Sorcerer will survive the encounter is anybody's guess. A dreadful fate if he dies, but the thought that the deadly spell was destined for use on me mitigates my sympathy somewhat.

Heart pounding for fear of encountering another monstrous alligator, I find the ladder. I haul my bulky figure up the creaking rungs as quickly as I ever scaled anything in my life. At the top of the shaft I push off the cover and drag myself into the street. All around people stare in astonishment as, filthy, bedraggled, wild-eyed and stinking, I emerge into the sunlit streets of Twelve Seas.

"Sewer inspection," I mutter to one inquisitive individual who nears me as I struggle on my way.

"What's it like down there?" he calls after me.

"Fine," I call back. "Good for a few years yet."

Chapter Twelve

I present a desperate figure as I march into Quintessence Street. The stink from my disgusting sewage-encrusted clothes is unbearable and I'm obsessed with the desire to be clean and to wash the terrible experience out of my system. Down a small alleyway is the public baths. I know the manager well but that doesn't mean she's pleased to see me striding in looking like an apparition from hell.

"Need a wash," I say as I march past her, ignoring her protests and admonitions for me not to go anywhere near her pool in my condition. Bathers scatter like the rats in the sewer as I make my appearance. Mothers grab their small children out of the water in panic as I walk fully clothed into the water. People scream abuse. There are calls for someone to fetch the Civil Guard to protect them from the plague carrier who's just poisoned their bath.

Ignoring them all, I sink under the warm water and

roll around, rubbing the filth from my skin and my clothes. As I let the heat take away some of the tension, I feel some gratitude towards the King. He doesn't do much for the miserable poor of Twelve Seas, but at least he built us a good bathing house. Some time later I emerge clean, my clothes in my hands. I wrap my now sadly bedraggled cloak around my frame and march out, still ignoring the abuse poured on me from all directions.

"Thanks. Pay you tomorrow," I grunt at the manager, Ginixa, who is loudly promising a law suit against me for ruining her business.

Makri gapes as I appear at the Avenging Axe. "What happened to you?"

"Bad day in the sewers," I reply, grabbing a thazis stick on the way up to my rooms. I'm still high on shock and fear, and the effects of my using the sleep spell are starting to show. Spell casting is a tiring business. Even without the subsequent pursuit, putting those Society men to sleep in the alleyway would have taken it out of me. The episode in the sewers has completely worn me out. I need to lie down and sleep, but I'm too worked up to relax. I smoke the thazis in three long draws. Makri arrives with a beer, and in between gulps I finish off the last of my klee. The strong spirit burns my throat as it goes down. Probably there are healthier methods of calming down than thazis, beer and klee, but none so quickly effective. By the time I've gone next door and dressed myself in some dry clothes I'm starting to return to my normal jovial self.

"Who was it?" enquires Makri.

"The Society of Friends. With a Sorcerer."

"They still think you've got the magic Cloth?"

I nod. There's a knock on the outside door. I answer it with a sword in one hand and a knife in the other. Outside is Karlox, the enforcer from the Brotherhood.

"What the hell do you want?"

"We hear you found the Cloth. Go a long way towards paying off your debts—" he begins.

"I don't have the damned Elvish Cloth!" I yell, slamming the door in his face.

"This is preposterous, Makri. Two Elves are paying me to find the stuff, and everyone else thinks I have it already. It's getting confusing. When I smoked that thazis I swear for a moment I started believing it myself. I'll kill that damned Kerk, it's all his fault. He spread the rumour that I stole it from Attilan."

I notice that Makri is no longer listening. The mention of the Elves has put her in a bad mood. I'm not certain why it's bothering her so much. Makri has experienced plenty of prejudice against her in the city, with customers downstairs always commenting on her Orcish blood. She doesn't like it but it doesn't usually make her unhappy for long. Often forgets it almost right after hitting the customer. What seems to make matters worse is the fact that it involves Elves. I guess Makri, being one third Elvish, and speaking their language, and detesting Orcs quite as much as they do, finds rejection by them particularly galling. I don't bother trying to cheer her up. Karlox's visit has put me in a pretty bad mood myself.

We light up some more thazis. Our mood improves a little.

"I think the Cloth is still in the city."

Makri points out that only yesterday I said this was impossible.

"I changed my mind. I don't know how, but that Cloth is in Turai. I can sense it."

"Very astute, Thraxas. Though I suspected as much myself when all these people started trying to kill you."

I tell Makri about the alligator.

"You're joking. There aren't really alligators in the sewers?"

I assure her there are. A wave of fatigue rolls over my body.

"I'm going to rest. The Society of Friends probably won't risk another open attack on me down here in Brotherhood territory, but if a Sorcerer with a sore leg comes looking for me, tell him I'm not in."

It's dark when I wake. A few thoughts of sewers and alligators come to mind but I banish them. More important business calls, namely I'm hungry. Really, really hungry. I launch myself downstairs to investigate Tanrose's cooking. It's now late evening, and drinking at the Avenging Axe is in full swing. Gurd is regaling some off-duty Civil Guardsmen with tales of the time he and a group of fellow mercenaries were trapped south of Mattesh and had to fight their way back to Turai through hundreds of miles of unknown terrain and whole armies of ferocious enemies. It's a true story actually, though I have noticed it does tend to grow in the telling.

Makri, chainmail bikini more or less in place, is gathering tankards and scooping up what looks like a fairly handsome tip from a group of sailors just back from the Southern Islands and full of the wonders they saw among the Elves. I head straight for the side of the bar where Tanrose sits selling her wares and cast a greedy eye over her food.

"Evening, Tanrose. I'll have a whole venison pie, a large portion of each vegetable and three slices of your apple pie with cream. No, better make that four slices. Tell you what, just give me the whole pie. And you'd better give me a bowl of beef stew as well. Stick a few yams on the side will you? What's in the pastry? Pork and apple? Give me two of them, and I'll take six pancakes to mop up the sauce. No, make that eight pancakes and four pastries. Any cake? Pomegranate? Good, I'll have a slice to finish with. A large slice. No, larger. Okay, I'll take the whole cake."

"Had a busy day?" grins Tanrose, piling up a tray.

"Terrible. Couldn't stop for a bite to eat anywhere. Better make that two venison pies. If I don't eat them Gurd'll only finish them off."

Vast tray of food in hand, I pick up a special "Happy Guildsman" jumbo-sized tankard of ale at the bar and retreat to a corner to eat. I have a powerful appetite. Satisfying it gives me intense pleasure.

"One whole venison pie feeds a family of four," comments Makri, passing with a tray.

"Not if I get there first," I reply, moving on to the pork and apple pastries, one of Tanrose's specialities. By now the beef stew has cooled sufficiently to let me mop it up with my pancakes, and I wash it all down with the rest of my ale, calling Makri over to bring me a second giant "Happy Guildsman" tankard to accompany my apple pie.

Some time later, pomegranate cake finished to the last crumb, third "Happy Guildsman" resting invitingly in front of me, I reflect that life is not so bad. Okay, you might get chased around sewers by the Society of Friends, but there's always Tanrose's cooking and Gurd's ale. Make a man glad to be alive. Makri appears beside me during her break. She makes a few snide comments about my appetite, but I wave them away benevolently.

"You have to stay slim, Makri. You need a good shape under that bikini to earn tips from sailors. Me, I need something more substantial. You can't solve crimes and face dangerous criminals with only a few morsels inside you. When people see me coming they know they've got a problem on their hands."

Makri grins. As usual she's carrying a purse on a long string over her shoulder for holding her tips, though I notice that today she has a new one, slightly larger than normal.

"Tips increasing?"

Makri shakes her head. "Same as ever. I'm using this to carry round some other money I've been collecting. Don't want to risk leaving it in my room."

"What money?"

"Contributions to the fund."

"Pardon?"

"You know. The fund for raising money to buy a Royal Charter for the Association of Gentlewomen."

This is the first I've heard of any fund, although I did know that the Association of Gentlewomen was applying for a Royal Charter, without which they cannot be recognised as an accredited Turanian guild, and take their place on the Council as a member of the Revered Federation of Guilds, and send an observer to the Senate.

"I didn't know you were that involved, Makri. How much have you raised?"

She snorts. "Only a few gurans. When it comes to the Association of Gentlewomen people round here are meaner than a Pontifex. Gurd won't let me collect in here but I've been going round the local shops. I wouldn't say your average Twelve Seas shopkeeper was keen to contribute. I have a few donations from local women though. Ginixa at the public baths gave me five gurans."

"If she sues me for ruining her business she might be able to afford a lot more. How much does the A.G. need for the Charter?"

"Twenty thousand."

"How much have they got?"

Makri doesn't really know. She's only collecting

money, and is not involved in the organisation in any major way. She thinks they still have a long way to go.

"And paying for the Charter is only one part of what we need. Before you even make the application, there's the large fee to the Revered Federation of Guilds to process the papers. And all the way along the line there's people to be paid and palms to be greased—the Praetor for Guild Affairs, the Deputy Consul, Palace officials and who knows who else. Apparently it's standard practice for the Consul's Secretary to demand a ten-thousand-guran bribe before he lets an application go through."

"That's going to add up to a lot of money."

"It does. And we're going to need twice as much in bribe money because of the opposition from the True Church and all the other people who don't want to see the Association of Gentlewomen make any advance. I heard the figure of fifty thousand mentioned. There aren't many wealthy women in Turai. Even the ones that do run their own businesses have a hard time surviving because the guilds won't admit them. Well, if they won't let us in to the Bakers, Innkeepers, Transport or other Guilds, they're going to have to face us on the Revered Federation Council when the Association of Gentlewomen gets its Charter."

"Who do you give the money to?"

"Minarixa the Baker. She's the local organiser. Care to make a contribution?"

"What will the Association of Gentlewomen do for me?"

"Get me off your back."

"Yes, well, maybe later, Makri."

"Why not now?"

I look around anxiously. "The place is full of Barbarians and dock workers. If they see me giving money to the Association of Gentlewomen they'll ridicule me half to death."

Makri sneers. I will give her some money later. Not right now though, not in public. I have an image to maintain.

"You should have asked the Princess, Makri. She must have a lot of money."

"She hasn't."

"How do you know?"

"Because I heard at last night's meeting that Lisutaris, Mistress of the Sky, already asked Du-Akai for some help."

"Lisutaris, Mistress of the Sky? She's pretty senior in the Sorcerers Guild. Works at the Palace too. Is she involved in your group?"

Makri nods. "All sorts of women are. But the Princess couldn't make a donation. The King controls her money. And they don't get on very well."

"I'm not surprised, if she lies to the King the same way she lied to me. I still wish I knew why she sent me to find that spell. Why would a Princess want to put a dragon to sleep? It's not like it's guarding anything. No reason to bother with it that I can see. Unless . . ."

I break off, and stare into space.

"Sudden Investigator's intuition?" says Makri, slightly sarcastically.

"That's right. You might want to put a dragon to sleep to make it easier to kill."

"Why would Princess Du-Akai want to do that? It's a present to her father. They don't get on that badly."

"I've been wondering how all this fits together, Makri. In my experience, when various troubles descend on me, they generally turn out to be connected in some way or other. No one knows how the Red Elvish Cloth was brought into the city. No one knows where it is now. And if the rumours of the Orcs buying it are right, no one knows how it's going to be transported to them.

Well, what if it was put inside something that was very secure, which was going back to them eventually?"

"You mean inside the dragon?"

"Why not?"

"How the hell would you stuff a roll of Red Elvish Cloth inside a dragon?"

"I don't know. But that Sorcerer who chased me through the sewers is powerful. He might have done it after he hijacked the shipment."

Makri scoffs. "Dumbest idea you've ever had, Thraxas."

"Oh yeah? Well, I trust my intuition. And my intuition tells me that the Red Elvish Cloth is right this minute inside the new dragon at the King's zoo. It's the perfect place—in fact it's the only place, because dragons are well known for disrupting sorcery. If the Cloth was inside that beast, our Palace Sorcerers wouldn't be able to detect it, Elvish marks or not. A very clever notion, Makri, very clever indeed. Hide the Cloth in the dragon, wait till it mates with the King's, then off it goes back to Gzak, taking the Cloth with it."

Makri considers this. Two Barbarians shout for beer but Makri gestures for them to be quiet. "So what did Attilan have to do with all this?"

"I think he learned of it somehow and decided he'd intervene. Steal the Cloth for his own country. King Lamachus of Nioj would be very pleased with him if he did. Which would explain what Attilan was doing with a spell for putting a dragon to sleep. A Niojan diplomat might be able to gain access to the zoo when it was closed to the public."

"Where did he get the spell?"

I admit I don't know. But I'm pretty sure he was killed before he used it. Which means the Cloth should still be inside the dragon, right under the noses of the Palace Sorcerers. Just waiting for me to recover it.

I notice Makri seems even more exposed than usual, and is bulging out of her bikini in a manner guaranteed to make even the most experienced sailor's jaw drop.

"Makri, how old are you?"

"Twenty-one."

"In which case, unless your unique parentage has produced some very strange effects, your breasts should have stopped growing."

Makri glances at her chest.

"They have. I took a couple of links out of my bikini to make it a bit smaller. I need to earn more tips, Samanatius the Philosopher is starting a new class and I have to raise the fee."

If Makri ever does make it to the Imperial University no one will be able to say she doesn't deserve it.

Chapter Thirteen

Next morning Derlex, the young Pontifex, arrives at my door, thrusting a collection box under my nose. He's come for a donation to the fund for repairing the tower on the local temple, recently damaged in a fire. I rummage around for a few coins. Always pleased to do my civic duty. Also it might get him off my back. It's making me nervous, the way he's always around these days, asking me how I am, encouraging me to go to church. There must be worse sinners than me for him to worry about. Makri appears and Derlex departs with a frown.

"To hell with him," sniffs Makri, which I guess is exactly what he's thinking about her.

Makri is reading today's copy of *The Renowned and Truthful Chronicle of All the World's Events*.

"Anything interesting?"

"Another Sarin the Merciless story. Apparently she killed a rich merchant in Mattesh and fled with his money. Fought off three Civil Guards who were after her."

I scoff at this. "I bet. These news-sheets, they exaggerate everything."

"How?"

I explain to Makri that I've tangled with Sarin the Merciless before. "I ran her out of town about six years ago. She was trying to set up some protection racket. The Transport Guild hired me to get her off their back. Bit of a joke, really. She's no killer, just some petty hoodlum with big ideas. The papers always like to build these people up. It gives them something to write about. If she fetches up in Turai I'll soon show her who's number one chariot around here. Hope she does, I could do with some reward money."

Makri grins. "Who's Mirius Eagle Rider?" she asks, glancing again at the news-sheet.

"Sorcerer," I reply. "Works for Rittius at Palace Security. One of the most powerful Sorcerers in the city, although not averse to dwa, from what I hear. What's it say about him?"

"He's been murdered."

I raise my eyebrows. That is news. Mirius Eagle Rider murdered? Mirius was not an obvious candidate for murder. There isn't much to the report. Palace Security have it under wraps for just now. But it does contain one notable fact. Mirius was found by one of his servants this morning with a bolt from a crossbow in his back. Strange. A crossbow is an unusual weapon for a murder. Pretty cumbersome thing to carry around as a concealed weapon. It would have to be concealed because it's illegal to carry one in the city. Too powerful, makes the Civil Guard nervous. Generally they're only used in wartime.

Deputy Consul Rittius isn't going to be pleased at such a senior Sorcerer being killed like that. The thought of the Deputy Consul not being pleased gives me some pleasure, although as a man's death is involved I don't get too carried away. Strange, though, that a Sorcerer like Mirius should have succumbed to any normal weapon, no matter how powerful.

"Dwa'd out of his head, I expect. Probably had an argument with his dealer. These Palace Sorcerers, they're all degenerate."

"Everyone in Turai is degenerate," opines Makri. "I met people with better manners in the Orcish slave pits."

With that she goes off to her early shift downstairs, and I head off to visit Jevox at the Guard Station to see if he has any information for me. I stop off at Minarixa's bakery and arrive at the station still wiping crumbs off my face. It's already too hot to be comfortable and I'm perspiring freely as I stroll inside. My sword is uncomfortable at my hip. It's chafing at my skin. I never used to notice that sort of thing when I was a young soldier.

Jevox is on duty at the desk. He's mopping his brow as I arrive. "Hotter than Orcish hell in here."

"Damn right it is." I ask him if he's learned anything.

"That Sorcerer who's been chasing you about, Glixius Dragon Killer. He had a big reputation in the west. Very bad, and very powerful. He was expelled from Samsarina a few years back. Involved in an attempted coup."

Samsarina is a large, wealthy country some way to the west, one of the strongest of the Human Lands. Glixius Dragon Killer. A name I'd never heard before Kerk mentioned it. It doesn't tell me much. Sorcerers always take on exotic names when they finish their training and don the rainbow cloak. He might be able to kill dragons. He might not. He's of aristocratic birth

though. Any man with a name ending in "ius" belongs
to an aristocratic family. It's one of these class distinc-
tions we have, just like anyone with "ox" or "ax" in their
name is low-born. Like Jevox the Civil Guard. Or
Thraxas the Investigator.

"Our Prefect got a report he'd been seen in Mattesh.
Left suddenly after the royal vaults mysteriously emptied themselves of gold."

I wonder if he survived the alligator attack.

"Who's got the Cloth?" Jevox asks me.

I tell him I don't know. I don't mention my theory
that it's inside the dragon.

"You know you're famous now, Thraxas?"

"Huh?"

"Prefect Tholius says you were mentioned in a
debate in the Senate. Senator Lodius was denouncing
the authorities for their incompetence and he cited you
as prime example. Wanted to know why you hadn't
been arrested and charged with Attilan's death. He
claimed there must be some sort of cover-up going on.
Is it true?"

I shake my head. I'm not important enough for
anyone to cover up for.

"In that case I reckon the Consul might swear out
a warrant for you just to shut Lodius up. He's not going
to want Lodius accusing the King and his ministers of
incompetence with the elections approaching. Maybe
it's time you found yourself a lawyer."

I'm sweating and thirsty so I visit the large street
market that separates Twelve Seas from Pashish and
buy a watermelon. When I've got most of it inside me
I notice Palax and Kaby, who often busk here during
the day. They're sitting on a small patch of waste
ground next to a fruit stall, talking to someone. As I
wander over to say hello their companion rises to leave
and I smile, because he's a giant of a man, completely

dwarfing the young buskers. He dwarfs me as well, in height if not in girth. He must be close on seven feet tall, with shoulders and biceps to match. Not a man to tangle with, though from the way Palax and Kaby are waving and grinning I guess he must be friendly.

"Who was that?" I ask, while accepting a draw on a thazis stick Kaby offers me. The mild narcotic is still technically illegal in Turai but since dwa swept the city the authorities don't bother much about it.

"That was Strongman Brex. We used to work with him in the circus, down in Juval. We played music while he smashed rocks with his bare hands. Sometimes he'd come busking with us. He'd hold us up in the air, one on each palm, while we played. We earned a lot of money like that."

"What's he doing in Turai? Is the circus in town?"

Palax shakes his head. Strongman Brex has apparently left the circus. He'd had enough of the life and came to Turai looking for proper employment.

"He's already got a job. Pity, he won't be able to busk with us."

"What's he doing?" I ask, passing the thazis back to Kaby.

"He got a job at the Palace. Working for Princess Du-Akai."

I blink. "Princess Du-Akai? What's she want with a strongman?"

"Don't know. But Brex likes it. He gets well paid and he doesn't have to smash rocks with his hands any more."

I leave them to their busking. People round here don't have much money to spare, and if they try playing up in the better areas of town the Guards chase them away.

Why would the Princess want a strongman? I wonder, as I haul myself up the outside stairs towards my office. Bodyguard? Can't be—Palace Security provides her with bodyguards. Maybe it's only temporary employment. Maybe she just needs someone strong enough to cut open a dragon.

I reach the top of the steps. I open the door and gape stupidly at my room. It appears to have been torn apart by a whirlwind. Papers, broken glass and smashed furniture lie strewn in an incredible jumble across the floor. The last of my precious kuriya is seeping through the floorboards. I groan, and rescue what I can. I do more than groan when I see my only bottle of klee lying smashed beneath a chair. I was saving that.

"Goddamn those Brotherhood pigs!" I roar, unsheathing my sword.

The noise attracts Makri. "What's happening?" she says, finding me about to march outside, sword in hand.

"That stinking Brotherhood is trying to put the frighteners on me!" I yell. "Well, I'm not having it!"

Madder than a mad dragon, I storm back down the outside stairs. Makri, perhaps feeling that a single-handed assault on Brotherhood headquarters is a little ambitious, grabs her swords and hurtles down the steps behind me.

I am practically blinded by fury. Gambling debt or no gambling debt, no one comes into my room and smashes my last bottle of klee. I don't have far to go to vent my wrath. There, coming round the corner, is Karlox and his gang, eight of them. They appear surprised as I confront them and start hurling abuse.

"Try threatening me again and you die, Karlox! Who do you think you're dealing with here?"

Karlox grunts angrily. He's a man of few words, too dumb to know many. He draws his own sword and the Brotherhood men fan out. I am ready to fight. Makri stands at my side. A landus wheels round into the street, kicking up a spray of dust and scattering the beggars.

A head appears from the curtained window. It's Yubaxas, local Brotherhood boss. He demands to know what's going on. I inform him that I'm about to administer some punishment to his thugs in retribution for wrecking my room.

Yubaxas actually smiles, something he rarely does. It doesn't suit him. "We didn't wreck your rooms, Thraxas. Not worth the effort. You know the position already. You have three days to pay up, then we wreck you."

He motions to Karlox and his cronies. "Get up to Kushni quick. We're needed."

The landus departs. The Brotherhood thugs trot after it. I'm left standing alone in the street, deflated.

"So, who did wreck your rooms?" asks Makri.

I shrug. I suppose Yubaxas could have been lying, but I can't see why. I don't imagine he was terrified at the sight of me.

Makri kicks a stone. Trudging back to the Avenging Axe, she is disconsolate. "I was looking forward to a fight," she says.

"Well, if I don't come up with the money in three days there'll be plenty of fighting to do."

Makri looks happier. I feel some relief that Makri, despite her weird predilection for studying philosophy, is a keen enough fighter and a good enough friend to automatically support me in a crisis, even though it's not her affair.

I begin the weary task of putting my rooms in order. I've got no idea who wrecked them, or why. I'm in a terrible mood.

Chapter Fourteen

———✦———

Gurd stumbles into the bar from the street outside clutching the remains of a box of tankards.

"There's a riot outside," he says, as he starts to barricade the door.

A riot. I see the elections are under way. It's always a difficult time in Turai. With the success of the Populares, or anti-monarchy party, things are getting more tense all the time. When Rittius won the position of Deputy Consul last year it was a sensational victory for the Populares, led by Senator Lodius. The Traditionals, covering the Royal Family, Consul Kalius and most of the Senate, regarded it as the end of civilisation. Civilisation is still here, but if Rittius holds on to his post this year, it might not be soon enough. The Royal Family can no longer sweep aside all opposition, but neither are they weak enough to be easily overthrown. Praetor Cicerius is standing for them against Rittius, trying to regain some of the lost ground for the Traditionals. He's an honest man though not particularly popular. Still, he has a chance of victory. Since he was elevated from Senator to Praetor, many people think he's done a good job, and he has the reputation of not taking bribes, which is almost unheard of in this city. People might support him in his bid for the higher post of Deputy Consul.

I muse on things, while the riot rages. Who killed Attilan? Trying to pin down some sort of lead, I decide to work backwards. Where, for instance, did a Niojan diplomat get an Orcish spell for putting a dragon to sleep? Not the sort of thing you can buy at the local apothecary. Could Attilan have obtained it from one of the Orcish Ambassadors at the Palace? Possibly. But if their Ambassadors are anything like our diplomats, they won't be magicians. Diplomats are always drawn from the oldest, most respectable families and they tend not to practise magic, regarding it as beneath them. Orcs have their class divisions and snobberies, just like us. Also, unless utterly treacherous to their country, they would not let such a vital spell fall into western hands. I doubt Orcish diplomats are capable of such treason.

Who else in Turai might have such a spell? There's always the dragonkeeper. Now there's an Orc who might well have such a spell, and could be bribable. Many Orcs are greedy for gold, another attribute they share with Humans. Sometimes I swear if they weren't so ugly I wouldn't be able to tell the difference. I catch sight of my reflection in the mirror behind the bar. I'm no oil painting myself.

I'd like to ask Pazaz a few questions. My Orcish is very rusty so I recruit Makri, who is a rather unwilling accomplice. She's still in a bad mood and it got worse when she was caught in the riot and had to kick her way through to her afternoon ethics class. The prospect of visiting an Orc appals her. Her hatred for

Orcs is such that she protests she may not be able to
prevent herself from attacking the dragonkeeper on
sight. I extract a promise that she will not kill him
without provocation but she flatly refuses to leave her
swords at home.

"Talk to an Orc without a sword at the ready? Are
you mad?"

"He's here under diplomatic protection, Makri."

"Well, he'll need it if he tries anything with me,"
retorts my young and hot-headed companion, fasten-
ing on her blade.

I absolutely refuse to let her bring her axe.

"We're visiting the Palace, for God's sake, Makri, not
going into battle. And take that knife out of your boot.
It'll be hard enough getting you into the Palace grounds
without you looking like an invading army."

The Orcish diplomats are housed in an Embassy
within the Palace walls. They never appear in public
for fear of causing unrest. We all hate Orcs here. Fair
enough. They all hate us. The dragonkeeper is billeted
in a small house in the grounds of the zoo, which are
open to the public during the day. It's forbidden to
speak to him, but I figure it's worth a try.

Makri is afforded some very strange looks by
Guards and officials at the huge Lion Gates that open
into the Palace grounds, and when it's learned that
we're going to visit the King's zoo there are some
unpleasant comments from some of the soldiers on
duty.

"Must be missing her dragons," says one.

"Orc," sneers another.

Makri scowls but manages to restrain her temper
until they require her to hand in her sword. They don't
insist on me turning in my weapon, and Makri is livid
about the prejudice against her. I pacify her the best
I can, which is hardly at all, and we enter the Palace

grounds with Makri angrier than a wounded dragon and threatening terrible vengeance on the next person to insult her.

The King's Palace in Turai is one of the wonders of the world. Many larger states than us have far less impressive imperial buildings. Since money started flowing in from the gold mines a few generations back, various Kings and Princes have turned their hands to building an ever more splendid residence for themselves.

Behind the huge Lion Gates, six times the height of a man, is a fabulous den of luxury. The gardens alone are famous throughout the Human Lands, with towering arbours, vast lawns, avenues of trees, banks and beds of flowers, all fed by streams and fountains that were engineered by Afetha-ar-Kyet, the great Elvish garden-maker of a few generations back. The Palace itself is a vast edifice of white marble and silver minarets. The courtyards are paved with pale green and yellow tiles imported from the far west and each wing is roofed with golden slates. The corridors and state rooms are covered with mosaics of gold leaf and coloured stone, and the private quarters were decorated by artists and furnishers drawn from all over the world.

I used to work here. When I was a Senior Investigator for Palace Security I had the run of the place. Now I'm about as welcome as the plague.

The grounds are vast and it takes us some time to reach the zoo. It's hot, and I'm tired. I don't much feel in the mood for seeing Orcs or dragons. I point out a few of the architectural glories which surround us to Makri, but she's in too bad a mood to admire them, even though architecture would be part of the University course. Her bad mood intensifies deeply when the call for Sabam rings out from a nearby tower and we are obliged to kneel and pray. I have to practically wrestle her to the ground. If we failed to make our prayers right here in the public grounds of the Palace we'd be up on an impiety charge so quick our feet wouldn't touch the ground.

I have trouble staying awake in the heat and doze off during the prayers. Makri unceremoniously boots me awake. I ignore her coarse witticism on my religious shortcomings and haul myself to my feet. The zoo is now in sight but as we approach its white walls a fearful commotion erupts and Guards and civilian officials start pouring this way and that. We hurry on and reach the zoo but the entrance is barred to all the people flocking round from every direction. I recognise various important Palace officials, including Kalius the Consul. The Niojan Ambassador arrives in a sedan, followed by another sedan with thick curtains and an odd, alien crest on the side. The Orcish Ambassadors. One of the Royal Princes hurries past with his bodyguard. What on earth is going on?

Behind the Prince comes, of all people, Pontifex Derlex. I grab the priest's arm and demand to know what's happening.

"The new dragon's been killed!" he yells. "It was cut open during prayers! Princess Du-Akai's been arrested!"

Chapter Fifteen

I have no opportunity for further enquiries as Makri, myself and everyone else are summarily evicted from the grounds. We share a landus home with Pontifex Derlex, who is so excited by the whole affair he doesn't seem to mind travelling with Makri, the demon from hell. It's a lot for him to be excited about, I suppose. Derlex is a fairly lowly local priest. He'd never normally be found at the Palace but he had been invited there as the guest of Bishop Gzekius, who was presiding at some religious ceremony for the Royal Family.

The sensational story soon spreads all over Turai. People gather on street corners and bars to speculate over the affair and study the latest reports in the special editions of the news-sheets. It's one of the most serious scandals anyone can remember, and it is bound to have great repercussions. Senator Lodius is already fulminating against corruption in the Royal Family. The Populare candidates in the forthcoming elections are

fighting to outdo each other in condemning the deca-
dence and graft that they say is gripping the city.
Personally I take little interest in politics, and any
enthusiasm I might have for reform is tempered by the
fact that Senator Lodius is in reality a nakedly ambitious power-seeker ready to use any means to attain
his ends. Deputy Consul Rittius belongs to his party,
which suggests how bad it is.

None of this matters to me right now. What does
matter is the sensational events at the King's zoo. The
dragon had its belly slit open, not the easiest of things
to accomplish, given that a dragon's skin is like armour.
Arrested at the scene along with the Princess was
Strongman Brex, with an axe over his shoulder. When
the Princess was found to be carrying a large quan-
tity of dwa it was presumed that she had somehow
drugged the beast before Brex hacked it open. As far
as I can learn, no one knows why they did it.

Naturally the Orcs are furious. The King is furious.
The population is in uproar. And when you consider
that the Niojan Ambassador is still threatening war if
the murderer of Attilan is not brought to justice, it
might be a good time for the faint-hearted to vacate
the city. Senator Lodius is going to exploit this to the
utmost, which means the elections will be more violent than usual. We're in for a tough time this summer, unless the Niojans just invade and get it over with.

Makri is hurrying her meal before rushing out to
tonight's class. Principles of geometry, I think. She's
wrapped in the all-over cloak she's obliged to wear at
the Institute to prevent her from panicking the young
scholars.

"What are you going to do?" she asks me.

"See if I can find out where the Princess has
hidden the Cloth. It hasn't come to light yet, and no
one else seems to realise that it was hidden inside

the dragon. I might still be able to recover it for the Elves."

"Aren't you going to help the Princess?"

"Of course not. She isn't paying me, and I don't owe her any favours." Sometimes Makri just doesn't understand the commercial nature of my business. I don't help people for fun. I do it for money. Anyway, the Princess may well be beyond help. If she's foolish enough to be caught slaying the King's dragon, that's her problem.

Of course, if I keep on looking for the Cloth it might be harder to convince those murderous people who think I already have it to leave me alone. But that's my problem.

This evening, life in the Avenging Axe is in full swing. Mercenaries, dockers, labourers, pilgrims, sailors, local vendors and shop workers drink heartily, washing away their troubles. Young Palax and Kaby arrive and get out their mandolins, flutes and lyres and start entertaining the crowd with some raucous drinking songs, stomping traditional folk dances and a few maudlin ballads for the tavern's lonely hearts. They're good musicians and popular with the crowd, which is just as well really, or they might suffer more than the friendly abuse they already get for that brightly dyed hair and those colourful clothes and pierced ears and noses. Gurd pays them with free drinks. Quite a good scam really. Makes me wish I played an instrument.

Despite all the jollity Gurd is looking as miserable as a Niojan whore and fails to respond when I clap him on the back and ask him if he remembers the time we faced fourteen half-Orcs in the Simlan Desert with only one knife between us and still came out on top. He looks at me gloomily then asks if I'll come and see him tomorrow.

I nod, though it's not something I'm looking forward to. The talk I imagine will be about the cook, Tanrose, with whom Gurd thinks he may be in love. As an old bachelor who's spent most of his life wandering the earth as a mercenary, Gurd finds this very confusing. He can't make his mind up what to do, not wishing to offer her his hand in marriage and then find out that what he thought was love turns out later to be merely an infatuation with her excellent venison pies. He frequently asks my advice on the matter, even though I've pointed out that I have a poor record in affairs of the heart. Still, lending him a sympathetic ear is always a good thing. Makes him more tolerant when I'm late with the rent.

People laugh, dance, gamble, swap stories and talk about the day's scandalous affair. By the light of the oil lanterns Palax and Kaby work up a furious rhythm which has the whole tavern either dancing or stamping their feet. I bang my tankard on the table in time to the beat, and shout for more beer. All in all, it's a fine night in the Avenging Axe; more fun with the poor of Twelve Seas than I ever had with the aristocrats at Palace social functions. I end up hideously drunk, which would be fine but, just as Gurd and Makri are carrying me upstairs, Praetor Cicerius arrives. He is Turai's most famed Advocate and a man of great influence in the city. He informs me that I have to come up to the Palace and interview Princess Du-Akai right away.

It takes me some time to realise what he means, and for a while I keep trying to tell the Praetor it's no good. I've heard the rumours about his wife but I don't do divorce work.

"There are no rumours about my wife," retorts Cicerius, who is not the sort of man you can have a laugh and a joke with. He's around fifty, thin, grey-haired, austere, and is famously incorruptible. I invite him to join in an obscene Barbarian drinking song I learned from Gurd. He declines.

"Why don't you sort things out in this city, Praetor?" I demand, suddenly aggressive. "Everything's going to hell and the government's about as much use as a eunuch in a brothel."

Colour drains from the Praetor's face. Gurd and Makri abandon me in disgust. The Praetor's two servants pick me up bodily and bundle me outside and into a landus, which Cicerius is allowed to ride at night as part of his senatorial privilege. I begin to enjoy the experience, and start bellowing the drinking song out the window as we ride through the quiet streets of Pashish. Cicerius looks at me with contempt. Let him. I didn't ask him to come visit me.

"No use looking at me like that," I tell him. "If the Princess chopped off the dragon's head, it's her fault, not mine. Bad thing to do. Poor dragon."

I fall asleep, and have only dim memories of being carried into the Palace. The servants are insulting about my weight. I insult them back. I'm not the first man carried drunk into the grounds of the Imperial Palace, though I may well be the heaviest. I'm deposited in some building I don't recognise and the servants start forcing deat down my throat. Deat is a hot herbal drink. Sobers you up. I detest it.

"Gimme a beer," I say.

"Get him sober," says Cicerius, not bothering to conceal his loathing and contempt. "I will bring the Princess. Though why she insists on seeing him is beyond me."

I drink some deat, fail to sober up, and start wondering exactly where I am.

"The reception room of the Princess's chambers," a servant tells me.

"Right," I grunt. "I suppose Princesses don't get thrown in the slammer like ordinary people."

I think of all the times I've been thrown in jail and get slightly maudlin. "Nobody loves me," I tell the servant.

Cicerius arrives back with Princess Du-Akai. I greet them genially. The Princess thanks me for coming. She doesn't comment on my drunkenness. Good breeding.

"I am in grave trouble."

"I bet you are."

"I need you to help me."

"Too bad," I say, again gripped by alcoholic aggression. "I'm all out of help for clients who lie to me."

"How dare you speak to the Princess like that," roars Cicerius, and we start to argue. Princess Du-Akai intervenes. She motions both the servants and the Praetor outside, and draws up a chair next to me.

"Thraxas," she says, in the most pleasant of voices. "You are a drunken oaf. Tales of your misdemeanours while working at the Palace do not do you full justice. In the normal course of affairs, I would have nothing whatsoever to do with you. You're so far below me in the social ladder I wouldn't notice if I stepped on you. That woman with the Orcish blood is better bred than you. As well as being a drunk, you're gross, and a glutton, both qualities I despise. You belong in your slum in Twelve Seas, and I'd much rather you were there than here in this room with me. However, I need your help. So sober up, stop playing the fool, and get ready to listen."

"I seem to be doing a lot of listening already. Why should I help you?"

"For two reasons. Firstly, I shall pay you extremely well. I understand you are badly in need of money. Gambling is another of your bad habits."

I curse. My gambling debt seems to be the most

talked about thing in this city. Even the Royal Family knows about it.

"What's the second reason?"

"If you don't help me, I will ensure that your life in this city is hell on earth. I may be heading for a secure cell in a nunnery but I'm still third in line to the throne, and I have more influence in my little finger than you have in your whole fat body. So listen."

She holds out a heavy purse. I listen.

Chapter Sixteen

When I'm finished listening I'm led into the next
chamber by a servant. Cicerius is waiting for me. He
is no more friendly than before. The fact that the
Princess thinks I can help her doesn't make him any
keener on me. Cicerius is not known for his affabil-
ity. Despite his unparalleled reputation for honesty he
is commonly regarded as a rather distant and austere
man. Senators rarely hobnob with commoners like
myself, and Praetors never do, except when they need
their votes.

As I enter he is in animated conversation with a
younger man whom I recognise as his son, Cerius. The
Praetor sees me enter but does not acknowledge my
presence so I sit down heavily and wait for him to
finish. I'm tired and want to go home and sleep.
Damned Princess.

Finally Cicerius turns to me. "I trust your interview
was satisfactory."

"Very satisfactory," I brag. "The Princess knows I'm number one chariot when it comes to investigating so she's decided to put the whole affair in the hands of a man who can get things done. Smart woman, the Princess."

Cicerius fixes me with a hostile gaze. He is famous for his oratory and advocacy in the law courts. Part of his considerable armoury while making speeches is his range of facial expression, and the expression he wears when looking at me speaks volumes, rather like a man peering at a rat crawling out of a sewer. No way to behave when he's trying to be elected to a public post, I would've thought, but I suppose he doesn't care too much about my vote.

If I am to help the Princess I'll need Cicerius to open a few doors for me. While we are discussing arrangements, we are interrupted by the arrival of a Captain from Palace Security.

"Praetor Cicerius," he says, "I have a warrant here for the arrest of your son, Cerius."

The Praetor masks his outrage, and demands quite coldly to know the reason why.

"A charge of importing dwa," says the Captain. He shows Cicerius and Cerius his warrant then puts his hand on Cerius's shoulder. Cicerius is left speechless as his son is led away. It's a cruel stroke and a well-timed one by his rival Rittius. Praetor Cicerius has just lost his family and the election at the same time.

I walk up to him. "Hire me," I say. "I'll help your son."

Cicerius glares at me with increasing loathing before marching swiftly out of the room.

"Only trying to help," I say to the servant as he guides me out.

It's around two in the morning when I arrive back at the Avenging Axe. I'm fairly sober, sober enough to

avoid stepping on the drunks and desolates who lit-
ter the night-time streets, or tripping over the wreckage
that's still piled up after the riot. I have a headache.
I'm tired. I can't stand any more aggravation. When
I reach my room it has again been wrecked.

I stare at the incredible mess with dumb fury. Every
piece of furniture has been reduced to matchwood and
everything I own is strewn over the floor. Who is
behind this? Whoever it is I swear an oath to run them
through and dance on their remains.

Makri's a light sleeper. She's woken by my cursing
and appears with a sword in her hand. She's naked.

"Shouldn't you get dressed before you challenge
intruders?"

"What for? They'd be dead before they noticed I
wasn't wearing anything. What's going on?"

"My room's been wrecked again," I say, needlessly.
Makri offers me the use of her couch. I shake my head.

"I wasn't planning on sleeping yet. I'm still working.
And I need you to come and speak Orcish. Cicerius has
arranged for me to see the dragonkeeper."

"Now?"

"Has to be. If things get any worse for Cicerius he
might not have enough influence to even get me into
the zoo."

"How come?"

"His son just got arrested for dealing dwa. But that's
his problem, he doesn't want any help from me. I'm
working for the Princess again. I'll explain on the way."

Makri nods, and departs to get dressed. She loads
up with weapons and I don't object. On our way back
to the Palace I fill her in with the details.

"Princess Du-Akai claims she's innocent. She admits
she was going to cut open the dragon to get the Red
Elvish Cloth. Which is why she wanted the sleep spell
originally. I asked her if she'd got the spell back but

she denied it. That's why she had the dwa, to try drugging the beast. Anyway, someone beat her to it. So when the King and his retinue walked in and found her and Strongman Brex standing beside the dead dragon with an axe and a big bag of dwa it naturally looked suspicious."

"Naturally. Where did she get the dwa?"

"She stole it from the apartments of her brother Prince Frisen-Akan, though she didn't tell the King that. He doesn't know what a degenerate his oldest son is. I reckon the King might have tried to hush it up about her killing the dragon but Senator Lodius was there on official business. Naturally he started raising a scandal right away."

"So what are we going to do?"

"Find out who really killed the dragon before the Princess is dragged in front of the special Royal Judiciary and sentenced to life in a nunnery. You see I was right about the Elvish Cloth, Makri, even if no one else realises. It was inside the dragon. Find that and we'll find the killer. Maybe the killer of Attilan as well."

"Are you hired for that?"

"Not exactly. But Turai badly needs to produce a culprit. Nioj is raising hell about it. Cicerius agreed that a reward would be forthcoming if I cleared the matter up. Praetor Cicerius is a pillar of the establishment, or was till his son was arrested. He's as cold as an Orc's heart but he's also one of the few men in Turai I'd trust. Incidently, he regards me as the scum of the earth. Just his bad luck I'm the only one who can help the Princess. Mind you, I'm not entirely sure the Princess didn't kill Attilan, or have him killed. She *was* having an affair with him. That's how she learned about the stolen Cloth and Attilan's plan to intercept it for Nioj. Attilan had heard about it from a Niojan agent who was spying on the Orcish Ambassador. The Orcs

initiated the whole thing. They hired Glixius Dragon
Killer to steal the Cloth and load it into the dragon
so they could ship it home later. Who else knew about
all this I'm not sure, but it's a safe bet others learned
of it. Turai is a hard place to keep a secret, especially
in diplomatic circles, with Sorcerers prying everywhere.
Anyway Attilan bribed the dragonkeeper to let him have
an Orcish spell for putting the dragon to sleep so he
could recover the Cloth. Princess Du-Akai decided it
would be a good idea if she did it instead, which is
why she sent me to recover the box with that phoney
story about the love letters. Which is where we came
in, more or less. I guess whoever ended up with the
spell took the opportunity of the Royal Family all being
at their religious ceremony to sneak into the zoo and
do the deed. I've no idea who it was though. Not many
people have access to the private zoo at that time of
day. Diplomats mainly. There again, the Brotherhood
and the Society of Friends are quite capable of bribing their way anywhere."

"How did the Assassins get involved?"

I shrug. That's a loose end I'm far from tying up.
Why Hanama wanted the Cloth is a mystery. But it is
never easy to interpret the actions or motives of the
Assassins. As far as I am aware they never hire out their
services for any purpose except murder, but who
knows? Maybe they've taken up investigating as a side-
line.

"I can't see an Assassin like Hanama wanting to be
an Investigator," says Makri.

"Why not? It's better than rowing a slave galley."

We're now almost at the Palace. Makri has digested
everything I've said, as she always does, being a smart
woman, but she does wonder why the Princess wanted
the Elvish Cloth in the first place.

"She wouldn't tell me, even in private. Maybe she

was acting from patriotic motives, to prevent the Orcs or the Niojans getting it. More likely, knowing our Royal Family, she's got secret gambling debts and needed the money. Probably planned to sell it to the Orcs herself."

"So who are you finding it for now? The Elves or the Princess?"

"I'm finding the Cloth for the Elves. And I'm clearing the Princess of dragon murder."

"You'll get confused."

"Confused? Me? When it comes to multiple investigations I'm sharp as an Elf's ear. Anyway, I need the money."

The landus enters the Palace gates.

"Time to meet an Orc," I say to Makri. "Keep your sword in its sheath, I need to hear what he's got to say."

Chapter Seventeen

Orcs are a little larger than Humans, and slightly stronger. But uglier. They're much given to wearing crude jewellery with motifs of eagles and skulls, and probably originated the nose-, lip- and eyebrow-piercing style with which Kaby and Palax now distress the respectable population of Turai. Craggy-faced with dark, inky-red skin, they generally dress in dark shaggy leather clothes of simple design and wear their hair long. They're usually savage fighters and, despite what Humans say, are not stupid. I know that their diplomats have proved to be shrewd negotiators. It's said in the west that most Orcs do not read, and there is no literature of any sort in any of their nations, but Makri claims this is not true. Nor, she says, is it true that they play no music; nor are they cannibals. She even says she's seen Orcish paintings, though I find this very hard to believe. Makri loathes all Orcs, but refuses to admit that Humans are much more civilised. I know little of their civilisation. The only time I've encountered Orcs has been in battle, and most of the ones I've faced have ended up dead before we had a chance for much conversation. I've never even seen a female Orc, or a child.

As is the case with the Human Lands, Orcs speak their own national dialect as well as the common Orcish tongue. Very few people in the west know any Orcish—it's regarded as very unlucky even to utter a word of it—so Pazaz the dragonkeeper is surprised and disconcerted when Makri addresses him in the common Orcish language. He's naturally suspicious, but as he's been told by his superiors to cooperate with the investigation, and we're bearing a letter from the Praetor himself, he answers our questions.

"He claims not to know anything about the killing," reports Makri, who is herself finding the conversation very unsettling. The last time she talked to an Orc, she was their slave, and she doesn't enjoy the memory. "He's upset though. He liked the dragon."

"He liked it?"

"Used to read it stories at bedtime."

"Ask him if he sold the sleep spell to anyone but Attilan."

Pazaz denies that he sold a dragon sleep spell to anyone at all but we tell him we know he's lying. I threaten to inform his Ambassador and he breaks down a little. He admits selling a copy to Attilan, but swears there was no one else.

It's difficult to know if he's telling the truth. I get a feeling with most suspects, but the emotions behind this craggy face are strange and unreadable. I lay some more of my cards on the table and tell him I know all about the plot to export Red Elvish Cloth to Gzak. Now he is really worried. Even though he's under diplomatic protection he'd find himself in an uncomfortable position if the population of Turai learned about it. There's enough bad feeling in the city about Orcs being here at all, without it being known that they've been trying to steal our magical secrets.

Nothing in his answers brings me any closer to learning who killed the dragon, or where the Elvish Cloth might be now. Praetor Cicerius told me that the religious ceremony attended by the Royal Family had lasted no more than half an hour. Whoever came here and killed the dragon must have had good inside information, but in a city as corrupt as Turai good inside information is available to anyone for a price. More interestingly, Cicerius also informed me that the Investigating Sorcerers from Palace Security have been unable to detect the aura of any unusual visitors to the zoo, which makes matters worse for the Princess. Still, with the dragon's disruptive effect on any magical field, it's not absolutely certain that no stranger has been here.

"It can't have been easy for anyone to kill the dragon and remove the Cloth, sleep spell or not. Has no one been around showing any unusual interest in its habits?"

No one has, according to Pazaz. No one talks to him at all, apart from Bishop Gzekius, who's made one or two attempts to convert him to the True Religion. I'm almost moved to sympathy for the Orc. Bishop Gzekius is always trying to put one over on his fellow Bishops. Probably wanted the Orc's soul as a trophy.

It's time to leave. Apart from having my suspicions about Attilan confirmed, I haven't learned much. Lights burn still in the Palace as we're led through the grounds to the gates. Inside I expect everything is in uproar, due to the arrest of the Princess. Times are changing. At one time a Princess would never have been arrested in Turai, no matter the crime. A Praetor's son wouldn't have been arrested either. Now, with Senator Lodius's Populares increasing in power, the upper classes are feeling the pinch. Do them good maybe, having to obey the laws of the land.

I am dead tired. The heat of the night weighs me down. I could happily lie down and sleep where I am. The stress of the day and my tiredness is making my head pound; the prospect of facing my room, once more in ruins, makes it worse. We travel back in silence to Twelve Seas. Makri's thinking about Orcs. She tells me later that Pazaz had seen her fight in the arena, which made her feel even more like killing him.

"The next time I meet an Orc it'll take more than diplomatic protection to keep his head on his shoulders," she says before lapsing into gloomy silence. Neither of us has any inspiration. The night is oppressively warm and all I want to do is clear a space on my floor and sleep. Which is something I can't yet do, because there at the Avenging Axe, in his blue-edged Praetorian toga, is Cicerius in a landus, with his customary severe expression and a couple of servants looking nervous to find themselves in Twelve Seas in the middle of the night.

I've had my fill of the upper classes. I'm so tired I can't even be bothered to be rude. I just ask Cicerius if he can wait till tomorrow for the progress report on the Princess.

He hasn't come for a progress report. He's come to hire me to get his son off the hook. I fail to stifle a yawn, and lead him inside. I help myself to a flagon of ale from behind the bar and try to concentrate on what Cicerius has to say. I could cope with being Turai's cheapest Investigator but I'm finding it hard being the busiest.

Chapter Eighteen

One thing abut Cicerius, he's a man for plain speaking when necessary. He apologises stiffly for his former brusque refusal of my offer of help, and admits that I am probably the man for the job.

"As you know, my son Cerius Junius has been accused of dealing in dwa."

One time that might have shocked me. It doesn't any more.

"Deputy Consul Rittius, acting on information, obtained a search warrant this evening. He visited my house while I wasn't there. In the course of his search he found dwa in Cerius's rooms."

"How much?"

"Two imperial pounds."

"Right. Too much for personal use. Who's he dealing it to?"

Cicerius looks pained. "I refuse to believe that my son is a dwa dealer."

I point out that these days even the most respectable families are finding themselves involved in dwa. Cicerius frowns. His famous eloquence departs him as he considers the prospect of his son ending his days in a prison galley.

"So what do you want me to do?" I ask, drinking some beer.

"Find out the truth. As you know, Rittius and I are bitter rivals and are standing against each other for the post of Deputy Consul. He has leapt at the chance to discredit me. If Rittius defeats me and remains Deputy Consul, great harm will come to the city."

By which Cicerius means that Lodius's Populares will gain the ascendancy. As a bastion of the Traditionals, Cicerius doesn't like the thought of that at all. Not being interested in politics, I don't much care.

"I'd say you're discredited already."

"Not quite. Consul Kalius has no wish to see my son ruined. Nor does he wish to see me discredited and the Populares gaining ground. With the political situation in Turai being so volatile these days, it is vital that Senator Lodius does not increase his influence."

"So the Consul is going to sweep it under the carpet? Then why do you need me?"

"The Consul will not sweep it under the carpet," retorts Cicerius with asperity. "All citizens in Turai are subject to the law. But he will see that the case is not brought to court if Cerius names the people he bought the dwa from, and whom it was intended for. That is standard practice."

True enough. Many small dwa dealers have wormed their way to freedom by selling out their larger partners in crime.

"Unfortunately Cerius absolutely refuses to speak. I cannot understand it. All he has to do to safeguard his reputation, not to mention his family's, is tell the Consul the full story. He refuses."

Poor Cicerius. You spend all your time being the most respectable politician in Turai then your son goes and gets arrested for drugs. Just goes to show that even the blue-lined Praetorian toga can't guarantee you happiness.

"You're the finest lawyer in Turai, Cicerius. I've heard you tearing people apart in court with your cross-examination. If you can't get anything out of your son, what makes you think I will?"

Cicerius looks pained. The whole episode has obviously come as a terrible shock to him. He admits that his courtroom techniques somehow don't seem suitable for dealing with his son.

"Also I have little experience of these matters. Even in these decadent times I did not imagine that a young man of Cerius's character would become involved in dwa. Furthermore, in the few hours since this happened, I have already invited Tuparius to investigate the matter. Tuparius could learn nothing from my son."

Tuparius. A high-class Investigator. Works out of Thamlin. I don't like him much but he's not a bad Investigator compared to some of the others that work up there.

"Is he still on the job?"

Cicerius nods. I don't mind too much. Frankly, in a case of dwa dealing I wouldn't expect Tuparius to come up with much. Not enough low-life contacts.

"Even if you can learn nothing directly from Cerius," continues the Praetor, "I shall expect you to find out full details of the business, including where the dwa came from and who it was for. Once that information is passed on to the Consul, Cerius will not be brought to court. If he is not brought to court, we may keep it from reaching the ears of the public."

"Rittius is down on you like a bad spell. He'll make sure it does."

Cicerius raises one eyebrow slightly. Which means, I imagine, that he still has enough influence around here to hush it up, providing there is no court case.

"How long do I have?"

"It generally takes one week till the preliminary hearing. After that it will be too late."

I point out that I am already busy, far too busy to be wading into another case.

Cicerius points out that the public scandal will undoubtedly hand the election to Rittius. Which isn't so good for me, I must admit. Even if I don't care about politics, my life would be easier if the Deputy Consul wasn't a man who hated me. If I help Cicerius here, and he wins the election, then the new Deputy Consul would be in my debt. I become slightly more enthusiastic. Maybe I'll get back into the Palace one of these days after all.

Really I'm too busy to take on the case. I think about the money I owe the Brotherhood. I'm not scared of Karlox, but I can't fight them all.

"I'll take the case."

I pick up my standard retainer and another thirty for expenses, and promise to get on the job first thing in the morning. The Praetor departs. Makri, waiting silently all this time, is of the opinion that I am foolish to take on more work.

"That's three difficult cases at once. You'll end up making a mess of all of them."

"I need the money. I got two days left to pay off Yubaxas, and who knows if I'll recover the Cloth in time to get paid before the Brotherhood come after me. I'm in no position to turn down employment. And don't bother lecturing me about my gambling, I'm too tired to take it in."

I clear the junk off my mattress and sleep, but not for long. Kerk wakes me up by kicking my door. He has some information to sell and badly needs his morning dose of dwa. The early interruption to my slumbers puts me in a foul mood.

"Make it quick," I snap.

"Well you look as happy as a dragon with a headache," mutters Kerk, and grins stupidly. "I got some information about Prince Frisen-Akan."

I frown. I've already had enough of the Royal Family. "What about him?"

"He's importing dwa."

I'm almost moved to laughter. That the heir to the throne should be a drug dealer is quite in line with our national character these days.

"What's that got to do with me?"

"He's a friend of Cerius."

Word has got around quick about this one. I don't bother asking Kerk how he knows about Cerius. He's generally well informed about drug-related matters in Turai.

"And?"

"Cerius was holding on to the dwa for him."

I frown again. It's going to be difficult clearing young Cerius's name if it involves implicating Prince Frisen-Akan. Hardly the sort of result Cicerius is looking for.

I place a small coin in Kerk's hand. He looks at it with contempt, and demands more.

"Or I won't tell you who else is involved."

I press another coin in his hand. His hand trembles. He needs his dwa, and quickly.

"Glixius Dragon Killer."

"That's all I need. You sure?"

"Absolutely. He's overseeing the operation in the city. He's working with the Society of Friends. And the

Prince is bankrolling them. They're bringing in Choirs of Angels. Very good. Very strong. And cheap."

I demand to know how Kerk knows all this.

"Simple," he says. "Cerius told me. He can't hold his dwa. Rambles like an old man."

Kerk laughs, but it costs his broken-down body a great deal of effort. I ask him who's supplying the Choirs of Angels, but Kerk doesn't know. He's becoming too desperate to speak much more. He holds out his hand urgently. I give him more money and he hurries off to buy dwa.

I head back to bed, not wishing to think about what I've just learned. Maybe if I just ignore it it will go away. Unfortunately my bedroom is already too hot to sleep in. I fling open the window. Outside a stallholder starts shouting about his produce and enters an argument with a customer. I shut my window in disgust. There's no getting away from the heat and the noise in Twelve Seas. I detest it.

My two Elvish clients pick this moment to visit me. As I open the door, the argument outside intensifies into a screaming match and several bystanders get involved in the uproar.

"Just ignore it," I say, shutting the door and motioning them in. They look round at the wreckage in bewilderment.

"Just tidying up," I say as I clear some space by kicking junk into the corners of my room. Young Kaby unfortunately chooses this moment to burst through my outside door with her boyfriend Palax in her arms. She lets him go and he falls to the ground, where he's sick on the rug.

"He's overdosed!" she wails. "Help him."

Out in the street people are screaming. My room is as hot as Minarixa's oven. Broken furniture is strewn everywhere. Palax's face is turning blue. Makri rushes

in with a sword in her hand to see what all the fuss
is about. The Elves are close to panic.

"So how are you enjoying your visit to the city?" I
ask, and offer them a beer.

Chapter Nineteen

The Elves pass on the beer. Callis-ar-Del, the younger of
the two, swiftly draws a pouch from his bag, crosses over to
the vomiting Palax, and places a small leaf in his mouth.

"Swallow," he orders.

Kaby brings water. Palax swallows. He stops being
sick. Colour returns to his features. Callis cradles his
head in his hands for a few moments, and concentrates.
Palax falls asleep.

"He'll be fine now," says the young Elf, gently
releasing his head.

I'm impressed. "You a healer?"

Callis nods, before turning to Kaby, who is squat-
ting beside her sleeping lover, still concerned.

"Don't worry," says the Elf. "He will be fine. The
leaf of the ledasa plant is very effective in clearing
poison from the system, and I have stabilised the
colours of his life energy. But he is very unwise to
partake of dwa. It is an evil drug."

"I know," says Kaby. "And Choirs of Angels is the worst kind. I didn't know he was taking it till I found he'd spent our week's earnings."

Kaby and Makri carry Palax down to the caravan. I thank Callis for coming to the rescue.

"Are these ledasa leaves any good for hangovers?"

He says they are so I grab a few off him. Clever, these Elves. Talk to the trees and cure your hangover. I fill them in on the case, though in reality there isn't much to fill them in on. I tell them about my theory that the Red Elvish Cloth was inside the dragon but have to report that, if it was, it was spirited away before I got there.

They listen with interest and seem quite willing to believe my theory. Well, they have heard that I am an honest and competent man. I still like that. They take their leave, satisfied at least that I am working hard.

Makri arrives back in my room and reports that Palax seems to be out of danger.

"More than he deserves," I say. "He should know better than to mess with this new dwa. It's too strong. Addicts all over the city are going to be taking their usual dose and ending up dead."

"But it feels good when you get it right," says Makri.

I glance at her suspiciously.

"Well that's what I'm told," she adds.

I hope she is not indulging in it herself.

"The Elves said to thank you for your help with Palax," I tell Makri. "They must be getting used to you."

"Well that makes me happy as a drunken mercenary," says Makri, wryly, and departs.

I clean up some of the mess and ask Gurd if he'll bring in a servant to do something with my rooms. He will, but it will cost me extra.

I head on out. I have an appointment at the Thamlin gymnasium, a place where aristocrats go to bathe, exercise and relax. It's a very respectable establishment. Senators and their families only. No young girls or pretty boys for hire, at least not openly. Just Senators bathing, reminiscing and talking about politics, while their sons look on respectfully. As in all gymnasia, women are not allowed, one of the many things which aggravate Makri about Turai, although she does claim that given the choice she would rather not see the naked bodies of Turai's rich and flabby upper classes.

There are some very flabby bodies here, though I'm not one to talk, and I feel self-conscious and annoyed as I'm obliged to waddle naked past young athletes disporting themselves in the water, or reclining on couches while servant rub oil into their bodies. I'd rather have kept my towel on but it's frowned upon. I feel more at home when I reach the room at the far end of the gymnasium where elderly Senators and their retinues are gathered, mostly as unfit as me. Also they have less hair. I may get mine oiled, brushed and perfumed while I'm here.

This gymnasium is, incidentally, another of Turai's architectural marvels. It has more than its fair share of splendid friezes, statues and sculptures, although I'm in no mood to appreciate them. I'm here to talk to Cerius. He doesn't want to talk to me. I drag him to a private alcove and shove him on a bench. He's long-haired and skinny and again I feel ridiculous without a good baggy tunic to cover my obesity.

"I'm working for your father."

Cerius immediately clams up, and stares at his feet. Incongruously, he's clutching a bag of grapes, which servants distribute for free.

"Tell me about it," I say.

Cerius remains silent and hostile. The inside of the marble gymnasium is marginally cooler than the baking city outside, but it's still uncomfortable. I get a

strong urge to walk away from this foolish young man
and leap in the bathing pool. I think about my gambling debts, and try again.

"You're going to court in a week, Cerius. Dwa
dealing's a serious charge. Your family's influence won't
get you off, because Deputy Consul Rittius is prosecuting and he's an enemy of your father. Do you want to
see your father disgraced?"

No reaction.

"You want to end up pushing an oar in a convicts'
galley?"

Cerius puts a grape in his mouth. I consider slapping him. Better not, with so many Senators around.
I just can't get him to speak. I don't understand it.

"Who are you protecting? The Prince? They'll find
out in court, so you might as well spill it while it can
do you some good."

Cerius sits slumped in sullen silence. This is hopeless.

"I'll find out, you know. I'll study your past in the
kuriya pool and see where the Choirs of Angels came
from."

All of a sudden the young man looks anguished.

"Don't!" he pleads.

"Why not? Who are you scared of?"

Cerius abruptly rises from his couch and rushes off.
He leaves his bag of grapes behind. I watch him go
then pick up the bag and help myself to the rest of
the grapes. I notice he's been doodling on the paper.
Odd, ugly shapes, scratched in ink. I rise slowly from
the bench. Across the hall there's a fresco of two
beautiful water nymphs frolicking with a young man
with wings on his feet. He floats gracefully over the
water. Lucky guy. I drag my body outside. I'm pleased
to leave. All these young bodies make me feel old.

I walk down Moon and Stars Boulevard till I reach

the centre of town then take a shortcut through the ruined temple of Saint Isinius. I'm passing a broken-down column when all of a sudden something smacks into the marble in front of me, sending splinters cascading around my head. I drop into a fighting crouch and spin round, sword in hand. No one's in sight. I pad softly round the column, then through the archway in front of me. Still no one. Not even a footprint in this dried-out ground. The ruins are silent and when I sniff the air I can't sense anything. Very carefully, I go back to the column. I have a shrewd idea what struck it.

Lying on the ground is a crossbow bolt, nine inches long. I stare at it, and I don't like it one bit. The crossbow is a lethal weapon, extremely powerful. It can send a bolt through solid armour, take a knight off his horse at a hundred yards. I finger the bolt uneasily, wondering who fired it. I've never heard of the Assassins using such a weapon. Nor the Society of Friends. Very strange. I place the bolt in my bag and hurry on, sword still in hand, which earns me a few funny looks when I pass out of the ruins and back into the main street beyond.

Back at the Avenging Axe, Gurd, a slow reader, is ponderously working his way through *The Renowned and Truthful Chronicle*.

"Bad weapons," he says.

"Huh?"

"Crossbow. Brotherhood boss got killed up in Kushni yesterday. Crossbow bolt through the neck."

I read the report. Apparently that was the second important Brotherhood man to be killed in two days, both by crossbow. It seems like the Society of Friends might be getting the upper hand in the drug war. Aided by the mysterious crossbow wielder. It has to be the same person who shot at me. The crossbow is a specialised art. You need a serious amount of training before you can start firing bolts through people's necks from a distance.

Later Makri wonders why the Society of Friends should be firing at me. It's not like I'm on the best of terms with the Brotherhood. I can't think of an explanation. If the Society still think I've got the Red Elvish Cloth, killing me outright isn't going to get it back for them. Maybe I'm just good for some target practice.

My rooms are back in some sort of order. Time I think for a little sorcery.

Chapter Twenty

I stare at the kuriya pool with fury. I'm looking at a picture of the Fairy Glade. I presume the magic pool is once more making a fool of me. Having spent a considerable time working myself into a trance looking for information all I get is a picture of the place where my ex-wife had her assignations with the young Sorcerer. I thought it was all in the past but it must still be troubling me to interfere with the kuriya like this. Any strong image in your own mind can cause interference. Sorcerer's Apprentices often get pictures of their favourite actresses. So do Sorcerers.

This is the last of my kuriya. A waste of money. I'm about to give up in disgust when the pleasant vision of grass and flowers suddenly darkens and a malevolent face begins to take shape. I try to break the connection but it's too late, I'm trapped and I lack the power to pull away.

"Bad mistake, Thraxas," growls the malevolent image. "You should know better than to meddle with me."

"And who the hell are you?" I demand.

"I am Horm the Dead."

I cringe. My skin crawls. I'm scared. I try not to show it. "Well, nice to meet you, Horm. But I've a few things to be getting on with—"

Horm rasps out some evil spell and my room seems to explode. I'm blinded by a searing light and flung against the wall. My desk bounces on to my chest and shards of broken glass rain down on my head as I crumple to the floor. Makri hears the noise and rushes in to find me lying hurt and confused with most of my furniture piled on top of me. She hauls the desk off me then helps me to my feet.

"What happened?"

It takes me a while to get my breath. "A message from Horm the Dead," I gasp, eventually.

Makri unsheathes her sword and whirls round.

"Not here. In the pool. He sent a spell through."

"Can you do that?"

"No," I reply. "Well, not according to what I learned anyway. I guess Horm the Dead might have some tricks we don't know in the west."

Makri bursts out laughing.

"What's funny?"

"You're covered in ink."

"Makri, I just suffered an attack from one of the world's most deadly Sorcerers. I don't see anything funny in that."

This makes Makri laugh some more. "You shouldn't have pawned your protection charm. Why is Horm trying to kill you?"

I really can't say. Just something I've blundered into as usual. But if Horm has been wrecking my room, I must have got closer to his business than he'd like.

Even Makri has heard tales of the malevolent power

of Horm the Dead. "Didn't I hear you say one time that you'd never go up against him?"

I shrug, pretending to be unconcerned. Makri is not fooled. She lectures me on the stupidity of getting involved in too many cases at once.

"You don't even know why people are trying to kill you any more."

"I keep telling you I need the money."

"You shouldn't have got in debt to the Brotherhood."

"You think I don't know that? Can't you do something useful instead of lecturing me all the time?"

I hate it when I find myself involved with powerful Sorcerers. I should stick to divorce work.

Gurd is furious about the room. Destroyed three times in three days. A new record. He mutters darkly about looking for a tenant who won't keep ruining his furniture, and I have to divert him by steering the conversation round towards Tanrose, which I don't really have time for.

Later I tell Makri about the latest developments with Cerius, and the crossbow attack.

"I used the last of my kuriya looking for some clues but all I got was a vision of the Fairy Glade."

"What's it like?"

"Like a puddle of black ink."

"Not the kuriya, idiot. The Fairy Glade."

"Oh. Well, it's idyllic, during the days. Fairies flying around, unicorns wandering through the trees, Nymphs and Dryads playing music, beautiful flowers, sparkling streams. You should go, Makri, you'd like it."

"Maybe. I could use a bit of peace after living in this stinking city for a year. But Gurd says no one with Orcish blood can get in."

This is true. The Fairy Glade is deep in the woods, a long way from the city, and it's protected from harm by various natural magics, one of which does not allow an Orc to enter.

"You're only one quarter Orc. And you're one quarter Elf. The Fairies are big on Elves. They might take to you."

Makri says she has had quite enough rejection from Humans to risk more at the hands of Fairies, Nymphs and Dryads.

I wonder where my wife and the young Sorcerer went after running off to the Glade all those years ago. They couldn't have stayed there long. No Human can spend a night there. Sleep comes on even if you fight it, and then the dreams drive you mad. Literally mad. Every year a few romantic or foolhardy young souls try it, and the result is always the same; they wander off to perish somewhere in the wilds or end up back in Turai begging aimlessly on street corners. The Fairy Glade is strictly for daytime visits only.

Makri says she keeps passing meetings with orators haranguing crowds in the streets, and earlier in the day she'd seen one meeting disrupted by a group of armed men.

"Election. Deputy Consul's post's coming up for grabs."

"Why?"

"Don't you know anything about the city you live in?"

"No."

I remember Makri hasn't been in Turai long enough to have seen an election, so I explain to her that the Deputy Consul is second only to the Consul, who's second only to the King, and that the post comes up for grabs every two years.

"The Traditionals, who support the King, always held the post but last time Rittius won it for the Populares. Since then Lodius's party has been gaining power. Something to do with the Royal Family bleeding the city dry, no doubt. Cicerius is trying to win it back for the Traditionals."

"So why all the fighting?" asks Makri.

"Politics is like that in Turai. No one wins an election without bribing some voters and frightening others. The Traditionals generally employ the Brotherhood as their strong-arm men and the Populares use the Society of Friends."

Makri asks if she's entitled to vote and I tell her no, women aren't allowed, which puts her in a bad mood, even when I point out that no one is worth voting for.

"Not even the Populares? Wouldn't some democracy be a good thing?"

"It might be," I admit. "But we won't get it from any party with Lodius as its leader. The man's nakedly ambitious and cold as an Orc's heart into the bargain. And he's going to make a bid for power one day, whether his party wins the election or not. The King should have had him assassinated years ago."

"Why hasn't he?"

"He left it too late and now he's scared. Lodius has powerful backing these days—rich merchants, disaffected aristocrats, ambitious generals and so on. I tell you, Makri, it's not worth getting involved."

We play a game of niarit. I win. Makri is displeased.

"What's this?" she says, picking up a scrap of paper.

"It's a bag of grapes. Minus the grapes."

"But it's written on."

"Written on?" I say, studying the meaningless scribbles.

"Don't you recognise Low Orcish when you see it?"

"No. What is it?"

"The language of the Orcish underclass. Not the common Orcish tongue, or any of their national languages, but a sort of pidgin Orcish they use in the

Wastelands where there are Orcs, Humans and a lot in between. They speak it in gladiator pits."

I have to hand this one to Makri. I would've recognised standard Orcish characters but I had no idea there was a written form of pidgin Orcish.

"What's it say?"

"Load, or consignment . . . in spirit grass place. Spirit Grass Place? I don't know what that means."

I sigh. I realise immediately what it means. "I imagine that Spirit Grass Place is Low Orcish for the Fairy Glade, Makri. You might be getting to see it sooner than you think."

Makri wonders out loud why Cerius, a Praetor's son, would carry around a message written in Orcish.

"I was wondering the same thing. If the Prince and Cerius are really importing dwa like Kerk says, I can't see them being involved with Orcs. Unless it's coming from Horm . . . which would explain the warning he sent me. If Cerius has got mixed up with Horm the Dead it's no wonder he's terrified. He terrifies me."

"Is Horm a dwa dealer?"

"He could be, He uses it himself, and it's profitable enough to interest him."

"There are two letters at the end of the message," continues Makri. "S and M, I think. Mean anything to you?"

I shake my head. Makri has the afternoon off from work and is due to attend a lecture on Theological Philosophy by Samanatius, one of Turai's leading thinkers. Much the same as myself, I reflect, downstairs in the bar, as I down a few beers and do some serious thinking.

A messenger from the Brotherhood arrives. "Yubaxas is getting impatient," he says.

I throw him out of the bar. "I have two days left. Tell Yubaxas he'll get his money."

Spurred on to action I return to my musings about the Cloth. I figure that I'm close somehow, and what's more, when I find it, I'm sure I'll be able to clear the Princess.

Praetor Cicerius walks into the bar in his blue-edged toga, to the general consternation of the assembled drinkers. They gape in amazement as he crosses over and greets me. Not bad, I reflect, having the Praetor himself call on me. Might earn me a little respect round here.

Upstairs in my rooms he has some grave news. "The Investigator Tuparius has learned that Prince Frisen-Akan is paying Horm the Dead to bring dwa into Turai. Furthermore the Prince has sent a letter of credit to cover the payment. If this becomes known to the public, the government will fall." The Praetor shakes his head sadly. "My son is involved in passing drugs from that renegade half-Orc Sorcerer to Prince Frisen-Akan. This is worse than anything I could have imagined. How can I explain this to Consul Kalius? Think of the terrible repercussions if word got out! It was bad enough before, when the Populares merely sought to discredit me. If the Prince is dragged into the affair, what chance do the Traditionals have in the election?"

Cicerius insists that he does not care about winning the post of Deputy Consul for himself, but only about the good of the city. Strangely enough, I believe him. He demands to know what I'm going to do.

"What's Tuparius going to do?" I ask.

"Nothing. After relating this information to me he was murdered on his way home. A crossbow bolt through the neck."

"You're not making this investigation sound too attractive, Praetor. How about calling in the Civil Guard?"

"That is not possible. Many of the Guards owe allegiance to Rittius. We can't risk this scandal getting out. You will have to retrieve the letter of credit and see that the Prince's name is kept out of the affair."

Cicerius notes my lack of enthusiasm and enquires in an acidic tone what the matter is. I point out that every man has his limits. Even me.

"If the case involves Horm the Dead, Glixius Dragon Killer and Prince Frisen-Akan, no wonder your son is scared. They scare the hell out of me. Look what happened to Tuparius. Anyway, what do you expect of me? The state should be handling the job, and is it? No, it's not, because half the forces of the state are in the pay of these people. If you want to stop Glixius Dragon Killer importing dwa from Horm the Dead, get someone else to do it."

"I am not asking you to do any such thing." retorts Cicerius. "But my son must not be convicted of these charges. And Prince Frisen-Akan must not be implicated."

"That's going to be difficult, seeing as the only way for your son to get off is by naming the Prince."

Cicerius fixes me with his steely gaze, and demands to know if I am aware of the importance of the affair.

"Yes. I'll probably get killed."

"There are things more important to this city than your life, or mine," he replies. "If Deputy Consul Rittius succeeds in prosecuting Cerius, and disgracing the name of the Royal Family, he will win the election. If Rittius is re-elected, more Senators will move over to Lodius's party. The Populares may gain control of the Senate. Turai will be torn apart. Lodius seeks nothing less than the overthrow of the monarchy, and he will stop at nothing to procure it. He has succeeded in gathering support for his party by promising democratic reforms, but his real aim is to seize power."

As I said, I take little interest in Turai's politics but I'm aware that Cicerius is putting forward a very one-sided view of things. Plenty of people support Senator Lodius's Populares for good reasons. The massed poor of the city have no representation in the Senate at all. The aristocrats are heavily taxed to pay for the Royal Family's luxury. Our merchants, some of whom have amassed vast wealth, are even more heavily taxed, and also have little representation, being allowed only observer status in the Senate. Among the Honourable Association of Merchants there can now be heard mutterings that, as they contribute so much in taxes to the state, they should have some say in how it's governed. This has spread to lesser guilds once renowned for fierce loyalty to the King. So the King faces an alliance of disaffected aristocrats, powerful merchants, and city artisans. He can't give in to this alliance but it's too strong for him to sweep away. Lodius has artfully harnessed these disaffections. Were I to give the matter much thought, I might well find myself in sympathy with him. After all, Turai has certainly deteriorated in the past twenty years. Unfortunately Cicerius has a trump card to play.

"Do you know that at this moment Deputy Consul Rittius is preparing a list of men who will no longer be allowed to trade in the city? Your name is on that list, Thraxas. If he is re-elected, your Investigator's licence will be withdrawn."

I'm not sure if Cicerius is telling the truth. He might be. "Okay, Praetor Cicerius, I'll see what I can do. You better write me an introduction."

"An introduction?"

"To Prince Frisen-Akan. I'll have to speak to him. Don't look so appalled, Praetor. I promise I'll be polite."

I down a few beers and head out, looking for Captain Rallee. I find him easily enough, directing the removal of a load of dead bodies from the corner of the street. Stals are fluttering around looking interested in the prospect of some profitable scavenging.

"Another attack by the Society?"

He nods. They are getting the upper hand in their war with the Brotherhood.

"It's that damned crossbow killer. He's now killed four Brotherhood bosses in the past two days."

The Captain tells me that Choirs of Angels is flooding into the city. It's now cheaper than standard dwa.

"Won't be cheap for long, of course. Just long enough for these poor fools to get addicted."

I mention Horm the Dead. The Captain is interested, although anything happening so far from the city is really beyond his power. No state has much control over what goes on in the Wastelands.

"The Society of Friends is cornering the market. The Brotherhood is going to have to strike back with everything they've got. Things are bad enough with the elections, without this happening as well."

"How come the Society can get away with such a large operation?"

The Captain shrugs, which might mean anything. The higher ranks of the Civil Guard are not above corruption. Nor are senior city officials. When dealing with his superiors, Captain Rallee never knows whether or not he might be talking to someone who's raking in drug money himself. It would be practically impossible to find any person of influence in the whole city who wasn't involved in some way or other. All Captain Rallee and his guards can do is try to keep the peace, and pick up the pieces when they fail.

"Is Glixius Dragon Killer still working with the Society?" I enquire.

"We never had any proof he was working with them in the first place."

"Well, he certainly was when he chased me through the sewers with a bunch of Society men at his back."

The Captain shrugs again. Glixius Dragon Killer is not on any wanted list, nor can he be proved to have committed any crime. Which makes me wonder who he's bribing.

"Excuse me," says the Captain, "I have work to do. A gang's been robbing pilgrims out at Saint Quatinius's Shrine. Wouldn't have happened a few years back. People used to have some respect. Since half the city got hooked on dwa everything's gone to hell."

A Civil Guard messenger thunders up on horseback and tells them they're needed fast up in Kushni where a major confrontation is again taking place between two heavily armed gangs. They depart on the double, and not long after I see Brotherhood men pouring out of the Mermaid with swords in their hands, heading north. Captain Rallee might be right. Everything *is* going to hell. What's more, the heat is absolutely unbearable.

Makri returns full of enthusiasm from the philosophy lecture given by Samanatius.

"A great man," she enthuses.

Perspiration is running down her neck and she douses her head and shoulders with water while she tells me about the lecture. It's something to do with the nature of eternal forms, and the human soul, but most of it passes over my head.

"I asked him a question and he answered right off," says Makri. "Without looking at me with contempt, that is. Incidentally, I just remembered someone whose initials are S.M."

"Pardon?"

"S.M. The Orcish initials on the bag, after the message. It might be Sarin the Merciless."

I laugh.

"What's funny?"

"Sarin the Merciless. Sarin the Pussycat more like. I keep telling you, I ran her out of town before. She's nothing. If she's the best muscle Horm can find I've got nothing to worry about. Just start counting out my reward. Now, I'm off to see a Prince."

Chapter Twenty-One

On the way home from the Palace I pass three corpses and numerous walking wounded. Two men demand to know who I'm going to vote for. I draw my sword.

"Put me down as undecided," I growl.

On the corner of Quintessence Lane a crowd has gathered. They're looking at the young guy who sells dwa there every day. He's out of business now, with a bolt from a crossbow embedded in his neck. I have a strong appetite for four or five beers.

"How did it go?" asks Makri.

I note with disapproval that she has had her nose pierced.

"Palax and Kaby did it for me. Don't you like it?"

I shake my head. I'm too old for these outlandish fashions.

"Shouldn't you be trying to look normal, Makri, to get into the Imperial University?"

"Maybe," she concedes. "But I like having a ring

through my nose. Do you think I should have my nipples done?"

"Who's ever going to see? You've never had a lover."

"I might have, if all the men in Twelve Seas weren't such scum. Do you think that Elvish healer will visit again?"

"Yes. But if he finds you with your nipples pierced he'll panic. Body piercing is taboo to the Elves."

Makri thinks she could probably change his mind. I refuse to discuss it any more.

"So what happened at the Palace? How's the Prince?"

I sigh. I can hardly bear to describe how he is. "All the stories about Prince Frisen-Akan are true. Besides being as dumb as an Orc he's the biggest dwa addict in the city. Not to mention a stinking drunk, a thazis abuser, a hopeless gambler, a heavy debtor and all-round degenerate piece of rubbish. I look forward to his accession to the throne with great anticipation. Incidentally I'm setting out for the Fairy Glade early in the morning."

"Why?"

"To recover the dwa the Prince is bringing into the city for Horm the Dead."

"What?"

I shake my head and tell Makri the full sorry tale. Not only has Prince Frisen-Akan sunk so deeply into drug addiction that he barely knows what he's doing any more, he's so deeply in debt to so many people that it's becoming impossible to hush up.

"So he was planning to sell the dwa to make some money."

Makri laughs at the thought. It is funny in a way. Some Prince.

"He was getting small amounts of the stuff from Cerius. Unfortunately that wasn't enough so he decided to try something bigger. He's putting up the money for this transaction. It's the behaviour of a lunatic—if the King finds out he'll exile him. Which wouldn't bother me a bit except the Prince dragged Cerius into this madness and if the story comes out then Cerius will probably end up taking the rap."

"Dump your client," advises Makri.

"I'd like to, but I can't. It's all got too complicated. If Cicerius's son goes to jail, Cicerius loses the election. If that happens, I lose my licence. Also, Cicerius has offered me much more money to intercept the dwa and bring it back safely. Or rather, bring the letter back safely."

"What letter?"

"The letter the Prince sent authorising payment."

Makri gapes. I gaped too when I heard about it from the Prince who, in a rare moment of lucidity, did realise that sending a letter authorising payment for six sacks of illegal drugs, and signing this letter with his own seal, wasn't the brightest thing he could have done.

If the public learns about it they might as well cancel the election. The Populares will walk it. The people of Turai will forgive the Royal Family for many things but not wholesale drug dealing with a mad Orc Sorcerer. Particularly as the Princess is at this moment awaiting trial for killing the dragon. Poor Royal Family. I'm almost starting to feel sorry for them."

"You shouldn't get involved," says Makri.

"Cicerius is paying me six hundred gurans if I can keep Cerius and the Prince out of it."

"I'll go and sharpen my swords."

We hire a couple of horses and set off early next morning. I don't know who is taking the Prince's letter of credit to the Glade, so I plan to arrive there first and intercept it. Either that or attempt to make off with the dwa myself and swap it later. Makri has her usual assortment of weapons including some small throwing stars I've never seen before.

"Assassins' weapons aren't they?"

She nods. "I saw them on Hanama's belt that night we had the fight. I thought I'd try them out."

The streets are still empty save for one or two dead bodies from last night's gang warfare, and the ever present beggars. I'm fairly immune to beggars now, though some of them are so pitiful it's impossible to be completely unaffected; mothers with misshapen children, men back from the wars with no legs and no army pension, hopeless itinerants going blind with cataracts in their eyes. Turai is no place to be old, sick or without friends or family. Which gives me a slightly bad feeling about my own fate. No one is going to nurse me through my dotage if I'm crippled on a case.

The Fairy Glade is a good two hours' ride from the city, east through the farmlands and the vineyards that skirt the hills. It's some way inside the huge forest that serves as the boundary between Turai and Misan, our small eastern neighbour. Nothing much goes on in Misan, which is made up of small villages and clusters of nomadic tribesmen. After that it's a few hundred miles of increasingly wild and lawless territory before you reach the lands of the Orcs.

Glixius Dragon Killer is meant to collect the Choirs of Angels from the Glade tomorrow. It's being deposited there by Horm the Dead.

"Why is the pick-up point the Fairy Glade?" asks Makri.

"Glixius insisted. He knows that as Horm is half Orc he won't be able to get into the Glade. I imagine Glixius doesn't trust him completely and wants the stuff delivered someplace he can examine it in peace without fear of Horm double-crossing him or just stealing the Prince's credit note without delivering the goods. Somehow we've got to intercept that credit note."

Whether or not Makri can get into the Fairy Glade remains to be seen. Whichever guardian spirits protect it, they won't be used to anyone with Orc, Elf and Human blood. I've told Makri to keep smiling and to think positive thoughts. That always pleases the Fairies.

The countryside is parched and dry. Around the city the land is irrigated with a series of small channels fed by the river but further on the fields are barren. Much of this land has been overfarmed and is becoming infertile, which is one more thing for Turai to worry about. Some way on, as the land rises gradually and the trees become more numerous, the vegetation looks rather healthier. More rain falls on these hills than falls on the city. Astrath Triple Moon explained the reason to me once but I've forgotten what it was. The vast forest is now visible on the horizon. I glance at the sky. I don't like it out here. I feel exposed in all this space. I'm too used to the city. I don't ride much these days and I'm already sore in the saddle. Makri rides without a saddle, like the Barbarian she is. She seems untroubled by the heat, even in her leather and chainmail body armour. Her axe is strapped to her saddle and her two swords form a cross on her back. We're both carrying light helmets with visors.

A small copse is in front of us, then the forest proper begins.

"I've never been in a forest before," says Makri.

Horm the Dead rides out from the copse followed by twenty Orcish warriors.

"It might be a very short visit."

Another twenty Orcs ride out from the trees along with a few heavily armed Humans. They encircle us. I curse myself for my carelessness but I wasn't expecting to meet Horm in person. Certainly not this side of the Glade. He must have deposited the dwa and come this way to wait for Glixius, or whoever is bringing the Prince's credit note. Makri slips her helmet over her face, takes a sword in her left hand and her axe in her right, and prepares to make her death stand. I'm still hoping to talk my way out of it.

Horm rides up. His face is deathly white and his features, not unhandsome, are immobile, set in stone. His malevolent black eyes stare at me. His thick black hair hangs round his shoulders, with dark eagle feathers woven into his plaits and black and gold beads tied into their ends. Even in this heat he's wearing his black cloak. His aura is so powerful that it's intimidating just to be near.

I put on a brave face. "Greetings, Horm the Dead. All is well with you, I trust?"

"I warned you to stay well away from me." He demands to know what brings me here.

"A letter of credit which the Prince very unwisely gave to Glixius Dragon Killer."

"That is for me, not you."

"I'm sorry, Horm. We just can't let such a thing fall into your hands. Praetor Cicerius offers to redeem it for the full amount."

This is a lie but I'm hoping to buy some time. Horm the Dead shakes his head. He isn't interested in selling us the Prince's note.

"I have other plans for it, Thraxas. Do you think I'd be such a fool as to sell it for its face value? Once I have it in my hands the Royal Family will find themselves paying me for the rest of their lives to keep the matter quiet."

"The King of Turai does not pay blackmailers," I say, with dignity.

Horm the Dead laughs. "He does if he doesn't want to be swept out of power by the Populares."

The Orcs draw in tighter around us. They're ugly. Ugly and well armed, with scimitars and hunting bows.

"How can you dare to confront me, Thraxas? You have so little power."

"People often say that to me. But I get by somehow."

I've taken a small ball out of my bag.

"What is that?" sneers Horm the Dead.

"A child's toy," I reply, and hurl it at the ground where it explodes with a flash of light and a series of powerful, reverberating crashes. The multiple firecracker causes Horm's horse to rear in terror. The Orcs behind him likewise fight to control their mounts. Makri and I need no encouragement. We're through their lines at a gallop and into the forest before anyone has time to loose an arrow at us.

"Nice move," yells Makri, yanking her visor back to see better in the gloom.

It was a nice move. Only a smart guy like myself would know that Turanian horses are used to firecrackers because they encounter them at our festivals. To an Orc's horse from the Wastelands, it must have come as quite a surprise.

We pound along the trail, slowing as the branches droop. Behind us we hear sounds of pursuit but this forest path is a difficult place to chase anyone, as the branches are too low and the undergrowth too thick.

"How far to the Fairy Glade?"

"About a hundred yards."

"What if I can't get in?"

"We'll plead with the fairies."

Suddenly we burst into a clearing, a beautiful stretch of grass and flowers with a sparkling stream running down into a rocky pool. Standing beside the pool is a unicorn.

"We're here," I say, and dismount.

"Wow," says Makri, as the unicorn looks at us, unconcerned, and carries on drinking. I join it, scooping up some water to splash over my face.

"Is it safe?"

"Everything's safe in the Fairy Glade, Makri. Provided you don't stay the night."

Four Fairies, each about six inches tall and wearing brightly coloured garments, flutter out of the trees and hover in front of Makri's face, examining her. Four more appear, and then more, till eventually Makri is completely surrounded by small silver-winged Fairies. They start to land on her arms, and walk over her head and shoulders.

"They like you. I thought they would."

Somewhere a flute is playing, very gently. The Orcs can't reach us here. Strange though it seems, we forget all about them, and sit down to rest and watch the Fairies, and the unicorns and the Dryads that appear from the trees, and the Naiads that surface from the pool to play with the butterflies.

"I like this place," says Makri, removing her body armour.

I like it too. I'm surprised. I thought I'd become too much of a cynic.

"What's that?" asks Makri as a half-man, half-horse trots into view.

"A Centaur. Pretty intelligent, by all accounts. Lascivious too."

The Centaur approaches. Like all the magical creatures here he seems completely unconcerned by our presence. He halts in front of Makri, staring appreciatively at her curves. Makri shifts a little uncomfortably.

"Seen enough?" she says querulously, as the Centaur keeps on staring.

The Fairies giggle.

"Pardon me," says the Centaur, pleasantly. "Force of habit."

He makes to leave. I remember what I'm here for. "Excuse me," I say. "We're looking for some sacks of dwa."

The Centaur frowns, and looks at me accusingly. "Bringing such a thing into the Glade is a violation."

"I know. That's why we're going to remove it."

I give him a brief rundown of events, stressing heavily that myself and Makri are on the side of law and order.

"Your city's law and order mean little to us."

"We believe in peace and love," says Makri, which is curious coming from a woman currently carrying an axe, two swords and God knows how many knives and throwing stars. I can't imagine where Makri picked up such an odd phrase but it seems to go down well. The Centaur likes the sound of peace and love. So do the Fairies. They're clustering round Makri like bees round honey, flying round her, walking over her, playing with her hair. Obviously they love her. Makri basks in the sunshine and the attention, happy as an Elf in a tree. The Fairies don't take much notice of me.

"I'll take you to the sacks," says the Centaur, who introduces himself as Taur. "We will be pleased if you remove them. Although they were not prevented from entering the Glade, we did not like the people who brought them. They were Orc friends."

We walk past the pool where the Naiads are combing their long golden tresses. The water spirits are young, beautiful and naked. Twenty years ago I'd have dived right in the pool. Oh to be young.

Taur leads us through the clearing and under the

shadow of some massive old oak trees. It's so cool and pleasant that I have a strong urge to sleep. I shake it off. It's only midday but we can't waste time. We have to be out of here before nightfall.

"We're making progress," I tell Makri. All we have to do is get hold of the dwa and we can trade with Glixius for the note."

"What about Horm the Dead?"

"I don't know. I'll think of something."

Taur takes us to the far end of the Glade and into the trees where the six sacks are partially hidden in the undergrowth. He then departs for an assignation with a Dryad. I'm almost moved to smile. Mission accomplished, as my old Commanding Officer used to say. Now I'm in a position to trade for the letter of credit. The Fairies stay with Makri while we load the sacks of dwa on to our horses.

"How do we get out of here?" enquires Makri. "I don't mind fighting forty Orcs but I can't guarantee I'll kill every one of them."

"You disappoint me. As they can't get in here, maybe we could stay just inside the boundary and pick them off? If we killed enough of them we could make a run for it."

Makri pulls out her throwing stars. "We might get a few of them. But Orcs aren't that stupid. Once they see what's happening they'll just withdraw far enough away that we can't reach them."

"Do you have a better idea?"

"No."

"So we might as well try it."

We hurry back to the clearing where our horses engage briefly in conversation with two Centaurs who greet us affably as we pass. It's strange being sur-rounded by these peculiar creatures, all of them with-out a care in the world, while our lives are in such extreme danger. We creep through the trees to the edge of the Glade, then separate. I get down on my belly and crawl forward, trying to spot the line of sentries. There's no sign of any. I can't find an Orc anywhere. Makri returns with the same tale. The Orcs are not guarding the Glade.

"Strange. They must be waiting outside the forest, watching the paths."

"I know this forest," I say, gaining confidence. "I can lead us north and out of the forest far away from the path. We'll be back in Turai before they know we've gone."

I'm surprised at such poor tactics from an experienced warrior like Horm the Dead. Dwa must be addling his mind. We hurry to make our escape. The Fairies still flutter along happily beside Makri. They seem to be enjoying it all. Centaurs call out appreciatively as we reach the clearing. Taur, back from his assignation, is just making some gracious comments about Makri's figure when he stops short, tossing his head in alarm and sniffing the air. The hairs on the back of my neck start to prickle. I can sense something very bad about to happen.

"What is it?" asks Makri.

"Horm the Dead. He's close."

"Horm can't get in here!"

I look up, shielding my eyes against the burning sun. High above, a monstrous shape is circling the Glade. As it descends its great wings beat the air like a vision of hell. The Centaurs wail. The Fairies shriek and fly into the trees and the Naiads disappear under the water. Horm the Dead and thirty Orcs are gliding towards us on the back of a dragon. A real war dragon. Not a small one like the one in the King's zoo. Not a half-grown thing like the one Makri fought in the slave pits. A proper Orcish war dragon, black and gold, vast in size, with terrible fangs, fiery breath, scales like armour and talons that can tear a man in two. The most frightening creature ever to draw breath, and it's coming our way, fast.

"A war dragon," I say to Makri. "God knows how Horm got hold of it but it looks like he's decided to smash his way into the Glade."

Makri stands firm with her axe raised. "I fought one before . . ."

The dragon circles closer.

"It was an awful lot smaller than that though," she admits. "Did you and Gurd really kill a dragon in the war?"

"Yes. Not nearly as big as this though, and the sleep spell gave us a couple of seconds to get its eyes. But you can't use magic here. My sleep spell won't work in the Fairy Glade."

"It's funny the way your spells tend not to work whenever we need them most."

"Yes, I've noticed that as well."

As the dragon nears we see that it's wearing a visor of steel mesh to protect its eyes. When the dragon is about fifty feet above the ground, and Horm and his troops are screaming at us and brandishing their swords, there's a terrific flash of lightning as it hits the protective magical field that covers the Glade. The dragon screams and a blast of flame belches from its nostrils. One Orc plummets to the ground but the rest hang on grimly, as the dragon furiously throws itself against the barrier. It screams and writhes, beating at the air with its wings and talons. Bolts of blue lightning split the sky and thunderous explosions rock the Glade. A tremendous flash lights up the forest as the barrier finally gives way. The vast golden bulk of the beast crashes to the ground and lies stunned in a great cloud of smoke and dust. There's a brief moment of silence, then with fierce war cries the Orcs emerge like demons from the smoke, and charge towards us, waving their swords and screaming.

I turn to flee. Makri stands her ground. I curse at her, and grab her arm. She brushes me off.

"I'm not running from Orcs twice in one day," she declares, gripping her axe and slipping on her helmet. Neither of us has had time to don our armour so Makri faces the charge wearing only her chainmail bikini and helmet whilst I'm standing in an undershirt hoping no one shoots an arrow into my belly.

An amazing thing happens. A great phalanx of fabulous creatures emerges from the trees, ready to fight to defend the Fairy Glade from the hated Orcs. Centaurs, unicorns and Dryads, with clubs and spears, rush forward to meet the Orcs' charge. The air is thick with furious, spitting Fairies, and odd Pixie-like creatures that ride on the backs of the Centaurs, brandishing knives.

Battle is joined. The Glade dwellers plus myself and Makri against thirty huge Orc warriors and the malevolently powerful Horm the Dead. Thank God the dragon is stunned. The air still crackles as Horm attempts to force his sorcery to work in the magic-dampening space around him. Bolts of lightning flicker from his fingers, powerful enough to drive back the Centaurs but not yet strong enough to spread destruction. The Orcs attempt to slash their way through us and their huge curved blades inflict some damage but they're driven back by stabbing unicorns and clubbing Centaurs, and Fairies who fly round them spitting in their eyes and pricking them with tiny, needle-like weapons.

Makri starts hacking her way through towards the Orc Commander, a huge creature with two massive swords who rallies his forces with an evil, screeching battle cry. I'm confronted by two Orcs and forced

sideways against a tree. I manage to strike one of them
down and before the other can attack he's transfixed
from behind by a unicorn's horn.

Horm the Dead is not one of those Sorcerers who
shuns battle. Seeing his Orcs hard pressed, he aban-
dons his effort to work his magic and lays about him
with a black sword to murderous effect. He sends a
Naiad flying backwards screaming and almost decapi-
tates a Centaur with a great curving blow. In the midst
of the mayhem, I glimpse some naked Naiads emerging
from the water and swiftly dragging the bleeding Dryad
away from the scene and into the pool.

The forces of the Fairy Glade have the Orcs out-
numbered. We start to outflank them, forcing the Orcs
to retreat towards the still unconscious dragon. The Orcs
form up in front of the gigantic, smoking beast, using
its bulk to guard their backs. Fighting is extremely fierce.
The Glade beings lose some momentum in the face of
determined Orcish resistance, and the outcome hangs
in the balance. Then Makri slays an Orcish warrior and
bursts through their ranks to mount a furious attack on
their Commander. He roars an Orcish curse at her and
assails her with his two huge swords. Makri parries with
her axe and sword, screams a curse of her own, and
buries her axe deep in his helmet. The Centaurs cheer
and charge forward with their clubs and the Fairies
renew their efforts at confusing their enemies, buzzing
and stabbing like a horde of tormenting insects.

The Orcs crumble under our final assault and are
hacked down in front of the dragon. Horm the Dead,
streaming with blood, screams in rage as he holds off
Makri and a Centaur. Summoning one last great burst
of energy, he shouts out a demonic spell and the air
around him crackles with fire as the spell struggles
against the magic dampening aura of the Fairy Glade.
Finally it bursts through, sending Makri and the

others spinning backwards. Horm screams a desperate command to the dragon, causing it to rouse itself with a terrifying roar. Makri picks herself up and sprints back towards the Sorcerer, but before she can reach him he scales the side of the dragon and orders it into the air. With a great beating of its wings the huge war dragon lifts off the ground. Makri, frustrated by the escape, whips a throwing star from her bag and hurls it at Horm. He screams as it embeds itself in his leg, but he hangs on. There's another terrific flash of blue lightning as the dragon crashes up out of the magical field leaving thirty dead Orcs below, and not a few casualties on our side.

We've won. Thraxas, Makri and the unicorns beat off Horm and a dragon. When I tell them about it at the Avenging Axe, they'll never believe me.

Chapter Twenty-Two

I'm completely drained. I can barely stand. I haven't been in a battle like that for a long time. I slump to the ground. The Centaurs and their friends take no rest, but immediately start dragging their wounded companions towards the pool. When I see the first badly wounded Dryad emerge healthily from the water just moments later I understand that the water has healing powers, and will protect the inhabitants of the Glade.

Makri has some wounds of her own. She has a gash on her arm and her nose is torn and bleeding where an Orcish blade ripped out her nose ring.

"Damn," she says, and winces in pain.

Taur trots over. He's looking pleased with himself.

"A fine battle," he says, as he scoops up water from the pool to rub on Makri's wounds. He carries on rubbing longer than is strictly necessary, but the bleeding stops, and Makri starts to heal right before our eyes.

"You have a strong constitution," says Taur. "And a fine body. Are you planning on staying?"

"Won't it drive me mad?"

"It drives Humans mad. But I'm sure that a woman of your extraordinary make-up would be quite safe."

"You hear that, Thraxas? A woman of my extraordinary make-up."

I snort. I'm getting fed up with this. She declines Taur's offer however, telling him that she must get back to the city. The Centaur is disappointed.

"Visit us again soon," he says.

"We love you," say the Fairies, and settle on her shoulders. Makri is happy as an Elf in a tree. A pleasant visit to the Fairy Glade and a good battle all in one day. She's particularly pleased to have killed the Orcish Commander.

"I knew him when I was a slave," she tells us. "He badly needed killing."

I drink plenty of water from the pool. Makri declares it to be the most refreshing thing she's ever tasted. I'm not entirely satisfied.

"Got any beer?" I ask Taur as we saddle up our horses.

His eyes twinkle. "Not exactly, Thraxas, but we do have some fine mead."

Mead. Alcohol made from honey. Not one of my favourites, but better than nothing I suppose. I accept the flagon from Taur and the rest of the Glade dwellers look kindly on us as we depart. They like us for helping protect the Glade against the Orcs, and for removing the dwa from their presence.

"Visit us again," calls Taur to Makri, waving goodbye. She waves farewell.

"You know, given that you're a social outcast in polite society, it's amazing the way some people take to you, Makri," I say, as we ride out into the forest path.

"Well, the Centaurs certainly liked me," agrees Makri. "And the Fairies. But they liked you too, I saw some of them resting on you."

"They were using my belly as a sunshade."

I guzzle down some mead. It tastes sweet; not unpleasant though no substitute for beer, and not nearly potent enough after my recent experiences.

"You want to be careful," says Makri. "We have a long way to ride and I don't want you falling off your horse."

"Pah," I snort, and drink more from the flagon. "It'll take more than Fairy juice to affect me."

By the time we're halfway home I am spectacularly, roaringly, hopelessly drunk. Taur's mead is obviously more powerful than I thought. As we pass some farm labourers I brandish my sword and sing a battle song to them. They laugh, and wave back genially. We pass through some lightly wooded hills and I let go with another fine old drinking song. Suddenly I feel overwhelmingly tired and fall off my horse. There is a loud thwack as something thuds into a tree next to me.

"What—?"

Makri leans over. "A crossbow bolt!"

It occurs to me, none too clearly, that it would have hit me had I not at that precise moment had the good fortune to fall off my horse.

I struggle to my feet. The bolt is embedded deep in the tree. Makri leaps from her horse, swords at the ready, and crouches watchfully. I grab my own sword and try to pull myself together.

A figure steps out from the trees to our right, a crossbow in his hands. He walks towards us with the shaft pointing at Makri. Fifteen feet away from us he halts. It's not a him, it's a her. A tall woman, plainly dressed, with her hair cropped very short, wearing, for some reason, a great many earrings. She turns her gaze on me.

"You drunken oaf, Thraxas," she says, with some contempt.

"A friend of yours?" enquires Makri, who is crouched ready to spring.

"I never saw her before."

"You have. I looked rather different then. I am Sarin. Sarin the Merciless. And you would be one dead Investigator if you hadn't fallen off your horse."

She laughs, mirthlessly. "But I can soon fix that."

Sensing Makri about to spring, she instantly turns the crossbow on her.

I can't quite make this out. Sarin the Merciless never used to be a deadly woman with a crossbow. Must have been taking lessons. I curse myself for drinking so much mead, and shake my head to clear it.

"What do you want?"

She fixes me with a stare. Her eyes are black and cold as an Orc's heart. This is not the same woman I remember at all.

"You dead would be a good start, drunkard. But that can wait. Right now I'll take the dwa."

Her black eyes flicker back to Makri.

"The Fairies liked you," says Sarin. "Strange. They didn't seem to take to me.

"They didn't like me either," I growl. "They probably guessed I've got a terrible temper. So get out of my way."

Sarin pulls something from her tunic. "I take it you are hoping to trade the dwa for this?"

It's the Prince's credit note, but Sarin doesn't seem keen to enter into negotiations.

"I've decided I might as well keep the note and take the dwa. Now hand it over. I'm very good with this crossbow. I'd say you're at my mercy. As you may know, that is not something I have much of."

She laughs.

Unfortunately Makri is not the sort of person you can rob and expect to put up no resistance. Her fighting code, not to mention her pride, just won't allow it. Any second now I can tell that she is either going to leap at Sarin or try and catch her with a throwing star or knife before she can shoot. I don't like this too well. Sarin the Merciless has proved she's skilful with that crossbow, and I'm not sure that she might not transfix Makri before she could come to grips.

A terrible wave of tiredness passes over me. Delayed shock from the war dragon. Or just too much mead. I take a quick decision to act before things get out of hand. I'm still carrying the sleep spell. I'll take Sarin out before she can do any harm. The fatigue is overwhelming. I can hardly stand. I bark out the spell. Makri looks briefly surprised, then crumples gently to the ground. I realise that I have rather messed things up. The effort of casting the spell finishes me off. I fall to the ground. The last thing I hear before passing out is Sarin's mocking laughter.

Chapter Twenty-Three

An Elf is standing over me. It's Callis, brandishing a lesada leaf. He must have guessed I've been drinking. I wash it down and struggle to my feet. Makri is still sleeping gently on the grass. Jaris has rounded up our horses and is leading them over.

"What happened?" asks Callis, as he goes to attend to Makri. I decline to comment. Callis tells me that when he appeared a tall woman was in the process of loading sacks on to her horse.

"She rode off. Was it the Cloth?" he asks.

"No. Something else. But related to your case," I add, just in case he thinks I'm not working hard enough for him. I curse. Everything has gone wrong. Now Sarin the Merciless has the dwa and the letter. It's just as well the Elves appeared before she used my sleeping figure for target practice. I wonder why the Elves did happen along, and ask them.

"We were looking for you," explains Callis. "Gurd

at the Avenging Axe told us that you had gone to confront Horm the Dead and we wished to help. Even in the Elvish Lands Horm has an evil reputation.

Makri wakes suddenly and leaps to her feet with a savage snarl and a sword in each hand. She looks round in confusion, wondering where the enemy is. When the realisation of what happened sinks in she is angrier than I've ever seen her. The Elves watch in bemusement as she berates me at length at my utter stupidity in misdirecting my sleep spell, sending her instead of Sarin crashing to the ground.

I can think of little to say in my defence and am forced to listen to her rage about my drunkenness, incompetence and general stupidity, after which she proceeds to fume about the disgrace to her fighting honour.

"I met sub-Human Trolls in the gladiator pits who were smarter than you! Number one chariot, are you? Sarin would have stuck you full of holes if the Elves hadn't rescued you. You're about as much use as a one-legged gladiator. You made me fall asleep in front of an opponent!" she yells. "I'll never live it down. That's it, I'm finished. Next time you want some help, don't bother asking, I'm busy."

And with that she leaps on her horse and gallops off without even acknowledging the Elves' presence. They look at me wonderingly.

"A very volatile character," I say, waving my hands in vague explanation. "Takes defeat too personally."

I ride back to Turai with the Elves. They are puzzled that a fine sorcerous Investigator like myself could actually misdirect a spell, thereby putting his companion to sleep, but after I explain about Sarin's own considerable sorcerous powers, and the spells she was throwing at me right and left, I don't think their confidence in me is shaken too badly.

Next morning I wake with the mother of all hang-overs, the Brotherhood beating on my door, and the city in violent uproar. Once again it is a poor start to the day.

"Money's due tomorrow," says Karlox.

"Fine," I grunt, avoiding some flying debris. "It'll be there. Which is more than you'll be if the Society of Friends keeps picking you off."

Karlox snarls. He doesn't like that. "We got their measure. And we got yours. You don't pay up tomorrow, you better make sure you've been saying your prayers."

I slam the door on him.

I don't say my prayers but it doesn't prevent young Pontifex Derlex from visiting me right after the riot calms down. The sun is beating down more ferociously than ever, making him sweat inside his black religious robe, but he declines my offer of a beer. The Pontifex is doing the rounds in his constituency, checking up on people after the riot. Makri pushes her head through the outside doorway and is about to say something when she notices the Pontifex and clams up. She departs. I notice Derlex's deep frown.

"Loosen up, Derlex. No need to look like your soul's in torment every time you catch sight of Makri."

He apologises, rather stiffly, but admits that Makri does make him very uncomfortable. "The Orcish blood, you know."

"She's got Human blood as well. Elf too. Probably a very interesting soul. You should try and convert her."

He looks uncomfortable again. "I don't think I am allowed to try. It's blasphemous to preach the True Religion to an Orc . . . even one quarter Orc might involve me in some heresy . . ."

I laugh at the thought, and tell him not to worry. Makri is not in line for any sudden conversion. After a little talk about this and that, he goes on his way.

I wander out into the corridor. A thought strikes me suddenly. Makri appears, heading downstairs for her first shift of the day. I ask her what she wanted earlier.

"To tell you never to speak to me again. Or communicate in any way. From now on, Thraxas, you don't exist."

"Makri—"

She walks stiffly past, tossing her head so that her long hair swings around her shoulders. Obviously she has not yet forgiven me for yesterday's escapade.

"It could have happened to anyone!" I yell at her departing form. Now I'm distracted. What was I thinking about? The True Church. Something about it is nagging me.

Downstairs I sit over a beer and a plate of stew and think things over. Why did Derlex visit me? Plenty of other people in riot-torn Twelve Seas must need his help more than me. Now I think about it, Derlex never stops visiting me these days. I never used to see him from one year to the next. What made the Church so interested in my welfare all of a sudden?

Thinking about the Church nudges my memory along and I realise what it is that's been bugging me. Pazaz. The Orc dragonkeeper. He said that no one spoke to him, apart from Bishop Gzekius. According to Pazaz, Gzekius tried to convert him.

"But that's impossible," I say, out loud to no one. "Derlex just told me it was blasphemous to preach the True Religion to an Orc. The Bishop couldn't have been trying to convert him. He's not going to lay himself open to a heresy charge just for one dragonkeeper. The other Bishops would be down on him like a bad spell."

I stand up, banging my fist on the table. Makri looks at me very coolly.

"That's it! That's why Derlex has been round here all the time. He's spying on me for the Bishop. And the Bishop is after the Cloth! The Church is behind it all! The Royal Family was attending some special religious service when the dragon was cut open. Which means that the Church would know exactly when the zoo was going to be empty. And the Bishop was talking to the dragonkeeper before that. He wasn't trying to convert him. He was pumping him for information! Just like Derlex has been round here pumping me for information! Derlex was at the Palace that day; he rode home with us in the landus. He probably had the Cloth on him then, passed to him by some other Churchman. And now I think about it, when I returned to Attilan's house to retrieve the spell there was another young Pontifex passing by. He could have stolen the spell, just before I came looking for it."

Makri raises her eyebrows. Sweat is running down her body, making her muscles glisten. She's been listening, but still refuses to acknowledge me.

I wonder why the Church would want the Elvish Cloth. There could be any number of reasons. Maybe just to sell it. Or perhaps the Bishop needs to do some secret planning without getting spied on by the other Bishops. Gzekius is an ambitious man, it's about time he made a try for the Archbishopric. It seems to fit together well enough. And if I'm right, then the Red Elvish Cloth should be somewhere in the Church's possession right now.

"It might even be in Derlex's church. And if it is, I'm going to find it! Are you free tonight?"

Makri glowers at me. "No. I'm studying. You're on your own."

She grabs a tablecloth, savagely wipes a few tables, then stalks off through the back to bring in a box of tankards. Tanrose appears carrying a large chunk of beef for the lunchtime stew. I buy a pastry and tell her about Makri being mad at me. Tanrose already knows all about it.

"She's angrier than a Troll with a toothache," says Tanrose. "But she'll get over it."

"I need her help tonight. Any suggestions for helping her get over it quickly?"

"Bring her some flowers," says the cook.

The suggestion is so strange that at first I fail to grasp what she means. "Flowers? What for?"

"To say sorry of course."

"Say sorry with flowers? To Makri? You mean go out and buy some flowers and give them to Makri as a present? As a way of saying sorry? Flowers?"

"That's right."

"Are we talking about the same Makri here? Makri the axe woman?"

"Just because a woman wields an axe doesn't mean she wouldn't appreciate a bunch of flowers."

"She'd probably attack me with them."

"You'd be surprised," says Tanrose, and gets on with hacking up the lump of beef.

Tanrose must be losing her mind. Flowers for Makri, indeed! The idea makes my head hurt. Right then Praetor Cicerius walks in, accompanied by the Consul himself. Well, well. I certainly get a higher class of visitor these days.

Cicerius tersely relates that the city is fast degenerating into chaos. The fighting between the Brotherhood and the Society of Friends has reached new heights and the Civil Guard is losing control.

"I've advised the King to suspend the constitution," says Consul Kalius, "and send in the Army."

I imagine the King will be hesitant to do this. The Populares might come out in open revolution. Various generals are suspected of being supporters of Senator

Lodius, and there's no knowing how obedient the Army would be.

"We're facing complete anarchy," complains Cicerius. "The Traditionals must retain power if the city is to survive. Did you get the letter?"

I admit that I didn't. This doesn't go down too well. I relate the events of the previous day, more or less. I don't explain exactly how Sarin the Merciless ended up with the dwa and the letter. Cicerius and Kalius are aghast and berate me for my failure. The Consul openly implies that I'm fabricating the whole story about the dragon in the Fairy Glade just to make my failure look better, and wonders out loud if I might not have sold the dwa for myself.

I haven't had enough sleep. I never get enough sleep. It's hot as Orcish hell in here. My head is pounding. I can't take much more of this. I point to the door and order them to leave. The Consul is shocked. As Turai's most powerful administrator, he's not used to being shown the door.

"How dare you!" he rages.

"Why not? I'm a free man. I don't have to listen to anyone calling me a liar, even the Consul. Especially when I've got a headache. I did my best. If that best isn't good enough, then tough. Now leave."

Cicerius waves this away. "This is no time for squabbling," he states. "If the Society of Friends obtains—"

I wave him quiet. I'm in no mood for speeches. "I know. Prince disgraced, your son disgraced. Traditionals disgraced, you lose election, Populares win, Lodius marches to power. That's the scenario according to you. I've heard it before. What do you expect me to do?"

"Find the letter," says the Praetor.

"I already failed."

"Then you must try again. Don't forget, my son

Cerius is your client. The letter will send him to prison."

I frown. I hate the way Cicerius keeps pulling the "can't desert a client" routine. I wish I'd never heard of the damn client. It's too hot to think clearly. What will Sarin the Merciless do with the damning letter of credit? She won't have any interest in using it for political means but she'll certainly know how valuable it is to the King's opponents. The Populares are the obvious people to sell it to, and easy for her to reach, because Senator Lodius is supported by the Society of Friends, and Sarin's associate Glixius is himself associated with the Society. I don't even know if they are still working together. It seems like Sarin might have gone off on her own. Double-crossing your associates is standard behaviour in the Turanian underworld.

"We still might be able to buy it back, but it would cost you plenty to outbid the Society. Be better if we could just steal it. Haven't your Sorcerers been able to locate her? She's carrying six bags of dwa. Someone should be able to pick up the aura."

"Tas of the Eastern Lightning has scanned the city without finding anything."

Tas of the Eastern Lightning has taken over from the murdered Mirius Eagle Rider as the Chief Sorcerer at Palace Security. He's powerful enough. If he can't find it by magic, probably no one can.

The call for morning prayers resonates through the city. The Consul and the Praetor are less than pleased to be obliged to kneel and pray in a tavern, but there's no getting out of it. I find myself kneeling in prayer beside a blue-edged toga and a gold-edged one. I notice my own tunic is frayed. I wonder if my prayers will have some extra effect, seeing as they're being offered up in such high-powered company. Afterwards we discuss things for a while and I agree to do my utmost to locate Sarin. They depart, still brushing the dust from their knees.

Makri reappears and starts cleaning the debris off the floor. I appeal to her better nature and tell her I could really do with some help tonight. She refuses to talk, and practically sweeps me up with the rubbish. I catch Tanrose looking at me from behind a vast cauldron of beef stew.

"To hell with this," I grunt, and storm out the front entrance. Baxos the flower seller has plied his trade on the corner of Quintessence Street for thirty years. I estimate it is twenty years at least since I availed myself of his services. He practically falls over in surprise when I march up and demand a bunch of flowers.

"Hey Rox," he calls over to a fish vendor on the other side of the road. "Thraxas is buying some flowers."

"Got a lady friend, has he?" yells back Rox, loud enough for the entire street to hear.

"Time you were courting again, Thraxas!" screams Birix, one of Twelve Seas' busier prostitutes. The cry is taken up enthusiastically by her companions.

I grab a bunch of flowers, toss some pennies at Rox and march off hastily, pursued by a great deal of ribald witticisms. I am in the foulest of tempers and will have more than a few harsh words to say to that idiot Tanrose.

Back at the Avenging Axe I practically crash into Makri and her mop. I thrust the flowers into her hand, figuring it's best to get it over with quickly.

"I'm sorry I put you to sleep in front of an opponent," I say. "Here are some flowers."

Makri gawps in amazement while I march swiftly onwards to the bar for a much needed flagon of ale.

Almost immediately I am tapped on the shoulder. It's Makri, who then proceeds to do a number of strange things. First she embraces me, then she burst into tears, and runs out of the room.

I'm bewildered. "What's happening?"

"The apology worked," replies Tanrose, in a satisfied manner.

"Are you sure?"

"Of course I'm sure."

"It all seems very strange to me, Tanrose."

"I wasn't surprised your marriage broke up, Thraxas," says Tanrose, as she shovels some stew on to a plate for me.

Chapter Twenty-Four

I spend the afternoon drinking a few beers, thinking things over, and swapping tales with a mercenary from the far north. He passed through Nioj on his way to Turai and from his account it sounds as if the Niojans are preparing for war.

"They say they heard some rumours that some Orcs were marauding on the borders."

It could be true. Or it could be a story put about to deceive our King into thinking they weren't about to attack us. It's bound to happen some time, and they still have the excuse of their murdered diplomat. Cities have fallen on flimsier excuses than that.

Could the Church have murdered him? Would Bishop Gzekius go that far? Maybe. I have no other candidates in mind.

Makri returns from her lunchtime logic class. She does appear to have been pacified by the flowers. Apparently no one ever gave her flowers before. Smart idea from Tanrose, I must admit, though Makri is embarrassed at bursting into tears and instructs myself and Tanrose never to mention it to anyone.

Makri reports that things are pretty grim outside. She had to fight her way through three street brawls on the way to the Guild College.

"I have a lecture in mathematics this afternoon," she says. "I'd better sharpen my axe before I go. Incidentally, Sarin the Merciless didn't seem quite so useless as you made her out to be."

"She got lucky. She's learned how to use a crossbow. Big deal. Just wait till I meet her again. I suppose I will, now the Consul wants me to find her. But it's going to have to wait because I'm going looking for the Red Elvish Cloth. Which is just as well maybe, because I've no idea where Sarin is. If Tas of the Eastern Lightning can't find her, how do they expect me to? I wonder if Rittius is really planning to take away my licence. Cicerius might just be saying that to scare me. You know it's rumoured Rittius is going to introduce a bill banning the Association of Gentlewomen?"

Makri nods. She attended an A.G. meeting last night and as a consequence has now gathered further knowledge of Turanian politics.

"It's confusing," she admits. "Some powerful women in the city are already campaigning behind the scenes against Rittius because he's against the Association. But a lot of the Association of Gentlewomen still support the Populares because they'd like to see some reform. The meeting ended with everyone arguing."

"I'm not surprised. No one in Turai can ever agree about politics. I'd like to take a holiday till it's all over."

"Where?"

"Anywhere I'm not wanted by the law. Which does limit the choice, now I think about it. I've violated statutes in every neighbouring state. Maybe I could travel to the furthest west and see what Kamara is like."

"It's not like you to admit defeat, Thraxas."

"I know. But I really can't think how to find Sarin. If Tas can't find her, then no magic of mine or even Astrath's is going to be any good. And I've got no influence in the north of the City. If she's with the Society, I'll never reach her."

A messenger arrives for me, bearing a brief note: *"Come alone to the Stadium Superbius at midnight if you want to bid for the letter,"* it says. It's signed by Sarin the Merciless.

"I suppose that simplifies things," I admit. "Might end up a good day after all. Burgle Derlex's church tonight and pick up the Cloth, then move on and buy the letter from Sarin. With any luck I'll be paying off the Brotherhood tomorrow."

Chapter Twenty-Five

"Feel like going to church, Makri?"

"If we must."

The streets are quiet, barely illuminated by the oil lamps on each corner. The whores have all gone home, and the only people in sight are the homeless beggars who sleep in doorways.

We make our way down to the end of Saint Volinius's Street, right by the docks. Behind us the huge hulks of triremes and quinquiremes float high in the water, ready to take on cargo tomorrow. The sight makes me pause. I saw a fair amount of the known world in my younger days, but it's been a good many years since I've travelled far from Turai. What would it be like, I wonder, to get on a ship and sail to Samsarina or Simnia in the west? Or further, to the distant, barely explored shores of Kastlin? South perhaps, to the Elvish Islands, where the sun shines on perfect white beaches and music floats through the trees? I shake my head. I'm too old to go travelling again. I guess I'll be stuck in this city for the rest of my life.

In front of us is the large and imposing Church of Saint Volinius, the only richly decorated building in Twelve Seas. So far the dwa addicts haven't started robbing the churches. It's only a matter of time. No lights show though a lamp is visible in the window of the small house in the grounds where the Pontifex lives. We hurry to the back of the church. I hesitate. I've never broken into a church before and I don't relish the prospect. Just because I can't be bothered praying doesn't mean I relish offending the Divinity. Makri sees my hesitation.

"If someone finds us here and I cut their head off the Divinity will be far more offended," she says, encouragingly.

I mutter the opening incantation. Nothing happens. Not surprising. You'd expect a Pontifex like Derlex to know the common minor incantations, even if the Church does disapprove of magic.

"Locking spell," I mutter, and get to work. It doesn't take long. I was picking locks as soon as I could walk. I have a natural talent for it. We hurry inside. Makri takes one of the huge candles off the altar and lights it from her tinderbox. I get the impression she's enjoying this sacrilegious behaviour but it's making me uneasy. Shadows from the statues around us loom out eerily as we pass and I half expect some ancient saint to step out from an alcove and reprimand me for desecrating church property.

We start to hunt, lifting up the altar cloth, peering under the pews, poking around in all the nooks and crannies of the church. We haven't got very far when we are interrupted by a faint noise from the door we came in. Makri swiftly blows out the candle and we disappear silently under a pew. A tiny glimmer of light flickers into view. I risk a quick glance, then put my mouth to Makri's ear.

"Glixius," I whisper. "And three others."

Concealed under the bench, we wait as the Sorcerer and the Society of Friends search the church. Obviously I am not the only person who suspects the True Church of the theft.

Again noises come from the door. Glixius's illuminated staff is extinguished and the four men conceal themselves somewhere in the far side of the church. I peek out from my hiding place. Entering the building, sword in hand, is Hanama. Watching her creep silently towards the altar I am again mystified by the Assassins' interest in the Cloth.

Hanama has even less time to search than Glixius. She is interrupted almost immediately by the sound of yet another party entering, and swiftly conceals herself behind the altar, disappearing only seconds before Yubaxas and five Brotherhood men steal silently into the church.

"I think I'm going to laugh," whispers Makri.

I shoot her a warning glance, though I have to admit it is funny in a grim sort of way. With us, the Society of Friends and an Assassin all hiding under chairs and suchlike, it's starting to remind me of one of the sillier comedies at the theatre.

When sounds of entry force Yubaxas and his companions to scurry for cover, Makri actually does giggle, though this is fortunately covered up by the voices of the new arrivals who are making no effort to be silent. A quick glance reveals Bishop Gzekius and four Curates with lanterns, led in by Pontifex Derlex.

"Where is it?" demands Gzekius, his voice booming through the church.

Derlex unlocks a side room. They enter, and emerge quickly with a large piece of folded Red Cloth.

"Excellent," says the Bishop.

I wait tensely. Are any of the people hiding here about to rob the Bishop? I certainly do not intend to, not even to clear the Princess's name and claim the huge reward. I'd be in endless trouble afterwards. It's disappointing that so many others worked out where the Red Elvish Cloth was, but I can live with the disappointment. It's better than being hauled up in court for burglary, and probably heresy and treason as well.

The back door flies open. Shockingly, four Orcs stride in. The Bishop cries out in horror. Orcs are quite definitely not allowed in a true church. I groan. I know what's going to happen now, but I'm powerless to prevent it. Makri leaps from under the pew and hurtles towards the Orcs, a sword in each hand and murder in her eyes. I drag myself to my feet and run after her. I can't let her fight four Orcs on her own.

"Thraxas!" yells Pontifex Derlex.

"Orcs!" screams Yubaxas, as the Brotherhood reveal themselves.

It goes badly for the Orcs. Makri and I engage with them while the Brotherhood and Hanama outflank them. Even the Curates lend a hand. The Orcs are quickly cut down.

"Orcish scum," spits Makri, and kicks one of the bodies.

"What are you doing here?" screams Bishop Gzekius.

Personally I'm stuck for an answer. The awkward silence doesn't last long. There's a huge thunder flash and everyone except me is flung to the floor. I remain upright, if shaky. One advantage of carrying a lot of weight—good centre of balance. Glixius Dragon Killer has emerged to enter the fray. He makes straight for the Cloth.

"I notice you didn't come out to fight the Orcs," I

say as he advances, and grab the Red Elvish Cloth from the floor.

"Allies come and allies go. Now give me that!" he shouts.

"Blasphemers!" yells Bishop Gzekius. "You'll all pay for this! Get out of my church!"

Glixius lunges at me. Makri sticks out her leg and he crashes to the floor. I take the Bishop's advice, and flee with the Cloth.

By the time I reach the alley outside Makri is at my shoulder and we're about fifteen seconds in front of Glixius and the Society of Friends.

"Look!" gasps Makri. At the far end of the dark alley are eight armed men.

Makri's swords appear in her hands.

"We're trapped," I groan.

Bizarrely, a manhole cover opens in front of us.

"In here!" hisses a voice.

It's Hanama. Typically, she slipped out of the Church unnoticed.

I hesitate. Meeting Assassins in sewers isn't all that attractive a prospect. And I haven't forgotten the alligator. Suddenly my senses go crazy. Glixius Dragon Killer has rounded the corner and is about to unleash a ferocious spell. I unfurl the roll of Cloth in an instant and hurl it over myself and Makri. The spell bounces harmlessly off us but Makri, taken by surprise by my unexpected manoeuvre, stumbles backwards into me and we both fall through the manhole into the stinking darkness below.

"Not again," I groan as I struggle to my feet in the filth. Two visits to the sewers on one case seems excessive.

"Let's go."

I bundle up the Cloth as quickly as I can and we head off, while up above there is shouting and confusion.

I don't know where we are. I've never been in this
part of the sewers before, so I let Hanama lead. She
carries a small lantern of cunning design which lights
our way.

I'm not sure why I'm following her. I don't think
we're allies. At least she's taking me away from Glixius.
I solemnly swear to myself that if I survive this night
then I will make every sacrifice, including beer, to buy
myself a new spell protection charm. They're hideously
expensive but I can't go running scared from Sorcerers all the time, not in my line of work.

"Where are we going?"

"Exit on the shore," replies Hanama, who seems
entirely at home down in the sewers.

"Keep a look out for alligators," I pant to Makri.

"I will," she replies, and even she seems slightly
worried by the prospect. We make good time. The level
of sewage is low due to the long spell of hot weather.
Water in Turai's aqueducts has already started to run
short. Hanama suddenly comes to a halt.

"We're close to the exit."

With that she abruptly douses her lamp. Before I
realise what she's up to she grabs the Cloth and tries
to yank it from me. I hold on grimly and in consequence we both fall over and start rolling around in
the filth, struggling for the Cloth. I'd say she was a
more skilful close-combat fighter, but I have a weight
advantage.

"Let go!" hisses Hanama. We struggle some more,
till my senses again pick up an ominous warning.

"Glixius," I yell. "Magic coming."

"What's that noise?" calls Makri, as a huge roaring
starts reverberating through the tunnels.

"It sounds like a flood."

"It can't be, it's summer."

Suddenly and terrifyingly a huge wave of water

surges through the tunnel, carrying us off with it. I'm buffeted and dragged along, unable to breath as the flood water carries us before it like rats. My last conscious thought is to curse Glixius Dragon Killer for unleashing such a thing. The man is completely heartless. I didn't even know there was a flood water spell. Eventually I pass out, with visions of my past life flickering before my eyes.

I drift back to consciousness somewhere on the sea shore, beached like a whale. I cough and retch about ten gallons of water out of my lungs and rise unsteadily to my knees. It's very dark and I can just make out the figure of Makri lying close by. As I struggle towards her she opens her eyes and turns on her side to spew out the water she's swallowed.

"Still alive?"

"Just about," mutters Makri, clambering to her feet. She's relieved to find she still has both her swords. She brought them with her from the Orcish gladiator pits, and they're fine weapons. Orcs might be hated the world over, but they make a fine blade. Then I notice something wrapped around my fingers. A strip of Red Cloth, ripped from the main roll. I stare at it glumly. I doubt if anyone will pay me a reward of six hundred gurans for this miserable fragment. I curse, and stuff it in my pocket. Hanama must have kept hold of the rest. As usual, she has now disappeared. With the Cloth. I curse.

"I can't shake that damned woman off. She's sharp as an Elf's ear at this investigating business. How the hell did she know to come to the church?"

I haul myself up the rocky beach. I come to a halt, surprised. Lying prostrate beside a pool is the small figure of Hanama. As we approach she rolls over and groans. Makri hurries and kneels down beside her.

"Someone's slugged her."

The Assassin has a nasty wound on the back of her head. She comes round at the sound of our voices. Makri cradles her head and drips a little water from her flask into her mouth.

"Thanks, Makri," says the Assassin. She struggles to her feet.

"What happened?"

"Someone hit me from behind. I was still spewing up water from the flood—"

"So where's the Cloth?" I demand.

Hanama stares coolly at me, and turns on her heel. She makes her way up the beach, unsteadily. I stare after her, but don't bother pursuing her. She wouldn't answer questions from me if her life depended on it.

Two of the three moons are visible in the sky. Light from them glimmers on a rock about the size of my fist. I reach down and find it is sticky with still damp blood. Whoever hit the Assassin didn't bother with anything fancy. I slip the rock into my pocket.

Makri and I reach the patch of waste ground that leads into the warehouses beside the harbour. Steam rises from my clothes in the heat of the night. At least the flood water washed off the sewage. We walk past a warehouse and turn the corner and there, right in front of us, is Glixius Dragon Killer. He looks bedraggled, as if he might have been caught up in his own flood.

"You—" he begins, and starts to raise his voice for a spell.

Nothing happens. His spells have run out. I smile.

"Too bad, Glixius," I say, and punch him in the face as hard as I can It's a good punch. There's a lot of feeling behind it, and a lot of weight. He goes down in a heap and stays there.

"Nice punch," says Makri, admiringly.

"Thank you."

After all this magic, there's something very pleasing about a good punch.

We walk on. Part one of tonight's mission is a failure. Let's hope the next part goes better. We have an appointment with Sarin the Merciless but we don't get far. Before we reach Quintessence Street three landuses hurtle up and screech to a halt beside us. Pontifexes, twelve of them, leap out and surround us. At least, they're wearing priestly garments, but as they're carrying swords and look like they know how to use them, I guess they belong to a fairly specialised division of the Church.

"Bishop Gzekius would like to see you."

Makri's hands go to her swords. I shake my head. "Fine. I'll be delighted to see the Bishop."

We climb in and the landuses take us off through the still dark streets of the city.

The Head of the Church in Turai is Archbishop Xerius, who has four equally ranked Bishops under him. Gzekius's parish includes Twelve Seas but he doesn't live there of course. He lives in a very large villa up in Thamlin, where he gets his relief from ministering to the poor by sitting by his swimming pool eating delicacies from his own private fish ponds.

Gzekius is a large, powerful man, around fifty with thick grey hair. Ambitious too, though he conceals it fairly well under his normally placid exterior. I say normally, because when we are led in he looks far from peaceful. In fact he's close to exploding and wastes no time in threatening me with arrest, excommunication and a lengthy visit to the prison galleys.

I regard him coolly while he thunders on about the desecration of churches and the general disgraceful state of the citizenry in Turai, particularly me. "It's all very well threatening me, Bishop," I say, when I can get a word in. "But I wouldn't say you're in too strong a position yourself. I doubt that the King will be very amused to hear that you stole the Cloth in the first place. Illegal for anyone but the King to have it, remember. And of course there's also the matter of Attilan. Your man stole the spell from the garden. Had he murdered the diplomat before I got there?"

"How dare you accuse the True Church of murder!" fumes the Bishop.

"Not forgetting stealing a spell, and putting the King's dragon to sleep then hacking it to death. I'd say you might be joining me on the prison ship."

I'd hoped to shake the Bishop with this. He doesn't look shaken, but he does calm down a little.

"Neither myself nor the Church had any involvement in the theft of the Cloth." He claims that he has no idea how the Cloth came to be in Derlex's church. "Do you seriously expect anyone to believe that one Pontifex stole a dragon sleep spell from a Niojan diplomat while another helped cut the cloth out of the dragon?"

"Yes."

"They won't. Not when the accusation comes from a man like you, Thraxas," he says dismissively.

"I might not be able to persuade the King or the Consul, Bishop Gzekius, though I'll have a good try. But I'll sure as hell persuade Praetor Cicerius. And remember, it wasn't just me that saw you and Derlex with the Elvish Cloth. So did an Assassin, the Brotherhood and the Society of Friends. And the Orcish Ambassadors must know you had it as well, because they sent their Orcs to recover it. That's a whole host of witnesses. None of them good witnesses I grant you, but more than enough to persuade the population that you've been up to something. A very juicy story for the *Chronicle*. Very poor publicity for the Church, Bishop, particularly at a time when Senator Lodius is on the rampage. He doesn't like you at all. What was it he called you last week? 'Bloodsucking parasites on the poor,' I believe."

We face each other in silence for a while. I help myself to a little wine. Makri stands mutely in a corner, uncomfortable in these surroundings.

"I don't know why you wanted the Cloth. Maybe you just needed some cash. But I think you might have been looking to make a magic-proof room for yourself. You're an ambitious man, Bishop Gzekius. The Archbishopric comes up for grabs soon. You are not favourite for the job, but everyone knows you want it. So it's going to take some serious plotting on your part to land it. The other Bishops in Turai wouldn't like it at all if you had a magic-proof room. Far too much of an advantage in plotting. So they'll believe my story anyway."

The Bishop raises his eyebrows slightly, which seems to signify that I've got through to him. He dismisses his attendants from the room. I help myself to some more wine. Tastes like a fine vintage.

"Where is the Cloth now?" he demands, when we're alone.

I tell him truthfully that I don't know.

"Disappeared down a sewer and it's probably not coming back. Which is bad for me, as I was meant to be finding it. But that's not my main problem. I'm meant to be clearing the Princess's name. That's what I've been hired to do. The rest doesn't bother me too much. Help me sort that one out and the whole sordid story will never pass my lips."

Bishop Gzekius sips his own wine, savouring it. "Are you telling me that you were not after the Cloth for yourself, Investigator?"

I shake my head. "Just doing the work I was hired for."

The Bishop looks at me for a long time. He's puzzled

by the thought that I might be honest. He transfers his gaze to Makri. He's wondering how far he can trust us.

"I have heard, Thraxas, that you do perform the job you are paid for. In an honest fashion. Perhaps I can trust you to keep your word. It would, in some ways, be easier than having you killed."

We stare at each other. It floats through my mind that Pontifex Derlex must have given him a reasonable report of my character, which comes as a surprise.

"And how would you suggest I help clear the Princess's name?"

I shrug. "Call in some favours at the Palace. From what I hear, the King owes you a few. The Cloth's gone now, it doesn't do you or the Church any good to have a major royal scandal."

The Bishop stares at me for a while longer. "I do have influence," he says, finally. "Enough to sway the King, possibly. And enough to make your life in Twelve Seas short and full of incident. So be sure never to trouble me again."

He dismisses us from his presence.

"What did that mean?" asks Makri, as we find ourselves again out in the warm night-time streets.

"I think it means he'll help the Princess. And give me hell if our paths ever cross again. Well, that'll do for now."

I glance up at the stars.

"About an hour till we're due to meet Sarin. We've just got time to go and see Astrath Triple Moon. It's high time I had some proper sorcerous help on all this. Someone slugged Hanama and took the Cloth and I want to know who. Also I wonder if he might locate Sarin. Tas of the Eastern Lightning couldn't find her but, whatever means she was using to hide, she might be out in the open now. If I knew where she was I might be able to take her by surprise and get the letter back for free. No point wasting thousands of Cicerius's gurans if we don't have to."

I glance at Makri. "Incidentally, when did you and Hanama become friends?"

"What? We're not friends."

"Oh yeah? The way you cradled her head when we found her unconscious seemed pretty friendly to me. And she said, "Thanks, Makri," when you gave her water. That's friendly for an Assassin."

Makri snorts dismissively. "So? She'd been hit on the head. You're rambling, Thraxas. I only met her one time, when she attacked you in your room."

I'm suspicious about this, but I let it lie, and we hurry down to visit Astrath Triple Moon. It's still the middle of the night. The streets are quiet, except for a few bakery workers on their way to light the ovens for tomorrow's bread.

Our visit to Astrath is unproductive. He doesn't actually mind too much that I wake him in the middle of the night, but when I ask him if he can locate Sarin he draws a blank. Likewise for the six sacks of dwa.

"She must have left the city."

"Impossible. She's due to meet us at the Stadium Superbius in half an hour."

The Sorcerer shrugs and asks if I've anything else he can look at. I still have the fragment of the Red Elvish Cloth but of course he can learn nothing from that. By now I am fairly sick of Red Elvish Cloth. The stuff is nothing but trouble. I hand him the rock I've been carrying, the one that was used to club Hanama, and ask him if he can learn anything from it.

"Take me a while, Thraxas. It's always difficult getting information from rocks. Auras cling to them very tenuously, if at all."

I tell him to do his best, and meanwhile ask if he can lend us his landus.

"You can't ride in the city at night."

"I have senatorial privilege."

"Really?"

"No. But I'm working for Cicerius, so I can pretend. And we're late."

"So which one of us is the Senator?" enquires Makri, as we thunder off in the carriage.

Makri knows full well that women can't be Senators. I'm starting to think she's going to too many of those meetings.

Chapter Twenty-Six

In the centre of the town Civil Guards are still out in force because of the tension that hangs over the city. Wild rumours abound about cancelled elections, planned coups, bribery and assassination. It's even whispered that the Royal Family has been buying drugs from the Orcs and selling them to the population.

The Guards challenge us. "Urgent business for Praetor Cicerius," I roar, and gallop on towards the Stadium. I have with me a bag of gold from Cicerius and instructions to bid as high as is necessary to obtain the Prince's letter of credit.

The Stadium Superbius is situated just inside the city walls, over on the east side of town. It's an enormous stone amphitheatre, built by King Varquius a hundred years or so ago, and it's a very important place. It's the setting for circuses, theatrical performances, religious ceremonies, gladiatorial shows and, cause of my recent misfortune, the chariot races. I love the chariot races. Twice a week during the racing season the amphitheatre is packed full of race-goers from every stratum of Turanian society. Praetors, Prefects, Senators, priests, society ladies, Sorcerers, high-ranking guild officials: all mingle with the huge mass of proletarian Turanians there to enjoy a day out and maybe pick up a little money on the side. Prince Frisen-Akan is an enthusiastic race-goer with his own stable of chariots. Even the King sometimes attends. Naturally, the Stadium Superbius also attracts a swarm of petty criminals, and most of the book-makers are controlled by the Brotherhood or the Society of Friends.

We dismount from the landus and stride into the giant, dark building. Makri has a torch with her. She lights it, casting weird shadows on to the old stone walls from the statues of famous gladiators and charioteers of the past. No one is in sight.

I take out the strip of Red Elvish Cloth I wrenched from Hanama's hands in the sewer, and rip it in two.

"Tie this round your neck."

Makri looks perplexed.

"If Sarin's here then so is her associate Glixius Dragon Killer. This strip of cloth will act as a spell protection charm."

"Are you sure?"

"Not sure at all. But it might."

We round the Triumphal Arch through which the victors parade at the end of the games. In front of us, in the shadows, a figure lies prostrate on the ground. We draw our swords and advance carefully. Makri kneels down.

"It's Sarin," she hisses. "She's been clubbed on the back of the head."

First Hanama and now Sarin. Someone's making my life easier. I glance around. No one's in sight, but down by the wall there is a small pile of dull white powder. I reach down, poke my finger in it and taste.

"Dwa. Looks like Sarin had the sacks with her and someone seized them."

Makri also pokes her finger in the powder and tastes it. This does not seem strictly necessary to me but I let it pass.

I kneel down and start searching Sarin. "She might still have the letter. No point paying for it if we don't have to."

Sarin has been clubbed quite viciously and I'd swear she'll be out for a long time but to my surprise she suddenly opens her eyes. To my further surprise she yanks my long braid in a very painful manner and sends me tumbling away in the dust. She leaps to her feet. Despite her recent lapse from conciousness and the ugly wound on her head, she faces me in a fighting crouch.

"Lost your crossbow?" I jeer, and charge in, aiming a blow of my own. A cunning street fighter, I feint with my left and land her with my right. At least that's the theory. Sarin avoids both blows and kicks me in the ribs, sending me hurtling backwards. I pick myself up, fairly puzzled at this turn of events. I hurtle in again, figuring to overpower her with my weight, but Sarin performs some fancy move which I don't exactly follow, except I end up on the ground again. I get pretty mad because I notice out the corner of my eye that Makri, instead of leaping in to help like she should, is actually laughing. I draw my sword. Sarin takes out a small knife. We circle each other. I can't find an opening. I can't understand it at all. I wasn't lying when I said I'd run her out of town before. How the hell she has returned as a hardened warrior is beyond me.

We exchange a few blows. I'm starting to get short of breath. I've been fighting and running around to excess in the last twenty-four hours and I don't seem to have eaten or slept. The heat is getting to me. I lunge at Sarin and she parries again and kicks my legs from under me, so I fall very heavily to the ground. I struggle up again and turn my head towards Makri.

"Will you stop standing there like a eunuch in a brothel and give a man some help?"

"Just giving you a chance, Thraxas. You told me you'd be down on her like a bad spell if she showed her face again."

I glare at Makri then make another assault on Sarin. I'll show her who's number one chariot round here. She parries my sword with her small knife then hits me so hard with the flat of her hand that I'm sent spinning into the wall where I once more slump to the ground.

Before Sarin can follow up, Makri decides she's had enough laughs for one day and appears above me with her sword drawn.

She confronts Sarin. "Thraxas tells me you can't fight."

I clamber painfully to my feet. "Well, she didn't used to be able to."

"Three years in the warrior monastery at Kvalir," says Sarin, and almost smiles.

"I take it you weren't studying religion," I say, grateful for the chance to catch my breath.

"No. Just fighting. I used to find it annoying the way people could defeat me. No one defeats me now."

"You weren't looking too good when we found you."

"Someone crept up behind me." Sarin the Merciless frowns, and looks a little puzzled. "Normally no one could do that."

"Maybe your pal Glixius Dragon Killer decided he didn't want you around any more."

She shakes her head. "Glixius is no longer my associate. Horm and Glixius double-crossed me. After I cleared the way for them with my crossbow, they tried to edge me out of the operation. They didn't like sharing their profits with a third party. Particularly a woman."

She shrugs. "So much the worse for them. I outsmarted them. And it was not Glixius who clubbed me. He wouldn't be capable."

She casts her eyes around, and looks troubled. "My horse has gone. And the dwa." She reaches into her tunic and produces the Prince's letter. "But I still have this. And it will cost you ten thousand gurans. Unless you would like to try and take it off me?"

I'd as soon not. I remain silent.

"To business," she says.

"I believe that letter is mine," comes a voice.

A tall figure in a rainbow cloak strides out of the darkness. It's Glixius Dragon Killer. He glowers at me with hatred in his eyes.

"I presume we are seeking the same item," he says. I grunt in reply.

"You are wasting your time, Thraxas. The letter is mine."

"You seem to be having trouble holding on to it."

"I was not expecting such treachery from Sarin the Merciless."

I turn to Sarin. "So what are you going to do now? I doubt if your warrior monk training is going to enable you to fend off me, Makri and Glixius."

Sarin sneers. I haven't impressed her.

"As representatives of the honourable politicians in this city, you make a sorry pair. An obese, drunken Investigator and a treacherous criminal Sorcerer." She holds up the letter. "For blackmailing a Prince. The opening price is ten thousand gurans. Who'd like to make an offer?"

Glixius Dragon Killer has no intention of bidding. He raises his hand to fire a spell at her. Seconds later

he is tossed to the ground and lies stunned. His spell
has rebounded on him. Another rainbow-clad figure
floats gently down from the top of the arch.

"Who's that?" says Makri.

"Tas of the Eastern Lightning," I reply. "Looks like
Palace Security are getting in on the act at last."

I'm expecting Tas to wrest the letter from Sarin and
possibly send her crashing into a wall with a spell for
good measure. What he actually does is stroll over and
kiss her lightly on the cheek. Makri and I look on in
amazement as she kisses him back.

"No wonder he said he couldn't find her. They're
in league now."

"Indeed we are," booms Tas, a tall man with long
brown hair tumbling down over his rainbow cloak.

"What's the matter with these Sorcerers in Turai?"
I snarl, cursing them all. "If they're not dwa addicts
or drunks, then they're psychotic criminals."

"Lucky you never finished your studies," whispers
Makri, eyeing the pair warily. "Is Tas more powerful
than you?"

"Like a tiger compared to a rat. Try not to upset
him. Remember what happened to Mirius Eagle Rider."

"Do I hear a bid?" calls Sarin the Merciless.

I offer her the ten thousand gurans. Glixius Dragon
Killer hauls himself to his feet and swears a savage
oath. He fires up another spell and Tas bounces it right
back, sending Glixius thudding to the ground again. It's
a sight I enjoy. I'd kick him while he's down but I
haven't the time.

"It seems you are the only bidder, Thraxas," says
Sarin. "Very well, ten thousand gurans to you."

Sarin holds out the letter. I hold out the bag of gold.
The transaction is interrupted by a bolt of lightning
which sears into the ground between us, sending everyone flying. I land on my back, staring stupidly at the sky.

Just discernible in the darkness is the vast shape of a
war dragon, something not seen this far west since the
war ended fifteen years ago. Its nostrils are red with fire
and riding atop the beast is the crazed figure of Horm
the Dead, long black hair and feather jewellery flying
in the wind. His shrill voice cuts through the night.

"The letter is rightfully mine, I believe."

Tas of the Eastern Lightning climbs calmly to his
feet. "Not yours, Horm the Dead."

With that Tas unleashes a spell that sends the dragon
spinning through the sky, screaming with rage and
bafflement.

"Wow," says Makri.

We're impressed. Horm the Dead and a war dragon
obviously hold no terrors for Tas of the Eastern Lightning. Horm regains control and flies back overhead.

"Save your energy, Tas of the Eastern Lightning,"
shouts Horm. "I haven't come for the letter, or the
gold, or to fight with you, though one day I will kill
you at my leisure."

"At your leisure," shouts Tas. "Then why have you
come?"

"To destroy your city, and all the Humans in it who
I have found so annoying of late. Humans such as
yourself, Thraxas."

Horm the Dead starts to intone a spell. A very long
spell, in Orcish, never before heard in the world. He
completes his incantation, waves us a mocking farewell,
then wheels his dragon up and away into the night. We
all stare at each other. Nothing seems to be happening.

"What was that all about?"

Tas of the Eastern Lightning looks very grim. He
takes Sarin's hand. "Get the gold. It's time to go. That
was the city-devouring spell. The Eight-Mile Terror.
Horm has remade it. Madness will now grip the population. Turai is going to be destroyed."

I should know better than to aggravate these mad half-Orc Sorcerers. You never know when they might come and destroy your city.

"I don't feel anything," protests Sarin.

"You're wearing a protective necklace," says Tas. "So am I. But the population isn't."

Outside a low murmuring is growing in intensity. We run from the Stadium Superbius and are confronted with the terrible sight of the city starting to burn. Yellow flames leap into the sky to meet the first rays of dawn. Sarin holds out the letter.

"The gold," she snaps.

I make the transaction, though what use it'll be once Turai succumbs to the flames of madness I don't know. Glixius Dragon Killer runs up behind me and tries to snatch the letter out of my hand. Sarin the Merciless executes a faultless kick to his head, worthy indeed of a trained warrior monk, and Glixius slumps unconscious to the ground.

"A bad mistake to double-cross me," she mutters. She takes out a knife and bends over him. I think she's going to finish him off but instead, with a malicious grin, she slits his protective charm and takes it from his neck.

"Happy awakenings," she says, putting her arm round Tas's waist. Tas mutters a spell and they rise into the air.

"You can't just leave Turai to be destroyed!"

"I believe Lisutaris, Mistress of the Sky, was working on a counterspell to Horm's Eight-Mile Terror," calls Tas, now high above us. "She might be able to save you all, if she can stay awake long enough."

They disappear into the blackness.

"Why wouldn't Lisutaris, Mistress of the Sky, be able to stay awake?"

"She's always stoned. Smokes her thazis through a big water pipe."

Glixius stirs.

"We better get out of here."

We run. Behind us Glixius screams like a maniac and starts bellowing out spell after spell, far more than he could possibly retain in his memory in normal circumstances. Statues start falling from plinths and walls explode in flame as the now insane sorcerer vents his wrath on the world.

"That Sarin is a mean woman!" I gasp, as we dive for the safety of the nearest buildings. "I don't give much for Tas's chances once he's outlived his usefulness."

All of a sudden we're surrounded by demented citizens waving clubs and swords and attacking anything that moves. An old woman with a stick charges at Makri. Makri boots her out the way but is obliged to gut a huge northern mercenary who flies at her with a battle axe. We flee into an alleyway and leap the wall at the end, seeking safety, though nowhere is safe. Between us and every city gate is a crowd driven mad by Horm the Dead's evil spell.

A hand appears from nowhere and grabs Makri. She disappears with a yelp into a doorway. I plunge after her and find her in the grip of a small dark figure. It's Hanama, Master Assassin.

"Oh God, not a mad Assassin," I cry, and leap at her throat. Hanama side-steps neatly and I thump against the wall.

"Not a mad Assassin," says Hanama coolly, and fingers her own protective necklace, made from the same Red Elvish Cloth as mine.

I don't know if this meeting is a coincidence or if Hanama has been following us. With the city starting to self-destruct there is no time to think about it.

The Assassin scans the crowd with distaste. "My guild dislikes too much social unrest," she says. "Some discontent is good for business, but too much always spoils things."

"True, Hanama. No one needs Assassins when everyone's killing everyone else anyway. I guess the investigating business will go downhill as well."

"We'd better try and reach Lisutaris' house," says Makri, and explains to Hanama that the Sorcerer may have a countermanding spell to the Eight-Mile Terror. Hanama agrees. I look at her with suspicion. Her behaviour of late has been strange, out of character for an Assassin. They usually keep themselves to themselves, apart from when they're killing people.

I have no great hopes of Lisutaris being able to end the riot but I don't have any better idea. Besides, it's possible that the Sorcerers up in Truth is Beauty Lane will be able to hold off the maddened crowds so it seems as good a destination as any. I can't say I'm pleased to throw in my lot with an Assassin though, and I tell her to depart.

Twenty or so soldiers, fully armed and fully maddened, charge up the street towards us. We flee, and I find myself keeping company with Hanama anyway, much against my will.

Unfortunately, Truth is Beauty Lane is a popular destination for the crazed inhabitants of the city. Even in their madness they see that it will be a fine place to burn. Everyone has gone violently insane. Apart from the Royal Family, only Sorcerers, senior officials and a few wealthy merchants have protective necklaces, and I wouldn't give much for their chances against the demented mob.

Makri and Hanama's fighting skills and my enormous body weight get us close. The resident Sorcerers are making a desperate effort to keep the crazed citizens at bay. The air crackles with magical energy as the barrier they've erected is subjected to a continual barrage of flaming torches and missiles. Not all of the Sorcerers in Truth is Beauty Lane are as powerful as Tas of the Eastern Lightning or Harmon Half Elf. Many of them are little better than astrologers, with few more resources than myself, and the effort is starting to tell on them. Gorsius Starfinder, and Old Hasius the Brilliant, Chief Sorcerer at the Abode of Justice, both powerful Sorcerers, stand firmly in the street repelling all comers, but several of their companions are starting to retreat, forced back by the weight of incoming missiles. A few firebrands penetrate the magical barrier and the houses at the end of the street start to burn. Of Lisutaris, Mistress of the Sky, there is no sign.

The crowd are fully occupied with the attack and make no attempt to prevent us drawing near. When we reach the end of the street I bellow at Gorsius Starfinder at the top of my voice, straining to make myself heard above the roar of the mob. Gorsius hears me. He stares at me dubiously. I hold up my protective necklace, screaming for him to let me in. He motions with his staff. The barrier flickers. Hanama, Makri and I plunge through.

"Bad place to come for refuge," gasps Gorsius Starfinder, who's standing flinging spells in his underwear, having not even had time to don his rainbow cloak. "We can't hold them off much longer."

"Where's Lisutaris?"

"Stoned, I expect," says Gorsius, ducking as a rock flies overhead.

"Tas of the Eastern Lightning told me she was working on a counterspell to the Eight-Mile Terror."

"The Eight-Mile Terror?" screams Gorsius. "Is that what has caused this?"

"What did you think it was? Something in the water?"

Gorsius groans. "Then there is no chance of it ending. Where is Tas? We need his help."

"He's not coming, I'm afraid."

In the distance flames are rising from the Imperial Palace. Another rock penetrates the barrier. Gorsius Starfinder crumples to the ground. His Apprentice runs up and drags him to safety but the Sorcerers are now harder pressed than ever. Some of the junior ones who've never been to war are losing their nerve. We sprint up the road to Lisutaris' mansion. Around it lie the bodies of her servants, subdued in their madness by the Sorcerers. The door is locked.

"The crowd just advanced," says Makri.

I charge like an elephant and the door splinters. Hanama, fleetest of foot, is the first to find the Mistress of the Sky, Sorcerer of vast power, and hopeless thazis abuser. She's lying beside her water pipe with a faraway look on her face. The room is thick with smoke, thicker than the Avenging Axe after an all-night celebration. The woman really does smoke far too much of this stuff. Once more I curse the degeneracy of our Palace Sorcerers.

"Try and rouse her, Makri. I'll look for the spell."

Makri starts shaking Lisutaris, while Hanama and I tear the house apart looking for the counterspell to the Eight-Mile Terror. From outside the roar of the crowd intensifies as more and more of the demented citizens break through the Sorcerers' barrier.

As I plunge into Lisutaris' workroom a crazed servant appears from somewhere waving a carving knife. I dodge the strike and slug him. He's too mad to feel it and comes at me again so I trip him up and break a chair over his head. If we survive Lisutaris can patch him up later. I start rummaging through the Sorcerer's books.

"Is this it?" asks Hanama, appearing with a freshly written parchment. I study it quickly.

"Afraid not, this is a spell for making thazis plants grow quicker." Hanama tosses it away in disgust and we carry on searching. A rock crashes through the window. The crowd are closing in. Gorsius Starfinder and his Apprentice stumble in through a back door, dragging Old Hasius the Brilliant with them. All three are cut and bleeding.

"The crowd's breaking through!"

Hasius the Brilliant is reputed to be a hundred and ten years old. He'll be lucky to reach a hundred and eleven if the counterspell doesn't turn up soon. I drag open another drawer, and uncover various newly worked parchments, which I scan frantically.

"Yes!" I scream in triumph. "A counterspell to the Eight-Mile Terror!"

Gorsius hobbles over to study it with me. As he reads through it quickly, he wipes blood from his face. More rocks crash through the windows. His face falls.

"She hasn't finished it."

I quit the room immediately and tell Makri to stop trying to revive Lisutaris, Mistress of the Sky.

"She hasn't finished the spell. There's nothing to do now but get out of here before the whole city goes up in flames."

"Well, so much for civilisation," says Makri, and makes to leave with me.

"Where are you going?" demands Gorsius Starfinder, appearing beside us.

"Anywhere. We're going to fight our way out before the city burns."

"You can't just run away," protests the Sorcerer.

"Only thing to do," says Makri, matter-of-factly. "We can't fight the whole population."

"Just buy us some time. Lisutaris can complete the spell."

Before I can reply the door crashes open and there stands Glixius Dragon Killer with madness in his eyes.

"Death to all Sorcerers!" he screams.

He leaps towards me, arms raised. I hope my spell protector is strong enough to resist his insane sorcery.

I don't get the chance to find out because instead of casting a spell Glixius punches me full in the face and I tumble to the floor. He screams with laughter.

"I enjoyed that," he says, and draws his sword.

Makri leaps in front to protect me and engages Glixius in combat. At that moment a horde of deranged rioters burst into the house waving swords and flaming torches. Makri and I flee the room, dragging Gorsius Starfinder and Lisutaris with us. We run back to the workroom where we find Hasius the Brilliant slumped unconscious and Hanama expelling two intruders from the back door.

We're surrounded. We barricade the doors with furniture, and look at each other, wondering what to do. Lisutaris, Mistress of the Sky, moans, and shows signs of coming round. The mad crowd hammer on the door and there's the sound of axes breaking it down.

"Can't all you Sorcerers do something?" demands Makri.

We can't. No one has any spells left. Mine went long ago and the collective power of all the others was dissipated in holding the crowd back in the street outside. We have no more power than anyone else. Less, given the condition of Hasius, Gorsius and Lisutaris. Smoke starts to creep under the door. The rioters have set the house on fire.

Chapter Twenty-Seven

Somebody is screaming, "Put the fire out, put the fire out!"

It's me. No one puts the fire out.

I don't believe it. Here I am, surrounded by Turai's most powerful Sorcerers, and I'm going to die in a house fire.

"Doesn't anyone have even one spell left?"

Gorsius Starfinder shakes his head. His Apprentice looks blank. Hasius the Brilliant is unconscious. Lisutaris, Mistress of the Sky, is still stoned. The smoke gets thicker. Flames lick under the door. Makri and Hanama try to wrench the door open but it now seems to be barricaded from the outside.

I lose my temper completely. I grab Lisutaris, haul her to her feet and give her a slap which nearly takes her head off. She opens her eyes, and grins stupidly.

"Hello!" I scream. "Anybody there? Listen good.

We're about to burn to death. No one else has any power left so it's up to you. Put the fire out."

"What?"

"PUT THE FIRE OUT!"

"No need to shout," says Lisutaris, showing some signs of coming back to reality. She waves her hand. The fire goes out.

"I'm really hungry," she says.

I beat the door down with a few mighty blows. Lisutaris' spell has ejected the rioters from the house but they are screaming outside, regrouping for another attack. I'm getting out of here. Unfortunately an even larger crowd of maniacs, including several heavily armed soldiers, now surrounds the house, occupying the Praetor's gardens like an invading army. All of a sudden a fancy landus careers into view. The driver is struggling desperately to control the horse as all around missiles fly and flames spurt into the sky.

The carriage thunders through an ornamental hedge and over some beds of flowers before scything its way through the crowd. Whoever is in it seems to be deliberately heading our way.

"Nice driving," mutters Makri, as the carriage veers round some trees at a furious pace. The driver is hunched down low, trying to avoid the rocks hurled by the rabid mob. It almost makes it to the house but comes shuddering to a halt when the front wheels get stuck in an ornamental pond.

"It's the Princess!"

"She's picked a poor time for a jail break."

Du-Akai, showing more spirit than I would have given her credit for, leaps from the driver's pillion, fends off an attacker and dashes towards us, crowd in pursuit. She makes it to the front door and we haul her in. She collapses on the floor, panting for breath. Unfortunately for her, her sanctuary is likely to be brief.

Maddened by her appearance the crowd charge the
house and start removing the door frame. Any second
now they'll be pouring through. I groan, and turn
quickly to Lisutaris.

"Finish your counterspell and make it quick!" I tell
her, then wearily get back to the task of preserving my
life against the mob. Hanama and Makri join me at
the door and we hold them off the best we can. Even
in their maniacal state, the sight of our three blades
is enough to deter some of the rabble, but the soldiers
seem to relish the opportunity for combat and fly at
us like we are hostile Orcs. It's a grim battle, and the
fact that we're being forced to slay innocent people
makes it worse. Horm the Dead has certainly wreaked
a terrible revenge. Makri should never have stuck him
with that throwing star.

I've just dispatched an opponent when Lisutaris,
Mistress of the Sky, shouts at us from behind. "What's
the Orcish for "peace"?"

I'm baffled by this interruption.

"What are you talking about?" I scream.

"I have to translate my counterspell into Orcish to
make it work. My Orcish isn't very good. What's their
word for 'peace'?"

"*Vazey*," yells Makri, kicking an opponent away from
her.

We carry on fighting.

"What's the Orcish for 'Harmonious Conjunction'?"

This takes Makri a few minutes, which is not surprising as she's locked in combat with a huge soldier
carrying a twin-bladed axe.

"*Tenasata zadad*, I think!" she screams back after
dispatching him.

Bodies are now everywhere but the attackers don't
let up. Their madness seems to be intensifying and
smoke is starting to drift into the room from the houses

burning in the street. I've got a serious cut on my face and another on my shoulder and I notice that Hanama isn't moving too well and seems to be wounded in the leg.

"What's the Orcish for 'All men shall be brothers'?"

"For God's sake, Makri, go back there and translate her damned spell. Me and Hanama will hold them off."

Makri sees the wisdom of this and hurries back leaving myself and the Assassin to fight on. In my vainer moments I've been known to claim to be the best street fighter in the city. This is an exaggeration, but I am good at it. So is Hanama. I wonder about the incongruity of fighting shoulder to shoulder with a heartless Assassin, but I don't wonder for long because a truly frightening opponent now leaps at me. He's one of the largest men I've ever seen and he's carrying an axe the size of a door. He attacks me with a ferocity that drives me backwards, and I find it almost impossible to block his axe. He's extremely fierce and strong and I'm too weary to fight much longer. I lunge at him and stick my sword in his shoulder, but he's madder than a mad Sorcerer and doesn't even feel it. His axe crashes on to my hastily raised blade and I'm forced to my knees. He chops at me again and my arm goes numb. I drop my sword. He slashes at my throat.

His blade stops right at my skin and he tumbles to the ground with Hanama's knife sticking in his back. I gasp out a thank you and haul myself to my feet, ready to meet the next wave of attackers. Behind me I can hear Makri, Lisutaris and the other Sorcerers bandying around Orcish and Elvish terms as they try to complete the counterspell.

Hanama's wounded leg gives way and she sinks to one knee, heavily pressed. Again showing some spirit, the Princess runs forward and clubs an opponent to the ground. I'm gripped with sudden fury about being forced to make my death stand in such a useless manner. I never figured I'd go out fighting a crowd of demented Turanian shopkeepers. I turn my head and bellow at the top of my voice.

"If you don't finish that spell, Lisutaris, I'll come and kill you myself before they get me!"

"Hold on," she shouts in reply. "Another minute."

We hold on for another minute. As Lisutaris starts intoning the spell I go down under the weight of six attackers armed with clubs, and pass out of consciousness.

Chapter Twenty-Eight

❧

When I wake it's dark and quiet. Either I'm dead or the riot's stopped. A door opens, letting light into the room, and Makri enters. Her head is bandaged, but she seems healthy.

"What happened?"

"Lisutaris' counterspell worked. The whole city started to return to sanity about three hours ago. Just in time for you and Hanama. Good fighting, incidentally."

"Thank you."

I notice that I'm not feeling too bad, considering what I've been through.

"The Sorcerers patched you both up. After they'd seen to the Princess of course. All the rioters have departed to put out fires and lick their wounds. Half the city's been burned but the Sorcerers that are left seem to have it under control now, And the Civil Guard is out in force."

"Where's Hanama?"

"Next door. It took the Sorcerers a long time to heal her wounds."

"Should have let her die."

Makri points out this is rather ungrateful of me. Without Hanama, the mad crowd would have overwhelmed us.

"Maybe. Maybe not. I figure I had things pretty well under control. Well, time to get back to work, I guess."

"Is it?"

I nod.

"I've got the Prince's letter back and probably gathered up enough information about the dwa dealing to keep Cerius out of court. Not sure about the Princess though. We'll have to hope that Bishop Gzekius comes through on that one and persuades the authorities that she didn't kill the dragon. And then there's the Cloth . . . I've been doing a fair bit of thinking about that . . . let's go and see Hanama."

Makri declines. She's keen to get back to the Avenging Axe and check on things there. She's concerned that someone might have made off with the funds she's been collecting for the Association of Gentlewomen during the riot.

"What if my philosophy notes have been burned?"

Makri departs in a hurry, leaving me to seek out Hanama. The diminutive Assassin is not in the room next door, but I find her in the wine cellar sitting on the floor with a bottle in her hand. Her black clothes are in tatters after the fight but like me she seems in good shape after her healing.

"Well well," I say. "That makes two surprising discoveries about you in one day."

"What?"

"Firstly, you can be sufficiently shaken by events to need a drink to calm you down."

"I do not need a drink to calm me down," says Hanama, coldly.

"Well, I do," I say, selecting a bottle and opening it with the corkscrew I keep on my key ring, and sitting down beside her on the floor. "We just fought off more maniacs than two Humans could reasonably be expected to cope with. A magnificent effort, though I say so myself. Anyone deserves a bottle of wine after that, even an Assassin, trained to be emotionless. Which brings me to my second discovery about you, Hanama. You're not emotionless."

"And why do you say that?"

"You saved my life. I'm touched."

"You shouldn't be. I merely saved you because I needed you at my side to fight off the mob."

I don't pursue it. She's probably telling the truth. "You know, Hanama, I seem to run across you a lot these days. I haven't worked out why that is yet. Still, I must say, for the number three in the Assassins Guild, you're not such a bad sort. A little distant, perhaps, but hey, for a woman who once scaled the sheer walls of Menhasat Castle in a snowstorm to assassinate Consul Pavius, you're not bad company. Is it true you once killed a Sorcerer, a Senator and an Orc Lord all in the same day?"

"The Assassins Guild does not discuss its work," replies Hanama.

"Cheers," I say, raising my bottle.

She raises her own a fraction, and we drink together. All around are wine racks stuffed with excellent vintages, though I can't see any beer. I finish one bottle and open another, selecting the finest I can find.

I don't bother asking Hanama why she has been after the Cloth as I know she will simply deny it. But I do express some surprise about finding her unconscious on the beach.

"Even though you'd just been half drowned in that
sewer I'd have thought it was impossible for anyone
to sneak up behind you."

She looks faintly troubled. "So would I. I swear I'd
have sensed an attacker, half drowned or not."

"Sorcery perhaps?"

She shakes her head. She didn't sense any sorcery
and a woman of her skills and training would have. I
didn't pick up anything at the scene either. It remains
a puzzling mystery. And a puzzling coincidence as well,
now I think about it, because it seems very unlikely
that anyone could sneak up behind Sarin the Merciless after the warrior monk training, yet they did.
Obviously someone very good at sneaking is going
around Turai clubbing people on the back of the head.
Does that mean, I wonder, that the same person who
took the Red Elvish Cloth from Hanama also took the
dwa from Sarin? An interesting thought.

"There was something, but . . ."

I look at her inquisitively.

"I can't put my finger on it. But at the instant I was
hit I thought I sensed . . . well I don't know . . . something not quite Human."

"Like an Orc?"

She can't say. It was too fast and she was half
drowned at the time. A dim memory rises inside me
but disappears before I can identify it.

Hanama takes another drink then rises gracefully.
It's time for her to get back to see how things are
at Assassins Guild headquarters. As number three in
the organisation, Hanama is important enough to wear
a special protection charm, but that doesn't apply
to all Assassins by any means. Must have made
it interesting when they all went mad with the Eight-
Mile Terror.

She leaves. I open another bottle of wine. The cellar

is cool and it's the first time I've been comfortable in weeks. I find myself drifting off to sleep and it's an effort to rouse myself and get back to work.

"I guess it's better than rowing a slave galley," I mutter, and haul myself to my feet.

Chapter Twenty-Nine

The Princess is wearing a new robe borrowed from Lisutaris and has brushed and plaited her golden hair. Her fancy arm bracelets are dented where she was struck by a rock, and she's lost an earring along the way, but all in all she looks not bad for a woman who had to fight her way through a riot. As I emerge from the cellar—to the well-deserved thanks and congratulations of the Sorcerers—she grabs an opportunity for a word. While not exactly apologising for her previous rudeness, she lets me know she thinks better of me now. I reply graciously. I can just about remember how from my days at the Palace.

The Sorcerers are recovering from the riot with a table full of delicacies and a generous selection of Lisutaris' wines, although I think Lisutaris herself is still a little on edge, probably because she feels that she is long overdue for a blast on her water pipe but doesn't actually want to smoke thazis while the Princess is still there. I don't expect the Princess would mind, what with the riot and everything, but a Sorcerer has to respect the forms of polite society if she wants to get on. Princess Du-Akai rises to leave. Lisutaris offers her a carriage and an escort back to the Palace, but it seems like the Princess has been waiting for my arrival because she declines the offer and elects to go with me. I grab a pastry off the Sorcerers' table and follow. Some servants haul the carriage out of the pond, fit a fresh horse on the front and I squeeze in behind her.

The sun is beating down even more strongly than yesterday. The ever present stals are wilting in the trees, what's left of them. After the coolness of Lisutaris' wine cellar it's hard to take.

"Hot as Orcish hell out here. Where exactly are you going, Princess? Back to captivity?"

She supposes so. When the riot broke out and she found herself trapped in a burning wing of the Palace she naturally decided that it would be a good idea to get out of there fast, but now it's all over it seems best to go back. She wouldn't get far if she fled for real. Too easily recognisable.

"I'll be locked up in my chambers again. Better than a prison cell, I suppose."

We make our way slowly up the debris-strewn road. The elegant pavement tiles are cracked and soot-blackened. The trees, specially bred to stay green through the fierce summer, are broken and burned. Suddenly I spot two familiar figures emerging warily from the shattered front of another villa. It's Callis and Jaris, my Elvish clients. They're followed out by a couple of young and rather shaken-looking Sorcerers.

We stop and greet them. The Elves tell me that they were fortunate to be in Truth is Beauty Lane when the riot broke out, and they took shelter with the nearest Sorcerers. As Elves the Eight-Mile Terror did not affect them directly, but being trapped in the middle of thousands of mad Humans has shaken them badly. They've had enough of city life. They're heading home and plan to take the next ship south out of the harbour at Twelve Seas. I'm displeased to have failed my clients but there's not a lot I can say. I came close to the Cloth but I didn't recover it. Clients are never impressed when you just come close, and neither am I. We bid each other farewell.

As we ride on the Princess expresses her disappointment at my failure.

I try to reassure her. "I didn't get the Cloth back but I found out who gutted the dragon and removed it."

I explain to her about Bishop Gzekius and the True Church. "I can't exactly prove it in court but I have a fair amount of leverage over the Bishop and I reckon he'll do what's necessary to show you're innocent. If he does then it all stays quiet. Otherwise I'll have no choice but to give a full report on his recent activities for *The Renowned and Truthful Chronicle*. It loves a Church scandal."

The Princess is grateful. She should be. Till I stepped in she was facing a lifetime in a mountain-top nunnery.

"Please also convey my gratitude to Makri for her efforts on my behalf."

"I will."

"This Cloth has proved to be very troublesome for Turai, Thraxas."

"Anything floating round that's worth thirty thousand gurans is bound to be trouble."

"Who ended up with it?"

The Palace is now in view. Smoke drifts above, but it's still in one piece, just about.

I admit I don't know who ended up with the Cloth.

"It was last seen in the hands of an Assassin but she was clubbed by something not Human."

"Not Human?"

"That's right. Which narrows it down I guess. Orcs, probably, or a half-Orc agent. Or . . ."

I feel some inspiration coming on. Right back at the start of the case, when I was being hauled away from Attilan's garden by the Guards. I sensed something there but couldn't identify it.

"Or someone very good at sneaking up on people. Someone renowned for stealth."

"Like?"

"Like an Elf. God damn it! The Elves. It was them all along! No wonder they keep popping up all over the place! Hiring me to help them indeed! Princess, can I borrow your landus?"

She nods. We're at the Palace grounds and soldiers and guards rush up to surround the Princess. I take a swift leave, dragging on the reins and sending the horse racing back the way I came.

I had been meaning to call on Cicerius and pick up some payment, but it'll have to wait. Is it today or tomorrow I have to pay my debt to the Brotherhood? I can't remember. Too much excitement. Too much all-night rioting.

The Elves have gone from Truth is Beauty Lane. I run through the ornamental gardens and hammer on Lisutaris' door. When a servant answers I run right over him and find Lisutaris consoling herself with her water pipe. Fortunately she doesn't yet seem to be too stoned.

"Lisutaris, I need a favour, and quick."

"Very well."

"Can you tell me where a couple of Elves are now?"

I describe them to her. Lisutaris closes her eyes for a few minutes. An expression of tranquillity settles on her face. My nose wrinkles at the powerful smell of thazis in the room.

Her eyes open. "They're at Twelve Seas docks. Boarding a ship."

She's a powerful Sorcerer, Lisutaris, Mistress of the Sky. Pity she smokes so much. I impinge on her for another favour, which she again is willing to grant, aware that I saved them all in the riot. So minutes later I am thundering through Turai on a fine horse from her stables, on my way to intercept two treacherous Elves.

The streets are chaotic. Rubble lies everywhere. Municipal horse carts are starting to collect the bodies but there are still plenty left to choose from. The streets to the south are flooded from a burst aqueduct. Steam rises in the burning sun. It takes me a long time to get down to Twelve Seas and I'm sweating and cursing by the time I'm in sight of the docks.

A giant figure strides in front of me, grabbing the reins and bringing me to a shuddering halt. It's Karlox, of all people.

"So you survived the riot," he growls. "Good. You got another three hours to pay up."

"Karlox. You are dumb as an Orc and you have no idea how much you annoy me."

I swing a hefty boot and catch him full in the face and he goes down in a heap. I spur my horse on, struggling through the hopeless crowds of Twelve Seas, many of whom have been burned out of their pitiful dwellings. There are huge gaps in the skyline where the six-storey slums have collapsed into smouldering rubble on to which municipal firemen are still pouring water. My horse is starting to protest. In the heat it finds carrying my bulk quite a difficult task. We struggle on.

"Thraxas!"

It's Makri, sword in one hand and a bag of manuscripts in the other. She's on her way to her mathematics class.

"Makri, you are a madwoman. There won't be any classes today. The Guild College is still on fire and the Professors are probably all hiding in their cellars, unless they're dead . . ."

She looks disappointed.

"Are you sure?"

"Of course I'm sure. Now, if you want to be in on the end of the case, get up on the horse."

She leaps aboard. The horse protests some more. No doubt Lisutaris will be able to nurse it back to health.

"Where are we going?"

"The docks. I'm chasing the Elves. They've got the Cloth. Probably the dwa as well."

Makri finds it hard to believe that the Elves are criminals. "Callis is a healer."

"He'll need healing when I get through with him. Can you think of anyone better qualified to sneak up unnoticed behind Hanama and Sarin? And don't forget the way the Elves mysteriously appeared when Sarin had us cold outside the city. They'd been following us. They've used me all along, Makri. Representatives of an Elf Lord indeed. They're after the Cloth for themselves."

"Crooked Elves?"

"That's right. I was a fool to take them on face value."

Makri asks me why I didn't check their credentials in the first place. "Because they handed over a load of money of course. Now, stop asking stupid questions."

We're next to the harbour. Just as well as the horse absolutely refuses to take another step. We dismount and look around. Several ships have been sunk in the harbour and a few more are smouldering at their berths. Only one vessel seems to be in good shape and

the captain is obviously keen to get out of the city fast
because he's preparing to weigh anchor as we approach.

He looks at us curiously: a large fat man, ragged and
filthy, dripping with sweat, and an exotic young woman
with a chainmail bikini and a sword sticking out from
under her cloak.

"Travelling far?" he says.

"Not travelling at all," I reply. "Just looking. For
Elves. Any aboard this ship?"

He stares at me blankly, the universal sign in Turai
that a bribe is called for. I pass him a guran.

"Just got on," he says. "Cabin at the front. We're
sailing in three minutes, with you on board if you're
still here."

Makri and I rush along the deck past various sur-
prised-looking sailors who are making ready to cast off.
Most of them are bruised from the riot but work away
busily. You have to be tough to sail these seas.

There's only one cabin door at the end of the ship—
most passengers on a trader like this would simply bunk
down wherever they found an empty piece of deck—
and we kick it open and stride right in. I'm not prepared for what we find and am rendered temporarily
speechless.

I unsheathe my sword almost involuntarily, although
there is obviously no one here to fight with. No one
here at all except two dead Elves, each with a knife
deep in his heart. They've both been stabbed in the
chest, I mean; I'm not absolutely certain if Elves'
hearts are in the same place as ours. They're dead
anyway.

I catch a momentary flicker of sadness passing over
Makri's face at the sight of the young healer dead on
the floor, but she's too hardened to death to show much
emotion. Myself, I'm not sad at all, but I'm sure as hell
puzzled. From the lack of outcry outside I presume that

no one on the ship knows what's happened, but it can't be an easy thing to kill two Elves without making the slightest sound. I study the weapons. Small throwing knives, unleashed with murderous accuracy before the victims knew what was happening.

"Looks like they met their match in sneaking," I grunt, and start searching the cabin.

They've stashed the dwa under their bunks. There's no sign of the Cloth. A call comes from the ship's mate that they're about to sail. I'd like to take the dwa but it's not strictly necessary and I don't want to draw attention to myself by struggling off heavily laden. I notice the healer's pouch lying spilled open on the floor. There's a few lesada leaves among a bunch of other herbs. I pick them up and stuff them into my own pouch.

"Shame to waste them," I tell Makri. "Very good for hangovers."

"You don't have to explain, Thraxas. I never expected you to have any qualms about robbing the dead."

We leave the cabin and stroll off the ship as though nothing has happened.

"Shouldn't we inform the Captain his passengers are dead?"

"What for? Just make trouble all round. For two dead Elves the authorities will be crawling all over the ship. It'll be weeks before he can sail. And we'll be answering questions from the Guard for a month. This way he gets to dump the bodies out at sea as soon as they're discovered. I expect they already paid for their passage. And he's got six bags of dwa to make up for his trouble. Much easier all round."

I'm more tired than a man should be. I have difficulty walking home.

Large parts of Quintessence Street are unrecognisable, mere burned-out shells. The municipal carts haven't got round to collecting the bodies from Twelve Seas yet, so the place is quite a mess. The Avenging Axe is badly damaged but at least it survived. When Gurd went mad and started swinging his axe around not many of the locals fancied taking him on.

I walk in, climb upstairs and fall asleep on the remains of my couch.

Chapter Thirty

—◆—

Karlox has a nasty cut on his face where I kicked him. I know, because he's standing over me with a sword in his hand.

"You ever consider knocking?" I growl.

"Door wasn't locked," says Karlox.

I'm still lying on the couch. The point of Karlox's sword is making it awkward for me to rise. He's got five men with him. They're looking for the money I owe. I don't have it.

"The Orc bitch went out," grunts Karlox, reading my mind. I was hoping she'd burst in and rescue me. "Got the money?"

"On its way. I'm just waiting for payment to arrive."

Which is true. Cicerius owes me plenty for clearing his son, and clearing the Princess. I can't really explain this to Karlox however, and I doubt it would make any difference if I could. For Karlox it's more fun if I don't have the money.

"Got a spell ready?" he asks, knowing full well that I haven't.

"No? Not much of a Sorcerer, are you? Not much of anything really. Apart from a gambler. A bad gambler. Very unlucky. And this is the most unlucky day you're ever going to have, fat man."

One of his thugs laughs. They advance and stand round me, swords drawn.

"What is going on here?" demands a now familiar voice. It's Cicerius. I never thought I'd be so pleased to see him. He strides into my shattered room, a grim frown on his narrow face.

"Well?" he says, going right up to Karlox and looking him squarely in the face. This is a little awkward for Karlox. Not only is Cicerius much too important for him to push around, but the Traditionals use the Brotherhood as muscle during the elections.

"Some private business, Praetor," says Karlox, uncomfortably.

"The gambling debt, no doubt," says Cicerius.

Of course. I forgot everyone in the city knew about it.

Cicerius motions to his attendant. The attendant draws out a purse, counts out some coins, and hands them over to the Brotherhood enforcer.

"Depart," orders the Praetor.

Poor Karlox. He's sadder than a Niojan whore at this turn of events. He was looking forward to doing a little enforcing on me. He departs, followed by his men.

I rise, grateful at this turn of events, and thank Cicerius. He looks at me with disapproval and gives me a brief lecture on the stupidity of gambling, particularly if I'm not good enough to win.

"The money will be deducted from your fee."

Praetor Cicerius, looking more incongruous than

ever in his crisp white toga in my shattered room, informs me that the Princess has been cleared.

"The Consul has been reliably informed that the dragon was in fact killed by Orcs from their Embassy. An internal Orcish power struggle, apparently. The Civil Guardsmen picked up their bodies here in Twelve Seas." None of this is true, of course. It's just the story circulated by Bishop Gzekius to clear the Princess's name, as promised. "The Orcish Ambassadors are not happy, but as several of their Orcs were found in a place they were forbidden to enter, a church, they cannot protest too much. The King is relieved to learn that his daughter has not been indulging in illegal activities. It's a satisfactory outcome. I don't suppose it's true?"

I tell him no, it isn't and fill him in on most of the details, including everything I know about the Bishop's misdemeanours. The Praetor is shocked to learn the extent of the Bishop's machinations. I imagine Gzekius will find his influence at court waning from now on. Of course Bishop Gzekius will now have it in for me in no uncertain fashion so it won't hurt to have Cicerius ranged against him. Despite being troubled by what I tell him the Praetor has to admit that I've done what I was hired to do. The Princess is in the clear. Soon everyone in Turai will hear rumours that the whole trouble was the fault of the Orcs trying to steal the Cloth. There's some truth in that, I suppose. They did start it when they hired Glixius to get it for them, although events quickly spiralled out of his control.

The Praetor informs me that he has already let it be known to the Niojan Ambassador that his attaché Attilan was killed by the rogue Orcs after he stumbled on their criminal activities. Clever of the Praetor. Gets Turai a bit of breathing space. Nioj will still destroy us one day.

Whether it was the Pontifex I saw at Attilan's house or the Elves that killed the attaché, I don't know. The Elves, I think. Now that the Orcs have been blamed, it doesn't seem to matter much.

"Of course our Elvish allies who sent us the Cloth are not fully satisfied. We may have shifted the blame for the theft on to the Orcs but there is still no sign of the Cloth. Do you know where it is?"

I shake my head. I've been expecting Cicerius to give me a hard time about this—I haven't forgotten Consul Kalius accusing me of lying—but he seems quite prepared to believe me.

"Well, I cannot expect you to do everything. I am already grateful to you for keeping my son out of court and preserving his reputation. And that of the Prince. However undeserved that may be."

He makes to leave, but halts at the door. "Princess Du-Akai wishes me to pass on her sincere gratitude," he says, and departs abruptly. As he opens the door the smell of smoke drifts in from the smouldering buildings in the street outside.

I muse on the Praetor's words. Not bad. The Princess likes me. Maybe I can do a little social climbing on the back of that. Anything to get out of Twelve Seas. Makri appears the moment he departs. Having returned half-way through his visit she has, of course, been listening at the door.

"Looks like your luck's changing, Thraxas. Everyone's pleased with you. The city officials, the Royal Family—even the Brotherhood is off your back."

I nod. It's true. Things do look better than a few days ago. My enemies are either pacified or departed. Apart from Glixius Dragon Killer—with my luck he will have survived the riot—and the Society of Friends, who will no doubt be mad as hell at me for messing things up for them. I can live with that.

I stub my toe on something on the floor. It's a bottle of beer. Must've been hidden under the sofa. I open it and take a long swig, then stare out the window at the wreckage outside.

"Somehow you don't seem too pleased," says Makri. I turn to face her. "I'm pleased enough, I guess."

"Well you're looking as miserable as a Niojan whore."

I take another drink. "I don't like being given the run-around, Makri. Not by anyone, but particularly not by you."

Makri raises her eyebrows. I tell her to stop acting innocent.

"The Association of Gentlewomen stole that Cloth, didn't they? Don't bother looking shocked and perplexed, you haven't been in civilisation long enough to fool an experienced liar like me."

Makri continues to look shocked and perplexed. She denies any knowledge of what I'm on about.

"Oh yes? I've wondered all along what Hanama's involvement in all this was. The Assassins don't hunt for stolen goods, they assassinate people. It seemed just possible that they would've wanted the Elvish Cloth for their guild, to make their own magic-proof room perhaps, but in that case why was it always Hanama who kept appearing everywhere? Why not some other Assassin? There are plenty of them. Way too many in fact. But it was always her. And she's a difficult woman to shake off, as the Elves found out last night."

Makri continues to be silent. I continue to talk.

"I knew immediately when I saw the Elves that Hanama had killed them. A knife throw to their hearts before they could even move. Very efficient. Difficult to carry out, of course, given that Elves are practically impossible to take by surprise, and they move pretty damned quick when they're in danger. But not beyond the powers of Hanama. They only outsmarted her before because she was half drowned in the flood. I wondered at first how she could possibly have known it was the Elves—after all, I'd only just worked it out and I swear no one did before me—then I realised. I mentioned it to the Princess just before I went after them myself. And to Lisutaris. One of them got a message to Hanama, and fast. Quite a group, this Association of Gentlewomen, Makri. Princesses, Assassins, Sorcerers. And barmaids."

I fix her with a stare.

"Are you suggesting I've been passing on information?" says Makri, not sounding too pleased about it.

"Well, have you?"

"No, I have not. And if the Association of Gentlewomen has been pursuing the Elvish Cloth it's news to me. Why would they want it anyway?"

"Same reason everybody else in this city wants things. For money. You told me you needed fifty thousand to buy a Charter. Taking a collection box round Twelve Seas isn't going to get you far. But a nice fat thirty thousand for the Cloth will."

Makri absolutely denies it. "I don't even believe that Hanama is in the Association of Gentlewomen. She's an Assassin."

"So? Maybe she feels she's not making out as well as she should. Held back from promotion by the men in the Assassins Guild. And, now I think about it, when she came round on the beach she called you Makri. Struck me as pretty friendly at the time, for someone you'd only ever seen once before during a fight. And the Princess passes on her best regards as well . . ."

We stare at each other across the room. Makri strides over to me and sticks her nose right in my face.

"Thraxas," she says, her voice clipped and hostile. "You might be right about the Association. Maybe Hanama was getting the Cloth for them. I hope she was. We need the money. But I wasn't in on it. I wouldn't pass any information about your business behind your back, because you're the only friend I have in this stinking city."

She glares at me angrily. I glare back at her. Seconds pass in hostile silence. It strikes me that I don't have too many friends in this stinking city either.

"You've been working too hard, Makri. Let's go downstairs. I'll buy you a drink."

Chapter Thirty-One

In the aftermath of the Eight-Mile Terror the violence that was gripping Turai fades into the background. The elections are still going ahead, and the Brotherhood and the Society of Friends are still struggling to control the dwa market, but in the face of the recent calamity most of the outright hostility is either toned down or suspended altogether. Everyone is too busy rebuilding the city, and rebuilding their lives.

Cerius is not brought to court, due to the evidence I present to the Consul. Prince Frisen-Akan's attempt to import narcotics on a large scale doesn't reach the ears of the public. Cicerius is pleased on both counts. Thanks to me he keeps his reputation. What's more, any sort of civic disaster usually unites the population behind the Royal Family, which will quite probably hand the elections to the Traditionals. Too good a politician to miss an opportunity, he makes a fine series of speeches in the Senate, urging everyone in Turai to pull together to rebuild the city. It does his election chances no harm at all.

The Renowned and Truthful Chronicle of All the World's Events notes that one of the sad losses to the city in the recent riot was one of its most powerful Sorcerers, Tas of the Eastern Lightning, found dead in an alley with a crossbow bolt in his back. The paper laments the fact that a mad rioter could have acquired such a weapon. It didn't take Sarin the Merciless long to get rid of him.

"I guess if you've extorted ten thousand gurans, it's better not to have to share it," said Makri when she hears the news. "Are you still keen to meet her again?"

"Absolutely. The sooner Sarin comes back to Turai the better. I could do with some reward money. I'll soon show her who's number one chariot around here."

The Avenging Axe is being knocked back into shape. Here, as in the rest of Twelve Seas, architects and builders are engaged round the clock to put things right. Workmen are busy everywhere, sweating in the heat. Flocks of stals, displaced by fire from their old perches, fight for nesting space on the roofs of the new buildings. The King opens the royal vaults to pay for much of the work, which is very generous of him, although cynics might say he was merely buying his supporters' victory in the elections.

Personally, I'm in good shape. A fat payment from Cicerius and an extra bonus from the Princess, not to mention the valuable double unicorn the Elves gave me as a retainer. Plus a solid reputation as a man who gets things done.

"So, are you moving back to Thamlin?" asks Makri, who is busier than ever, with thirsty bricklayers, roofers, glaziers and architects clamouring for drinks all day.

"Not yet, Makri. The Traditionals might think I'm a good Investigator but they don't want me as a next-door neighbour. It'll be a while yet before I'm invited back to the Palace."

"Who's going to win the election?"

"Probably Cicerius. Which is good for me. Except Senator Lodius and the Populares now really dislike me. Which is bad for me. I never have any problem making new enemies."

In between shifts Makri has been studying hard and spends long hours in her room with her books and scrolls. Undeterred by her experience in the Fairy Glade, she's had her nose pierced again by Kaby. It keeps her happy.

I take out two necklaces, and hand one to her. She stares at it suspiciously.

"It's the Red Elvish Cloth we wrapped round our necks on the night of the Eight-Mile Terror. It worked pretty well then, so I asked Astrath Triple Moon to treat it with a spell which means we now have strong protection against sorcerous attacks. It's illegal to keep it, but now it's woven into these necklaces no one's going to know.

Makri puts it on. "Not that I need it," she says. "I'll trust my swords against magic any day. But you could do with it. Try not to pawn it this time."

"I'll do my best."

Kaby and Palax wander in looking tired. They're busking on the streets again. I don't envy them. It's too hot to work. Fortunately, I don't have to. Not for a while anyway.

"Another 'Happy Guildsman,' if you please, Gurd."

He passes over a tankard but I notice he's looking glum. "Tanrose is annoyed with me," he complains. "She says I never pay her any attention. What can I do?"

"For God's sake, Gurd, don't you even know the basics? Take her some flowers."

The ageing Barbarian looks puzzled.

"Flowers? Will that help?"

"Of course it will," I state with confidence.

And it does.

THRAXAS
and the
warrior monks

Makri steps into the Avenging Axe, her sword at her hip and her philosophy notes in her hand. Perspiration runs down her neck.

"It's hotter than Orcish hell out there," she complains.

I grunt in agreement. I don't have the energy to do much more. It's hotter than Orcish hell in here too. It's as much as I can do to get my beer up to my mouth.

Makri is due to start her shift as barmaid. She takes off the man's tunic she wears outdoors and tosses it behind the bar, then sluices some water from the pitcher over her face and neck. It runs down over her tiny chainmail bikini, a garment that displays almost all of her physique and guarantees a healthy flow of tips from the dockers, sailors, Barbarian mercenaries and other low-life who drink in this tavern.

Makri lives in a small room upstairs. I also live here, in a couple of rooms further down the corridor. My name is Thraxas, and when the heat isn't so fierce that it's impossible to move, I work for a living as a Private Investigator.

Finest Sorcerous Investigator in the City of Turai

says the sign on my outside door. Okay, I admit my
sorcerous powers are now limited and diminishing all
the time, but while I might not be able to perform like
a high-class Palace Sorcerer I still know a spell or two.
I still have the finely tuned senses you develop when
you study magic. And I'm a determined man when I'm
on a case. So I figure the sign is accurate enough.

I don't bother mentioning that I charge cheap rates.
Everyone knows that already. Since I lost my job at the
Palace I wouldn't say my life has worked out especially
well.

I raise my hand limply, motioning for another beer
from Gurd, ageing northern Barbarian and owner of
the Avenging Axe.

"No intention of doing any work, then?" enquires
Makri.

I wave my hand dismissively. "Still going strong on
the last fee."

Six weeks ago I helped out Praetor Cicerius, and
Cicerius is an important man in this city. More important than a Senator. More important than a Praetor now
in fact, because he just won the election for the post
of Deputy Consul, which makes him the second most
senior government official after Consul Kalius, who
answers only to the King.

"Yes," I reflect, raising my beer. "Old Cicerius was
pretty generous with his money, I have to admit. As
he should've been, of course. He wouldn't have won
the election if I hadn't saved his reputation."

Makri scoffs. Makri scoffs at a lot of what I say.
I don't mind, usually. For one thing, she's one of the
few friends I have in this filthy city. For another thing
she often helps me out in my work. Not with the
investigating exactly. More with the fighting. Here in
Twelve Seas, the poor and crime-ridden dockland
neighbourhood, people generally don't like being

investigated. Most times I'm on a case I figure I'm going to have to use my sword at some point or other. Which is okay. I'm pretty good with it. But Makri is an escapee from the Orcish gladiator pits and consequently one of the most lethal swordswomen ever to walk the earth. I don't exaggerate. Makri may be only twenty-one and working as a barmaid to put a little food in her mouth and pay for her classes at the Guild College, but place her sword in one hand, her axe in the other and a row of enemies in front of her and the carnage can be quite incredible.

For seven years she fought in the Orc slave pits. As well as honing her fighting technique to near perfection, this has also given her powerful hatred of Orcs. Of course all humans hate Orcs, despite the peace treaty in force just now. But Makri's hatred is particularly fierce. Which makes the fact that she actually has some Orc blood in her veins all the more difficult for her. As well as some Elf blood. She's certainly an unusual mixture, unusual enough to take considerable abuse for it, although when she's serving drinks with her long dark hair swinging round her bronze shoulders and her small metal bikini clinging to her perfect figure, I notice the drinkers tend to forget their prejudices.

"You'll put on weight," says Makri.

I pat my large belly in a satisfied manner.

"Let him be," says Gurd, grinning, as he pulls me another flagon. "Thraxas doesn't like to work too hard when it's hot. I remember, back in the Orc Wars, we could never get him to do a decent day's fighting when the sun shone."

I ignore this quite untruthful slur on my reputation. Back in the Orc Wars I fought damned hard, I can tell you. Let them mock. I deserve a rest. This time last year I was pounding the docks looking for a crazed

Half-Orc who had killed eight men and damn near made me the ninth. Now, with a fat payment from Cicerius and no need to work through the rest of the burning hot summer, I'm as happy as an Elf in a tree.

"Another beer, if you please, Gurd."

Gurd is about fifty. His face is weather-beaten and his long hair is completely grey, but his muscles are undiminished with age. They bulge as he pours the drink and passes it over the bar.

"Not tempted to get involved in this?" he asks, pointing to an article in *The Renowned and Truthful Chronicle of All the World's Events*, the thin, badly printed news-sheet that specialises in reporting all of the many crimes and scandals that infest Turai. I glance at it.

"Death of a Sorcerer? No, I can live without it. He was only a minor Sorcerer, anyway."

The *Chronicle* reports that the said Sorcerer, Thalius Green Eye, was found dead yesterday at his house in Thamlin. Poison is suspected and his household servants have been taken into custody. I remember Thalius from my days at the Palace. He was a fairly unimportant figure, more interested in casting horoscopes for young aristocrats than practising any serious magic. Which isn't to say his death will be treated lightly. Being a Sorcerer has proved to be unusually hazardous in Turai recently. Only last month Tas of the Eastern Lightning was killed along with Mirius Eagle Rider, both of them connected with the case I was working on. As Sorcerers are important to any state, particularly a small one like Turai, and as they're not in endless supply, I imagine the Guards will be working away busily on the case. Let them. If old Thalius annoyed his servants enough that they went and poisoned him, he probably got what he deserved. Degenerate, these Palace Sorcerers. Dwa addicts, most of them. Or drunks. Or both.

"Another beer, please, Gurd."

I read the rest of the *Chronicle*. There's enough crime, but that's always the case in Turai. A Praetor's been indicted for smuggling dwa into the city, a wagonload of gold from the mines in the far north has been hijacked on its way to the King's treasury and the house of the Simnian Ambassador has been burgled.

I toss the news-sheet away. Let the Civil Guard sort it out. That's what it's paid for.

The door slams open and two unfamiliar characters walk in. Fighting men, but not the normal mercenaries we get round here on their way to join up with the King's forces. The pair of them march up to the bar and order beer. Gurd pours them a couple of tankards and they make for a table to rest from the heat.

The taller of the two, a rough-looking individual with closely cropped hair and a weatherbeaten face, halts as he passes my chair. He stares at me. I glance back casually. I recognise him. I was hoping he wouldn't recognise me. It would have made my life easier. Under the table, my hand slides automatically towards the pommel of my sword.

"Thraxas," he says, spitting out the word.

"Have we met?" I enquire.

"You know damn well we met. I spent five years on a prison galley because of you."

"Because of me? I didn't force you to rob that Elvish Ambassador."

I suppose I did gather the evidence to put him away. He draws his sword with well-practised ease. His companion follows his lead and with no further discussion they leap towards me with murder in their eyes.

I'm out of my chair fast. I may be forty-three years old and have a fat belly, but I can still move when I have to. The first attacker slashes at me but I parry and riposte to send him hurtling backwards with blood spurting from his chest before whirling round to face the other assailant.

The other assailant is already lying dead. In less time than it took me to dispatch my opponent Makri has grabbed her sword from its place of concealment behind the bar, leaped into the fray and slain him.

"Thanks, Makri."

Gurd now has his old axe in his hands and looks disappointed there is no one left for him.

"Getting slow," he mutters.

"What was that about?" asks Makri.

"They robbed an Elvish Ambassador to the Imperial Palace. Took his money when he was lying drunk in a brothel in Kushni. Civil Guards couldn't find them but I tracked them down. About five years back. They must have only got off the prison ship a couple of months ago."

And now they're dead. Every time I put someone away they swear to get me, but they never usually carry out their threat. Just my bad luck this pair happened to walk into the Avenging Axe. Or their bad luck, I suppose.

I frisk the corpses from habit, with no results. Nothing linking them to any of the City's criminal gangs. Probably they were just enjoying their freedom before embarking on a life of crime again. I'd rather not have had to kill them but I don't care too much. Next time they were convicted of anything they'd have been hanged anyway. One of them has a purse hanging round his neck but it's empty. Not even a coin. Their next robbery wouldn't have been too far away.

Blood oozes over the floor.

"I'll deal with this mess," says Makri, returning her sword to its hiding place, where it rests alongside her spare axe and a few knives and throwing stars. Makri likes weapons.

She mops up the blood then bends down to pick up the empty purse that I've discarded on the floor.

"Nice embroidery," she says. "I could do with a new one."

She puts it round her neck. Seven years in the Orc gladiator pits has left Makri fairly immune to the effects of death. No qualms about putting a dead man's purse round her neck, provided it's handsomely embroidered.

Gurd and I drag the bodies outside. No one takes much notice. Corpses on the street are not an especially unusual sight in Twelve Seas. Most people are too busy scratching a living to pay them much attention.

I grab a passing child and slip him a coin to take a message to the Civil Guards informing them of what has happened. They won't be too bothered about the affair either but as I'm a licensed Investigator, it pays to keep on the right side of the law.

Back inside Makri has cleaned up the floor and is polishing the bar. I get myself another beer and sit down to rest. It's getting hotter by the minute. The bar starts to fill up. The city suffered riots recently and, as much damage remains in the streets, much construction is going on to repair it. Come lunchtime the tavern is full of workers seeking refreshment from their morning shifts on the scaffolding. It's good business for Gurd. Good business for Tanrose as well, who makes and sells the food in the tavern. She's a fine cook and I purchase one of her large venison pies for lunch. With plenty of money left after my last case I've sworn to survive the rest of the burning hot summer without working. This morning's fighting came too close to work for my liking.

"What was an Elvish Ambassador doing drunk in a brothel in Kushni?" enquires Makri, later.

"Enjoying himself. His Elf Lord called him back to

the Southern Islands right afterwards in disgrace and it was all hushed up here in the city. The King never likes anything that might damage our relations with the Elves."

I order myself another beer and wonder if I should have another venison pie. Unexpected activity tends to give me a powerful appetite.

"Everything gives you a powerful appetite," says Makri, grinning, as she carries on cleaning the tables.

After I finish my venison pie, I load up with a few of Tanrose's pastries and buy another beer to take upstairs.

"You're drinking too much," says Tanrose.

"Needed a hobby after my wife left."

"You took it up as a hobby long before that."

I can't deny it.

I have two rooms at the Avenging Axe, one for sleeping and one for working. The workroom has an outside door with steps down to the street outside so clients can visit without coming up through the tavern. I'm planning to sleep the afternoon away but before I can settle down a frantic banging comes at the door. I open it and a young man rushes in, bouncing off me and ending up in the middle of the room looking scared and confused.

"They're going to hang me!" he cries. "Don't let them do it!"

"What? Who?"

"I didn't kill him! It's a lie! Help me!"

I glare at him. My rooms are in their usual mess and he's not helping any. He's in a real state and for a long time I can't make head nor tail of what he's saying.

Eventually I have to fling him in a chair and tell him to start talking sense or get the hell out of my office. He quietens down, but keeps glancing anxiously at the door, as if he's expecting his pursuers to burst in any second.

I walk over to the door and mutter the few short sentences that make up the standard locking spell. It's a common minor spell and you don't have to be particularly skilled in magic to perform it, but the young man seems reassured.

"Now, tell me what's going on. I'm too hot to stand around guessing. Who are you, who's after you, and why?"

"The Guards! They say I killed Drantaax!"

"Drantaax? The sculptor?"

He nods.

Drantaax is a well-known man in Turai. Best sculptor in town. One of the best anywhere. Well respected for his work, even by the aristocracy, who generally look down on artisans. His statues decorate many of Turai's temples, and even the Royal Palace.

"Drantaax was murdered last night. But I didn't do it!"

"Why would anybody think you did? And who are you anyway?"

"I'm Grosex, Drantaax's apprentice. I was working with him last night. We're busy finishing off the new statue of Saint Quatinius for the Shrine. We've been working on it for days . . . but now he's dead. He was stabbed in the back."

"Where were you at the time?"

He was next door. He came through to the workroom and found Drantaax lying dead with a knife in his back. Then Drantaax's wife Calia arrived and starting screaming.

"Calia called the Guard. All the time she was shouting at me, saying I'd stabbed him. But I didn't."

He hangs his head. He's running on nervous energy and it's making him ill. I offer him a thazis stick. Thazis, a mild narcotic, is still illegal but everyone uses it—well, everyone in Twelve Seas anyway. As he inhales the smoke his features relax.

I demand more details. I frown when I learn that instead of waiting for the Guards he fled the scene. And he mentions the interesting fact that the knife sticking in Drantaax belonged to him. I raise an eyebrow. It's not exactly hard to understand why everyone might think he did it. He's spent the night hiding in alleyways, wondering what to do, and now he's here, trying to hire a detective who, frankly, is not too keen to be hired. I'm still too hot, I don't need the work, and for all I know he's guilty as hell.

He looks pathetic. Even though I'm hardened to most things in Turai, I almost feel sorry for him.

There's more banging on my door.

"Open up, it's the Guard."

I recognise the voice. It's Tholius. As Prefect of Twelve Seas he's in charge of the Civil Guard in the area. Naturally enough he despises me. Guards don't like Private Investigators. It's odd that the Prefect himself is here. Normally he'd consider himself too important to get out on the streets and do police work.

I ignore the banging. It doesn't go away.

"Thraxas, open up. I know Grosex is in there."

"No one here but me."

"That's not what our Sorcerer says."

I glance at Grosex. If the Guards reckon the case is important enough to track him with an official Sorcerer he's certainly in bad trouble.

I'm still deciding what to do when the matter is taken out of my hands. The door groans as the Prefect orders his men to break it down. It's not much of a door, and my locking spell is not much of a spell.

To my extreme annoyance it caves in under the weight of heavy Guards' boots and they flood in to my rooms.

I explode with anger. "What the hell do you think you're doing, smashing your way into my rooms? You can't break your way in here without a warrant!"

Prefect Tholius waves a warrant in my face and brushes past me. It's probably not filled in properly, but I don't bother arguing.

"One false move out of him—arrest him," he orders his Guards.

He confronts young Grosex. The apprentice, worn out from worry and still dressed in his dust-covered work tunic, cowers before the yellow-edged official toga of the Prefect.

"You're in serious trouble," rasps Tholius, grabbing Grosex roughly by his tunic. "Why did you kill the sculptor?"

The apprentice hopelessly protests his innocence. Prefect Tholius sneers, then shoves him into the waiting arms of two large Guards.

"Take him away. If he tries to run, kill him. And as for you, Thraxas . . ." He turns on me. "Don't dare interfere with the law again. If I so much as hear a rumour you're involved in this case I'll be down on you like a bad spell."

He turns to go, but halts at the ruined door.

"Feel free to file a claim for compensation from the authorities," he says, laughing. Any such claim would have to go to the Prefect for authorisation.

After bagging his suspect and insulting me the Prefect is as happy as an Elf in a tree and walks off smiling. The Guards depart, dragging young Grosex with them. My last sight of him, he's being hauled down the stairs into a covered Guard wagon, still pathetically protesting his innocence.

I shut what's left of my door. I finish the rest of my beer, then head downstairs to see Makri.

"I'm working," I tell her. "Got a case."

"Since when?"

"Since Prefect Tholius smashed down my door and dragged a client of mine away to prison. I didn't want to work, but I am now angrier than a wounded dragon and I will consequently move heaven, earth and the three moons in order to demonstrate to Tholius that I am not a man to be treated in this way. I'm off to investigate. See you later."

I march out into Quintessence Street with my sword at my hip and grim feelings in my heart. When I was Senior Investigator at the Palace people used to treat me with respect. I've fallen a long way since then but I'm damned if I'm going to let some petty tyrant like Prefect Tholius walk all over me.

It's hotter than Orcish hell out here and the stink of fish from the harbour market hangs thick in the air. I have to pick my way over mounds of rubble around the site of some new construction where the old houses were destroyed in the riots. In their place a contractor is raising new blocks of tenements on either side of the narrow street. Four storeys is the legal maximum in Turai but they'll probably go higher. More profit for the builders and slum landlords. And Tholius. Prefects oversee the building in their area and Tholius rakes in a fair amount in bribes by turning a blind eye to things. Perks of his job. Most Prefects are the same. So are the Praetors. Corruption goes a long way up in this city. The building contractors themselves are in league with the Brotherhood, the criminal organisation that runs the south of the city. They have to be. You can't do much around here unless the Brotherhood is involved.

There are two Civil Guard stations in Turai. The main one nearby is commanded by Prefect Tholius and a smaller one down by the docks is under the charge of

Captain Rallee. I know him well, but he resolutely refuses to allow any of his men to pass on any information to me. I also have a contact at the main station, Guardsman Jevox, who's not above passing me the odd fragment of information since I got his father off a rap a few years back, but I can't risk running into the Prefect again so soon. Tholius doesn't spend too much time here—most often he's lounging around in some brothel or bar in Kushni, spending the gurans he's extorted—but he might well still be around, questioning poor Grosex.

The matter is decided when Guardsman Jevox comes out of the station and makes a frantic warning face as he sees me. I step out of sight around the corner. Peering round, I catch sight of Tholius and two Guards leading Grosex in handcuffs into a covered wagon. They drive off, with Jevox forming part of the horse escort. My official enquiries will have to wait. Which brings me swiftly to some unofficial ones. I walk on, ignoring the beggars. There's too many of them to do anything else.

At the end of Quintessence Street I turn into Tranquillity Lane, a miserable and filthy little alleyway full of prostitutes and dwa addicts. The prostitutes ignore me. The dwa addicts hold out their hands, begging. Since dwa, a powerful drug, swept the city a few years back there are more and more addicts loitering on the streets, making Twelve Seas a dangerous place to walk around after dark—or at any time, really.

Some way along Tranquillity Lane is the Mermaid, a tavern so disreputable that no one with any sense, breeding or dignity would go within a mile of the place. I seem to end up here often. Kerk, an informer of mine, can usually be found here, slumped at a table or lying on the floor if the dwa has got to him. Kerk deals dwa to support his habit and comes across much useful information, which he sells, also to support his habit.

I find him outside the tavern, lying on the sun-baked earth. There's an empty flagon of ale by his feet and the air around him has the distinctive aroma of burning dwa.

I nudge him awake with my foot. He stares up at me with his large eyes, eyes that suggest that somewhere along the line there's Elvish blood in his family, which wouldn't be all that strange. Elves visiting the cities of men are not above romantic liaisons with the prostitutes that work here. The Southern Islands of the Elves are paradise on earth, but they're short on prostitution. I guess the young Elves have to satisfy their urges somehow.

"What do you want?" mumbles Kerk.

"You know anything about Drantaax?"

He holds out his hand automatically. I drop a small coin into his palm, a tenth of a guran.

"Sculptor. Got killed last night."

"You know anything else?"

"Stabbed by his apprentice. So they say."

By the expression in his eyes I guess he knows a little more. I drop another coin into his palm.

"The apprentice was sleeping with his wife."

"Is that rumoured or certified fact?"

"Rumour. But a strong one."

The sun beats down. In the narrow confines of Tranquillity Lane it is close to unbearable. I've marched over deserts that were cooler than this. Kerk knows nothing else but says he'll keep his ear to the ground. I give him another coin and he hauls himself to his feet, now having sufficient money to buy some dwa.

I turn and leave. Not much news from Kerk, but interesting enough. Always makes things more interesting when the apprentice is sleeping with the master's wife. Unfortunately it also makes it more likely that Grosex did kill him, which is something I don't want to be true, though I've no real reason for holding him to be innocent, apart from a vague feeling that he wasn't lying. And my intense dislike of Prefect Tholius.

Stals, the small black birds that infest the city, sit brooding in the heat along the walls of the alley. They rise in the air, squawking, as they are disturbed by a stone tossed by a youth wearing the yellow bandanna which marks him out as a member of the Koolu Kings, the local youth gang. He picks up another stone.

"Toss that in my direction, kid, and I'll ram it down your throat then rot your guts with a spell."

He backs off. Being an Investigator, I'm not exactly popular with the Koolu Kings, but they know not to mess with me. When I'm on a case on a hot day like this I'm not a man to laugh and joke with.

He sneers as I walk past. I sneer back. Kids. They used to steal fruit from the market till dwa swept the city. Now they rob people at knifepoint to buy drugs. Turai is going to hell, and quickly. If the population doesn't just riot, steal and drug its way to extinction then King Lamachus of Nioj will sweep down from the north and wipe us off the face off the earth. All he needs is an excuse, and not a particularly good one at that.

Having at least made a little progress I decide to call back in at the Avenging Axe before heading off to see what I can find out at Drantaax's studio. If I've got a whole day's investigating in front of me I need a beer, and maybe some food. It's also in my mind that I should check a few spells in my books. I freely admit that I'm not much of a Sorcerer these days—I even find it too tiring to carry the standard protection spell around in my head—but I am still able to work a trick or two. It annoyed the hell out of me that Prefect Tholius was able to waltz in and arrest Grosex right under my nose. Very bad for my reputation, if my clients get dragged away like that.

I'm preoccupied with dodging the rubble in the street outside so it takes me a second or two to focus on the figure that greets me as I walk into the tavern. I'm used to fairly strange spectacles on the streets of Turai: chanting pilgrims, hulking northern Barbarians, the occasional green-clad Elf. Closer to home, Makri herself is an exotic sight with her red-bronze skin bulging out of her chainmail bikini. Furthermore she has recently had her nose pierced with a ring, a very unusual sight in this city, and one that I strongly disapprove of. It was done for her by Palax and Kaby, a pair of travelling buskers and musicians who are an even more colourful young pair, with their hair dyed bright colours, their clothes even brighter and multiple facial piercings to boot. But it doesn't prepare me for the sight of a young woman in bare feet—a ridiculously dangerous thing to do given the state of the streets—wearing a long skirt dyed with the signs of the zodiac and a garland of flowers woven into her hair.

I blink stupidly as she stands in front of me. I can't think of any reason she would not be wearing shoes.

"Hey, Thraxas," says Makri, appearing with a tray. "This is Dandelion. She wants to hire you."

Before I have time to object that no one can possibly be called Dandelion she takes my hand, stares deeply into my eyes and pronounces that's she's sure she's come to the right man.

"I can tell you have a sympathetic soul."

Makri is sniggering somewhere in the background.

"You want to hire me?"

"Yes. On behalf of the dolphins."

"The dolphins?"

"The dolphins that live in the bay."

"The ones that can talk to humans," chips in Makri.

I grunt. It's said that the dolphins can talk. Personally, I find it hard to believe.

"They sing as well," adds Dandelion, brightly.

I'm struggling to keep my temper under control.

"I'm a busy man. Is there any point in this wildlife lecture?"

"Why, yes. The dolphins are in terrible trouble. Someone has stolen their healing stone. They want to hire you to get it back."

"Their healing stone?"

"That's right. It's very precious to them. It fell from the sky."

Dandelion smiles sweetly. I abandon all efforts to keep my temper.

"Will you move out the way, please? I'm a busy man and I'm working on a case. A real case. A murder. I've got no time to stand here and listen to some fool with flowers in her hair ramble on about dolphins and a healing stone that fell from the sky. Now, excuse me."

I brush my way past. Dandelion leaps in front of me.

"But you must help them!"

"Find another Investigator."

"The dolphins want you. They've agreed that you're in tune with them at a very deep level."

It's as much as I can do to avoid slapping her. Makri, I note, is finding the whole thing highly amusing. Fine. Let her go and help the dolphins. I have a murder to investigate. I march up the stairs, not even stopping for my beer. I need something stronger and hunt out a bottle of klee, the spirit distilled locally in the hills outside the city. After my recent successes I've bought a better brand than I could normally afford. It still burns my throat as it goes down. I shake my head, and take another drink. Talking dolphins indeed. I've enough problems with Orcs, Elves and Humans. The fish can look after themselves.

After the distraction of the ridiculous Dandelion and her dolphin ramblings I return to the real world and head off towards Drantaax's workshop. I've already walked more than enough in this heat so I hire a landus and sit back and let the small horse-drawn carriage take me out of Twelve Seas and north into Pashish. Pashish is a calmer area than Twelve Seas, home to the poor but respectable workers and their families who keep this city going. There isn't much wealth here but the streets are a little wider and less sordid than those close to the harbour. My friend Astrath Triple Moon, the Sorcerer, lives close by and I'll probably call in on him later.

While riding I'm thinking about two things. One, who killed Drantaax? Two, who is going to pay me to find out? As the heat of my anger from Tholius's invasion of my rooms fades a little, it strikes me that I have plunged into a case without receiving a fee, which is unusual for me. I don't do this for fun. It's my living. Technically I don't even have a client. Grosex was apprehended before he had time to hire me. The worrying thought occurs that being a young apprentice he might not have any money. He might have spent all his meagre wages on presents for the sculptor's wife.

I'll have to hope for the best. Just because I'm not actually desperate for money doesn't mean that I've suddenly come over all charitable. The way my life goes these days, I'll be poor again soon enough. Probably right after the next chariot race.

The landus is halted at a corner by a passing group of chanting pilgrims on their way to visit the shrine of Saint Quatinius over on the west side of the city. I reach out and grab a news-sheet from a vendor. *The Renowned and Truthful Chronicle of All the World's Events* is always keen to report lurid goings-on and the death of the sculptor is a major story. Murder is common in this city, but Drantaax was well enough known for it to be big news. A number of different artists work in Turai, attracted by the wealth that still circulates among our decadent upper classes, but none was as renowned as Drantaax.

The news-sheet says that the statue he was working on, a life-size figure of Saint Quatinius on horseback, was partly funded by the True Church in Nioj. It describes the crime without much detail, then goes on to report that the statue is missing. I presume this must be a misprint. We have many smart criminals in Turai but I can't imagine anyone making off unnoticed with a life-size bronze statue of a man on horseback. God knows what it would weigh. The Niojan angle is bad news though. Nioj is a fundamentalist state. Their King is also their Chief Pontifex and a religious fanatic to boot, so this will give them plenty of reason to be annoyed with Turai.

Drantaax's house is located at the far end of Pashish, where things start to get a little more comfortable. The streets are clean and the pavement is in good repair. I dismount a block away, pay the driver, and walk up.

The house and workshop are guarded outside by two Civil Guards. When I inform them I'm here on business they stare at me stony-faced and refuse to budge.

"That's all we need," comes a voice from behind me. "Thraxas poking his fat belly into Guard matters."

I turn round. "Hello, Captain Rallee. Glad to see you're on the case."

"Well, it's not mutual. What do you want?"

Captain Rallee and I go back a long way. We fought together in the Orc Wars. Along with Gurd, we had some hair-raising times, which I still regale an audience with while drinking in the Avenging Axe. After the war, when I was Senior Investigator at the Palace, Captain Rallee also spent a lot of time there before falling out of favour with Deputy Consul Rittius and finding himself once more pounding the streets. His Guard station down at the harbour is in one of the toughest patches in town, which is saying something. Rallee doesn't mind that's it's rough—he's not the sort of man to flinch from his duty—but he feels a man of his experience should have moved on to something better by now.

Though we were once fairly close and were also both bounced out of the Palace by Rittius, we've grown apart in the past few years. I'm freelance now, and Rallee's a Guard, and these two breeds are never comfortable with each other. The Captain has done me the odd favour and he knows I'm no fool, but finding him on the case is no guarantee of any inside help.

"How's life in the Civil Guard?"

"Better than rowing a slave galley. There again, with you around, maybe not."

I tell him he's looking well, which is true. He carries his age better than I do. His hair hangs down his back in a thick pony tail, as does mine, but his is blond and shining. So is his moustache. Mine is starting to show signs of grey. I imagine the ladies still like him.

The Captain brushes aside my compliment. "You working on this or just poking your nose in for the sake of it?"

"Just earning a living, Captain. Grosex hired me before Tholius got to him."

"The apprentice? He hired you? What with?"

"He paid my standard retainer," I lie.

The Captain snorts and tells me it's well known that Grosex didn't have a penny to his name, never mind a thirty-guran retainer to hire an Investigator.

"So is it true he was having an affair with Drantaax's wife?"

The Captain shrugs. "So they say. Something was making Calia happy anyway, according to the servants."

"Where is he now?"

"Prison. And you're not going to see him. Tholius has him locked up tight and he's not going to risk any of his credit for a quick arrest by letting you interfere. This is bad, Thraxas. The True Church in Turai spent a long time persuading the Niojan Church to help fund the statue. They were going to invite some Niojan clerics down for the inauguration ceremony. Meant to help us get along better I guess. Now the sculptor's dead and the statue's gone. King Lamachus won't like that at all."

"Where's the wife? I need to speak to her."

"You can't."

I'm getting annoyed at this. "What's eating you, Captain? Since when is an Investigator forbidden to talk to a witness?"

"No one's forbidding anything. You can't speak to her because she's missing. Took a hike before we got here."

According to the Captain, Calia sent a servant to alert the Guards after Drantaax's body was found. When they arrived she'd gone.

"No one saw her leave. Calia slipped off amid the confusion. So now we have one dead sculptor, one missing wife and one missing statue."

"The statue is really gone? How could anyone move it?"

The Captain shrugs. "No idea. But it's gone all right. All two tons of it."

"Tholius traced Grosex to my place with a Sorcerer. Can't the Sorcerer find the statue?"

"Apparently not. And no, before you ask, no traces of sorcery were found at the scene. Our men went over the whole place without finding the slightest trace of anything magical. How the statue managed to disappear is a mystery. The servants swear that Drantaax was working on the statue that morning. Drantaax's wife found the body right after he was killed, so there was no time for the statue to disappear. But it did."

"Why is Tholius so sure Grosex did it?"

"Grosex's knife was sticking in the corpse."

"So? That doesn't mean anything. Anyone could have used his knife."

"Maybe. We'll see what our Sorcerer says when he examines the weapon, but I figure he'll find Grosex's aura on it all right. Now, I'm busy. If you don't mind I'll get on with my work."

"I need to see inside."

"Go to hell."

Captain Rallee used to be liaison officer between the Abode of Justice, which controls the Civil Guard, and Palace Security. A nice comfy job, though after many years at the sharp end of crime in Turai he deserved it. Now he's back pounding the streets and he doesn't like it at all. He is rarely in the best of moods.

"Come on, what's the matter? I have a right to go in."

" 'What's the matter?' What's the matter is I have

Prefect Tholius on my tail looking for this one to be wrapped up quickly so we can keep Nioj and the True Church happy and I already have Consul Kalius on my tail about the King's hijacked gold shipment, as well as a million other things, from pilgrims being robbed at the shrine to eight dwa-related killings in Kushni in the past two days. Is that enough for you?"

I make sympathetic noises but point out that as the official representative of Grosex I have a legal right to examine the scene of the crime. The Captain ponders for a while. He doesn't want me inside but, to be fair to him, he's not a man to flout the law.

"Take a look, then. If Tholius appears and chucks you in jail, don't come crying to me."

At this moment, as we are about to enter the house, the call for afternoon prayers rings out from the many towers scattered throughout the city and we are all obliged to kneel with our heads bowed to the ground. There's no avoiding this in Turai. Three times a day we have official prayers and anyone not found kneeling is in trouble with the authorities. So I kneel and pray next to Captain Rallee and the two Guards, which is funny in a way, though often while working I've found myself obliged to pray in far stranger company. I've even found myself fighting an opponent when the call rang out, and been obliged to kneel down beside him, pray, then stand up again and kill him. At least he went to meet his maker well prepared.

The heat is intense and I have to struggle to stay awake. When the call for the end of prayers rings out I drag myself wearily to my feet.

"You're getting slow, Thraxas," says Captain Rallee. "It's time you got off the streets. Try opening a tavern."

"I'd drink myself out of business."

We enter the house, and I quickly get down to examining the scene of the crime under the watchful eye of a Guard who's assigned to follow me and make sure I don't do anything I shouldn't.

Drantaax's house is a standard enough building, a little grander than most but nothing special. If it wasn't for the exquisite statues decorating the rooms, garden and central courtyard it could be the dwelling place of any moderately prosperous businessman. The statues are beautiful though. Even an untrained eye such as mine can tell at a glance that they are of a higher quality than most things you find around our cities temples and libraries.

Drantaax's large workshop is joined on to the back of the house but there isn't much to see at the scene of the crime, other than a faint blood stain where the body was and a large empty space where the statue ought to be. I concentrate to see if I can detect the aura of magic, but I can't. I'm pretty sure none has been used here in the past few days. According to Captain Rallee the statue was definitely here yesterday. It was seen by the Pontifex from the True Church, sent to see how it was progressing.

The statue was a bronze cast. Drantaax carves it out of plaster, then sends it to a foundry who casts it for him and ships it back in six pieces. After that the sculptor puts the pieces together, files it down, makes any final adjustments, and there you are, one bronze statue. Statues of that kind are hollow inside but Drantaax had finished assembling it so it must have weighed a couple of tons, saint, horse and plinth.

And now it's gone. Vanished. No one saw a thing. When the statue was finished it would have taken six men with lifting gear and a specially strengthened cart to move it out. I study the winches at the end of the workshop designed for moving the heavy artifices. A cumbersome process, I'm sure. Not something you could do in a hurry. But someone did shift it, and no one saw a thing. None of the neighbours or any bystander the Guard has been able to trace saw anything unusual in or around the house. A beggar sits across the street every day and he swears that no wagon left the yard on the day of the murder.

"It can't just have disappeared."

Captain Rallee informs me dryly that he'd already worked that out for himself.

"And Old Hasius the Brilliant says no sorcery was involved? Very strange."

Other statues are in the workshop, some still being worked on, others now complete. Fine statues, valuable, I imagine, to a collector. All of them are smaller, some of them only busts that one man could carry. So why did the thief choose to take such a massive thing with him instead? It would be impossible to sell, even in Turai, favoured home of the crooked merchant.

Outside the workshop is a flowerbed where a small sculptured Wood Nymph reclines in a bed of red flowers. The flowers have lasted well in the fierce summer heat, but are now starting to wilt. Petals cover the path, making a small red patch. With a tiny piece of yellow in the middle. I bend down for a closer look. There are a few yellow petals in among the red. I glance at the flowerbed again. None of the flowers there are yellow. Strange. Maybe there were only a few yellow petals and they all fell off? Maybe not. I pick up the yellow petals and place them in the small pouch at my hip I carry for such occasions.

I look around a short while more without learning anything. Captain Rallee tells me he has no leads on the whereabouts of Drantaax's wife. If he knows anything, he isn't saying. He has all three of Drantaax's servants locked up for questioning and there doesn't seem any immediate prospect of me being able to see them. I figure it's time to leave.

I need to see Grosex quickly but as I'm close to the home of Astrath Triple Moon I decide to call in there first. Astrath is a Sorcerer, and a good one, and he might be able to help.

While walking down the street it strikes me that I'm being followed. I can always tell, have an instinct for it. It's part of the sensitivity I developed as a young Sorcerer's Apprentice and it served me well when I was a mercenary. The feeling is still there when I reach Astrath's house. As I ring his bell I quickly look round, but no one is in sight.

A servant leads me into the house which is a great deal smaller than you would expect for the home of a powerful Sorcerer like Astrath Triple Moon. Like me, he's come down in the world. Astrath found himself in trouble a couple of years ago and is lucky to still be in the city at all. He was employed as official Sorcerer at the Stadium Superbius, with responsibility for seeing that all the fights and chariot races were above board and not influenced by magic.

The citizens of Turai are very sensitive about this— no one wants to bet on a chariot and then find it's been hexed—so the resident Sorcerer has an important job. After a series of strange results the word went around that Astrath was taking bribes to turn a blind eye to sorcerous interference. He was in grave danger of a lengthy prison sentence or possibly a public lynching till I dug around a little and cleared his name—well, not exactly cleared his name, as he was in fact guilty as hell, but I muddied the water enough that no proof could be brought to court. Astrath consequently managed to avoid expulsion from the Sorcerers Guild but he was compelled to quit his job. The scandal forced him out of his lavish villa in Thamlin and landed him here in Pashish, ministering to the needs of the poor.

I often ask him for advice. He might have a weakness

for taking bribes but he's sharp as an Elf's ear on all things sorcerous. He's also a generous man with his food and drink, and generally pleased to see me. None of his old buddies in the Sorcerers Guild would come within a mile of him these days, which leaves him short of intelligent conversation.

As I walk in he's already instructing a servant to bring in wine and fruit. His small front room is crammed full of books, potions and other magical paraphernalia and he has to brush several rolls of paper away to make space for the decanter.

"How's life?" I ask.

"Better than rowing a slave galley, but not much. If I have to draw up another horoscope for the local fishwife I swear I'll poison her next catch. Gets me down, Thraxas. The woman has fourteen children and she wants to know everything the future holds for each one of them. How the hell am I meant to know if her seventh daughter is going to make a good marriage?"

He sighs, and pours some wine. We chat for a while about affairs in the city, speculating whether things might improve now Cicerius is Deputy Consul, and if war with Nioj or Mattesh is likely.

"You hear about Drantaax?"

Astrath has. "Fine sculptor. As soon as I heard about it I checked the conjunctions to see if I could learn anything, but they're way off."

Powerful Sorcerers such as Astrath Triple Moon can sometimes look back in time. Fortunately for the criminals of Turai, it's a very difficult feat, and completely impossible if the three moons were in the wrong phases when compared with their current position in the sky. Occasionally the Sorcerers at the Abode of Justice have pulled off a spectacular coup in difficult criminal cases by peering through time and identifying precisely who was there and what happened, but it's a very rare occurrence. Most often the Guards have to pound the streets asking questions, the same as me.

I fill him in on what I know of the case and ask him about the statue. "Any ideas how it could have been moved?"

He strokes his beard. Beards are uncommon in Turai but they're favoured by Sorcerers and a few other guilds, like the Tutors and the Storytellers for instance.

"No sign of magic at all?"

"None. Guards didn't find any and I'd swear nobody had uttered a spell there recently. I might not have made it much past Apprentice Sorcerer but in my line of work you learn to recognise it."

"A good Sorcerer might be able to hide it, Thraxas. Which Guard Sorcerer checked the place out?"

"Old Hasius the Brilliant."

"Old Hasius himself, eh? Must be important if the Guard got him down from the Abode of Justice. Well, that changes things. No Sorcerer could hide all traces of his aura or his spells from Old Hasius. He's a cranky old soul, but he knows his magic. The statue must have been carried out manually."

"Impossible. There wasn't time. It was there in the morning. Various people will swear to it. And Drantaax's workshop is on the main street in Pashish. There is no way that someone wouldn't have seen it being removed on a wagon. It would have taken six men and an hour to load it. Major operation. But no one saw a thing. The statue just vanished. I know that Old Hasius the Brilliant's been scanning the city for it, but he can't find a thing."

Astrath agrees that the whole thing is very odd but can't offer any suggestions. "When it comes right down to it, Thraxas, does it matter to you what happened to the statue? If you just want to clear Grosex of the murder, I mean."

"Good point, Astrath. It might not matter at all if I can find some other angle. But the Prefect has him locked up tight and it's hard to get a lead. I guess if I knew where the statue was I'd probably find out what was behind it all. And it might produce some results for the Guard Sorcerers once they had a good look at the aura."

He agrees to scan the city himself to see if he can come up with anything.

Before I go I ask him if he has any suggestions for preventing a repeat of this morning's debacle where Tholius walked in and took Grosex away.

"An invisibility spell?" he suggests. "Make your client unseeable by the authorities."

"Way beyond me, I'm afraid. I could never get it to work. My powers don't rise much above the sleep spell for knocking out opponents these days."

"Hmm."

He takes his grimoire off a shelf and hunts through the index. "How about this? Temporary bafflement. Simple little spell. Makes anyone searching your rooms very confused indeed. Not foolproof, of course, if you're up against anyone strong-willed enough, but it should be enough of a distraction to let you conceal anyone from nosy Civil Guards."

That sounds like it might work. I thank him, finish up my wine and take my leave. After the coolness of Astrath's house the evening streets are still unbearably hot, and walking home I am followed again. I don't try to shake them, preferring instead to discover their identity, but the culprit is tricky and I fail to get a glimpse of him.

Back at the Avenging Axe Makri has finished her shift and is about to disappear up to her room to study mathematics, which is part of her course at the Guild College. It is Makri's ambition to attend the Imperial

University. This is impossible as the Imperial University does not admit women students. It only admits the sons of Senators or the richest of our merchants, and it is certainly not likely to accept anyone with Orc blood in her veins. Despite this, Makri refuses to be deterred.

"The Guild College didn't want to admit me either," she points out. "And look how well I'm doing there."

"Last week you had a fight with *eight* of your fellow students."

"They insulted my ears."

One consequence of Makri's unusual parentage is that her ears are rather pointed, though as her hair is so long and thick, they're usually hidden from view.

"So? I've insulted your ears plenty of times."

"You're a drunken oaf who doesn't know any better," counters Makri. "Students ought to be polite. Anyway, I wouldn't really call it a fight. Most of them just ran away. And I passed the philosophy exam right afterwards."

I notice that Makri has secreted a few thazis sticks from behind the bar among her sheaf of papers. I take one from her as we walk upstairs.

"Better not let Gurd catch you stealing his thazis."

"He should pay me better. Why wouldn't you help the dolphins?"

"Help the dolphins? You mean work for Dandelion? You must be joking. I'm an Investigator on a murder case. I haven't the time to traipse round after some social misfit with flowers in her hair listening to some so-called talking dolphins bleat about their healing stone. The woman was obviously insane."

Makri laughs. "I liked her."

"Only because you always like people that outrage me."

"Like who?"

"Like Hanama the Assassin, that's who. Woman

damn near killed me and now you go to meetings with her."

This is a slight source of friction between myself and Makri. Makri has become involved with the Association of Gentlewomen, a group formed to advance the rights of women in Turai, which, it must be admitted, are rather limited. Can't join the guilds for one thing, apart from a few specialised ones like the Sorcerers and the Assassins. Can't join the Honourable Association of Merchants either, which puts a serious block on business opportunities and such like. Can't vote, can't sit in the Senate. Nor are they allowed in the luxurious baths and gymnasia up town. Which, I must admit, never troubled me unduly till Makri became involved with the Association and started making a big deal about it.

I'm willing to go along with her views, I guess. It's no skin off my nose. As long as I contribute a guran or two to Makri's collections, it keeps her off my back. However, as I learned to my cost recently, membership of the Association of Gentlewomen has grown alarmingly recently. It would be a great surprise to most citizens of Turai if they knew, for instance, that not only did the Association have the support of the likes of Minarixa the baker and Chiaraxi the herbal healer, but it can count on the covert support of Princess Du-Akai, third in line to the throne. The King certainly won't be amused if he finds that out. Nor will the True Church, who regard the Association as an abomination.

Lisutaris, Mistress of the Sky, a very powerful Sorcerer when she can stay away from her waterpipe, is another supporter. Strangest of all, I'm pretty sure that Hanama, number three in the Assassins Guild, is in there as well. The thought of Makri attending secret meetings with these people makes me worry that possibly some people in the city who shouldn't know my business might occasionally be learning a few things they oughtn't. Not that Makri would ever knowingly betray any of my secrets, of course, but she's only been in the city a year and remains unsophisticated in the ways of civilisation. She sometimes gets cheated in the market. She finds it awkward using cutlery. I can still lie to her and get away with it.

Makri goes off along the corridor to study. I go to sleep.

Next day I'm awake so early I almost catch morning prayers, which I haven't done for years. Despite my prompt start it's a morning of complete frustration. I take a landus up to the prison but I can't get to see Grosex. All prisoners have the legal right to see their representatives, which in this case includes me, but in Turai legal niceties aren't always respected and I'm turned away at the prison with the abrupt news that Grosex is not seeing anyone. When I protest loud and long about it an official asks me to produce evidence that I have in fact been employed by Grosex to investigate his case.

"Prefect Tholius dragged him off before he could write my authorisation."

And that doesn't get me anywhere at all. Obviously the authorities want this wrapped up quickly without the bother of anyone constructing a reasonable defence. Grosex's trial is scheduled for next week and if this situation continues he'll certainly hang. Drantaax was valued by the city, and public opinion is baying for his killer's blood.

I curse my lack of influence with officials in this town. I have plenty of contacts in the underworld, but

since getting booted out of the Palace many powerful doors have been slammed shut.

It strikes me that Cicerius, our new Deputy Consul,
might be willing to go out on a limb for me after the
good service I rendered him recently, but Cicerius is
away on official business in Mattesh, so I am for the
moment stuck.

If I can't see Grosex then I should certainly see
Drantaax's wife but all my enquiries lead nowhere. No
one saw her go and no one has any information as to
where she might be. She has one relative in town, a
brother who works in a warehouse down at the docks.
He can't tell me anything and doesn't seem to care
much. They never got on, apparently.

"Was she having an affair with the apprentice?" I
ask him.

"Probably," he replies, indicating it's time for me to
be on my way. I hang around to be awkward but learn
no more than the fact that we're bringing in a lot of
wheat by ship these days.

I'm interested that Drantaax's wife Calia comes from
a family of dock workers. Means she married above her
class. Drantaax isn't an aristocrat but a successful sculptor
ranks some way above your standard manual labourer.
Everybody in Turai is conscious of such a distinction.

I visit the Guard station when Tholius is away but
Guardsman Jevox doesn't know where Calia is and
doesn't think the Guards have any real leads.

"It can't be that easy for a woman with no family
to hide in the city. Where would she go? The servants
claim she couldn't have taken any money with her. And
why did she disappear?"

"Maybe she killed him so she could set up with the
apprentice," suggests Jevox.

"Well, if she did it was pretty careless to use his
knife and get him hanged as a result."

I wonder about Calia and Grosex. If they were really having an affair it seems strange that she would take to her heels and leave him in the lurch.

Jevox tells me he used to know her when she still lived down by the harbour. He remembers her as a very beautiful young woman.

"No surprise when she married a wealthy sculptor. If she'd held out she could probably have gone even higher."

Jevox is busy. Tholius is giving his men a hard time because Senator Lodius, who leads the opposition party, the Populares, is using the recent wave of crime as a stick to beat the Traditionals with.

"Foreign Ambassadors' houses burgled!" he roars in the Senate. "Gold stolen from the King! Honest citizens murdered in the streets! Dwa spreading like a curse through the city! And what are our representatives doing about this crisis?"

There's more more to the speech, as reported in the *Chronicle*, and it naturally makes every city official from Consul Kalius downwards uncomfortable. Senator Lodius's Populares suffered a slight reverse in the elections a few months back, but he's still a powerful man in the city, capable of causing any amount of problems if he stirs up the mob. So the Civil Guards are all working overtime to try and solve a few outstanding crimes and they're none too pleased about it. I leave Jevox staring glumly at a pile of witness reports concerning a dwa-related murder at the docks. None of the witnesses seem to have seen anything, which is usually the case when powerful dwa gangs commit violence.

If I had something belonging to Calia I might be able to work a spell to locate her but I have nothing. I go back to the sculptor's house but it is now locked tight and guarded and nothing I can say will get me inside. I curse myself for not taking something when I had the chance before. However, the Guards' Sorcerers won't make any progress in this direction either because the moons won't be back in the right conjunction for several months. Grosex can't wait several months.

I complain about this to Astrath Triple Moon.

"Any time I need to find someone in a hurry the moons are in the wrong alignment. Sorcery's a bust when it comes to solving crimes."

"Not always. I've got you some good results in the past."

That's true enough. Anyway, it's just as well sorcery can't solve all the crime in the city, otherwise I'd be out of a job.

Astrath scans the city for the statue, without success. Which seems to make it certain that it's gone far away, but how remains a mystery. Back in the Avenging Axe I complain about my lack of progress to Makri.

"The only thing that's happening is I'm getting followed."

"Followed? Who by?"

"I don't know. Haven't caught so much as a glimpse. But I can feel it."

"Have you tried the kuriya?"

I shake my head. Kuriya, a dark and mysterious liquid, will sometimes yield up a picture in reply to a question, provided the enquirer has been trained in the process. It's something I can still do with reasonable results on occasion, though it completely drains me these days. However, it doesn't always work and the liquid, imported from the far west, is hideously expensive, so I'll only really be able to try it once. I'd rather get information about Grosex than whoever is tailing me. I'll look after them in person when they show their faces.

I finish my lunchtime ale. I can't see Grosex and I can't find any witnesses to what went on and I need to know. I turn my thoughts back to Drantaax's wife Calia. Perhaps the kuriya might give me a hint. Worth trying. I'm not getting anywhere without it.

It takes a long time to put myself into the required mental state. Ideally a Sorcerer should work in a peaceful environment but there is precious little quiet in Twelve Seas at the best of times, with fish vendors, dwa dealers and whores all competing to advertise their wares. Stray dogs growl and fight with each other, children play noisily in the dirt and women shout at the stallholders as they bargain for their cheapest vegetables. Apart from this uproar there's the additional noise of the builders everywhere. It's not easy to sink into a trance. I do my best.

In front of me is a saucer full of the precious black liquid. The one merchant who imports it from the far west claims that it's dragon's blood. This is not true— I've seen dragon's blood—but it gives him a reason to charge such a ridiculous price for it. Whatever its origins, it can respond to the searching mind of a skilled Sorcerer. And even me, though I never made it much past Apprentice.

I've drawn the curtains and illuminated my room with a large red candle. The shiny black liquid reflects the light. I concentrate on the flame, and think about Drantaax's wife, and where she might be.

For a while, nothing happens. Almost long enough to think that nothing will happen. I stay in my trance. Time passes. The room goes cold and I can no longer hear the noise outside. Finally a picture starts to form: a house, a large house, a white villa on a wooded hill.

I'm straining to see more clearly when my concentration is affected by a tiny nagging feeling of unease. I don't know what it is. I ignore it. It won't go away.

I try and concentrate on the picture, but it's slipping. Deep in my trance, I realise that someone is in my room. A bolt of fear shoots through me, the horrible terror of being helpless in front of an enemy. I emerge from the trance with a frightened roar, leaping to my feet confused and disorientated and whirling round frantically to see who's there. My vision spins crazily for a second and then focuses sharply on two figures just yards from where I was kneeling. One of them is engaged in going through the papers on my desk while the other one keeps look-out. They're both wearing red robes. They both have shaven heads. Monk burglars?

"Who the hell are you?" I roar.

They turn and head for the door. I leap after them and grab the nearest one by the shoulder, spinning him round.

"What's going on?"

He pulls away. Still shocked by the interruption to my trance, I have even less patience than usual. I let fly with a blow that should send the monk through the wall. He blocks it. I'm surprised. I try again. He blocks it again, automatically, with no apparent effort. When I aim a third clubbing blow at his face he touches my arm and I find myself facing the other way, God knows how. Then I'm propelled across the room by a mighty slap between the shoulder blades. I bounce into the far wall and crumple on to the floor.

Makri charges in and finds me lying confused and disorientated. She rushes to the outside door, but there's no one in sight. My assailants have departed as swiftly and mysteriously as they appeared.

"Who was it?" asks Makri, helping me to my feet.

"Just two warrior monks out for a little fun," I gasp, and sink down on the couch, exhausted from looking in the kuriya. Having to confront two warrior monks on top of that is way too much.

"What are warrior monks?"

"Monks who are also warriors. They spend half their time in prayer and meditation, and the other half learning how to fight. Excuse me, Makri, I have to lie down."

My head swims. The blow winded me. I lie on my couch till it clears. Makri brings me a beer and I start getting back into the real world.

"Damn them. I was just starting to get a picture when they arrived."

I strive to remember what the house in the kuriya pool was like. A villa on a wooded hill. Could be any one of a number of places up on the edges of the rich suburb of Thamlin where the land rises up towards the Palace. But it might be somewhere else—another city even.

"No, Calia couldn't have made it so far away. If she'd taken passage on a ship the Guards would have heard about it. And I don't believe she galloped off on a horse. Rallee tells me they've made a thorough check on everyone who hired out horses that day. Checked the trading caravans leaving the city as well."

Makri wonders why the Guards are so keen. "They're taking a lot of trouble over this, aren't they? For a run-of-the-mill murder?"

"Perhaps. But Senator Lodius is making speeches about the city going to ruin again, so the Guards are working flat out to try and prove they're not the waste of space he accuses them of being. Poor Jevox was looking forward to a week's holiday and instead he's up to his eyebrows in witness statements and is consequently about as miserable as a Niojan whore about everything. The Guards need to do a good job on Drantaax and reckon they're off to a flying start having actually arrested someone so quickly. They won't want to risk messing up the trial of his killer."

I ought to get up to Thamlin and see if I can find that villa. Damn those monks for interrupting.

Gurd knocks and pokes his head round the door.

"Makri," he says, "you should be working. And Thraxas, there's someone downstairs to see you."

"Who?"

"I think her name was Dandelion."

"Tell her I've gone out," I say, rising hastily. "Important investigating. Stop looking at me like that, Makri. I am not going to look for the dolphins' healing stone that fell from the sky, and that's final. If you're so concerned, take Dandelion to one of your Association of Gentlewomen meetings. They'll sort her out."

I grab a sword, pick up some money to buy a loaf of bread at Minarixa's bakery, and head on out.

As soon as I hit the street I know I'm being followed. I frown. I'm getting fed up with this. I jump in a landus and instruct the driver to take me to Thamlin quickly. He does his best, but, with all the construction work, the potholes in the roads and the market traffic, we move slowly and I fail to shake off my tail. I regret not dealing with this earlier.

Thamlin is a different world to the filth of Twelve Seas. Here the streets are clean and paved with pale green and yellow tiles. The luxurious villas stand behind leafy gardens and white walls manned by members of the Securitus Guild. Civil Guards patrol the streets in numbers, keeping them safe from the rabble. No one disturbs the calm. Even the stals, the small black birds which infest the city, look better fed. Anyone wandering up here to do a little begging is soon chased away so as not to disturb the peace of our aristocracy.

I used to live here. Now I'm about as welcome as an Orc at an Elvish wedding.

Having no particularly good idea as to where to start my search I halt the landus in Truth is Beauty Lane, where the Sorcerers live, and stroll on up the gentle slope towards the wooded area adjoining the grounds of the Imperial Palace. All around me are houses similar to the one I saw in the kuriya pool. I strain to recall any distinctive features but nothing comes to mind. Just another luxurious villa where the occupants can lie around in the shade drinking wine from their own vineyards and eating fish from their private ponds. I frown. A fine piece of investigation this is turning out to be.

I notice a Guard standing outside one of the smaller villas set back from the road. No one else is in sight, no servants trimming the lawns or tending to the flower beds. It strikes me that it is very probably the house of Thalius Green Eye, the recently killed Sorcerer.

It's nothing to do with me. I should stay away. So I wander over for a look. The Guard isn't paying much attention to anything. He doesn't notice me slipping over the small wall and into the garden. I don't know why I'm doing this. Just naturally curious about Sorcerers being murdered, I guess.

The gardens are well tended but empty. Presumably all of the dead Sorcerer's servants are still in custody, answering questions about their knowledge of poisons. I walk swiftly through some tall trees till I reach a small ornamental pond at the back of the house. Unlike some of our wealthier residents, Thalius didn't keep it stocked with fish. A well-stocked fish pond is a big status symbol in Turai; an aristocratic matron couldn't ask a member of the Royal Family to dinner unless she could produce a first course from her own private source. Takes some money to maintain though.

I'm now close to the back door, painted yellow with a small statue of Saint Quatinius at each side. Yellow is regarded as the luckiest colour to paint your back door in Turai. The front one should be white.

Virtually everyone falls into line on this one. Even if you're not superstitious, why tempt fate?

I'm closing in on the door when a noise inside sends me hurrying to hide behind a large bush. Another noise from behind sends me deeper into the undergrowth. I watch with interest bordering on amazement. First, the back door opens and out come three shaven-headed and red-robed monks, very quietly indeed. They glide through the portal warily, checking that they are unobserved before moving off towards the far end of the grounds. They are not unobserved, however, because from the undergrowth behind me emerge four other monks, equally shaven-headed but garbed in yellow. They immediately rush at the first group and attack them without warning.

The silence is broken as battle is joined, and a very athletic battle it is too. People talk of the fighting prowess of warrior monks but I've never seen such a demonstration myself. I watch in astonishment as kicks fly head high and crunching blows send opponents spinning great distances over the lawn, until the recipients of these blows leap athletically to their feet and run back into the fray. Most of the blows are accompanied by peculiarly intense shouts so the whole neighbourhood must surely hear what is going on.

It doesn't take long for the Civil Guard from the front of the house to arrive. When he sees the seven warring monks he wisely decides not to get involved, but blows a piercing whistle to summon help.

Hearing this, the monks disengage. They eye each other with hatred, then the uninjured help the wounded and they make off in different directions. Again, they display great agility in leaping over walls and various other obstacles between themselves and freedom.

More Civil Guards will arrive at any second. I just

have time to make my escape. I ought to get as far away from here as I can. So instead I walk over to the back door and step inside. I'm a fool sometimes. My overwhelming curiosity—or nosiness—has landed me in trouble since the day I was born.

At least there's some relief in here from the baking sun outside. I sluice some water over my neck from the pitcher in the kitchen, and head on into the house. In the first room I enter—a wide, white, calm room with pastel tapestries on the walls—I meet a young woman with a knife in her hand who challenges me in a spirited manner and attempts a vicious slash at my belly before she trips over the empty bottle of klee at her feet and falls down in a drunken heap on the floor.

Another unexpected development. I frown. I'm sure Thalius wasn't married, yet she's wearing a toga suitable for the woman of the house. Must be his daughter.

She looks up from the floor and demands to know what I'm doing here.

"Investigating the death of Thalius," I lie.

"You're not a Guard." She climbs unsteadily to her feet. "Just as well. Guards won't get anywhere finding out who killed my father. Guards are as much use as a eunuch in a brothel."

I'm surprised to hear this expression spoken in her cultured voice. She reaches for another bottle of klee on the shelf behind her. She's already had more than enough but I figure it's none of my business so I don't try and stop her. I think I can hear noises outside suggesting more Guards have arrived.

"The Guards will be here any moment. I'm an Investigator. I'll help you if you tell me about it."

It comes out sounding sincere. It might even be sincere. I'm feeling kind of sorry for her, drunk and alone with her father freshly buried.

"What's to tell?"

"Who killed your father?"

"His dwa dealer, I suppose."

This takes me completely by surprise. Not the fact that Thalius Green Eye took dwa—that's common enough among all classes of people and Sorcerers seem particularly prone to it. But there was no mention of any drug connection in the reports of the killing.

"I thought he was poisoned by a servant."

She laughs, stupidly, drunkenly. "So they say. Didn't want another drug scandal to rock the Palace. Too many already. My father wasn't poisoned. He was killed by a crossbow bolt. Couldn't pay the dwa dealer."

There are footsteps outside as the Civil Guards enter the house.

"Hire me to find the killer," I say, urgently, but it's too late. At the same moment as she falls unconscious to the floor the Guards enter the room led by Prefect Galwinius himself, their chief in Thamlin.

Prefect Galwinius knows me well. He dislikes me just as much as Prefect Tholius does. More, possibly. He takes one look at her outstretched body before ordering my immediate arrest and I am loaded into a wagon and carted off to jail.

It's not unusual for me to be carted off to jail in the course of an investigation but when I reflect that I have been carted off this time because of something I wasn't even investigating, I wonder if even at my stage of life it might not be too late to curb my natural inquisitiveness.

The worst thing about being in jail is the heat. And the smell. And you can't get a beer. The company's always bad as well. There's plenty wrong with being in jail.

I'm sitting in a small cell with a fellow prisoner who won't say a word and lies on his bunk looking miserable as a Niojan whore. It's actually a relief when the prayer call rings out. Gives me something to do.

My requests to the Guards for the legal representation to which I am entitled are routinely ignored. I don't actually have my own lawyer (though in my line of business I should), but as a citizen of Turai the state is meant to provide me with a Public Defender. They don't. It's well into the evening before anyone official pays me any attention at all. Two Guards thrust the door open and take me along a corridor into an interview room where Deputy Prefect Prasius is sitting stony faced behind a desk.

I'm moderately pleased to see Prasius. He doesn't like me any better than the Prefect, but he's not quite as stupid. He's younger than his boss Galwinius, and well spoken, as you would expect. You don't get promoted or elected into official posts in Turai unless

you're well born and your name ends in the aristocratic '-ius'. A name like Thraxas marks you out as
low born. There is no legal reason why a man from
the lower classes can't be elected to high office, but
the aristocrats have the Senate pretty much sewn up
with money and patronage and it's extremely rare for
a new man to break through.

"So, Thraxas. You want to tell us what you were
doing in Thalius's house?"

"You want to tell me where my Public Defender is?"

Prasius looks round at his Guards. "He wants to
know where his Public Defender is. Anyone seen his
Public Defender?"

The Guards shake their heads, which makes the
fancy tassels on the shoulders of their tunics sway back
and forward.

"Looks like no one's seen him."

"I've a right to representation."

"You've a right to shut up about lawyers and start
answering questions. Now, what were you doing in
Thalius's house? And why did you attack his daughter Soolanius?"

I lean forward and stare at him.

"Prasius. Is it a qualification for every official in this
city that they have to be as dumb as an Orc? Do you
really think you can intimidate me? Go to hell. Bring
me my representative, and I might talk. Or I might
not. Depends how I feel. Meanwhile, you better just
take me back to the cell. If you want to keep holding me illegally, then do it. I'll expect a fat payment
when I haul you through the law courts."

This is not the way to talk to the Deputy Prefect
if you want to get out of jail, but I'm damned if I'll
ever knuckle under to these people. I'm taken back to
my cell. My fellow prisoner is still lying on his bunk
and he doesn't look any happier.

Later on I pay a Guard to give me today's copy of *The Renowned and Truthful Chronicle of All the World's Events*. There's nothing much in it unless you happen to be interested in the current leading scandal about the Senator's wife and the Army Captain, which I'm not. And the editor spends some time lambasting the Civil Guard for its inefficiency in not being able to find a two-ton statue. The statue of Saint Quatinius was meant to be dedicated at an important religious ceremony next month, attended by delegates from various other city-states. The paper fulminates over the fact that anyone could fail to find such an enormous object, and hints strongly that bribery and corruption must be involved. Fair enough, although I haven't had any more success than the Guards, and no one's bribing me.

Twelve Seas gets a mention on the back page, with a small news item on the burning down of one of our local taverns, the Boar's Head, and the death in the fire of the landlord, Trinex.

Lousy tavern, the Boar's Head, full of dwa dealers and exotic dancers. I won't miss it at all. I never liked Trinex either. The tavern was run by the Brotherhood and Trinex was a member of their organisation, which makes the affair interesting. The Brotherhood doesn't like it when one of their money-making establishments gets burned down. Very bad for business.

I'm used to being in a cell—it's happened to me enough times—so it doesn't particularly bother me, but it's frustrating to know that I've got nowhere with Grosex and time is running short. After doing the standard magical tests the Guard Sorcerer detected Grosex's aura on the knife. Only his aura, no one else's. And that's enough to convince the Guards and probably a jury that the apprentice killed the sculptor. The city law courts can push through a capital case in five days if they have the inclination. Unless I find out who really killed Drantaax then Grosex could be hanged in less than a week. And when I'm freed I'll be no further on really. I can't recognise the white villa the kuriya pool showed me. Even if I could there's no guarantee that Drantaax's wife would be there. I seem to be drawing a blank on this one.

I mull over what happened at the house of the Sorcerer Thalius. Even though I have no involvement in the case it's a curious chain of events. Why was it said that he was poisoned by a servant, when his daughter says he was murdered by a dwa dealer? And was he really killed by a crossbow bolt? That's a very unusual weapon in Turai. It's illegal to carry one inside the city walls. Although I recently encountered a very deadly crossbow killer named Sarin the Merciless who had some involvement in the dwa trade. I wonder if she might be back in Turai? I'd be interested to meet her again. She's a wanted woman and I'm always keen to collect a little reward money.

Most interesting of all, in view of my recent experiences, is the appearance of the monks. What were they doing there? Connected with the dwa trade? That wouldn't be a surprise. Practically everyone else in the city brushes up against dwa since it took over so many people's lives. But it could be something else entirely. Maybe Thalius had some religious artefact they wanted? But Thalius was strictly a small-time Sorcerer, unlikely to be in possession of anything very important. Maybe they just came to get their horoscopes read.

I wonder who the two groups were and why they were fighting. It's an odd coincidence that one day I find two strange monks burgling my rooms and the next thing you know there are monks slugging it out on the lawns in Thamlin. I speculate on what I might have blundered into, but I can't think of anything to fit the facts. I don't know much about warrior monks. There again, who does?

I spend the night in the cells. The next day it's hot as Orcish hell. The food is not what I'd call fit for humans and I'm desperate for a beer. I'm about to vent my frustration by kicking the door when it opens and Thalius's daughter walks in. She's steadier on her feet but I can tell she's been drinking. I'm not a man who'd condemn her for it. If you can't have a drink when your father gets murdered, when can you?

"Thraxas. They tell me you really are an Investigator. I thought you were another crook."

She'd woken up from her prolonged drinking bout to find her house being searched by monks in red robes. Naturally this was disconcerting. She apologises for trying to stab me and I wave it away.

"Finding monks burgling your house is enough to unsettle anyone. Believe me, I know."

She gets to the point quickly. The Guards are getting nowhere with the death of her father and she wants to hire me.

I glance round at my cellmate. He seems to be sleeping but I don't want to discuss anything in front of him. It's not beyond the intelligence of Deputy Prefect Prasius to have put one of his own men in here to spy on me.

"I'll take the job, but we can't discuss it here. You'll have to get me out of this cell first."

She takes a small flask from her bag and sips from it. She's a pretty young woman, with a mass of dark hair and striking green eyes. Pretty enough to compliment were I not too old, overweight and generally washed up to be handing out compliments to young women.

"Can I get you out?"

"Sure. Just tell the Deputy Prefect I was in your

house by your invitation. They don't have anything else to hold me on."

This goes smoothly enough. Deputy Prefect Prasius makes me wait while he consults with Galwinius. They don't like it at all, but if Soolanis says she invited me in there's nothing they can do about it. I wasn't committing any other crime. Eventually a Guards Sorcerer accompanies us to the front entrance where he utters the necessary spell to open the door. I walk out into the scorching sunlight.

"I need a beer."

So does Soolanis. We stop off in a tavern on the edge of Thamlin, a higher-class establishment than I would normally frequent. The landlord looks at me suspiciously but seems reassured by the presence of the obviously well-bred Soolanis until she starts knocking back glasses of klee in a manner quite unbecoming to a lady. Eventually I have to bundle her back into a landus and we head south.

Turning into Quintessence Street we pass the still smouldering ruins of the Boar's Head. Not a timber is left standing. Whoever set it alight did a good job, not that it's too hard to start a fire among rickety wooden buildings of Twelve Seas dried out by the fierce summer sun. Fire is a continual danger in the city. It's probably only because the space beside the tavern had already been cleared prior to reconstruction that there wasn't a far larger conflagration. Casax, the local Brotherhood boss, and Ixkar, a senior official in the Innkeepers Guild, are standing next to the ruins, grim-faced. They don't look like they're discussing plans for a summer outing. I wouldn't like to be the arsonist when they get hold of him.

Soolanis is half asleep as we ride to the Avenging Axe. She only makes it up the outside stairs with some difficulty. Once inside she slumps on to my couch and falls fast asleep. I stare at her with some frustration. She might at least have stayed awake long enough to pay me my retainer.

I have a large jug of water in my bedroom. I walk through to throw some on my face. The jug is empty and there's a young whore asleep in my bed. I know she's a whore because of the red ribbons in her hair. I've never seen her before.

I go looking for Makri. Makri comes looking for me and we meet at my door. She glances at Soolanis, sprawled out on my couch.

"You finally found a girlfriend who drinks as much as you."

"Very amusing. Who the hell is that in my bed?"

"In your bed? Right. That'll be Quen, I expect. She's a whore."

"I know she's a whore. I saw the ribbons. Is this some kind of joke?"

Makri shifts a little uncomfortably. "I wasn't expecting you back just yet. I thought you might be longer in prison . . ."

I explode. "Damn help you are, Makri. Other people might do something like finding me a lawyer to get me out of jail. Not you. You fill my room with whores and hope I won't be back for a while. Get her out of there!"

"I can't," wails Makri, and starts to look distressed. "Everyone's after her."

"Who's everyone?"

"The Guards. And the Brotherhood. And the Innkeepers Guild."

A horrible suspicion starts to form in my mind. "You don't mean she . . ."

Makri nods. "She burned down the Boar's Head. But she didn't mean to kill the landlord. She was just teaching him a lesson."

"Well she certainly taught him a good one. Okay,

now I know who she is. I still don't know what she's doing here."

"She just turned up. In a panic. She was looking for me. We met before, at a meeting."

I gaze at Makri with horror. "You knew her before? And she came into the downstairs bar? She just walked in after burning down the Boar's Head only a hundred yards away? And you led her up here? Why didn't you just put up a big sign saying *Wanted: arsonist hiding in Thraxas's room*? Get her out of here this second!"

"But she's safe here."

"She is far from safe. The Brotherhood has eyes everywhere. God knows how many people will have seen her come in here. And even if no one did, the Brotherhood will use a Sorcerer. Ten to one Casax has one of them working on it now."

Makri was unaware that the Boar's Head was owned by the Brotherhood. She realises that it makes it more serious. Not that it would be any light matter if it was just Civil Guards and the Innkeepers Guild in pursuit. Like most guilds, the innkeepers have some powerful connections.

"What can we do to help her?"

"You can do what you like, Makri. I'm doing nothing. Just get her out of here. And quickly."

"But the landlord assaulted her!"

"I sympathise. It must be a hard life as an exotic dancer. Now, are you going to get rid of her or do I have to throw her out myself?"

Gurd rattles the door and sticks his head in. "Thraxas. The Guards are downstairs looking for you. You want me to stall them?"

I nod. He departs.

There's a fierce banging at my outside door.

"Thraxas," comes a voice I wish I didn't recognise. "It's Casax. I need to talk to you."

Well, that's fine. The Guards are downstairs and the local Brotherhood boss is outside. I glare at Makri with loathing. She shrugs, and draws a long knife from her boot.

"Got an axe anywhere?"

One thing you can't take away from Makri, she's always prepared to make her death stand. Personally, I need a little more notice.

"Stall him," I say, and start rummaging in my bag for the spell of bafflement I borrowed from Astrath Triple Moon.

Casting a spell for the first time is no simple matter. It takes time, thought and preparation. However, with Gurd holding off the Guards downstairs and Makri stalling Casax by pretending she doesn't speak the language very well, there's no time for any of that. I just drag out the scroll, hurry into my bedroom and chant it out over the sleeping form of Quen. Nothing happens, not even the customary cooling of the surrounding air when magic is used, so whether it's worked or not is anybody's guess. By the time I get back to my office Prefect Tholius is clumping through the inside door with six Guards in his trail and a very angry Casax is confronting Makri at the steps with some of his brutes.

Casax, the boss of the Brotherhood in Twelve Seas, is new to the job. He was Yubaxas's number two and took over the leadership when Yubaxas was killed a couple of months ago by the Society of Friends, the Brotherhood's rivals, who run the north of the city. Casax is keen to assert his authority and he is not pleased to have been kept waiting.

"Who is this squeeze that doesn't speak the language?" he demands, which makes Makri frown. Being called a squeeze is not something she enjoys.

"It's his Orcish friend," says Karlox. Karlox is a

Brotherhood enforcer, a massive man, stupid, aggressive and hostile. Casax, no angel himself, stares round the room suspiciously.

Prefect Tholius meanwhile is unsure of how to proceed. As Prefect of the Twelve Seas, he should in theory be in charge here but he knows that in practice he can't order Casax around. Wishing neither to offend the Brotherhood boss nor to acknowledge his inferiority to Casax, the Prefect looks perplexed.

Casax is far from confused. He's a dangerous character and looks it: large, muscular, never known to smile. He's around forty, with long black hair tied back neatly in a braid, a plain brown tunic and a large gold hoop dangling from each ear. Unlike some gang bosses he doesn't go in for ostentation and apart from the earrings he wears no jewellery. His sword is sheathed in a plain black scabbard. He rose through the ranks of the Brotherhood, which doesn't happen unless you're smart and ruthless.

"We're looking for a woman named Quen."

"Never heard of her. You know anyone called Quen, Makri?"

Makri shakes her head. She has her knife in her hand and she's madder than a mad Sorcerer about Karlox calling her an Orc. It wouldn't take too much now for her to attack them all and damn the consequences. If they find Quen and try to take her away, she certainly will.

Casax signals and his followers start searching. The Brotherhood boss greets Prefect Tholius without showing much respect, and enquires what brings him here.

"We are also seeking the woman called Quen. On a charge of murder and arson."

Casax grunts. "After we've got hold of her there won't be much left for a trial."

"Who is this?" demands Tholius, motioning to Soolanis, still slumbering peacefully on the couch.

"A client."

"Your clients always sleep in here?"

"Only when they get tired."

The Brotherhood men enter my bedroom, followed by two Civil Guards. My heart is pounding. I mentally snarl a curse at Makri. If she had to bring a murderer and arsonist here, why did it have to be one who'd offended so many important people? Between the Brotherhood and the Civil Guards, I'm finished in this city. Things couldn't be worse if I'd challenged the King to single combat. Rivers of sweat drench my body.

I conceal my nerves. I've no more desire than Makri to bow down to these people. The Brotherhood might be stronger than me but I'm never going to treat its thugs with respect. I grab a bottle of klee from my cupboard and take a hefty slug, then offer it to Makri as if there was nothing wrong at all.

Casax is staring at me. "You drink too much, fat man."

"Is that so?"

The searchers emerge from the bedroom. One of the Brotherhood men starts to speak but seems to forget how to. The other does it for him.

"In sir no one."

"What the hell d'you mean, "In sir no one"?" rasps Casax, scowling.

The man shakes his head. "I mean no one in there, sir."

One of the Civil Guards nods in agreement.

"Search the rest of the tavern," orders Casax. Prefect Tholius instructs his men to do the same.

What do you know? The spell of bafflement worked. No stranger entering the room can find Quen.

Casax strides over to confront me. He towers over

me. His skin is bad. "If you're hiding the whore, you're in big trouble, Thraxas. She burned down one of our places. Killed one of my men. The Brotherhood can't allow that sort of thing to happen."

"But you can allow one of your men to seriously assault a young woman," says Makri, striding over in turn to confront Casax. He shrugs.

"Part of the job."

"Really? I work in a bar too. Try sending some of your men over here to assault me." Makri's eyes narrow slightly. She's still gripping her knife. Casax is surprised to find himself confronted by a young woman, but unperturbed.

"I've heard of you. You must be Makri. Part Human. Part Elf. Part Orc. You got pointed ears under all that hair?"

"Why don't you take a look?" says Makri, who would certainly gut him if he tried.

Casax grins. "I hear you're a good fighter. Very good with a blade. But don't get ideas above your station. You're wasting your talents here, you know. Come and work for me. Earn you a lot more money. Maybe pay for the University."

Karlox guffaws at the idea of Makri going to University, but I'm not entirely sure that Casax's offer isn't serious.

Makri looks slightly disconcerted to learn that Casax knows so much about her. She doesn't reply. She keeps her knife in her hand and her attention on her enemies.

"Sorcerer traced the whore to this tavern, Thraxas."

"Maybe he was mistaken. The Brotherhood don't use magic often, do they?"

"We use it when we have to. Now, where is she?"

"I've never seen her."

Annoyance flickers over the Boss's face. After the search of the tavern produces no results there is a moment of tension while he stares at us as if making up his mind whether to order his thugs to attack us there and then. He decides against it.

Before leaving Casax informs us that we will be under surveillance and if we are found to be sheltering Quen then he'll kill us. He says this quite matter-of-factly.

"No doubt Prefect Tholius will protect me with the full weight of the law," I suggest.

The Prefect leaves without saying anything.

When they've all left Makri thanks me for helping and apologises for landing me in this mess. I wave it away. I'm too worn out to be angry any more.

"Anyway, it's good to put one over on the Brotherhood. It bugs me the way they're always going round like they're number one chariot around here."

"I thought they were."

"Well it annoys me anyway."

Soolanis has slept though all of this and shows no sign of coming to life. I explain who she is to Makri, and wonder out loud what we're going to do with Quen. We certainly can't move her right now, yet it is very unsafe for her to stay. My bafflement spell isn't going to fool a prying Sorcerer for long, though it's true that the Brotherhood generally rely on muscle and fear rather than magic and may not be using a top-class Wizard.

"Incidentally, Makri, why did you put her in my bed? Wouldn't she be more comfortable in your room?"

Before Makri can answer the door opens. Dandelion appears.

"Did you persuade him yet?" she says.

"There wasn't room," explains Makri. "I, eh . . . said Dandelion could stay for a while."

I groan. Dandelion starts talking about dolphins but I'm already on my way downstairs.

"A beer, Gurd, and quickly."

"Trouble with the Brotherhood?" says Gurd, seeing the shaky state I'm in.

"I can cope with the Brotherhood," I tell him. "It's the sisterhood that's getting to me."

I need to send a message to Astrath Triple Moon to see if we can do anything to boost the spell of bafflement to keep Quen hidden till we decide what to do about her. I can't go myself. Walking straight out of here and round to a friendly Sorcerer would be a sure sign of what I was up to. The same goes for Makri, and anyway she doesn't want to miss her afternoon lecture in rhetoric. Gurd and Tanrose can't leave the bar and Palax and Kaby are out busking on the streets. Which is the sum total of people I can trust.

"Dandelion could go," suggests Makri.

I let forth some abuse about Dandelion, pointing out that a woman who walks around Turai in bare feet with flowers in her hair is likely to be as much use as a one-legged gladiator when it comes to practical matters.

"She casts horoscopes for dolphins, for God's sake."

"The Brotherhood won't suspect her."

True enough. We send Dandelion with the message.

"You know, Makri, two days ago I was sitting here without a care in the world. How did all this happen?"

"You got annoyed because Prefect Tholius dragged Grosex out of your room."

So I did. Foolish of me. I didn't need to do anything. Wasn't even hired to do anything. And now I'm looking for a two-ton statue and trying to find the wife of a murdered sculptor. Which led me into the affair of Thalius Green Eye and his inebriated daughter, again entirely my own fault.

"But Quen was nothing to do with me. You landed me in that one. What did the landlord do to her anyway?"

Makri doesn't want to go into details, though she seems satisfied that burning down his tavern and him in the process was a reasonable act of retaliation. She's hopeful that if she can protect her from her immediate danger then some of the more powerful women in the Association of Gentlewomen will look after her, maybe providing funds for her to leave Turai and set up somewhere else.

Soolanis finally wakes just as Makri is taking her leave, wrapped in the large cloak she is obliged to wear at the Guild College. Her chainmail bikini proved to be far too distracting for young students and old professors alike, and even her man's tunic showed off too much of her legs, apparently.

"What's the matter with these people?" complains Makri. "If it's not one thing it's another. Now I have to sit at the back of the class wrapped up like a mummy just because they can't concentrate on the lesson."

Soolanis needs a drink. I pass her some water. If she wants to drink herself to death that's her affair, but I need her to stay sober long enough to tell me some details of the case. She drinks the water with the same lack of enthusiasm I might show in the same circumstances.

"Where did you get that?" she asks abruptly, rising to her feet and pointing at Makri's purse.

"I took it from the neck of a man I killed."

"It's my father's," says Soolanis. "It has his name embroidered on it."

I study the purse. And indeed, the name of Thalius Green Eye is embroidered in tiny letters in one of the arcane magic languages normally reserved for spells. It's something I should have spotted earlier, though the writing is very small and intertwined with the rest of the needlework.

Soolanis is highly agitated. Myself, I'm puzzled. What's the connection between the man who walked into the bar and tried to kill me, and Thalius Green Eye?

I ask Makri to leave the purse behind, and she does so. Quen is still sleeping in my bedroom. I leave her be for the moment, but when night comes she's going to have to go and struggle for space in Makri's room. I surrender my bed for no one. And I don't share it with anyone, either.

"All right, Soolanis. Tell me everything you know about your father's death."

Soolanis tells me that Thalius was always in trouble with money. He was a minor figure at the Imperial Palace, outshone by the talents of the other Sorcerers, and even his business of drawing up horoscopes for lesser aristocrats was on the wane. It's expensive living in Thamlin and the upkeep of his villa in Truth is Beauty Lane soon led him into debt.

"He didn't know where to turn. So he turned to dwa."

The dwa made him forget his problems but the natural consequence was that his problems worsened. Less work, more expense. He couldn't even face going to the Palace unless he was full of dwa, and when he made it there he was in no state to draw up a horoscope.

"After a while it took over his life."

I get the impression that somewhere at that time drink took over for Soolanis. When the neighbours started talking about Thalius she found it almost impossible to face the world without fortifying herself.

Despite the poor state Thalius was reduced to, he was never forbidden to enter the Palace, which suggests that he might have been taking something there that someone important wanted quite badly. Prince Frisen-Akan has already been in trouble because of his liking for dwa.

"You think your father was killed because he couldn't pay his dealer?"

"Probably. That's what happens, isn't it?"

She claims not to know who his dealer was. Because Thalius was killed by a crossbow I question her about Sarin the Merciless, but the name doesn't ring a bell and she doesn't recognise my description of her. For the past four months she's been so obliterated by alcohol that she can't recollect much of what's been going on around her.

She looks sadly at the small purse. "He liked this. Never let it out of his sight. Do you have any wine?"

I shake my head. I never developed a taste for it. I take her a beer, which serves just as well.

"I'd say it was unusual for a Sorcerer to be killed over a dwa debt. Not impossible, but the dealer would rather have the money, and there must have been stuff in the house your father could have sold. Unless it wasn't just a small debt for his own dwa. Perhaps he owed much more. Was he dealing himself?"

The thought of her father actually dealing dwa brings tears to Soolanis's eyes. She admits that it's possible, but she doesn't know.

I muse on these things. If Thalius was a rather larger player in dwa than his daughter realised it might explain why the Guards have covered up the facts of the case. Drug scandals have already come too close to the Palace, particularly in the person of Prince Frisen-Akan, and the authorities wouldn't want any more trouble. Consul Kalius has already had to hide the Prince's shortcomings from the public. The politics of Turai are in a perpetually fragile state and Senator Lodius, the leader of the anti-royalist Populares, is always quick to pounce on any scandal he can use for his own ends.

Prince Frisen-Akan is keen on dwa and I have no doubt that he's not the only one among his circle who is. If Thalius Green Eye was supplying them it would explain why he wasn't thrown out of the Palace and also how he might have accrued enough debts to get himself killed. Taking a shipment of dwa and failing to make the payment is a stupid thing to do, but it happens surprisingly often, with inevitable results.

I'm considering the possibilities of Thalius taking dwa into the Palace when an odd thought occurs. Why was he so fond of the purse? This one is nothing special. All sort of things can have sentimental value, but I don't recall meeting anyone who was overly attached to their purse.

I study it. It's small and the top fastens with two drawstrings, the sort of thing for holding a few gurans. No room for anything else. I mutter a word in the old Sorcerers" language, a common word for commanding something to open. I sense a fractional cooling in the air. I draw on the two strings and the purse opens, and keeps opening. It opens an impossible amount.

Soolanis gapes in astonishment as I draw the small mouth of the purse further and further apart till it eventually reaches the length of my outstretched arms.

"What is it?" she asks, disconcerted by the impossibility of what she's seeing.

"The magic space," I reply. "Or rather an opening

into the magic space. Another dimension, whatever that means. This is no ordinary purse. It's a magic pocket."

I look into the large hole I have now opened. My face goes cold as it nears the interface between the normal world and the magic space. Inside everything is tinged with a purple hue and my eyes take a while to adjust.

Anything put in magic space to all intents and purposes will lose all weight and volume. Which would be a very handy way for a Sorcerer to take a large bag of dwa into the Palace for instance. My eyes adjust to the odd light. I reach down, stretching my whole arm into the purse. Anyone looking on would think that my limb was vanishing into thin air. I'm expecting my fingers to settle in soft-powdered dwa. Instead they encounter something hard, cold and metallic. I take my hand out and look again. It's a head. A bronze head. With a body attached. And it's sitting on a horse.

I withdraw my head from the magic space and look at the purse in my hand. Even for a man who's used to magic, it is very strange to realise that I am at this moment holding a two-ton statue of Saint Quatinius right in the palm of my hand.

"Well, that explains a lot," I mutter.

I'm fairly pleased with myself. The Guards are looking all over the city for this. Sorcerers at the Abode of Justice have been hunting for it. And I've found it. Which, I believe, means a handsome reward is now owing to me. Well done, Thraxas. Not only have you found the statue, you've enabled the religious ceremony to go ahead and also smoothed over a very awkward breakdown in relations between Turai and Nioj. They might even give you a medal.

More importantly, I've probably found Drantaax's killers. If the two men who arrived in the Avenging Axe were carrying his statue it seems a safe bet they killed him to get it. Too late to question them but with the Sorcerers at the Abode of Justice that's not always necessary. If they were at Drantaax's workshop there's a strong chance a few things like dust will have stuck to them. A good Sorcerer will be able to pin it down, linking them to the crime. I just have to get the bodies examined.

I waste no time. The bodies, once deposited in Quintessence Street, were picked up by the public refuse service. I informed the Guards of what had happened but, for a pair of known crooks, the Guards won't have taken much trouble. The bodies will have been sent to the morgue in Twelve Seas for burial or cremation. Fortunately for me, there's been a backlog ever since the riots. Beggars who die in the streets now have to wait up to two weeks before it's their turn to go.

Captain Rallee is at his Guard station. When I tell him I think I've found Drantaax's killers he's full of questions, most of which I decline to answer.

"So it just so happens that the two guys who attacked you in the Avenging Axe also killed Drantaax?" he grunts, suspiciously. "How come you just discovered that?"

"Can't reveal my sources, Captain. You know that. It won't matter to you anyway when we get the bodies checked and they turn out to be the killers. It'll be a feather in your cap. Also, it'll put Grosex in the clear."

The Captain says he'll believe it when he sees it. We take the short walk to the morgue. The Captain sends the attendant through to the back to check his files.

"I still reckon the apprentice did it."

"That poor little guy? Come on, Captain, does he look like a murderer to you?"

"Yes."

After some time, the morgue attendant comes back. "Cremated the bodies yesterday."

My jaw drops in a foolish manner. "Yesterday? What do you mean yesterday? There's a two-week delay."

"Not any more. Prefect Tholius provided us with the funds for more workers. We've been clearing up the backlog. The Consul figured it was time we got this city back in order after the riots."

I turn to the Captain. "But they did it."

The Captain raises an eyebrow. "And now they're gone. Very convenient, Thraxas. Look, I know you have to try and clear your client, but I'm a busy man. I don't have time for this. If you have a fight with some other thug and he miraculously turns out to be Drantaax's killer as well, don't tell me about it."

The Captain thinks I've made the whole thing up. Probably suspects I checked that they were cremated first before coming to him with my theory.

"You were a good soldier, Thraxas, but as an Investigator you're about as much use as a eunuch in a brothel."

He departs, leaving me frustrated, cursing my luck that the Consul should at this moment decide to assign more money to the city's morgues. If these two did kill Drantaax all traces of the connection have now gone up in smoke. I trudge back to the Avenging Axe. What to do?

I still have the statue but that isn't much use any more. There seemed an excellent chance it would carry decisive clues to the murderer of Drantaax. During their manhandling, the killer or his accomplices would have left traces of their auras which a Sorcerer could detect. Not now though. The aura will have been irretrievably washed away in the magic space. From what I remember of my lore physical objects survive unscathed in the magic space, but all magic vanishes, including remnants of auras. Spectacular find or not, it hasn't moved me any closer to clearing Grosex. With my number one suspects now gone, I'm not sure how I'm ever going to clear him.

"Just keep digging around, I guess," I mutter to no one in particular as I order a beer. Thinking about it, even if the two newly departed crooks were in on it, I doubt if they masterminded the whole operation.

Soolanis is at the bar, so I ask her a few more questions.

"Where did your father get that purse?"

Soolanis doesn't know. She thinks he brought it back with him from his travels in the west when he was a young man.

"It's an extremely rare item. You know it's illegal to have one in Turai? As far as I know there are only two in the city and they're both owned by the King. If Thalius had been caught with this he'd have ended up rowing a prison trireme."

They're banned because they make the King nervous. Too easy to seek an audience then suddenly pull a sword out of thin air. It wouldn't be the first time a King had been assassinated that way. I suppose Thalius was safe enough using it to take dwa into the palace. Magic purses like this can be detected by Sorcerers, but only with difficulty, and only if they're looking for it. Who would expect a wash-out like Thalius to have such a rare and valuable item?

Soolanis finishes her beer and looks around for another.

"So, Soolanis, it looks like whoever killed your father also killed Drantaax. I had a couple of suspects but I can't get to them now. Maybe someone else was in on it. Did anyone know he had this purse?"

Soolanis doesn't know. She doesn't know much about anything. All she wants to do is drink. The Avenging Axe is home from home for her. I offer to call a landus to take her back to Thamlin. She says she'd like to stay a while. As a Sorcerer's daughter from Thamlin, she's never been to a tavern on the wrong side of town before. She likes it.

"I've never had beer before. We always had wine at home."

I leave her to her beer and climb the stairs to my office. As I enter a knock comes at my outside door. I ask who it is. It turns out to be three monks. Unlike the last ones that visited, they ask politely if they can enter. They're wearing yellow robes. I figure that's okay. It was the red ones that burgled me. I let them in. Two young monks, plus one old and venerable. The young ones stand respectfully as I clear some junk off a chair for their master to sit down. Despite his obvious great age he walks quickly and easily, and when he sits his back is straight as a broomstick.

He greets me in a voice far stronger than you'd expect from such an old man. This is a man who's lived a healthy life. I doubt if he's ever drunk beer or smoked thazis.

"Forgive us for calling without sending warning of our coming. We are not often in the city and felt it was best to take the chance of finding you home."

Politeness always makes me suspicious. I stare at him. "How can I help you?"

"We wish to hire you to find a statue," says the venerable monk.

Now there's a coincidence. And me with a large statue right here in my pocket. "Tell me about it," I say.

The old monk is called Tresius. The Venerable Tresius. The others are not introduced. I'm not sure if the two younger monks were among the ones I saw fighting outside Thalius's house. With their shaved heads and yellow robes they all look much the same. I don't mention the incident. Neither do they.

Tresius tells an interesting tale in a sonorous voice reminding me of a kindly old Sorcerer I used to take instruction from. He taught me how to levitate. Between the ages of fifteen and sixteen I could raise myself four inches off the ground. Didn't last for long. I seem to remember I lost the art almost immediately after having my first beer.

"We are members of the Cloud Temple. We live and practise in a monastery in the hills."

I nod. Various isolated religious establishments are found in the far northern hills that border on Nioj, though it's a long time since I was up there, fifteen years or so, during the last war with Nioj, in fact. The thought evokes some powerful memories. Turai was stronger then, and not just because I was in the Army. All citizens were obliged to do military service. We used to be proud to do it. A man couldn't get anywhere in this city unless he'd fought for his country. Now half the population bribes their way out and King Reeth-Akan hires mercenaries instead. Many of our Senators have never even held a sword. A generation ago that was unheard of. It'll lead us into trouble one day.

I remember the day far up in the hills when we fought the invading Niojan troops to a standstill, destroying one legion and then another. We were holding out at a pass. Captain Rallee was there, a young soldier like me. We stood in our phalanx with our long spears in our hands and when they were broken we kept them at bay with our swords. We would have driven them back completely if more of their legions hadn't made it through another pass and outflanked us. After that it was a bloody retreat and a desperate fight right outside the walls of our city. And even there we held them off despite the huge superiority of their forces. The Niojan Army was four times the size of ours, even then.

Finally we were driven back into the city and were under siege with ladders and towers at every wall, fighting for our lives. Our Sorcerers exhausted their spells and took up weapons to join the defenders. So did the city's women. Even children joined in, hurling stones and slates from the walls at the sea of enemies swarming up from below. And then, just as the Niojans were starting to spill over our walls, news came that the Orcs had invaded from the east, rolling over the Wastelands with the largest army ever seen in the history of the world. Orcs, Half-Orcs, Trolls, Dragons, Sorcerers, unnamed beasts, everything they could gather under the leadership of Bhergaz the Fierce, the last great Orcish warrior chief to unite all their nations, all heading west with the intention of wiping us off the face of the earth. So the war between Turai, the League of City-States and Nioj ended abruptly as everyone combined in another desperate campaign to drive the vast Orcish Army back. Captain Rallee and I found ourselves fighting shoulder to shoulder with Niojans that only yesterday had been trying to kill us.

The Orc Wars were long and bloody. Battles raged on our borders and around our cities for months. With the help of the Elves we finally drove them out but at great cost. The population of some states has never recovered and several once fine cities are deserted ruins. There's been an uneasy peace ever since. We've even signed a treaty with the Orcs, and exchanged Ambassadors, but it won't last. It never does. Orcs and Humans hate each other too much. The Orcs waste their energy fighting among themselves, but once another leader powerful enough to unite them comes along, they'll be back.

It's barren land, around the hills. Cooler than the city though. Probably quite a suitable spot for meditating. I banish the wartime memories from my mind and concentrate on the monk's tale.

Most of the religious establishments up there are branches of the True Church, the state religion of Turai, but a few fall outside its authority. As Turai is more liberal in religious matters than some other states this is generally not a problem, providing they don't go around spouting heresies and spreading unrest. If that happens the King sends up a battalion and expels them from the country. I guess we're not that liberal in religious matters. I haven't heard of the Cloud Temple before.

"We have only been established for a short time. Until last year myself and the other monks were brothers of the Star Temple. Unfortunately there was a falling-out. I will not go into details—the disagreements were of a theological nature. While of great importance to us, they are not really relevant."

"Let me decide what's relevant."

"Very well. The dispute hinged around a debate on the nature of consubstantiality, concerning the exact way in which the Divinity relates to the substance of which the temporal world is made."

"Okay, skip the details. What happened after you started arguing?"

"Great bitterness arose, leading to divisions among us. There was even a danger of fighting. We are, as you may know, warriors as well as monks. The ability to fight is part of our spiritual training, disciplining us for the rigours of worship and sacrifice. Eventually, to bring an end to the terrible dispute, myself and some others left the Star Temple to found our own monastery, well away from our former brothers."

Tresius had been number two monk in the Star Temple, whose Abbot was Ixial the Seer. The way Tresius tells it, this parting of the ways went smoothly enough, but I have my doubts. Even if he's next best thing to a saint, no Abbot is going to like it if half of his monks suddenly go off and worship somewhere else.

I have my suspicions about the real cause of the schism. In my experience of human nature—admittedly based on a knowledge of the lowest forms—fancy disputes about fine points of detail in any organisation are liable just to be excuses for a good fight about who's really in charge. The way I read the situation, Tresius challenged Ixial the Seer for leadership and the result was too close to call, so he quit, along with half the monks.

I'm getting bored with this tale of quarrelling monastics when Tresius finally reaches the interesting part.

"During the struggle that took place before we left, the statue of Saint Quatinius that stood in the court-yard of the monastery was toppled from its pedestal and destroyed. This was a bitter blow for everyone. The statue was an ancient and beautiful work, carved in marble from the quarries of Juval. It is vital for a monastery of warrior monks to have in its possession a statue of Saint Quatinius."

Quatinius was a fighting saint, killed at war with the Orcs some hundreds of years ago. Warrior monks consequently regard him as an inspiration for their calling.

"We of the Cloud Temple did of course face the founding of our new monastery without such a statue. But we were aware of that, and have already commissioned the sculpting of a new one. Marble is no longer imported from Juval, so we commissioned one of bronze from Drantaax."

I raise my eyebrows.

"It would have taken some months to complete, but now that Drantaax is dead we will be forced to recommission it elsewhere, which will of course mean a delay. Sculptors of his skill are rare, and always have work already in hand. For our fledgling monastery, this delay is a serious setback. Are you aware of the Triple-Moon Conjunction in three months' time?"

I am. I still remember enough of my sorcerous training to recall the most important astrological phenomena. When the three moons line up in the sky every ten years or so, it's a major event. We have a festival. Everyone sings hymns and gets drunk at the chariot races. I've always enjoyed it.

"If we do not have a statue at the time of the conjunction it will mean a serious loss of face."

"How serious?"

The Venerable Tresius turns his head to his two followers and makes some slight movement with his eyes. They bow, and depart. Left alone, he inclines his head towards me.

"Very serious indeed. We cannot perform our Conjunction ritual without it. If Ixial the Seer has replaced his own statue by then, monks from the Cloud Temple may be placed in a difficult situation."

"In plain language, no statue, no monks?"

He nods.

"But Ixial and the Star Temple don't have a statue either. Have they commissioned a new one?"

"I believe not. I believe that they are responsible for the theft from Drantaax."

"Are you saying that Ixial, who's an Abbot, actually connived in the murder of Drantaax just so he could nab a statue for himself?"

"Quite possibly. Ixial is ruthless. I do not believe that his monks would have set out to commit murder but who knows what may have gone wrong when they tried to purloin the statue that was intended for the shrine? Alternatively, he may have hired others to do it for him, and been unaware of what might happen. Either way, with the twin events of the theft and the murder Ixial has struck a devastating blow against me. Drantaax's death means that our own icon will not be ready and he may gain an impressive new one for his own monastery. If that is the situation when the Triple-Moon Conjunction comes then his temple will gain dominance over ours."

"Meaning you lose out?"

"Exactly. And I do not wish my followers to return to Ixial."

I mull this over. I grab a beer from the crate on my shelf, open it, drink and mull it over some more.

"What exactly are you wanting to hire me to do? If I find the statue, I can't hand it over to you. It's being made for the shrine and it belongs to the city authorities."

The Venerable Tresius is aware of this. He doesn't

mind it being returned to the city authorities; he just doesn't want it going to Ixial. Apparently if no one has a statue that is not too bad. Of course if it turns out that Ixial was behind the murder and I prove it, then that removes Ixial and Tresius won't mind that at all.

"If he was not behind it, and you return the statue to the city, then each of our temples may flourish according to our merits."

"But if no one recovers the statue and it ends up at the Star Temple then your young monks will take a hike?"

He nods.

"You know I'm involved in this case already? I haven't been hired to find the statue, but I'm looking for the killer of Drantaax."

"Is it not likely that in the course of your investigation into the murder you will find the statue?"

"Sure it's likely. I'll put Ixial in jail as well if it turns out he was responsible for killing the sculptor."

The Venerable Tresius doesn't look too despondent at the thought of Ixial in jail. He gives the impression that Ixial is capable of anything. This consubstantiality argument must have been pretty bitter.

I ask him if he has any idea where the statue might be now. It's in my pocket of course, but I'm curious about how much Tresius knows.

"No, but I believe it has not yet reached the Star Temple."

"Why?"

"I have means of obtaining information from that establishment."

"You mean you have a spy there?"

He declines to answer this.

"So, basically, Tresius, you want to prevent Ixial from getting this statue. You're hiring me to find it and hand it back to the authorities."

He nods. I don't see any reason not to take his money. I'm going to hand it back to the authorities anyway, when I've finished with it.

I take my standard thirty-guran retainer.

I ask him if he's come across any of the Star Temple monks since he's been in Turai. He says that he hasn't. Which is a lie, given that I saw them fighting.

"One last thing. Why is he called Ixial the Seer? Is he a prophet?"

"Not exactly. But he does see very far in all directions. There is very little that he does not know."

Tresius takes his leave. At the doorway he meets Dandelion.

"Nice robe," says Dandelion, looking admiringly at the yellow cloth.

Tresius smiles serenely and departs, his warrior monk training providing him with enough inner strength not to flinch at Dandelion. Myself, I stare at her bare feet and flowers with renewed disgust.

"Astrath Triple Moon said to tell you that he is sure he can help," she reports.

She liked Astrath. Particularly his rainbow cloak and the colourful hat he wears on special occasions.

"I'm not sure if he knows too much about the stars, though. He didn't believe me when I told him that everyone born under the sign of the dragon was going to have a lucky year. I promised I'd go back and talk to him about it."

Poor Astrath.

Dandelion starts rambling on about the dolphins. Apparently they are really suffering without their healing stone. She can't understand why I won't help.

"They are very upset that you won't help them."

"Oh yes? And how do you know that?"

"They told me, of course."

The dolphins can't really talk. It's just a story for

children. I get a bleak mental image of Dandelion at the seashore, gibbering in the direction of some bemused-looking dolphins. Poor dolphins. I tell her I'm busy and banish her from my office. I've got things to think about.

Grabbing this rare moment of peace and quiet, I consult my book of spells and load the sleep spell into my mind. It is an unfortunate facet of magic that the spells don't stay in your memory, no matter how good you are. Once you use them, they're gone, and you have to learn them all over again.

Once I have the sleep spell learned I feel better. I have an uncomfortable feeling that before too long I am going to be involved with a lot of warrior monks and after seeing them flying through the air aiming kicks at each other's heads, I've no intention of getting involved in hand-to-hand combat. Anyone aiming a flying kick at me is going to find himself sleeping soundly before he lands.

Quen appears. I intimate that she's about as welcome in my room as an Orc at an Elvish wedding, and throw her out.

"Go and hide in Makri's room. If you're short of space in there then sit on Dandelion's shoulders. See if she can predict how you're going to escape the city."

I settle down with another beer, and think about things.

When I tell Makri about Tresius she's impressed. "It's your ideal case, Thraxas. Someone hires you to find something you already have. I take it you'll be spinning it out for a few weeks so you can charge him more?"

"Very amusing, Makri. Guild College has improved your sarcasm tremendously. The reason I didn't tell him I had the statue is that I haven't finished with it yet. I'm still trying to clear Grosex, remember. This is evidence."

Makri is even more impressed when I show her the huge statue inside the small purse.

"I like the look of the magic space. Everything's purple. Can we go in?"

"Definitely not. Entering the magic space is a very bad thing to do. My old teacher forbade it."

"You think this Ixial the Seer did kill Drantaax?" I've been filling in Makri on the details.

"It looks like he might be behind it. Which is fine with me. If I can prove it I'll get Grosex out of jail and it'll be one in the eye for Prefect Tholius. But it doesn't explain why the statue is here, though. Why did it end up in that man's purse? If the thugs that

305

tried to kill me were working for Ixial, why didn't they give him the statue?"

"Maybe they just couldn't wait to attack you."

"Possibly, I'm that kind of guy. But how come they had the purse with the statue?"

"Maybe just coincidence," suggests Makri. "They might have stolen it, or bought it in a tavern. After all, whoever took it from Thalius Green Eye might not have known what it was."

This is possible. Bit of a coincidence, but it's not that unlikely that my old adversary robbed Thalius and then headed for Twelve Seas to lay low for a while. I'm not convinced though. I figure that Soolanis is wide of the mark when she says that her father was killed over a dwa debt. I reckon the purse was the main reason. Which makes his killer a very ruthless person, if he was murdered merely to provide a means of exporting a statue from the city without anyone noticing.

"I'm dealing with a brutal killer here, Makri. Murdered a Sorcerer and the city's top sculptor. You know Thalius was killed with a crossbow?"

"I thought he was poisoned by a servant."

"Just a cover-up by the authorities. He was involved in dwa, probably taking it up to Prince Frisen-Akan at the palace. Consul Kalius won't want to reopen that scandal. It's only two months since the Prince's drug habit was nearly exposed to the population. Remember a ruthless killer with a fondness for crossbows?"

"Sure. Sarin the Merciless."

Sarin the Merciless. I ran her out of town years ago when she was all mouth and no action. She showed up recently in a far more deadly fashion, having honed her fighting skills for four years in a monastery with a group of warrior monks. I remind Makri of the warrior monk connection and she agrees that we could be dealing with Sarin once again.

"You keen to meet her again after last time?"

"What do you mean 'after last time'?" I demand.

"Didn't she win?"

I scoff at the suggestion. "Win? Against me? Please. I only let her go because I was busy with other things, like saving the city from destruction. If she shows her face around here again I'll be down on her like a bad spell. Anyway, freeing her was a smart move. Boost the reward money when I nail her this time. No cropped-haired, crossbow-wielding killer is going to get away from me twice."

Makri lights a thazis stick, inhales a few times and passes it to me. I pour us a little klee. Makri's eyes water as it burns her throat on the way down.

"Why do you drink this stuff?" she demands. "We'd have rioted in the slave pits if they tried serving it to us."

"This is top-quality klee. Another glass?"

"Okay."

There's a commotion outside as a stonemason gets into an argument with an architect. I hear that the master craftsmen have been complaining to their guilds that they're being provided with sub-standard materials, which wouldn't be a surprise. The King opened up the public purse to pay for many of the repairs to the city but by the time the Praetors, Prefects, clerks and Brotherhood take their cut I doubt there'll enough left to pay for superior stone or marble.

"You know, Makri, this whole thing stinks. According to the Venerable Tresius the statue is important to the Cloud Temple and the Star Temple because young monks regard an Abbot without a good statue of Saint Quatinius as about as much use as a eunuch in a brothel. But I'm not sure if I believe that. After all, why didn't Tresius think of that before he split off and set up his own temple?"

"Tresius said he commissioned his own statue from Drantaax. Ixial could have murdered Drantaax to prevent him from finishing the statue—or to steal it for himself."

I'd forgotten that. Still sounds dubious though. "I guess it might be true. But the Venerable Tresius lied about not meeting any other monks in the city. What if he's really after the statue for his own temple and is using me to locate it for him? Wouldn't be the first time some criminal tried to use me as a means of finding something. Wouldn't be the tenth time in fact."

"That's what you get for being good at finding things. Still, you have the statue so I don't have to worry too much about the details. Just make sure Tresius doesn't steal it. What are you doing about Grosex? I hear the trial starts in two days' time."

This makes me frown. I suddenly notice the heat again, and the dry, choking air. Every summer this damned city is like this. You think it can't possibly get any hotter, then it does. Two stals flop down on the window sill outside, too exhausted to fly any further. I glare at them moodily. I'm not fond of them.

"I was hoping Astrath could pick up the killer's aura if I found the statue but now it's been in the magic space that won't work. Which brings me back to the mundane matter of looking for witnesses. I need to speak to Drantaax's wife. Whatever she knows might be enough to fit together with what Tresius says and provide evidence against Ixial the Seer."

It's puzzling that Calia hasn't appeared yet. It's not so easy for a person to hide in this city unless they are well versed in covering their tracks. I can't imagine that she would be. But with no relatives apart from her brother and no friends that anyone knows of, where would she go? Lodging houses cost money. Anyway, the Guards have been checking them.

"I must speak to her. Maybe she knows who the murderer was and she's scared to come forward."

"Maybe she knows who the murderer was so the murderer thought he'd better kill her as well," suggests Makri, which, I have to admit, is a possibility. But the picture in the kuriya pool gave me the impression she was alive. Alive in a white villa. There are a lot of white villas in Thamlin.

Whoever murdered Drantaax must have had the magic purse ready to put the statue in, which does make it fairly certain that they murdered Thalius first. My head starts to swim. I can feel myself getting involved in too many cases at once, a bad habit of mine.

"So don't ask me about the dolphins. I don't have time to even think about them. And keep Quen out of my sight. The Brotherhood are stepping up their search. We better just hope Astrath Triple Moon really can boost the bafflement spell and keep her hidden. We might be able to move her in a day or two when the heat's off."

Makri has heard that the Innkeepers Guild has been complaining in high places about the Guards' failure to locate the killer of the landlord.

"They're demanding that the Abode of Justice assigns a higher-grade Sorcerer to the case."

"Great. Where did you hear that?"

"Association of Gentlewomen. We have a member who works as a cook in the Abode of Justice."

I growl. Innkeepers don't have a particularly high social status in Turai but their guild is surprisingly well connected. Not so surprising, I guess. Even Praetors and Senators like to go out for a drink every now and then. And as the Innkeepers Guild shares various business interests with the Brotherhood and the Society of Friends, it's not really safe to meddle with them. If the

Civil Guard gets going on this as well I'm in deep trouble.

Then there's the monks. Maybe Sarin the Merciless too. A lesser man might go to pieces. I go downstairs for a helping of Tanrose's stew and some more beer. If I'm going to find Drantaax's wife, I'll need plenty of energy.

Makri isn't due to work till this evening. She was planning to spend the afternoon practising a speech for her rhetoric class. This has been causing some mirth around the Avenging Axe, with heartless individuals, like me for instance, pointing out that while Makri's voice might be excellent for bellowing death threats across a gladiatorial arena, it doesn't seem all that suitable for the fine art of oratory. Makri ignores the mockery, but agrees to postpone her practice and come out with me, saying that she's been short of activity of late, and saving me from a band of deadly warrior monks might be good exercise.

I strap on my sword and stick a knife in the small scabbard concealed at the back of my waistband. Makri wears both her swords, more or less hidden under her cloak, and slips a long knife into each of her boots. As usual, she is not entirely comfortable without her axe, but it's too conspicuous. There is no legal reason why a woman can't walk around Turai carrying an axe, but it isn't exactly an everyday sight. A fully armed Makri—lithe, strong, and a blade sticking out in every direction—presents a very worrying sight for the Civil Guard. She tends to get stopped and questioned, which is inconvenient when we're on a case. Also, we get refused entry to high-class establishments.

She's still grumbling as we head out through the potholes, fish heads and assorted debris of Quintessence Street.

"You never know when you'll need your axe. Once, in the slave pits, I was fighting four Orcs and my first sword broke and then my other sword got stuck in the second Orc's rib cage. I had to finish off the other two with my knife and when I stabbed the last one my knife blade broke as well. I mean, bad luck, or what? Actually, it might have been sorcery because by this time I was supreme champion and some of the Orc Lords were getting jealous of my success and the way I kept killing their gladiators. So, right then, just when I didn't have a weapon, they threw in this enormous Troll carrying a nine-foot spear and a club the size of a Human. So that just goes to show."

"Goes to show what?"

"That you should never be without your axe."

"We'll just have to hope we don't meet a giant Troll at the end of Quintessence Street. What happened? Did you kill the Troll with your bare hands?"

"No. Trolls are too strong for that. I vaulted up the wall to the Orc Lord's gallery. His chief bodyguard ran in front of me so I took his sword off him, stabbed him with it, and leaped back into the arena. After all this the Troll was confused and I was able to hack him to pieces. By now the Orc Lord was angry I'd killed his chief bodyguard, so all the rest of his bodyguards started leaping down into the arena, eight of them, all in chainmail. It was a pretty close thing for a while, what with eight of them chasing me around and me with only one sword to defend myself. But after I disposed of a couple I managed to pick up another sword and once I had one in each hand I just mowed them down. Should have seen the crowd. They were going completely berserk. I had the longest standing ovation ever granted to a gladiator."

I glance sideways at Makri. When she arrived in Turai about a year ago one of her notable features was her inability to lie. But she's been learning recently, mainly from me.

"Is that story true? Or are you just practising for your speech at the rhetoric class?"

"Of course it's true. Why wouldn't it be? You think I can't defeat thirteen Orcs and a Troll? Now you mention it, though, it would make a good speech."

"What subject are you meant to be talking about?"

"Living peacefully in a violent world."

"Best of luck."

"I'll need it. Last rhetoric exam, I didn't do very well at all."

We take a landus up through town. The streets are hot as Orcish hell and as the day wears on it doesn't get any cooler. I call in on the small room in a tenement where Grosex lived on his own. No one in the building seems to know anything about him. The neighbours hardly saw him and don't think he's got any relations anywhere. The neighbours also hope that he'll be hanged. After all, he's just murdered our most famous artist.

I search his room, with no results. Nothing of interest, criminal or otherwise. Just a shabby little room for an apprentice who can't afford anything better. The floor boards are bare. The walls are stained with candle smoke. From upstairs come the screams of a misbehaving child and the hopeless shrieks of an enraged mother. I shudder.

"Lets get out of here. It's depressing me."

Poor Grosex. No friends or relations. Living in that miserable little room on his own. I can see he might have enjoyed some diversion in the shape of Drantaax's wife.

We head north. We're on our way to see Lisutaris, Mistress of the Sky. Lisutaris is a powerful Sorcerer, and unconnected with any of the official bodies in

Turai. She has a large independent income so she doesn't have to work at the Abode of Justice or the Palace, or draw up horoscopes and lucky charms for private citizens. This is just as well, as Lisutaris smokes raw thazis through a waterpipe all day and is permanently stoned.

I helped her out a few months ago so she might be willing to help me now though I'm not counting on it. Makri is more hopeful. They've met at a few Association of Gentlewomen meetings and the Sorcerer has appeared friendly enough, unlike some other well-born women Makri could name. Even the Association of Gentlewomen is not without its share of prejudice against anyone with Orc blood. Several Senator's wives have refused to sit in the same room as her.

Our landus comes to a halt in a narrow street as a large cart full of vegetables stops in front of us. Our driver shouts some abuse to no effect. The other driver seems to have disappeared and the vegetable cart stays where it is. We look round as our driver considers the tricky option of reversing his horse and cart down the narrow street. Standing behind us are five red-robed monks who by this simple manoeuvre have now cornered us. They stare at us quite calmly. The one in front, a small individual with boyish features, waves his hand in greeting. Makri and I leap down from the landus to confront them.

"What do you want?" I demand.

"The statue of Saint Quatinius," says the small monk, quite placidly. I notice that he is not sweating in the heat, like the rest of the population.

"What's that got to do with me?"

"We know that you have it."

My temper starts to boil. Who does he think he is, hijacking my landus when I'm out on a case? I tell him to go to hell. He doesn't. Instead he just stands there placidly, which annoys me more than ever. I try and shove him out of the way but he somehow avoids my push. I lose my temper completely and throw a punch at his annoyingly peaceful face.

He dodges it. And then throws a punch, not at me, but at the thick plank of wood at the rear of the landus. To my astonishment the small man's fist snaps it in two, sending splinters into the air.

"Where is the statue?" he repeats.

I try to draw my sword but before it's out of its scabbard he hits me and I fly backwards into the landus. A spar catches me in the ribs and I tumble on to the ground, gasping for breath.

Makri figures this is enough provocation for anyone and draws her swords. The monks take out some curiously shaped knives, each with long guards curving out from their handles, which they use to deflect Makri's blade. And they do indeed block her blade, something I've never seen before. They move with lightning speed, so that Makri is quickly encircled. Despite landing a cut on one opponent's shoulder, she is brought down by a kick from behind that she has no room to avoid. She's on her feet in an instant, landing a good kick of her own before thrusting herself against the nearest wall so they can't get behind her. Standing with her twin swords forming an impenetrable guard, she waits for them to come on to her.

I raise myself off the ground and walk a few yards so Makri is not in my way. I have my own sword in my hand and for all their fighting skill I'll fight five people with Makri at my side any day. But right now I don't have the time and it's too hot. So I let go with the sleep spell. The five monks crumple instantly to the floor.

Makri looks round angrily at me—I know she will regard this magic as a dishonourable way of dealing with opponents—but she doesn't protest. She's not used to meeting anyone who can land a kick on her and is looking puzzled.

Our landus driver is looking more than puzzled. He's quaking in his seat.

I ask him if he can clear the vegetable wagon from in front of us. He does this readily enough, leaping on the horse and taking the reins while I search the monks. I don't find a thing. They don't even have any pockets and none of them is carrying a bag. Just their curious knives. Makri takes all five for her collection.

The way is now clear. There are only a few minutes left till the warrior monks wake up. Less, if they have strong constitutions, which they probably do. We set off with as much speed as is possible through the crowded streets.

Makri's face is dark with fury.

"You annoyed because I put them to sleep?"

She shakes her head.

"No. I'm annoyed that I underestimated them. I can't believe I let someone kick me from behind."

She lapses into gloomy silence for the rest of the journey.

"Don't worry about it," I tell her. "No doubt you'll get to meet them again soon. There'll be plenty of opportunity to kick them back."

Lisutaris, Mistress of the Sky, is about the same age as me but much better preserved. I suspect that female Sorcerers have their own arcane beauty secrets to fight the ravages of time, but they've never shared them with me. She has long fair hair, woven in braids, which are piled on her head before trailing down her back. It's all held in place by a sort of tiara, silver, studded with pearls, in a style quite common among aristocratic women.

Well-born Turanian women spend much time and effort on their hair. Makri, with her vast unruly mane, affects some scorn at this. There is no denying, though, that on Lisutaris it is quite fetching, as is her rainbow cloak, which is of a finer cut and cloth than the standard Sorcerer's garment.

The last time I was here howling mobs were outside trying to burn the villa down, and wounded Sorcerers lay all over the floor. Lisutaris was lying on the floor as well, but her stupor was because of thazis rather than injury. I found a spell in her workroom for making the plants grow faster, which I suppose goes some way to explain why Lisutaris spends most of her time attached to a large waterpipe

inhaling the fumes from her specially grown private supply.

Thazis is still illegal in Turai. Only six or so years ago the Civil Guards were hot on tracking down offenders, if only to gather enough of the substance for themselves to smoke in private. Senators used to make impassioned speeches denouncing its use and blaming it for the moral decay that was gripping the nation's youth. Since dwa swept the city, no one bothers any more. Most people smoke thazis as a mild relaxant and antidote to their worries, though few are so enthusiastic and overindulgent as Lisutaris. She is notorious in certain circles for inventing a new kind of waterpipe. It could be worse. At least she isn't a dwa addict. That's turning out to be quite a popular occupation among the city's Sorcerers.

We are greeted hospitably enough when we arrive. A servant leads us through long corridors to a large airy room with green and gold Elvish tapestries on the walls and plants of all kinds surrounding a bay window overlooking the extensive gardens. Everyone has extensive gardens in Thamlin, and a team of gardeners on the payroll. If you don't, you lose status. Another servant brings us wine and announces that Lisutaris will be down presently.

From what I've seen of the villa, Lisutaris has followed the current Thamlin fashion of bringing in an interior designer, probably from Attical. I can remember when Sorcerers' houses were perpetually strewn with sorcerous junk which no amount of servants could keep entirely clean, but a fashionable woman such as Lisutaris would no longer be satisfied with that. Since Turai's gold mines started bringing in the wealth, everyone in Thamlin is much more concerned with style. Senators used to gain status from their prowess on the battlefield. Now they attain it through

modish living rooms and exquisitely tended gardens.
I don't approve of this, but I'm old-fashioned.

I'm not quite sure how to approach Lisutaris with
my requests. It is not the done thing to apply to a
Sorcerer for help in locating people, unless the Sorcerer actually hires himself out for that sort of thing,
which very few do. Apart from odd outcasts like myself,
who never finished his training, and Astrath Triple
Moon, who is now in disgrace, Sorcerers in Turai don't
go in for much private enterprise. They either work
for the King or the Consul or follow the standard
lifestyle of the idle upper-class citizen who doesn't have
to work at anything. Investigation is deemed to be
below them, a job best left to the Civil Guards. Or me.
Like the rest of the population, Sorcerers are very
conscious of their social standing.

The brief wait for Lisutaris to appear turns into a
long one. My patience quickly wears thin. The wine
is excellent, but I don't have the time to enjoy it. Makri
is still brooding about letting someone land a kick on
her, and she sits stiffly in her chair.

"Lighten up, Makri. Just because you're number one
chariot when it comes to fighting doesn't mean you
have to be invincible. There were five of them and
they're all specially trained. Some of these monks spend
their whole lives in monasteries, doing nothing else
expect fighting and praying."

"Well, they'll have something to pray about next time
we meet," says Makri. She mutters a few dark threats
about what she has in store for them.

Lisutaris arrives eventually, a faraway look in her
eyes. A servant leads her to a chair trying to conceal
the fact that he's actually holding her upright. I sigh.
What is it about being a Sorcerer that makes these
people indulge to such an excess?

"Can I bring you anything?" enquires the servant.

I notice my goblet is empty. "Another bottle of wine if you don't mind."

Lisutaris eventually focuses her eyes. When she sees Makri she smiles in recognition.

"Hello . . . ?"

"Makri."

"Hello, Makri."

The Sorcerer looks at me. I can tell she doesn't remember me. I remind her of the riot.

"I was the one who slapped you."

That didn't sound quite right.

"To bring you round. To put out the fire."

She gazes at me vacantly.

"And then I fought off the crowd that was trying to kill us. Well, me and Hanama the Assassin did. Praetor Cicerius later described it as a heroic effort."

Lisutaris continues to look vacant. "My memories of that day are a little hazy. So much happened, with the fire and the riots, I just . . ."

Her voice trails off and her eyes drift to her Elvish tapestries. Lisutaris is laden with pale silver jewellery of Elvish design and she plays absently with one of the many slender bangles that adorn her wrists. We sit in silence as the Sorcerer drifts off in whatever thazis-fuelled dream she has found in the tapestries. As an experienced and reputable Sorcerer, Lisutaris, Mistress of the Sky, will have spent a fair amount of time among the Elves. Our Sorcerers always visit the Southern Islands when they are young, to study and learn.

I've been to the Southern Islands myself, which few other Turanian citizens can claim. Very beautiful. Not much crime. They have good wine, but beer is hard to find. Lisutaris carries on gazing at the tapestries and I start to feel a little awkward and somewhat annoyed. I saved this woman's life a few months ago. I don't especially care that she's forgotten, but it makes asking her for a favour more difficult. I'm about to do it anyway when Makri leaps in ahead of me.

"Can you help us find someone?" she asks.

The Mistress of the Sky withdraws her gaze from her tapestries and looks at Makri, surprised. Makri, of course, does not realise that it is a rude question.

"Look for someone?"

A trace of annoyance flickers over the Sorcerer's face. For a second I think she's going to throw us out. Then she shrugs, and smiles.

"If you wish. Who are you looking for?"

I let Makri do the explaining. I'm interested to learn that their acquaintance in the Association of Gentlewomen is sufficient reason to break a social taboo. The Association is going to land itself in hot water with the King and the Church one day.

Lisutaris, Mistress of the Sky, reaches languidly for a silk bell rope and summons a servant. She tells him to bring her some kuriya. He departs, soon returning with a golden saucer on a silver tray with a small gold bottle beside it. He places a small table before Lisutaris and puts the tray down where she can reach it.

Lisutaris sips some wine before reaching over to pour the black kuriya from the bottle into the saucer. Without any preparation at all, she waves her hand over the liquid. Within seconds a picture starts to appear.

I'm envious of her power. It takes me a long time to get myself into the required mental state to summon up a picture yet she can do it instantly, even when she's stoned. I should have studied more.

"Is this the house you mean?"

I study the picture. It is. Lisutaris concentrates for a few moments.

"It belongs to a man called Osicius. It's situated near to the fountain that stands outside the southern wall of the Palace."

I thank Lisutaris profusely. She glances back into the dark pool.

"I see that Osicius has been going through some troubles recently. The aura of the house is disturbed. I also see that he is known by another name."

For the first time she looks as if she is straining. "Akial?" she says finally. "Or Exil perhaps?"

"Not Ixial surely?" I say, quite loudly. "Ixial the Seer?"

"That's right. Ixial the Seer. Well, he can't see me."

And with that the mighty Sorceress gets a very inappropriate fit of the giggles and starts rolling around in her chair in hysterics. The picture fades from the kuriya pool. While I wonder at the very unexpected discovery that Drantaax's wife is concealed in the town house of Ixial the Seer, Lisutaris keeps right on laughing, interspersed with the odd burst of "He can't see me," which seems to strike her as the funniest thing in the world.

She pulls the bell rope and orders the servant to bring her waterpipe. She offers to share some thazis with us. Makri is keen to try the waterpipe. I whisper to her that she'll look silly if five hostile warrior monks appear while she is laughing uncontrollably.

Makri's eyes harden at the thought and she refuses the offer. We thank Lisutaris, Mistress of the Sky, and take our leave. Outside we hail a landus and head on up to the south side of the Palace. Behind us Lisutaris is still finding things very amusing.

"Is she like that at your A.G. meetings?" I ask Makri.

"I cannot tell anyone anything about our meetings," Makri replies.

"I know."

We ride on.

"Actually she's worse," says Makri. "I'm surprised to see she's such a good Sorcerer. That was good sorcery, wasn't it?"

"Certainly was. I couldn't get pictures like that in the kuriya pool if I meditated for a month. Lisutaris is as decadent as the rest of our upper classes but she's sharp as an Elf's ear when it comes to magic. Good wine cellar too. Next time you run into her at a meeting see if she'll invite us to dinner. She might bring out the Elvish vintages. Incidentally, where do you hold your meetings?"

"I'm not meant to say."

"You know that Archbishop Xerius made a speech to the Senate last week in which he roundly condemned the Association of Gentlewomen as a wicked and ungodly organisation?"

Makri says something rude about the Archbishop.

A few important people ride past in fancy carriages, but the streets are far quieter here than elsewhere. Far cleaner as well. Even the stals look better fed. Makri wonders out loud why Ixial the Seer, Abbot of a monastery in the mountains, would have a villa in Thamlin. It's a good question. And why has Calia fled there?

The villa is precisely where Lisutaris said it would be. We ride past without stopping. There's nothing to see. No one in sight, not even a gardener. No sign of anyone from the Securitus Guild either. It's quite common for these villas to be protected by their own private Guards but this one doesn't seem to be.

I ask the driver to drop us off some way past. Makri and I leave the main street and enter a park which I think leads to the back of the villa's garden. After some uncomfortable scrambling over thorns and bushes, we find ourselves confronted by a wall eight feet high topped with metal spikes.

"Here we are. The house is on the other side of this wall."

"What are we going to do?"

"Take a look."

The heat is still oppressive but I feel sharp. I become frustrated when things get too complicated but when it comes down to the basics of investigation—like sticking my head over a wall and taking a good look—I feel in control.

The park was busy with nannies and tutors taking their young charges for walks and young Army Captains meeting chaperoned young ladies, but we've come far enough into the wooded area at the edge so that no one can see us. Makri offers to give me a boost up the wall, but I decide against giving her an opportunity to criticise me about my weight and stick a convenient log where I can stand on it. This gives me just enough height to see over.

"No one in sight," I whisper. "Let's go."

Makri is looking dubious. "Are you sure?"

"Of course. What's wrong?"

"I don't know. I suppose I'm just not used to climbing over other people's walls.

I was forgetting. Makri is dauntless in battle but she isn't used to the nitty-gritty of investigating such as sneaking round places you're not meant to be. I reassure her that I do this sort of thing all the time then lay my cloak over the metal spikes and haul myself over the wall. I drop down gently and slip behind a tree, where Makri joins me. There is still no one in sight. The light is fading as the sun sinks over the roof of the Palace in the distance, sending brilliant rays shooting from its golden towers.

"Are we going inside the villa? What do we say if someone catches us?"

"We'll just make some excuse. I always think of something. And keep your swords in their scabbards. If you kill anyone it'll just make things more complicated."

Keeping low, we head from tree to tree, taking cover and watching as we make the long trek towards the villa.

"Big garden," whispers Makri.

"They always are in Thamlin. Mine was huge. Further than I could walk."

The night comes quickly. Only one of the moons is in the sky, low down to the east, and it casts little light into the grounds.

Near the villa a large clump of bushes makes excellent cover and we crouch in the undergrowth before making our final approach to the house. It is now dark, but no lights burn inside. Very strange. Even if the owner was away there would always be servants left to take care of things. I feel some slight unease. If everyone inside is dead I'd as soon it wasn't me that found them. Such things happen to me way too often and the Guards always give me a hard time about it. "Dead Body Thraxas" they call me.

Suddenly the back door opens and figures emerge carrying candles. They walk in silence. I strain my eyes in the dim light to make out what's happening. They're carrying something. It looks like a corpse. Dead Body Thraxas strikes again. I go tense, wondering what I've stumbled into. They proceed towards us in silence. Four figures, carrying another.

"Monks," whispers Makri.

She's right. Monks with shaved heads. I can't distinguish the colour of their cloaks. They approach. The figure they're carrying starts to show signs of life as the monks carefully lower him on to the ground where he kneels as if in meditation. Eventually the other monks kneel in front of the figure they have deposited, and stare at him by the dim candlelight. From their reverential attitude I guess that this must be Ixial the Seer.

My eyes start to adjust. There is someone else beside him. Not a monk. Too much hair. It's a young woman. Calia, I presume.

Ixial holds up his hand and seems about to speak. Something catches his attention and he pauses. He swivels his head towards us.

"Who is there?" he demands.

We freeze. I'd swear he couldn't see us here in the bushes, in the darkness.

"Come out," he orders. "You cannot hide from Ixial the Seer."

"Fine," I say, stepping out into the open. "It was getting cramped in there anyway. You've got sharp eyes. But then I guess you would have, Ixial the Seer."

The four attendant monks rise swiftly to stand between me and their leader.

"What do you want?" demands Ixial. "And what is the meaning of entering into this garden uninvited?"

There's something odd about the way he's sitting. It's almost as if the woman beside him is actually supporting him. My first thought is that he is yet another dwa enthusiast but his voice seems too clear and firm.

"What do I want? Some conversation with the lady, mainly. About Grosex. One-time apprentice to the lady's recently departed husband Drantaax, and now languishing in prison awaiting a swift trial and execution. And after that I might like a few words with you about why your monks have been following me around the city, burgling my rooms and attacking me in alleyways."

Several more monks emerge from the house and advance in the gloom to stand close behind Ixial. I wonder how many are in the house. I've used up the sleep spell and I'm not sure how many warrior monks Makri and I can handle at once.

Ixial starts to speak but halts, giving the faintest of

groans. His face contorts. He is obviously in some pain and is fighting to control it. His followers turn their heads in concern. This is one sick Abbot. As Ixial slumps forward, Calia takes a small bottle from her bag and starts dabbing his lips and forehead with some liquid. None of the monks seems to have any idea what to do. They are all young, and I sense that they're frightened by their leader's distress. I step forward, brushing the monks aside.

"What's the matter with him?"

Calia looks up at me with despair in her eyes. No one tries to prevent me as I take a candle and reach down to move the blanket which covers his legs. His legs are a mess, twisted and broken. Each is protected by splints and bandages but blood oozes out from gaps everywhere and where the skin shows through it is black and putrid. If gangrene hasn't set in already, it isn't far away. I'd say that Ixial the Seer has about twenty-four hours to live, maybe less.

"We're waiting for the healers to arrive," says Calia. Her voice is desperate, almost without hope. No healer is gong to save Ixial. So twisted and broken are his legs that I assume only his willpower and rigorous training have kept him alive this long. With injuries like that most people would have given up and died by now.

"What happened?"

Calia doesn't answer. I look down at Ixial. He opens his eyes for a moment. He struggles briefly with the pain then his head lolls forward as he loses consciousness.

More lights appear in the house as the healers arrive. Two women, each with the green canvas bags commonly used for carrying medicine, are led into the gardens, along with a man in a flowing robe. An apothecary, a herbalist and a healer. Good luck to them.

I withdraw to Makri's hiding place in the shadows. The monks are gathered in a circle around their leader as the doctors examine him.

"No chance," I mutter. "They should have brought an undertaker. It would have saved time."

Makri is wary of the monks. Only hours ago they were trailing us through the city. Now they seem too concerned with their leader's plight to bother about us.

"I need to speak to Calia. Dying Abbot or not, I'm here to clear Grosex."

Oil lamps have been lit for the healers. While they go about their business Calia stands to one side in the shadows, ignored by the monks.

"She doesn't look in a mood to talk," says Makri.

"I never let that bother me."

"You want me to come?"

"Yes. She might feel better with another woman around."

"Even an Orc with pointed ears?"

"I'm sure I never called you that."

We circumnavigate the healers and the monks.

"I need to talk to you."

"Not now," says Calia.

I can see that she deserved her reputation as a Twelve Seas beauty but I can also see that she's been under immense strain. Her husband was killed only a few days ago. But I get the impression that he isn't uppermost in her mind.

"It has to be now. Unless you want Grosex to hang."

She looks up sharply. "Grosex? Hang? Why?"

"For murdering Drantaax, of course."

"That's ridiculous. He wouldn't have killed Drantaax."

"That's not what you said when you found Grosex standing over the body. I heard you were screaming out he'd stabbed him."

Calia brushes this off. "I wasn't thinking clearly. Who would be? I don't know who killed my husband, but I'm sure it wasn't the apprentice. He was far too loyal."

"It was his knife."

"Someone else must have used it."

"The Guards don't think so." I ask her who did and she says she doesn't know. I don't think I believe her.

"Tell me what's going on. What happened at the workshop? And why did you run here? What's your connection with Ixial?"

This gets no response.

"You'll feel better if you talk about it," I add. I often find this a useful line, but it doesn't work for Calia. I change tack.

"What happened to Ixial?"

"They attacked while he was meditating."

"Who did?"

"Tresius. The Cloud Temple. They sneaked up on him while he was praying and threw him from the walls."

"What happened to his seeing powers?"

"Ixial is a religious man," retorts Calia. "He does not distract himself with seeing while he is praying."

I see. That's not the way Tresius told it. According to Calia, Tresius and his followers had been apprehended trying to steal the monastery's statue before they departed in disgrace. The statue had tumbled to its destruction from the walls. But Tresius had later returned with the intention of killing Ixial and stealing his followers. During this altercation the Cloud Temple was repulsed but Ixial, taken by surprise, was himself tumbled from the walls, suffering the terrible injuries he now has.

"The monks brought him to the city to try and save his life."

The despair on her face shows quite clearly she knows it's hopeless. Any normal man would have died by now. Every healer, herbalist and apothecary in Turai isn't going to be able to put Ixial's twisted and broken legs back together. Nor could they cure the gangrene that'll kill him if loss of blood doesn't do so first. Even Sorcerers are powerless against gangrene.

Calia is more forthcoming. She tells us that she'd

been involved with Ixial a decade ago when he was
nothing more than a poor young student living in a
garret in Twelve Seas, reading scrolls of philosophy
by candlelight. She was in love with him then, and
still is. When he went off into the wilderness to take
up the life of a monk, she'd despaired of ever being
happy again. Eventually she ended up marrying
Drantaax, having no better prospects and parents keen
to get their hands on the dowry from a famous and
wealthy sculptor.

She tells me she spent ten years with Drantaax
during which time her life was comfortable but desperately dull. And so it might have remained, had she
not received a message from Ixial the Seer asking her
to meet him at a villa in Thamlin.

She went to meet him. And started an affair, I
imagine, though she doesn't come right out and say it.

This all raises some interesting questions. How did
an Abbot of a mountain monastery find the money
to buy a large villa in Thamlin, for instance? And
what was he doing with it anyway? Warrior monks
live in harsh conditions, training their minds and
bodies with rigorous exercise. I don't think they make
exceptions for their Abbots. They're not meant to
adopt false names, pretend to be aristocrats and hang
around in villas in wealthy parts of town. I don't think
they're meant to have affairs with married ex-lovers
either, although different sects adopt different views
on celibacy and such like. But I have to leave these
questions for now, and concentrate on Grosex. Now
that Calia has opened up a little, she tells me what
she knows. Simply put, she arrived in the workshop
to find Grosex standing over Drantaax's body and the
statue gone.

That's the same story as the Guards so far.

"Why did you flee?"

"I panicked. I knew there were stories about me having an affair. People thought I'd been seeing Grosex when really I had been seeing Ixial. I thought the Guards would accuse me of killing my husband so Grosex could have his business. So I fled. I didn't know they'd suspect Grosex. I liked him. I didn't mean to bring him any harm, but I had to get away."

"Sounds like you were glad of the chance."

"So what if I was?"

She puts a great deal of feeling into that. Maybe it's unbearable being married to a busy sculptor.

"You don't sound shattered with grief about his murder."

"I'm sad. I've got other things to be sadder about."

"What happened to the statue?"

She claims not to know. If she is aware of the goings-on with the magic purse, she's not letting on. I point out to her that the statue thief must surely be the murderer, and Ixial and the Star Temple were currently minus one statue. Which does make them a strong suspect.

She shakes her head. "Ixial would not have harmed my husband. Why would he? And anyway, when Drantaax's statue went missing Ixial was already close to death. It's taken his monks four days to transport him from the mountains to the city."

"Injured or not, he was still giving out orders, because his monks have been searching the city. Searching my rooms anyway."

"I know nothing of that."

Ixial calls out in pain. Calia hurries over to him. I look at the young monks, trying to gauge their reaction to her. Are they aware of her relationship with their leader, or has he deceived them with some story? I see no signs of disapproval on their faces.

I turn to Makri. "What do you make of it?"

"I'm completely confused," she replies. "Who did kill Drantaax, then? And who stole the statue and put it in the magic purse?"

I admit that I don't know.

"I don't understand that woman," continues Makri. "If she didn't want to marry Drantaax, then why did she? She didn't need a husband. She could've got a job in Minarixa's bakery."

"I don't think Calia is the type to spend her days in a bakery."

The healing goes on by the light of the lamps. Ixial drifts in and out of consciousness. Finally he lapses into a deep sleep, or maybe a deep coma. The healer, the herbalist and the apothecarist exchange glances, which are not hard to interpret. Ixial will be handing in his toga pretty soon. Several of the younger monks have tears in their eyes. If I was a man of sensitivity I'd leave them all to their grief. But I'm not. I grab the sleeve of one monk whom I think I recognise as one of the burglars at my office.

"Why did you think I had the statue?"

He yanks his sleeve away and hurries off to join his fellows. I question another with similar results.

"You're not going to learn anything more here, Thraxas," says Makri. "They're all too worried about Ixial. I feel kind of annoyed really. They owe me a fight."

As if on cue the silent garden suddenly erupts. Yellow-clad monks pour over the walls, and they haven't come to talk about consubstantiality. They charge towards the monks of the Star Temple yelling war cries and waving short sticks and curious knives. The Star Temple monks react quickly, forming a human shield around Ixial. More of their brothers hear the uproar and rush from the house. Soon eighty or so monks are battling away in the garden, punching, kicking, and flying through the air in their now familiar acrobatic manner. It's quite a sight. Makri and I withdraw to the bushes to watch, slightly bewildered by this turn of events. I start to suspect that there may be no more reason behind any of this apart from the two Temples' hatred of each other. Maybe they just fight all the time anyway, and the statue is no more than a side issue.

"Interesting religious dispute," I mutter to Makri as a monk bounces off a tree and crashes into the bush beside us. "They should try it in the True Church. Certainly liven things up a bit."

It's hard to be sure in the dim light, but I think I can see the Venerable Tresius in the thick of things. If it is him he's even better preserved for his age than I thought. I swear he leaps eight feet from the ground to hurtle over an opponent, kicking him as he does so, and lands behind another one whom he scythes to the ground with another kick to the legs. He finds himself surrounded by a group of red monks but leaps clear after sending two of them hurtling backwards into the pond.

Cries of anger and pain ring out from all sides as the monks surge this way and that. While some knives are in view most of the fighting is done empty-handed. Everyone seems to be doing their best to maintain the warrior monks' reputation as masters of unarmed combat. I wince as a pile-driving blow sends another young novice crashing into the bushes to lie unconscious at our feet.

"Should have kept your guard up," murmurs Makri who, I suspect, is enjoying the spectacle.

"Should we join in?" she asks.

"Of course not. Why would we?"

"I don't know. I just thought maybe we should."

"Just because there's a fight doesn't mean you have

to get involved, Makri."

"I suppose not. It just doesn't seem natural not to."

The yellow-robed monks of the Cloud Temple seem to have the upper hand, mainly because of the presence of the Venerable Tresius who carries everyone before him. None of the young monks in red can stand up to his furious fighting technique. Bodies literally fly into the air in front of him as he smashes one young novice after another out of the way. He fights his way to the edge of Ixial's bodyguard and keeps right on going. His followers fan out and start to attack from all directions.

The healer, the herbalist and the apothecarist have wisely fled the scene but I think Calia is still by Ixial's side, ready to defend him to the last. The power of love, I reflect. I have to admire her for it.

The brothers of the Star Temple put up a desperate defence. They're brave and unflinching but Tresius is just too much for them, brushing them out of the way like a dragon going through a squadron of poorly paid mercenaries. I wonder if he intends to kill Ixial? As an Investigator, sworn to uphold the law, I should act to prevent such a serious crime being committed right under my nose, but it's not really my affair when it comes right down to it.

Suddenly I sense someone close to us in the bushes. So does Makri. We turn round as one to the place where a dark-shadowed figure has moved in silence. The figure notes our presence but pays us no more attention. He raises something I can't quite discern. There's a sharp twang and a brief humming sound and the next thing I know one of the yellow monks cries out in pain and slumps to the ground. I recognise the humming sound. A crossbow. I don't need an introduction to know who the figure in the shadows is.

"Sarin the Merciless," I whisper to Makri.

The crossbow is both powerful and unwieldy. It's good for defending a city or launching an assault from cover but not much used on the battlefield because of its slowness to load. But in less time than I've ever seen it done before, Sarin has another deadly bolt in the groove. She fires it off, killing another of the Cloud Temple monks. As their second man goes down the yellow monks start to realise that something is wrong and pause slightly in their attack, unsure of what's happening. Another bolt flies from the crossbow. Another monk goes down.

"In the bushes," yells the Venerable Tresius, gesturing with his hand.

The interruption helps the Star Temple regroup and they re-form a solid defence around Ixial. Monks of the Cloud Temple are now running towards the bushes. I watch as Sarin the Merciless coolly loads another bolt into her weapon. This time she takes more careful aim. She fires at Tresius.

Tresius does something that is not humanly possible. He seizes the bolt out of the air before it hits him. I gasp in astonishment. A bolt from a crossbow has enough power at close range to go in through one wall and out through another. It's not possible to grab it out of the air in mid-flight. You can't even see it. And yet Tresius just did.

His followers reach the bushes. I step further back into the shadows. Sarin calmly fires a final bolt into the nearest of her attackers then engages the rest with an unarmed combat technique which matches theirs. Her boast that she'd spent four years studying in a monastery must have been true. She's up against three opponents and acquitting herself well, sending one spinning backwards, then circling round the other two, denying them an opportunity to attack.

Whistles sound in the distance. The Civil Guard

has been alerted. You can't stage a large battle in Thamlin without the neighbours complaining, and when the neighbours complain in Thamlin, the Guards take notice. There are screams and yells and whistles and the sounds of horse-drawn wagons arriving at the front of the house. Seconds later men wearing the black tunics of the Civil Guard are swarming into the garden.

"Time to go."

We depart swiftly, finding ourselves running towards the far wall in the company of various monks. I think I notice another figure in the shadows, a small figure, not a monk. Reminds me of someone, but I can't think who. By the time we're across the wall and into the park we're on our own.

"That was quite a night."

"Great fight."

We hurry away from the scene. Having once lived here I know my way around even in the dark. I lead us down a little-used lane between two villas till the sound of the uproar fades away. We now face a long walk home. Horse travel is forbidden in Turai at night. The night is still too hot to walk comfortably, and I realise I haven't eaten or drunk for some time.

"Did you learn enough to clear Grosex?" Makri enquires.

"I'm not sure. I'll need a while to sort it all out. Right now I need a beer. Why don't they have more taverns up here? First one we reach, I'm going in."

It's well past midnight. As nightlife in this district is not particularly raucous, we don't find a tavern open until we're almost out of Thamlin and into Jade Temple Fields, which is a fraction more lively. Jade Temple Fields takes its name, naturally enough, from the old temple with jade columns built as a present from the Elves three hundred years ago after we helped them in a war with the Orcs. Turai sent the biggest contingent of ships with the fleet of the League of City-States and we crushed the Orcish Armada at the famous Battle of Dead Dragon Island. That put an end to Orcish sea power for a long time. Turai's great Navy was formidable in those days, despite our relatively small size. Not any more. We used to be an important member of the League of City-States. We still are in theory, but everyone knows the Army and Navy are not what they were.

The League isn't what it was, either. It's protected smaller city-states from the aggression of our larger neighbours like Nioj for the last four centuries but it's been falling apart for the past twenty years. Now we're in a permanent state of alert over the silver mines that border on our supposed ally Mattesh in the south. If we end up at war with them the League will disintegrate and Nioj will eat us all for breakfast.

Jade Temple Fields is home to government workers, lesser civil servants and the like. We finally find a tavern where the lights are still on. Makri looks at it suspiciously.

"It'll be fine," I reassure her, and march in.

We're confronted at the door by a large individual wearing a green tunic signifying him as a member of the Securitus Guild, hired to keep out undesirables. Not like the Avenging Axe. Gurd will let anyone in.

The doorway is illuminated by a flaming torch. In the flickering firelight Makri's skin looks even redder than usual. The Guard is a mountainous individual. He stretches his arm out, preventing us from entering.

"No swords in here," he grunts, looking at Makri. "And no Orcs."

So Makri, without any hesitation whatsoever, hauls off and punches him in the face. He crumples to the ground.

I stare at her. "Couldn't we even have discussed it first?"

"What's to discuss? He insulted me."

True enough. But I badly wanted a beer.

"We'll find another tavern," says Makri.

The Guard is lying unconscious in the doorway. I'm tempted to hurdle the body and rush inside for a quick flagon of ale anyway, but decide against it. It'll only lead to trouble if he wakes up while I'm at the bar.

We trudge on through the hot night.

"I really think you ought to work on controlling your temper, Makri."

"I'll start on it tomorrow. Good punch, wasn't it?"

Makri has cheered up and is no longer looking as miserable as a Niojan whore, which she has been ever since the monk kicked her. Which is quite probably why she punched the doorman. Just keen to have some unarmed combat practice in case she meets them again.

Next day I sleep late and wake up with sore legs and a nasty hangover. I struggle out of bed and make straight for my small store of lesada leaves. These come from the Elvish Islands and are very effective against hangovers. I acquired them from an Elf who hired me a couple of months ago. He turned out to be a treacherous criminal and ended up dead, but at least he left something useful behind.

Hanama the Assassin killed him and his companion, and the thought jogs my memory. That small dark figure I glimpsed in the gardens last night reminded me of Hanama. That would be all I need, the Assassins Guild mixing itself up in things.

The lesada leaf quickly starts to take effect. As the hangover recedes I realise I'm stiff all over. It was a long walk home last night, interrupted by a lengthy stay in a tavern in Kushni. No problems for Makri there. The tavern was so disreputable I doubt they'd have turned away the King of the Orcs provided he had a few gurans in his pocket.

The Kushni quarter in the centre of town is a crime-ridden, dwa-soaked collection of taverns, brothels and gambling dens run by and fought over by the

Brotherhood and the Society of Friends and habituated by the assembled lowlife of Turai. I come here often in the course of my work. Makri, who doesn't have much spare time for socialising, isn't quite so familiar with it. I suspect she was taken by surprise by the potency of the alcohol served. She claimed she wasn't drunk but I swear it took her fifteen minutes to climb the outside stairs when we arrived home and she wouldn't have made it at all if I hadn't hauled her up the last flight myself.

So I'm slightly gratified when Makri crawls into my room about lunchtime and begs a lesada leaf from me. She's wrapped in an old blanket and looks like she has a bad dose of the plague. I don't mind Makri being number one chariot when it comes to fighting and she can be as sharp as an Elf's ear with her studies in philosophy and rhetoric, but I'd really take offence if she started outdrinking me.

Her hand shakes as she raises a goblet of water to her lips.

"You're looking as green as the leaf," I comment cheerfully. "I told you that mountain klee was too powerful for you. Needs a strong stomach like mine to take that beverage in."

"What the hell was it made of?" groans Makri.

"Oh, grapes, yams, corn . . . Who knows? Up in the mountains they just distil whatever comes to hand."

She shudders. "Don't you feel bad?"

"Of course not. Take more than a couple of bottles of mountain klee to affect me. I was up bright and early for morning prayers."

"Nonsense," says Makri, wincing with the effort of speaking. "You just got to the lesada leaves first."

Makri washes her leaf down with some difficulty then lies back on the couch with her arm covering her eyes.

"I don't think I can make that morning theology class."

I clear some junk off my table. Makri uncovers her eyes and looks at me with some ire.

"Stop bustling around. I know you're just trying to show the drink didn't affect you. I'm going to kill Dandelion."

"What?"

"I'm going to kill her. As soon as I feel better I'll run her through with my Orcish blade."

Dandelion has apparently been droning on about the dolphins again. Makri, normally sympathetic, found it hard to take in her weakened state.

"Though I could do with the healing stone right now. I'm never going drinking in Kushni again."

She lapses into mordant silence and waits for the leaf to do its work. Despite the heat of the morning she huddles miserably in her blanket and continues to look green. Poor Makri. I decide not to remind her that she actually sat on the lap of a young dwa dealer and attempted to kiss him before being thrown out the tavern. I'll save that one till she's stronger.

Downstairs Gurd and Tanrose are already at work. I study Tanrose's menu, selecting a few items for a hearty breakfast. I choose the fish. Tanrose cooks a fine plate of fish. I notice Gurd stiffening slightly as I order. Fish always puts him in a bad mood. The local fishmonger, quite a prosperous man by the standards of the neighbourhood, has had his eye on Tanrose for some time, and always gives her a good deal when it comes to buying his wares. This makes Gurd jealous. Poor old Barbarian. Having spent most of his life marching round the world fighting for anyone willing to pay him, he still can't get to grips with the idea of romance. He has got a crush on Tanrose that isn't getting any better. She doesn't mind this at all, but

Gurd unfortunately can't quite bring himself to do anything about it. Too used to being a bachelor. Meanwhile he suffers like crazy whenever the fishmonger comes around and starts giving Tanrose big discounts.

By the time I've finished my breakfast Makri has appeared downstairs, bright-eyed and healthy.

"The leaves of the lesada tree," she states, "have miraculous powers. How many more do you have?"

"Not many. And they're almost impossible to get hold of in Turai. Next time I have an Elf for a client I'll ask for some in payment again."

Makri points out that these weren't actually part of my payment from the last Elf.

"You just helped yourself after we found him dead."

"Much the same thing."

"I'm a bit hazy on the details of last night. Did we meet Sarin, or did I imagine it?"

"We met her. And she killed some monks with her crossbow. I've been trying to figure out what it all means. She's obviously on the side of the Star Temple. I presume she once trained under the tutelage of Ixial. I wonder if she killed Drantaax? It would be hard to prove because she's too smart to leave evidence lying around. Grosex goes on trial today. I finally got permission to see him, for what it's worth."

"How come?"

"Deputy Consul Cicerius came back into town at last. He arranged it for me."

I helped Cicerius's son out of trouble a few months back.

"That turned out to be a smart move," says Makri. "He's the first friend in a high place you've had in a long time."

"That's true. Though I wouldn't count him a friend. Cicerius is too austere to actually have friends. Also, he probably remembers that I insulted him when I was drunk. But at least he'll ensure that my legal rights are upheld when it comes to court matters. And Grosex sure needs some help from somewhere. He's been assigned a public defendant, so if I don't dig something up they might as well take him out and hang him now."

Makri gets herself outside of some fish. I take a lunchtime beer and consider the situation. I can't exactly interpret what's going on with the monks. Obviously the Venerable Tresius wasn't entirely straight with me. He neglected to mention that his followers had mortally wounded Ixial the Seer for one thing. So where does that leave me? I still have the purse with the statue in it. Tresius has hired me to find it. Maybe it doesn't matter exactly who did what to whom as far as the monks are concerned. I guess I'll pick up the fee for that anyway.

I'm troubled by meeting Sarin, though. She is a dangerous woman, and no mistake. If Ixial dies I imagine the Star Temple will disband and the monks will go over to the Cloud Temple. But if that doesn't happen and the red monks come looking for the statue again, I'll have Sarin to deal with as well. And then there's Thalius Green Eye. Who killed him? He was murdered with a crossbow which makes Sarin the obvious suspect, but it's not impossible that someone else might be trying to cover their tracks.

"Well, I reckon I've narrowed down the suspects for killing Drantaax to the monks of the Star Temple, the monks of the Cloud Temple, his wife Calia, Sarin the Merciless, and the domestic staff. Maybe a hundred people all told. If Grosex can keep from getting hanged for another year or two, I might whittle it down to single figures."

Palax and Kaby have been out early busking with a mandolin and a flute. They look as peculiar as ever.

Not only do they wear the strangest collection of bright
and ragged clothes ever seen in Turai, their hair practically defies description. They grow it long and thick
and dye it with food colouring and herbs into bright
colours quite unsuitable for a person's head. To make
things worse they're also well advanced in the matter
of piercings. Many people in Turai sport pierced ears—
in some guilds it's a mark of rank—but young Palax
and Kaby, for some unfathomable reason, have rings
through their noses and lips. Most shockingly, they wear
rings through their eyebrows too, a style never before
seen in the lands of Humans, and possibly too bizarre
even for an Orcish whorehouse. I suppose street
entertainers are allowed to be a little odd. Having
grown up in an Orcish slave pen, Makri is lacking in
public decorum, and asked them to pierce her nose
a few months ago. Appalling behaviour, as I immediately pointed out to her, and hardly the sort of attitude she should adopt if she ever wants to get into the
Imperial University. As the University already has
enough reasons not to accept her, there seems no
reason to provide them with another one. But Makri
likes the ring through her nose, and figures the University will be able to get used to it.

The young musicians sit down wearily at a table.

"There's a Sorcerer outside," says Kaby.

"Doing what?"

"Looking puzzled."

"He's with that new Brotherhood boss, Casax."

Bad news. I go to the door and look. As reported,
there is a Sorcerer outside, looking puzzled. He's young,
and while his rainbow cloak distinguishes him as a fully
qualified Sorcerer, I don't recognise him so he probably hasn't been qualified for long. Beside him are
Casax, Karlox and a few other Brotherhood men, all
looking expectantly at the Sorcerer.

Casax spots me and strides across the dusty road towards me.

I greet him civilly. He greets me with an icy stare.

"We're looking for Quen."

"Who?"

"The whore that burned down the Boar's Head."

"I expect she's left the city by now."

"Not according to Orius Fire Tamer, she hasn't. He reckons she's still around here somewhere."

I study the young Sorcerer.

"Orius Fire Tamer? He's new, isn't he? Must've qualified recently. You know, Casax, you can't really trust such a young Sorcerer. He comes fresh out of his apprenticeship thinking he knows everything, but it takes a while to adjust to the ways of a city like Turai. Sure, he's followed Quen's aura this far, but so what? Everyone knows she was around here somewhere. When everyone's talking about someone it can create a false aura. Enough to confuse a young man just starting out in business. Quen is long gone by now. If you want to trace her you'll have to hire a more experienced man. Or woman. Lisutaris, Mistress of the Sky, is very good, so I hear."

Casax isn't given to blustering. He looks at me quite coolly and informs me that the Brotherhood only tolerate my presence in the area because I never really get in their way. But if he finds I've got anything to do with hiding Quen then he'll be down on me like a bad spell.

"You'd better make sure you have another city to go to, and get there fast."

"I'll bear it in mind. Maybe Deputy Consul Cicerius could suggest somewhere." By which I mean I am not without powerful friends in this city.

"Maybe you better ask him quickly," replies Casax, by which he means that I'm not fooling anyone.

Young Orius Fire Tamer is still standing in the street looking puzzled. His powers have brought him this far but wily old Astrath Triple Moon's improved spell of bafflement is preventing him from precisely locating Quen. Casax returns to his side and speaks to him briefly. He's too important a man to spend his time hanging round in Quintessence Street, so after ordering his thugs to carry on the search he departs. Karlox scowls over at me, large, vicious and dumb as an Orc. There's nothing he'd like better than for Casax to order him to run me out of town. Let him try. I scowl back before shutting the door and rejoining Makri.

"We have to do something about Quen. The Brotherhood is close. Astrath's got their Sorcerer baffled but if the Guards bring Old Hasius the Brilliant in on the case we're sunk."

"Are they still watching the place every night?"

I nod. "But we might be able to sneak her away somehow. Maybe Astrath could work an invisibility spell for us. It's a lot to ask, though. Astrath has his own life to lead. We can't expect him to move heaven, earth and the three moons to help some young woman he's never met, especially as he risks getting into trouble with the Brotherhood."

"If we do sneak her away," enquires Makri, "will she still be hidden by his bafflement spell?"

"No."

"Then we can't do it."

"What do you mean we can't do it?" I protest, getting angry. "She can't stay here forever."

"We can't just give her up to the Brotherhood."

I suppose we can't. Not that I've grown attached to Quen or anything—she's a surly young woman as far as I can tell—but it would go against the grain to give up anyone or anything to Casax. I'm left with nothing much to say, so I just give Makri some abuse for landing me in this situation.

I notice that Palax has fallen asleep over his plate of food at the next table. It's a hard life being a busker. But I also notice Kaby is looking madder than a Troll with a toothache, which generally means only one thing. Palax did promise her he'd give up dwa, I seem to remember. It's a hard thing to give up. I grab a beer and take it upstairs with me where I lie on my couch and think about monks and statues and drift off to sleep.

I am awakened by a gentle knocking at my door.

"Who's there?" I call.

"Soolanis," comes the reply.

I wondered where she'd disappeared to.

I go and open the door.

Soolanis is there. So is Sarin the Merciless, with a knife at her throat. Sarin shoves her inside and steps in after her.

"You could just have knocked."

"I never like the thought of being turned away," says Sarin, knife still in her hand.

Sarin the Merciless is a tall woman with her hair cut unusually short, rather austere in appearance apart from the many gold and silver rings in her ears. She wears a man's tunic. Her eyes are as black as Makri's but they lack that friendly twinkle. She stares at me, as if wondering whether to knife me on the spot. My hand is on my sword, just in case.

"I'm looking for a statue," she says.

"That's a popular pastime round here these days."

"Well? Where is it?"

"No idea. I presume you're talking about the statue that vanished when Drantaax was murdered? No one knows where it is."

"I figure you do."

"You figure wrong."

"I know you've been hired to find it."

"I'm puzzled, Sarin. What makes you think I'd discuss this with you?"

"I'll kill you if you don't."

Sarin never has been one for working out unnecessarily subtle plans.

"You want it for the Star Temple?"

"That's right."

I point out that Ixial the Seer will be dead soon.

"I think he'll live. And even if he doesn't, I'll help his followers."

I ask her why. She confirms my suspicion—she studied fighting and meditation under Ixial, so she owes her loyalty to him. But I very much doubt if Sarin the Merciless feels loyal to anyone.

"Did you kill Drantaax?"

"I didn't come here to answer your questions. I came for the statue."

"The statue weighed two tons. How could I have it?"

I study her face to see if she is aware of the magic purse, but Sarin is as cold as an Orc's heart and her face is impossible to read.

"Did you kill my father?" blurts out Soolanis.

"And who would that have been?"

"Thalius Green Eye."

"No. And don't interrupt me again."

Sarin turns to me. "I want that statue, otherwise I'll kill you."

"Well, thanks for the warning. I'm always happy to spend time with cheap killers. Which is what you are, skulking round corners with your crossbow. I'd run you in now if there was a reward on your head. Now get out."

Sarin shows no signs of anger at my insults. She simply departs. I turn to Soolanis, who looks shaken by the affair.

"That may well be the woman who killed your father and she wouldn't think twice about killing you. Don't go to any more taverns on your own," I warn her. "Go home to Thamlin."

"I don't want to go home," she says miserably.

"Then get drunk downstairs."

Needing no further encouragement she departs to do just that. I take the purse out of my pocket and stare at it. Inside this purse is a large statue which numerous people seem very keen to get hold of. Too keen, you might think. I mean, how fascinating can a statue be? I'm finding it increasingly hard to believe that the monasteries want it for their religious ceremonies. There must be easier ways of acquiring a statue, even at short notice. So why is everyone so eager to find it? It's only a lump of bronze. Bronze is moderately valuable, but not valuable enough to go around killing people for. By the time it was melted down and transported anywhere, it would hardly be worth the trouble.

All things considered, I'm starting to feel rather suspicious about this statue.

"You're going to what?"

"I'm going to smash the statue. Bring me a sledgehammer."

Makri looks concerned. "I know you're in a tough spot but there's no need to take it out on the statue. Couldn't you just talk things over with someone?"

"I'm not taking anything out on the statue. I want to see what's inside it."

"Isn't it hollow?"

"Maybe. But I'm starting to have my doubts. Okay, it's a nice work of art. Okay, a monastery full of warrior monks needs a statue of Saint Quatinius or they can't show their faces at the monastery next door. And the Triple-Moon Conjunction is coming up soon. But why this statue? The True Church doesn't require anyone to observe their ceremonies in front of a particularly fine statue. Quite the opposite. They specifically say that worshippers can make do with virtually any old representation of the saint, which is why poor people everywhere observe the Triple-Moon Conjunction in front of cheap plaster artefacts. You can buy them in the market. You wouldn't expect that warrior monks, noted for their austerity, would absolutely have to have some fancy statue made by Turai's top sculptor. Doesn't make sense. As for Sarin the Merciless, she says she wants it for the Star Temple out of loyalty to Ixial. If you'll believe that you'll believe anything. That woman has about as much loyalty as a bokana snake."

"I fought a bokana snake bare-handed in the arena one time."

"Makri. Will you please stop this habit of reminiscing about the arena every time I mention some species of wildlife?"

"Sorry."

The more I think about it, the more convinced I am that this is no ordinary statue. I'm determined to take a closer look. And by doing so I will yet again be breaking the law, because it is heresy to interfere in any way with a statue of Saint Quatinius and if the True Church knew I was about to assault one with a sledge-hammer they'd have me up before the special Religious Court and off to a prison galley in less time than it takes Bishop Gzekius to guzzle down his evening decanter of fine Elvish wine.

"We can't let anyone see us or there'll be trouble. You make sure Soolanis, Quen and Dandelion are out of the way and I'll find a suitable heavy tool."

Soolanis, Quen and Dandelion. Just saying the names makes me feel uncomfortable. How did I end up playing host to these three young women? And did they have to be a drunk, a whore and a freak of nature? Sometimes I don't know what the city is coming to.

"When I was young you'd have been locked up for walking round with flowers in your hair," I grumble, heading downstairs to the courtyard at the back of the tavern.

There's a shed here, in which Palax and Kaby stable their horse. Behind this is their caravan. The sight makes me shudder. Normal people have plain wooden caravans painted white, with perhaps a little picture of Saint Quatinius in a yellow frame to bring them luck. Palax and Kaby's contraption is decorated with murals of God knows what in colours bright enough to sear the eyeball. With those young women upstairs and this pair of weirdos out here, I'm starting to feel annoyed. I marched through deserts and fought battles for these people. You think they might show some respect. Dress normally and get jobs, for instance.

I grab a weighty hammer from Gurd's tool collection and head back upstairs. I'm now thoroughly in a mood for smashing something. A large statue of the Blessed Saint Quatinius on horseback will do nicely.

Back in my room I carefully pull down the top of the purse. The head of the statue appears from out of the magic space. I have to be careful here, exposing enough of the statue for me to hit while keeping its base inside the magic space. If the statue were to appear fully in my room its weight might go right through the floor and kill half of the drinkers downstairs.

Makri is still dubious about the whole operation.

"It is a good statue," she points out. "Didn't you say it was an important work of art? Drantaax was a fine artist. I don't think it's right to destroy one of his works. Especially the last one he made before he was murdered."

I brush her objections aside. Five months studying at the Guild College and she thinks she's an art expert.

"Stand well back."

"You'll break your arm."

I hadn't considered this. I'm not backing down now. I let go at Saint Quatinius's head, aiming at the hardly visible point under the chin where bronze panels have been soldered together. I give it a mighty blow, putting all my weight into it (and that's enough weight for anyone).

There is an almighty clang. A small dent appears. I hit it again. The dent gets bigger. I let go with another furious blow and this time the bronze panel falls right off, landing with a great clatter on the floor. And there, staring out at us like an angel from heaven, is a beautifully moulded golden face.

I practically yell in triumph. "Gold! It's gold inside! That's what everybody's after."

I'm happy as a drunken mercenary at getting this one right. "This must be the missing gold, hijacked last month on the way from the mines to the King's treasuries. And I'm in a for a fat reward."

I look at the golden head. Underneath it, still covered in bronze, will be a golden body. I doubt if there's ever been so much gold in Twelve Seas before. Worth so much I couldn't even calculate it. And no one knows I've got it.

Makri and I study it thoughtfully.

"Never see that much gold again," I muse.

"Definitely not."

"The King has an awful lot of gold already."

"And they're digging more out of the ground all the time."

I sigh, and start pulling the edges of the purse over the statue. It's a tempting thought but someone would find out eventually. I'm too old for the life of a fugitive.

"I guess I wouldn't want to leave Turai right now," says Makri. "The city stinks, but it has the best university in the west."

The statue has now disappeared into the magic space. I put the purse back in my pocket.

"I suppose you could maybe just remove a finger before you give it back?"

"Absolutely not."

Actually, that's not such a bad idea. I'll see how the money situation is. Of course, I'm due a big, big reward now. The King is as mad as a dragon over the loss of his gold and the Palace has offered a thousand gurans for information leading to its recovery. I could take the purse to the Imperial Palace right this minute and demand payment, except I'm still working to clear Grosex and find Thalius's killer, which means I still need the statue.

"Do you think the Star Temple and the Cloud Temple know that the gold is inside?"

"Yes."

"Who put it there?"

"I'm not sure yet. Whoever it was, the monks want it badly. So does Sarin. So we can now expect all hell to break loose."

That's fine with Makri. And it's fine with me right now, when I'm feeling pleased with myself for solving part of the mystery. I pick up a knife, toss it in the air so that it spins, catch it by the handle, and slip it into its scabbard in one easy movement. Then I get out my grimoire and start memorising the sleep spell.

"If they want it they're going to have to come and get it off me. I'll soon show them who's number one chariot in these parts."

I take a bottle of klee from my table. It's empty. I seem to be going through it pretty quickly. I haul out another from my secret supply under the couch and share a couple of glasses with Makri. She shudders as it burns her throat.

"You're getting me into bad habits."

"What bad habits? Incidentally, what's so great about fighting a bokana snake? I killed plenty of bokana snakes when we marched through the jungle. They're not *that* scary."

"They grow much bigger in the Orc Lands. Deadlier poison as well."

"Naturally."

The sun's beating down and I'd be happy to spend the afternoon sleeping but I've work to do. As I strap on my sword and head on out, I remember I swore I wasn't going to work any more this summer. So much for that. If I pick up a nice reward for the stolen gold I'm going to spend the autumn and winter propping up Gurd's bar swapping war stories with anyone who cares to join me.

I notice two Brotherhood men in the area, still nosing around, looking for Quen. And someone else I recognise as an Investigator from uptown, probably hired by the Innkeepers Guild. I scowl. All I need now is for Sarin to pop out from behind a wall and start firing crossbow bolts at me.

The main law courts are close to the business area of Golden Crescent. It's an important part of town and the law court itself is a splendid building with thirty columns at the front and a portico of gleaming white marble. It's situated in a large public forum with a fountain and statues of assorted saints and past kings. The whole thing was built for the glorification of the city a couple of hundred years ago by King Sarius-Akan after he defeated Mattesh in battle and arrived home with a fair amount of booty to spare.

I used to come here often when I was Senior Investigator at the Palace. Any time I walked in, attendants would greet me politely and barristers from the Abode of Justice would rush to meet me to see what news I brought of my investigations. Those days are long past. If anyone here recognises me, they don't show it. There's no point in being polite to a man who's lost all social status, and you can't lose much more social status than I did when I was bounced out of the Palace for drunken misbehaviour.

I finally get to see Grosex, in the underground cells. He's sitting on a small wooden bunk and looks as if he hasn't slept or eaten for some time.

"How did the first day of the trial go?"

"Badly."

"How's your public defender?"

"Still reading up on the case."

Grosex is pale and noticeably thinner than he was a week ago when they arrested him. I can tell he's a man who's given up hope. I try and reassure him, telling him I'm following up a number of leads and so on.

"I expect to have the real killer soon."

"Soon enough to stop them from hanging me?"

"Of course."

That's close to a lie. The trial probably won't last more than another two days. If he's convicted he'll be executed soon after that. Turai's judiciary waste no time once they've found someone guilty. As a full citizen of Turai, Grosex will have the right of appeal to the King if sentenced to death, but the King never likes to buck public opinion by being too lenient. He's worried it'll give Senator Lodius's Populares a stick to beat him with, with crime being so bad in the city these days.

I question Grosex intensely for an hour and I don't learn anything. As far as he was concerned, it was just another day at the workshop till he found Drantaax with a knife sticking in him.

"When did you last use the knife?"

He doesn't remember exactly, but he used it at work frequently so it was bound to have his aura on it. I tell him not to worry.

"There's plenty of ways to fake a man's aura on a knife. I'll get to the bottom of it."

I wonder out loud if Calia might have killed her husband, but Grosex doesn't think this is likely. He knows she was bored, but she didn't hate him. On the contrary, she was rather grateful that she didn't have to live in Twelve Seas any more.

"You know anything about some illegal gold?"

He looks at me blankly. I don't tell him the full facts about the golden statue, but I let him know that Drantaax was mixed up in the gold heist somehow.

Grosex vehemently denies that the sculptor could have had any part in the crime. I'm certain that Drantaax couldn't possibly have filled up the bronze statue with gold in his workshop without his apprentice being aware of it so I tell him not to bother putting on an act.

"Drantaax is dead, so you don't have to defend him. And you haven't much time left. Figuring out where Drantaax acquired the gold might get me to his killer more quickly, so if you know anything you better spill it right now."

Poor, thin, pale Grosex seems to give up completely. He slumps on the hard wooden chair, his head in his hands, staring at the bare stone floor.

"I knew he would never get away with it," he sighs. "Now he's dead. If you expose him he won't even have his reputation left."

"You like his reputation more than your own life?"

Grosex considers it. Finally he decides that he likes his life better but it's a closely run thing. He doesn't feel like struggling any more. I think he might even be starting to regard the noose as a welcome release. I never like it when my clients get like that.

"It was the gambling that started it."

"Gambling?"

"Drantaax would bet on anything. He was never away from the Stadium Superbius in the chariot season. Other times he'd place bets on the out-of-town tracks. It got so he was in so much debt everywhere we could hardly get a delivery of marble any more."

I start to warm to Drantaax. He doesn't sound like such a bad guy for an artist.

"Did he drink?"

"Way too much."

You think these artists are dull and they turn out to be okay after all.

"He'd remortgaged the house, and he was about to lose it. Calia knew nothing about it and he was desperate she shouldn't find out." He laughs ruefully. "Not that she would have cared particularly. Poor Drantaax was crazy about her, but she didn't care anything for him. I figure she was involved with someone else, but I don't know who. People thought it was me, but they were wrong."

So Drantaax, heavily in debt, addled by drink and desperate for a way out of trouble, was more than interested when a solution presented itself in the form of a visitor who made the unusual enquiry as to whether the sculptor could hide a large amount of gold inside a statue. The new statue of Saint Quatinius to be precise.

"Why Saint Quatinius?"

"Because it's heretical to interfere with a statue of the saint. Even if Sorcerers from the Abode of Justice were scanning the city looking for the gold, they would never look inside a statue of Quatinius. It would be blasphemous."

That's true. It hadn't occurred to me before. Sorcerers have a shaky relationship with the True Church at the best of times. No Sorcerer is going to risk the wrath of the Church by interfering with its most important religious icon.

"The plan was to let the gold stay in the statue when it was placed outside the city in the shrine, then remove it later when the heat died down. Drantaax was paid enough to cover his debts and get his business back on its feet."

"Who was behind it?"

Grosex doesn't know. He never even saw the person who made the arrangements. Drantaax told him about it as it was impossible to hide the operation, but Grosex is very hazy on the details. He has no idea who might have killed Drantaax. He doesn't seem to know much about anything, and I can't prise any knowledge of the monks or Sarin from him.

"Who else knew about the gold heist?"

"No one. Drantaax swore me to secrecy. I never breathed a word."

"Didn't it bother you to get caught up in this? Even if Drantaax hadn't been murdered, you were quite likely to end up in jail as an accessory to stealing the King's gold."

"What could I do? Go and report my employer to the authorities? No other sculptor would ever take me on to finish my apprenticeship. I'd have been in trouble with the authorities anyway. No one would have believed I wasn't involved. Besides, Drantaax was the greatest artist in the city. One of the greatest anywhere. I didn't want to be the man responsible for sending him to a prison ship."

A Guard enters the cell to tell me that time is up. I discreetly slip Grosex a couple of thazis sticks before I depart. Might cheer him up a little. I care for my clients. It's illegal, of course, but what can they do to a guy they're going to hang soon anyway?

"I'll have you free in no time," I say in parting, as much to impress the Guard as anything. A brief depression settles on me. Ever since I saw the miserable little room in Twelve Seas where Grosex lived, and learned that he had no friends or family, I've been trying to avoid feeling sorry for him. Seeing him sit there in his cell waiting to be hanged, it's impossible not to.

"Well, you look as miserable as a Niojan whore," comes a robust voice.

It's Captain Rallee. I scowl at him, and stop looking miserable. I'm not going to let Captain Rallee know that I've started to pity my clients. He tells me I'm just the man he's looking for.

"Still trying to clear Grosex? Leaving it a bit late, aren't you?"

"I'd have been further on if Prefect Tholius hadn't arranged things so I couldn't see my client."

The Captain shrugs. "Tholius never bothers with the fine points of the law. He's a fool. Dumb as an Orc in fact. But it makes little difference in this case because Grosex is guilty, as you probably know by now."

"No evidence he did it."

"No evidence? It was his knife, and his aura was all over it."

"Come on, Rallee. There's plenty of ways to fake that."

"No. There are only a few ways to fake it. And they all need grade-A skills in sorcery. Are you saying that some high-level Sorcerer went all the way to Drantaax's workshop just so he could stick a knife in the sculptor and blame the apprentice? Not too likely. Anyway, it didn't happen, because Old Hasius the Brilliant says no sorcery was used in the workshop and I'll take his word above yours any day. So will the court."

"What motive could he have?"

"Calia probably. Kill the employer and set up with his wife. It's not smart, but it's not uncommon either. I remember you covered a couple of cases like that before you got slung out the Palace. Face it, Thraxas, you're on a loser with this one. When it comes down to pulling dumb strokes like trying to get me to believe that two thugs off the street who attacked you also killed Drantaax, it's time to hand in your toga. But that's not

what I wanted to see you about. What's going on with
the monks that are infesting the city?"

"Monks infesting the city? I hadn't noticed."

"Sure you haven't, Thraxas. Except you have one for
a client. The Venerable Tresius. Better make sure you
don't annoy him, he was empty-hand-fighting champion
of the Northern Army forty years back. I hear he hasn't
withered with age. What's he hired you for?"

Captain Rallee should know by now that I never
discuss my clients' affairs with the Civil Guard.

"He didn't hire me. He just dropped in to swap a
few ideas about consubstantiality. "

"And what the hell is that?"

"A complicated religious matter relating to the
precise nature of the Divinity."

"Funny, Thraxas, funny. Is that what you were discussing when you were hauling your fat butt over the
wall up at the villa in Thamlin the other night? Don't
look so surprised. You're not so hard to identify. Neither is Makri. The Guards who saw you going over the
wall tell me you still move well for such a big man. What
was the fighting about?"

"Sorry, Captain. I really don't know what it was
about. Myself and Makri were just out on some private business and we happened upon it."

"No good, Thraxas. Whatever the monks are up to,
you're involved in it. Taking a lot of work on, aren't
you? The Venerable Tresius, Thalius's daughter . . . and
Quen."

I almost jump when the captain says this, but I
control myself. I'm appalled that the Captain knows
about Quen. Maybe I should've expected it—he's a
good man with any number of contacts—but the news
that I am being linked to Quen comes as a blow.

"If you're hiding her, Thraxas, you're in for a whole
lot of trouble. She burned down that tavern and killed

the landlord and she's due a short trip to the gallows. She won't even make it as far as the gallows if the Brotherhood find her first. And neither will you. What did you get involved for?"

I can't think of a snappy answer so I remain silent.

"If you know where she is, Thraxas, and you're holding out, I really advise you to think again. Tell me and I'll take her away quietly so that no one connects it with you."

Distant memories of us fighting the Niojans and the Orcs together must be stirring inside Rallee. He's trying to do me a favour here. Prevent me from falling foul of the Brotherhood. While I'd certainly like Quen off my hands, I'm not turning a friend of Makri's over to the authorities for them to string her up. I stay silent, and make to leave.

"I think you're being unwise on this one, Thraxas. You have too much on your plate already. These monks are tearing each other to pieces. Whatever your involvement, you'll probably end up getting torn apart yourself. Especially now Ixial's back on his feet. A dangerous man, Ixial the Seer."

I gape in astonishment. "Ixial the Seer? Back on his feet? He was next best thing to dead a couple of hours ago."

"Maybe. But he's walking around just fine now. I've seen him. We had him in for questioning about the fight in the garden. And I know one other thing I'll tell you for free. There's an Assassin's contract out on him."

"How do you know that?"

"We have our sources."

"If you've got a spy in the Assassins Guild it's liable to be a very short stay. Have they really been hired to assassinate Ixial?"

"Yes. I'd stay well out of it if I was you, Thraxas.

If you can find who killed old Thalius Green Eye, good luck to you. I'd even wish you good luck if you could come up with anything to clear Grosex, even though he's guilty as hell. But you ought to steer clear of those monks. And ditch Quen before the Brotherhood starts getting annoyed or the Abode of Justice assigns a proper Sorcerer to hunt for her."

I walk out of the law courts with much on my mind. Ixial is alive. He can't be, but he is. And now there's a contract out on him. From who? And for why? Damn these monks. I wish I'd never met any of them. And damn that Quen as well. If she had to go and burn down a tavern, couldn't she have just climbed on a horse and ridden out of town, instead of coming to the Avenging Axe and making my life difficult?

I meant to ask the Captain if the Guard was making any progress on the missing gold. I forgot. It's hot. I find a tavern next door and push my way through the scribes and jurists and petitioners of the law courts to get one beer to quench my thirst and another to encourage some serious thinking.

Makri flops down on my couch. Perspiration runs down her shoulders and she rubs her skin where the chainmail bikini has been chafing in the heat.

"Stupid garment," she mutters.

It certainly is. No protection at all in a fight. Makri has an excellent set of lightweight leather and chainmail body armour which she brought with her from the gladiator pits. Orcs are skilful metalsmiths and their armour is easily a match for ours, if not quite up to the standard of the Elves. Makri's light mail will turn most blades, but it doesn't turn heads—or earn tips, hence the bikini during working hours. All fairly undignified, I suppose, but as Makri regards all men in Twelve Seas as scum she doesn't really care. She is, however, starting to care about the congestion in her room.

"Throw Dandelion out," I suggest, hopefully.

"No. I said she could stay."

"Doesn't she live anywhere?"

"She doesn't seem to. She's been sleeping on the beach recently."

"Well, at least she's close to the dolphins."

Makri won't go back on her word, so Dandelion stays for the meantime, but she does admit that it's starting

to be a strain. Dandelion keeps wanting to do her horoscope and Makri doesn't really have the time for this
sort of thing. Also she lit some perfumed candles which
dripped wax all over Makri's axe. Which was annoying
for a woman who loves her axe.

"Why do you put up with it?"

"I like her, sort of. I never met anyone before who
thought trees were as important as people. Anyway, I
don't have any friends in this city. Except for you, I
suppose. It's good to have someone else to talk to. At
least she's friendlier than Quen—Quen never speaks.
You'd think she might be more civil, seeing that I'm
saving her life by letting her live here."

I suggest that Quen might have been too soured by
her experiences as an exotic dancer to be friendly to
anyone any more. Or maybe she's too scared of the
Brotherhood to think about small talk.

"Maybe. But all she does is sit there in silence. It's
a bit of a strain. How come I've ended up with Soolanis
as well?"

"I think she's too unhappy about her father being
killed to go back home. I expect it gets lonely in a villa
on your own."

"Couldn't she sleep in here?"

"Absolutely not. I need the couch for whenever I
can't make it into the bedroom. You're too soft, Makri.
If you don't want her around, just throw her out. No
one's trying to kill her."

Makri grunts. "Well she's not much trouble. Just lies
around drunk all day."

It's interesting the way she's gathered a group of
troubled young women around her. She could start
holding her own branch meetings of the Association of
Gentlewomen. Provided they allowed for wide interpre-
tation of the word "Gentlewomen." They let Makri in,
so I guess they must.

Makri has come along to study her notes for her next class, as it's too crowded in her own room to concentrate.

"What are you studying?"

"Elvish languages."

"You speak Elvish already."

"Only the common tongue. I'm learning the royal language."

I'm not sure how come Makri speaks Elvish. She's quarter Elvish of course, but I assume the Elvish grandparent wasn't around in the gladiator pits. She never volunteers information about her upbringing, and I've never asked.

"What's that?" she enquires, noticing that I have a sheet of paper in front of me on the desk.

"I've been making a list of everything I need to deal with. It's something I do when I get too many things going on to remember at once."

I pass it over and she reads it out.

"Monks, statue, gold robbery, Drantaax, Grosex, Thalius, Assassins Guild, Quen, Sarin, Ixial, Tresius. You're right. You do have too many things to remember. Funny how you weren't going to do any work this summer."

"Hilarious."

"You can cross Ixial off now anyway."

"No, I can't. He's walking around healthy."

"Don't be ridiculous."

I assure her it's true. Makri is just as astonished as me. She knows as well as I do that Ixial should be dead by now. Even if he somehow managed to cheat death, he'd be recuperating for months. There is just no way he could be up and about.

"Sorcery?"

"No sorcery I've ever heard of can cure gangrene and heal wounds like that. I just don't know."

"What's the Assassins Guild doing on the list?"

"They've been engaged to kill Ixial. Don't know who by, but it's reliable information. He's not going to be an easy target from what I hear. If your friend Hanama gets the job, she'd better watch out."

Makri stiffens slightly at the mention of Hanama, wondering if we're going to have our standard disagreement about the subject, but the moment passes without dispute.

"And take care when you're out. Sarin the Merciless is threatening to shoot on sight if I don't hand over the statue."

"I will. Are you close to digging up anything to clear Grosex?"

"Not really. I strongly suspect those two guys we fought here but now they're gone up in smoke there's no way of connecting them with the crime. Even if they did carry out the killing, I figure someone else organised it. If I could prove that I'd still get the apprentice off. Everything revolves round the statue, which does point towards Ixial and the Star Temple, but now it's turned out to be full of gold who's to say it wasn't someone else altogether? Maybe whoever organised the heist fell out with Drantaax and had him killed. It could just be a coincidence that right at that moment the Star Temple came looking for a statue. Or else Ixial knew about the gold and was in on it all along. I just don't know. I can't turn up in court with some wild story about monks and statues. If the Consul found out I had the gold he'd be more likely to hang me than clear Grosex."

I take a drink of beer and a mouthful from a pastry I got at Minarixa's fine bakery. "What I need is some inspiration. Or a stroke of luck. Either will do."

"How long till they hang Grosex?"

"Two or three days."

"Well, at least there's no hurry. Have another beer."

I note that Makri's sarcasm is coming along nicely. She settles down with her Elvish manuscript and I stare vacantly out of the window, waiting for inspiration. I've got too much information. I can't sort it out. I'm confused. I go downstairs and bring up another beer.

Some hours later I'm still staring out of the window, though now I have a pile of empty flagons at my feet. Makri, who has been busy reading all this time, finally rises from the floor and folds up her manuscript. She casts a glance at the empty flagons.

"It's been a pleasure to watch you at work," she says, grinning. She heads downstairs to the back yard for a little weapons practice before her Elvish languages class.

I sigh. Inspiration never arrived. And I gave it every opportunity. I suppose I'd better just go out and see if I can stir things up a little. I'll go and visit Ixial the Seer. Even if I don't learn anything new about the case, he might let me into his health secrets.

I load up with a vast tray of stew and assorted vegetables from Tanrose. Just audible from outside are the sounds of a young woman attacking a target dummy with an axe and assorted swords and knives.

"Makri tells me she's making good progress at the Guild College," says Tanrose.

"Yes. She'll be talking to the Elvish Royal Family in their own language soon. I wonder if they'll talk back to her?"

Tanrose's stew fails to provide me with the pleasure it normally does. I take an extra pancake to mop up my plate, but my heart isn't really in it. In a morose mood I head out into the afternoon heat to see what I can dig up.

"Better than rowing a slave galley I suppose," I mutter to myself, striding up Quintessence Street.

A bunch of young Koolu Kings are hanging around at the first corner, trying to look tough. They stare at me as I go past. I stare back. They'll all be in the Brotherhood soon enough, ready for the real world of crime, unless war breaks out and they get conscripted, in which case most of them will be dead. Or the plague strikes like it did a few years back—another good way of emptying the slums.

I find a landus quickly and direct the driver to the villa in Thamlin. I'm in two minds as to whether to make a direct approach to Ixial or whether to try sneaking quietly in the back. I decide on the direct approach. I've had enough of sneaking for now.

My direct approach achieves results. After marching up to the villa and banging on the front door loudly enough to wake Old King Kiben it's answered by Calia herself. It's odd the way there don't seem to be any servants here. I suppose the monks must look after themselves. At any other abode in Thamlin the women of the house would rather die than actually answer the door themselves, but I suppose that Calia, coming from Twelve Seas, doesn't mind so much.

Calia informs me no one is in. She stands in the door in a manner to suggest I'm not welcome to come in and check. I notice she's looking happier with life.

"I hear Ixial got well."

She nods.

"How?"

"Through his great powers of recovery."

"Amazing powers. Almost makes me want to take up meditation. Where is he? Looking for Tresius?"

If she knows she isn't saying.

I tell her I'd like to ask a few questions about Drantaax. She doesn't want to talk till I point out that she's still wanted by the Guards for questioning and I'm not above turning her in. This gets me inside the door, but not much further. According to Calia she knows no more than she told me before. She doesn't know who killed her husband, and she doesn't seem to know anything about illegal gold.

"You know Drantaax was heavily in debt?"

"No he wasn't. He was the most successful sculptor in the city. He had commissions for years to come, all of them worth money."

"Maybe, but he liked to gamble. The way I hear it he'd remortgaged the house to pay off the bookmakers, and he was about to lose everything."

For the first time Calia looks surprised, then angry. She insists I must be mistaken.

"Drantaax didn't gamble. He might not have been so dull if he did. And he didn't drink. I don't know who you've been talking to, but none of it's true."

So Drantaax managed to conceal his debts from his wife. And his drinking. Lucky man.

"If he wasn't in debt, why was he so worried about finishing this statue?"

"He wasn't worried," claims Calia. "It was on schedule. We took a few days off in the country right before he was killed. That's how worried he was. Now, excuse me, I have things to do."

"Like what?"

"Packing. I'm leaving with Ixial."

"You're leaving Grosex to hang."

"There's nothing I can do about that. Nothing I can tell the Guards would clear his name."

"Ixial being arrested for murder would clear his name."

She falls silent. I can't get anything more out of her. Quite possibly she has nothing more to tell. Before I go I warn her about the Assassins. Ixial's welfare doesn't concern me but I hate the Assassins Guild for being a bunch of cold-hearted killers, and I'll frustrate them

if I can. Besides, if they kill Ixial I'm never going to
bring him to court.

"Ixial the Seer can look out for himself."

"I'm sure he can. But pass on the information anyway. The Assassins Guild is no joke. If Hanama takes
the case, I don't reckon much for his chances. She
won't bother marching up for a fair fight like the
Venerable Tresius. She'll put an arrow in his back or
use a poison dart while he's sleeping."

As I'm leaving the villa I have the slight impression that there's something close by that doesn't
belong. Something or someone. I can't quite make out
what. The sensitivity that I developed during my
Sorcerer's training rarely lets me down even now. It
wouldn't surprise me if there was an Assassin in the
garden. Well, I warned Ixial. If he ignores me, that's
his problem.

I figure I should check on the gambling debts. I call
in on Starox, the bookie, who operates from an illegal shop between Pashish and Twelve Seas. Starox is
a Brotherhood man but we're on good terms, largely
because I've lost so much money to him. To my surprise Starox tells me that he never took a bet from
Drantaax.

I can't work out why not. If the sculptor wanted to
gamble then Starox is the obvious person for him to
transact his business with. What's more, Starox is of
the opinion that if Drantaax was making large losses
with any other bookmaker in town he'd have been
bound to know about it.

"I know every heavy gambler in Turai. I don't figure the sculptor as a gambler, Thraxas. He was a well-
known man and as far as I know he never made a bet."

I thank Starox. I also place a couple of bets before
I leave. It's not the racing season in Turai—it's too hot
for the chariots to run at the Stadium Superbius—but

there's a small amphitheatre and track further down the coast where they catch the breeze off the sea and they're holding a race meeting this week. I was planning to go before I got bound up in this affair.

My next stop is the Public Records Office, which isn't far from the law courts. It's another place I used to be welcome but where the officials now pretend not to know me. To hell with them. I find a young clerk with time on his hands and we hunt through the scrolls in the records room till we find a document relating to Drantaax's property in Pashish.

"Who owns it?"

"Drantaax."

"But who's holding the mortgage?"

"No one. According to the city records it isn't mortgaged."

I take a look myself. He's right. Drantaax owned it outright. No problems with his finances are recorded here.

No debts and no gambling? Then why did Grosex think he was in such trouble? Stranger and stranger. I walk home, stopping off at a market stall to buy a watermelon which I eat, very messily, as I walk along.

It strikes me that if Sarin the Merciless carries out her threat then a bolt from her crossbow would go through me about as easily as the watermelon. There's not much I can do about that except be careful and rely on my senses to give me some sort of warning. I can't walk around wearing a breastplate in this heat. It'd kill me just about as quick as the crossbow. I could place the personal protection spell in my mind I suppose, but that's a large spell and I find it tiring to carry it around these days. Also, I like to have the sleep spell handy when I'm on a case, and I can't carry both. I just don't have the capacity any more.

I finally manage to track down one of Drantaax's

servants, a groom. The Guard had been holding him
as a material witness but his father has some influence
with the Horse Masters Guild and managed to spring
him. He doesn't tell me much I don't already know,
but he does confirm Calia's story that Drantaax seemed
to be in no trouble. The statue was coming along on
schedule and he doesn't know of any debts. The groom
had accompanied Drantaax and Calia on their short
break to Ferias, a small town further down the coast
where it's a little cooler in the summer. People with
money to spare often take a break there at this time
of year. Lucky them, I reflect, as the sweat pours down
inside my tunic and my leather sandals start to feel as
if they're made of wet rags.

I wonder if Drantaax had a bank account? Most of
the population never have enough money to worry
about banking it, and small businessmen usually just
keep their own safe or hide their takings somewhere
in their property but a relatively well-off man like
Drantaax might possibly have kept an account up in
Golden Crescent where the upper classes transact their
business. I have few contacts in that area but I might
be able to nose something out. It would answer the
question of whether or not Drantaax was in debt. I'm
preoccupied with these sort of thoughts so I don't
notice Makri till she stumbles into me in Quintessence
Street.

"Hey, watch your feet, Makri. What's the matter, the
heat getting to you?"

"Sorry."

She tells me she's just back from her class in advanced
Elvish languages, which she finds stressful because the
Professor always stares at her as if she shouldn't be
there.

"I hate him. But listen."

She says something in the Royal Elvish language.

"What did that mean?"

"Welcome to my tree."

"Very good, Makri."

"Are you impressed?"

"Yes. So will the Elves be if you ever sail down south and start talking it to them. Very few Humans learn the royal language."

Not many Humans know any Elvish at all, though the Elves have no objections to people learning. Makri's Common Elvish is quite fluent already, and mine isn't too bad. You study some when you start off as a Sorcerer's Apprentice, and I had a chance to practise it when I visited the Elves.

One thing that Makri actually admires me for is that I've been to the Southern Islands. Few men have. We trade with them of course, but apart from the ships' crews, few citizens would ever venture that far, deeming it much too dangerous a voyage. It might not be worth the trouble anyway. We like the Elves here, but they don't welcome too many visitors.

"I will sail down there one day," says Makri.

I'm surprised.

"What's brought that on? The last Elf you saw went as white as a sheet when he sensed your Orc blood. You swore you'd never even try speaking to one again."

"Well, they'll be pleased to see me one day."

Perhaps they will. For a social outcast Makri does have a surprising capacity for winning people over. And legendary creatures. When we visited the Fairy Glade a few months ago the Centaurs couldn't get enough of her. Of course Centaurs are, frankly, interested in any woman as well developed as Makri, no matter what her breeding.

"Kaby has a ring through her navel," says Makri. "I like it. Do you think I should get one?"

I'm bewildered by this sudden change of subject.

"You told me body piercing was taboo for the Elves," Makri explains. "Were you making it up?"

"No, it's true."

"Well, I suppose I could always take it out when the time comes. Do you think I should get my nipples done?"

"Only if you want to completely panic the Elves. And what the hell would you want to do it for? No one's ever going to see."

Makri has never had a lover. She says she might be interested if all the men in Twelve Seas weren't so disgusting. I admit she has a point.

"Kaby has her nipples pierced. She was showing me—"

"Could we please change the subject? Guild classes are fine. Intimate bodily detail I can live without."

Makri claims to be puzzled. "Is this another of your 'civilisation' things?"

Suddenly the call for Sabav, evening prayers, rings out.

"Now see what you've done, Makri. If you hadn't started rambling on about body piercing we'd have made it home before prayers. I could be sitting on my couch with a beer. Now we have to kneel down here and pray."

There is no getting around this. Wherever you are when the call comes from the tall towers, you pray.

Most people, more aware of this obligation than myself and Makri, have departed either to their homes or a temple, either to pray or to hide until it's over, but there are a few other stragglers and, along with the people who live on the streets and don't have anywhere else to go, we kneel down. It's annoying, especially as the Avenging Axe is now in sight, but there's nothing to be done about it. Makri is particularly unwilling to carry out this act of devotion as she doesn't believe in the True Church, but no exceptions are allowed and failure to comply means arrest.

I mumble my way through the evening prayers. The sun is still beating down and the ground is hard on my knees. I console myself with the thought of Gurd's ale only a few minutes away. After what seems like a long time the call comes for the end of prayers. At that very instant I get a strong feeling that something is wrong. Some danger is very close. I'm halfway to my feet but I fling myself to the ground. There's the whizzing sound of a crossbow bolt and I feel a sharp pain in my arm as something nicks it. On my way to the ground I crash into Makri and we fall in a heap. I look up. There's blood on my arm, but I'm otherwise okay.

"Damn that Sarin," I say, drawing my sword.

I notice that Makri isn't moving. She's lying face down in the dirt. I roll her over gently. There's a crossbow bolt sticking in her chest. Sarin's bolts are nine inches long. This one has penetrated about eight inches into Makri. Blood pours from the wound. I put my hand to her throat. I can't feel a pulse. I put my face next to her mouth; she isn't breathing. The lethal bolt aimed at me has smashed its way through her breastbone. Makri is dead.

For the first time in my life I'm frozen with horror. I don't look up to see if Sarin is in sight. I don't even try to get out of the way of another bolt. I just stare at Makri lying dead on the street in front of me.

Some people who were praying close by edge towards us. I take no notice of them as I pick up Makri's body and start walking helplessly back to the Avenging Axe.

"Call the Guards," shouts someone.

It's too late for the Guards to do any good. I can't believe that this has happened. Makri's body is light in my arms and hangs limply as I take the last few steps to the tavern. Blood seeps from her chest over my arms. In the early evening the tavern is quiet. I walk to the bar, where Gurd, polishing tankards, looks up at me. His mouth falls open. I stand there stupidly, not knowing what to do next. I can hardly even speak.

Tanrose appears.

"Makri's dead," I say eventually.

Tanrose takes my arm and leads me through to the room at the back and I lay the body on a table.

Gurd is as much in shock as myself and also cannot speak. Tanrose asks what happened.

"Sarin shot her," I say.

Now I'm going to kill Sarin. But I can't bear to leave Makri's body.

Tanrose bends over her. Her eyes fill with tears. As the initial shock wears off my eyes start to brim over too. I feel sick. Gurd groans and sits down in despair.

I look at the body.

"She can't just be dead," I say.

Makri suddenly coughs and blood spurts from her mouth. She groans faintly, then her body goes limp again.

"She's still alive!" cries Tanrose.

I waste no time talking. The second Makri coughs I'm off through the tavern on my way to Chiaraxi, the healer. Chiaraxi lives not far away. She's a skilful woman, ministering to the needs of the Twelve Seas poor for little reward but a great deal of gratitude. I run like I haven't run since I was a young man in the Army. At the entrance to Chiaraxi's tenement I find a queue of people waiting to go in. I barge my way past them into the apartment. There's a young woman there taking appointments in a waiting room. She looks up and starts to speak but I'm past and into the healer's room before she has a word out.

Chiaraxi is bending over a patient.

"Makri's got a crossbow bolt in her chest. She'll die any minute."

I'm half expecting an argument and am quite prepared to pick up Chiaraxi and carry her to the Avenging Axe. To her credit, however, she nods, mutters something to her patient about seeing him tomorrow, and grabs her bag before hurrying out into the street at my side. We run back to the Avenging Axe, and I rush her through to the back room.

Makri shows no sign of life. Her skin has taken on a peculiar hue.

When Chiaraxi sees the crossbow bolt buried deep in her chest she glances questioningly at me.

"She's still alive," I state. "Do what you can. I'll get Astrath Triple Moon."

I hurry out the back and saddle up Gurd's old horse as quickly as any old soldier in the country would. Then I leap on, ram my feet into the stirrups and ride furiously up Quintessence Street, careless of the pedestrians who scream abuse at me as I bowl them over. I make it from Twelve Seas to Pashish in record time and I don't waste any words on Astrath's servant as I shove him out the way at the front door and charge into Astrath's private room.

Less than a minute later we're heading back to the Avenging Axe. Astrath doesn't specialise in healing like some Sorcerers, but he has much knowledge and power. I'm praying he'll be able to help.

The horse protests as I mercilessly urge it on. It's on its last legs when it deposits myself and the Sorcerer at the tavern. I hurry Astrath through to where Makri lies motionless with Chiaraxi standing over her. She's stopped the bleeding.

"Is she alive?" I demand.

"Just."

"She shouldn't be," mutters Astrath, as he studies the wound, and Chiaraxi agrees with him. Astrath takes out a small clear crystal. It's a lifestone, carried by most Sorcerers. One of its properties is that when held next to a person's skin it glows with a green light. Unless they're dead. Then it doesn't glow at all. Astrath presses it on Makri's forehead. We strain to make out any colouring in the crystal. At first nothing happens and then, with painful slowness, the tiniest flicker of green appears.

Astrath stands up, looking troubled. He doesn't seem to want to say anything. I tell him to spit it out.

"No one recovers from that," he says, glancing at the crystal, which has already returned to its colourless state.

It seems clear that only Makri's great inner strength, derived from her mixed blood, has kept her alive. Even that is fading now.

"Take the bolt out!" screams Gurd suddenly, as his emotions pour out in a great burst.

Chiaraxi shakes her head. The bolt is buried in the bone. Even attempting to move it will kill Makri for sure.

"I've given her amacia herb," she says. "It'll strengthen her. I can't do any more."

Astrath speaks a spell over the body. I recognise it as a spell for strengthening the body's resistance. Very good if you have the plague. Not so helpful if you have eight inches of crossbow bolt buried inside you. Astrath and Chiaraxi hold out no hope. The amacia herb and the spell will do no more than delay the inevitable, and not for long. They can't even estimate how long Makri will stay alive, as she should be dead already. So I can't think of anything to do but wait till she dies then go and kill Sarin.

"What's happening?"

It's Dandelion. She yells in horror when she sees Makri. I'm too upset by events to care. My sleeves are still wet with Makri's blood.

Dandelion turns to me. "The dolphins' healing stone!"

So desperate is the situation that I'm prepared to grasp at the straw. "The healing stone? Is it real?"

"Of course it's real. I keep telling you. It will heal anything, but it was stolen."

A flash of inspiration strikes. One that should have struck before. Ixial the Seer. He couldn't recover from his wounds, but he did.

"What's the healing stone like?" I demand.

"I don't know."

"What do you mean, you don't know?" I roar.

Dandelion quails, thinking I'm about to strike her. I might.

"I never asked them what it was like. I just know it's their healing stone."

I want to rush off and find Ixial but I force myself to calm down and think. No use running blindly around town not even knowing what I'm looking for. The dolphins that talk live out in the bay. It's about a twenty-minute ride there. Too long.

"I could try calling from the harbour," says Dandelion. "They sometimes swim close enough to hear."

I agree to try. And I ask Astrath if he can locate Ixial for me.

"Maybe, if you have something belonging to him. Otherwise, maybe not."

I don't have anything. Or anything he's touched. I rack my brains for inspiration. There's the gold in the statue. If he was behind the bullion robbery he might have touched that.

I take out the magic purse and drag the top of it down. In the general horror about what has happened to Makri no one even gasps as the statue appears.

Astrath Triple Moon shakes his head. "No use, Thraxas. It's been in the magic space. Any lingering aura will be wiped off."

I step outside and return with the sledgehammer, then smash more of the bronze covering off, revealing a fresh piece of gold. "How about that? It's been covered all the time it's been in there."

Astrath fingers his short grey beard. "I might get something."

"Do what you can, then meet me at the bottom of Moon and Stars Avenue."

Gurd's old horse won't make another journey with two people on its back. I hurry along Quintessence Street with Dandelion, looking for a landus. The first one that trots past has some sort of minor official in the back. I grab the reins, bringing it to a halt, then brandish my sword.

"Need this landus," I say.

He leaps out, uttering threats. I punch him, and he falls down.

"Take us to the harbour and make it quick," I tell the driver.

I'm still carrying my sword. He takes us to the harbour, and he makes it quick.

Dandelion says she once talked to a dolphin at the furthest edge of the longest pier. We head there, out past the triremes and biremes docked for loading and unloading. The hulks are quiet in the evening, each burning only a small harbour light at the bow and stern. A few Securitus men, hired by the harbour authority, patrol the docks at night, but we encounter no one as we run along the pier. I don't run too far these days, as a rule. I feel my heart pounding with the effort, but I ignore it. Dandelion stumbles and falls. I drag her up. She's cut her foot on a sharp piece of metal and leaves a blood-stained footprint behind as we rush on. At the furthest part of the harbour is a breakwater which juts far out into the sea, providing shelter from the wind for incoming vessels. We stop when we can go no further.

"Well?" I demand.

Dandelion looks out over the dark sea. The sun has dipped over the horizon, its last rays casting a dark red hue over the water. Like wine, as I believe an Elvish poet once said. Dandelion tilts her head slightly and emits a very strange sound, a high-pitched whine with clicks and gurgles mixed in. We wait. Nothing happens.

She does it again. I glance at her with fury. If this is her idea of a joke I'm going to throw her into the sea.

"Where are the dolphins?" I practically scream.

She makes the noise a third time. I'm about to turn on my heels and go off looking for Ixial when she suddenly calls and points. Right underneath us a dolphin has poked its head through the surface and looks at Dandelion expectantly.

"What'll I say?"

"Tell it I'm here to find the healing stone. And tell it I have no time to waste."

They gurgle and whistle to each other for what seems like an eternity, though I suppose it's reasonably fast for a conversation between a dolphin and a human. Dandelion finally turns to me and tells me that the dolphins' healing stone is vaguely cross-shaped, made of black stone and about the size of a man's hand. That seems like enough to be going on with.

"It was on the altar of their undersea temple far off in the bay and a diver took it when they were all playing out at sea. The temple is—"

"Tell me the details later," I grunt. I head off, leaving the barefoot Dandelion to commune further with the dolphin.

Now I know what I'm looking for. If Astrath has done the business with the gold in the statue he might be able to tell me where to search. He's already waiting for me in a landus at the corner of Quintessence Street and Moon and Stars Avenue. Gurd is there too.

"Any luck?"

"Yes. Ixial the Seer's aura is all over the gold. I scanned the city and found him in Twelve Seas."

"Twelve Seas? You sure?"

"Yes. He's at the official residence of Prefect Tholius."

Prefect Tholius. That's probably something that's

going to make sense when I have time to think
about it.

"What are you going to do?" says the Sorcerer.

"Find the healing stone. Kill anyone who gets in my
way."

"Lets go," says Gurd.

His axe hangs at his hip. It's good to have Gurd
along. It's a long time since we fought anyone together.
I tell Astrath he doesn't need to come too. If he gets
involved in a brawl with Prefect Tholius he'll never be
readmitted to the Sorcerers Guild. But he wants to
come anyway. There's no time to argue so we set off
fast for Tholius's official residence in Tranquillity Lane
which, apart from the church and the public baths, is
the only decent building in Twelve Seas.

I'm trying to think of the best way to approach
matters. I just don't have time for anything fancy. If
I'm lucky Ixial will gladly hand over the dolphins'
healing stone, but it's not too likely. For one thing he'll
want to keep such a useful item for himself. For
another, it would mean publicly admitting to theft from
the dolphins. While that isn't actually a crime, it's a
taboo act and would effectively end his career as head
of a monastery.

I seethe with frustration as heavy traffic hinders our
progress. We ride in silence, knowing that every second we are away Makri is very likely to die.

When we reach Tranquillity Lane and turn into the
side street leading to the official residence we have a
stroke of good fortune. Prefect Tholius himself is walking towards us in the company of Ixial the Seer. They're
alone, without bodyguards, and they're taken by surprise
as we screech to a halt and leap from the landus.

Suddenly confronted by an Investigator, a Barbarian and a Sorcerer, all apparently mad, the Prefect is
taken aback. He demands to know what we want.

"The healing stone. And I want it now."

"What are you talking about?" demands Tholius.

I ignore him and turn to Ixial. "The healing stone."

Gurd slips beside him and raises his axe. Ixial prepares to defend himself. I remember his reputation as a fighter. I don't have time for this.

"Kill them with the heart attack spell," I say to Astrath Triple Moon.

Astrath raises an arm.

"Give him the healing stone!" yells Prefect Tholius, clutching nervously at his chest.

"He is not carrying a heart attack spell," says Ixial calmly, proving that he can indeed see many things. He strides towards Astrath. I slug him hard on the back of the head as he passes by, and he falls to the ground unconscious.

"You didn't see that," I mutter. I start to search him while Gurd keeps his axe close to the Prefect's neck.

"You know you're going to a prison ship?" rasps Tholius with impotent fury.

I find the healing stone. Small, black and shaped roughly like a cross.

"I'll see you on board," I reply. "Get in my way and I'll have to get you involved in the golden statue affair."

Tholius's eyes widen and he suddenly finds he has nothing to say. I figured it was a safe bet he was involved somehow along with Ixial. It makes sense of his keenness to dispose of Grosex without answering too many questions. Makes sense of some other things, but I can think about that later.

We jump back into the landus. Gurd takes the reins and we set off. I pass the stone to Astrath and he studies it as we make all possible speed back to Quintessence Street. Dust floats up from the sun-baked earth and more pedestrians are forced to scatter as we pass.

"Worked it out yet?" I ask the Sorcerer. The Avenging Axe is now very close.

"I have never seen anything like it before. The dolphins say it fell from the sky?" He turns it over in his hands, studying it carefully. "I don't really know what it is. It certainly feels powerful though."

Darkness has fully descended as we arrive back at the Avenging Axe. I estimate I've been gone no more than an hour. I send up a quick prayer as I run with the others through to the back room where Makri still lies on the table with the terrible wound in her chest. Now gathered in the room are Chiaraxi, Tanrose, Dandelion, Soolanis, Palax and Kaby. Only Quen is absent. Misery pervades the scene.

"I've got the stone!"

I expect this to produce some signs of hope. No one shows any signs of hope.

"You're too late," sighs Tanrose. "Makri died."

"No she didn't," I protest. "She just looks dead."

She does indeed look very dead.

"She has a strong constitution," I say. "Elf blood. Orc blood. Human . . ."

Chiaraxi shakes her head.

Astrath Triple Moon places his hand on Makri's brow then takes out his lifestone and touches her skin. It doesn't glow, not even a flicker.

"Try the dolphins' stone," I scream.

He places it first on her forehead and then on the wound. He touches it to the area just below her navel, where the centre of energy is located. Nothing happens, apart from Kaby expressing a great wail and slumping to the floor.

Astrath looks around helplessly. I grab the healing stone and try myself. Still nothing happens, though when I touch the stone I feel a warm glow in my fingers.

"It's not working. Piece of junk."

Astrath, calmer than me, takes the stone back. Noticing that Dandelion's foot is still bleeding from the accident at the harbour, he bends down to touch the injury. Before our eyes it heals up wondrously. In a matter of seconds the blood stops flowing and the skin has regenerated itself.

So the stone does work. And Makri is still dead.

"Is she really?" says Tanrose.

"I'm afraid so," replies Astrath, and Chiaraxi nods in agreement.

I take the healing stone again and place it on Makri's wound. Nothing happens. I stand there stupidly for a long time, waiting for her to come back to life. She doesn't. There doesn't seem to be anything else to do.

I take a tankard, walk through to the beer taps, fill it up, drain it, fill it up again, then walk back to where Makri lies and slump on the floor myself. No one speaks. The only sound is Kaby's sobbing, with a few others joining in as the mood takes them. Soolanis has drunk herself sober and sits rigidly in a chair with a bottle of klee, trying to get drunk again.

It flickers dimly in my mind that I now probably know most of what has been going on with the statue and Drantaax, but I'm in no mood to piece it all together. I have only two things in mind. One, I'm going to get drunk. Two, I'm going to kill Sarin the Merciless.

Heavy boots sound outside. Captain Rallee enters. If he's come to harass me about something he's picked a poor time. I stand up to confront him, ready to take out some of my anger.

He hasn't come to harass me. He's heard about Makri. Someone reported to the Guards that a strange young woman was shot down in Quintessence Street and he guessed the rest. He's come to pay his respects.

"I'm sorry about this," says the Captain, looking sadly

at Makri's body. Kaby is now crying uncontrollably. Without really registering the fact I notice that her boyfriend Palax's head is lolling on his shoulders and his eyes have the vacant look indicating a heavy dose of dwa.

"Who did it?"

"Sarin the Merciless."

"What's behind it?"

"The King's gold," I mumble, seeing no reason to conceal anything from Captain Rallee any longer.

I lead Captain Rallee through to the front of the tavern, now empty of customers. There I take the purse from my pocket and draw down its edges, exposing the statue underneath. The gold shines through, glinting in the light from the torches on the walls.

"That's the King's gold?" says Rallee.

I nod.

The front door opens.

"Correction. My gold."

It's Ixial the Seer. He walks forward. Behind him the massed ranks of the monks of the Star Temple file into the tavern.

The upstairs door bangs open.

"The statue is mine," says the Venerable Tresius, from the top of the stairs. He's slipped up the outside stairs and come into the tavern through my rooms. Behind him are gathered the massed ranks of the monks of the Cloud Temple.

The yellow monks descend the stairs in silence. The red monks fan out to meet them. Gurd, hearing the conversation, arrives to see what's happening. Captain Rallee looks questioningly at me.

The front door slams open to a heavy kick. Standing there is the bulky figure of Tholius, Prefect of Twelve Seas. He strides in with a great gang of armed men. Some of them I recognise as Civil Guards, though none are in uniform. Tholius is not wearing his Prefect's yellow-edged toga. I guess this is not an official visit. He's come to take the gold and kill any witnesses to his involvement.

Tholius surveys the scene briefly.

"Everyone out," he orders.

No one leaves. His men takes their weapons from their scabbards. Ixial the Seer studies the Prefect, as if trying to judge whether they're still partners. I could tell him the answer. A man who feels no qualms about robbing the poor of Twelve Seas is not going to share a golden statue with a monk.

There's a commotion outside and yet more people force their way in. A very tough-looking group of people, led by Casax. He's brought his strongest fighters from Twelve Seas and from the looks of the rest I'd say they've recruited from the gang lords of the surrounding areas. I'm puzzled why. If he's finally tracked Quen to the Avenging Axe he hardly needs an army to recover her.

Casax is briefly surprised at the sight of the Star Temple, the Cloud Temple, Prefect Tholius and Captain Rallee, but he adapts quickly. He laughs, in fact.

"I've come to pick up a little stolen gold," he announces to the multitude. "I see I'm not the first. Well, I'd advise you all to leave before you get hurt." He looks pointedly at Prefect Tholius. As the government's representative Tholius should be in charge here but in practice the Brotherhood boss has more power. Tholius is well supported in the bar, though, and he shows no inclination to leave. Neither do the monks.

Casax turns to me, and grins. "We've been looking for that gold ever since it was stolen. We had word the monks had something to do with it. And we had word you've been meeting with some monks, Thraxas."

He looks at me sharply. "You should know you can't hide anything that goes on in Twelve Seas from me. I guess we'd have got here quicker if you didn't have that bafflement spell to hide Quen."

"Have you taken her?" I demand.

"Taken her? What for? Quen works for me, fat man. And very clever she is too. We figured you'd lead us to the gold. As soon as she saw you showing off the statue she came back and reported it."

Casax doesn't have to brag about it, but he likes to let people know when he's outsmarted them. Just another of his character traits.

"I hear the Orc girl's dead," adds Casax. "Sorry about that. Nothing to do with me. Anyway, if you'd all like to step aside while my men get hold of that statue."

Captain Rallee strides in front of the Brotherhood boss. "What makes you think you're taking the statue, Casax? I represent the law here, and I'll arrest any man who tries to remove it."

Casax guffaws with laughter at the thought of a Civil Guard Captain getting in the way of a Brotherhood boss, particularly a Brotherhood boss with a full array of fighters in tow. They all laugh. The laughter grates on my nerves. With Makri lying dead next door I don't want to hear anyone laughing right now. I stand next to the Captain. I'd planned to kill Sarin but going down fighting these scum doesn't seem too bad an alternative right now. I feel like killing someone, and I'm not too particular.

"Come and get the statue," I say, motioning to where it stands, half in and half out of the magic purse.

Everyone in the room waits to see who's going to make the first move. At this moment Soolanis lurches through from the back. Oblivious to everything and everyone around her, she navigates her way behind the bar, takes a bottle of klee from the shelf, and lurches off again. You have to admire the woman's single-mindedness.

Captain Rallee again demands that everyone depart and let the law take over. At this Prefect Tholius advances towards him and angrily demands that the Captain stop interfering. "Twelve Seas is under my jurisdiction."

"So it is. But I work for the Abode of Justice and a Guard Captain has a responsibility to uphold the law in every part of the city. Are you here on official business? If so, why are your men out of uniform?"

Rallee turns to Tresius who's waiting quietly at the foot of the stairs. "And what do you want?"

The Venerable Tresius remains silent.

"They're all here for the statue, Captain," I explain.

"Even Tholius?"

"In on it from the first. He provided Ixial the Seer with inside information about the gold shipment. And he provided Ixial with a nice house in Thamlin where he could meet Drantaax's wife and learn everything he needed to know from her."

"Kill them," grunts Tholius.

The place erupts.

When I was nineteen I was expelled from the college for young Sorcerers. Having no money, no family and nothing better to do, I joined a company of mercenaries on their way to the war in the far southeast between the small city-states of Juval, Abelasi and Pargada. That was how I met Gurd, a large Barbarian of twenty-five or so who'd travelled down from the frozen north to see life in the civilised lands. That's what he said at the time anyway, though some years later he admitted to me that he'd actually been chased away by the outraged clan of a young woman he'd become rather too involved with.

Events in the south were confused, with the cities at war with one another. To make matters worse, each city had at least two claimants to the throne. On one occasion our company, in the employ of a Prince of Juval, ambushed some troops belonging to another Prince of Juval in the middle of a dense forest. At that very moment, the Army of the People's Democracy of Abelasi took us in the rear. While Gurd and I were still trying to work out which way our spears should be pointing, a joint force from the recently deposed King of Abelasi arrived along with his allies, the

Pargadan Army. No one knew what the hell was happening. In the dark tangled forest the companies of spearmen were soon splintered and disorganised, leaving a heaving mass of men struggling and fighting for their very lives with opponents they could barely make out. Panic set in as soldiers fought with enemies and allies alike in the confusion. There was nothing for me and Gurd to do, apart from hack our way through anyone and anything who stood in our way and hope that some time or other we'd arrive at an empty space where we could gather our wits, find a couple of horses, and get the hell out of there. Which we did, eventually.

I'm reminded of this day twenty-four years later as battle is joined in the Avenging Axe. Everyone wants the statue but only the last man left standing is going to carry it away. The monks of the Cloud Temple and the monks of the Star Temple lay into each other furiously, their lust for the gold fuelled by their bitter rivalry. The Brotherhood, enraged that anyone could even consider pulling off a criminal coup in their part of town, throw themselves into the fray. The gang members are not trained warriors like the monks but many of them served in the Army and they're all very experienced at the art of close-range street fighting.

Prefect Tholius meanwhile urges his men on. The Prefect has the most to lose perhaps, as his position in town is fast becoming untenable. Once word gets out that he was an accomplice in the gold theft he'll be stripped of his office and on his way to a prison ship faster than he can blink. Prefects can get away with many things in Turai, but not stealing gold from the King. Surrounded by his personal bodyguard of off-duty Civil Guards, he mounts a violent attack, determined either to wipe out all witnesses to his crime or make off with the loot to some other nation where he can live in luxury beyond the reach of Turai's laws.

Myself, I'm just caught in the middle. I don't want the statue. I wanted to solve a murder, but since Makri's death that's slipped well down my list of priorities. At the thought of her corpse lying next door blood fury rises in me in a way I've not felt for a very long time. I'm pleased for the chance to vent my wrath on whoever comes near.

Captain Rallee, as the only official upholder of the law in the premises, finds himself hard-pressed. He fights at the shoulder of Gurd and me, with the half-exposed statue protecting our backs. A howling monk of the Star Temple falls before his blade. I see he hasn't lost any of his old fighting skill.

Four Brotherhood men burst through the melee and set upon us. I parry a thrust, stick my sword through my opponent's thigh then gut him as he stumbles. Gurd chops a man almost in half and Rallee skilfully deflects a strike before running his sword up his opponent's blade and into his chest. The fourth Brotherhood man backs off, and we find a brief moment of space inside the madness.

"Couldn't you have brought a company of Guards with you?" I snarl at Rallee.

"Just came to pay my respects," he says. "And I want a few words with you when this is all over. Who do you think you are, withholding evidence? That statue should have been turned over to the Guard."

"I was just getting round to it," I grunt, and then it's back to the fray. Gurd's furnishings suffer heavy damage as people pick up whatever is nearby to use as weapons. Torches, tankards, chair legs and whole benches fly everywhere. Tholius himself picks up a huge wooden table and flings it at us before urging his men on towards the statue. Captain Rallee goes down under the impact. Gurd hauls him to his feet while I hold off two opponents with my knife and my sword. Everything is confused. I lose sight of both my opponents as a gaggle of monks flies in between us, screaming and cursing as they kick and punch each other senseless. I notice a young monk deflecting a sword thrust with his bare hands before delivering a neck-breaking blow to a Brotherhood man before himself falling to a sword thrust from behind. His companion screams in fury and leaps high over the sword then smashes his foot into the killer's face with such violence that his neck snaps like a twig.

Ixial the Seer and the Venerable Tresius struggle to close with each other, but are prevented by the mass of struggling bodies between them. Finally Tresius, who's seventy if he's a day, takes a jump from a standing position that any young athlete would be proud of. He rises, somersaults in the air while flying half the length of the tavern, brushes aside a few adversaries on the way down and finally stands directly opposite Ixial, at which Ixial smashes Tresius in the face, or tries to, but Tresius glides out the way. They then engage in spectacular combat, each master displaying to the full the fighting skills they've developed in a lifetime of study, but neither can get the upper hand.

Another table pounds down on top of us and this time it's my turn to get knocked to the floor. Gurd manages to deflect the thrust of a long spear just before it impales me. I leap up and set about defending myself, but the situation is fast becoming hopeless. There's only three of us and we are now beset by Tholius's men on one side and Casax's on the other while monks rage everywhere in between. All of us have taken wounds and the floor underneath us is slippery with blood. Bodies lie everywhere and we stumble over them as we're forced back against the huge lump of marble.

I remember that Astrath Triple Moon is still in the background somewhere and I wonder if he might be preparing some mighty spell to get us out of this. Probably not. I dragged him out of his house so quickly he didn't have time to place any spells in his memory. He'd need a grimoire to read in a new one. If he has any sense he'll have disappeared out the back door taking Soolanis and Dandelion with him. So we're relying on sword power only, and that's starting to flag. I'm using my blade to parry the opponents on my right, while desperately deflecting blows from the left with my knife. I hack down another of Tholius's men, but the next one presses in on me immediately. I can't keep this up for much longer.

"Face it, Thraxas, trying to fight with two blades you're as much use as a eunuch in a brothel," comes a voice in my ear.

I whirl round in astonishment. It's Makri, a sword in one hand and an axe in the other, and she's looking pretty damned healthy.

"What happened?"

"I got better."

"Well, you took your time. You expect me to fight the whole of Turai on my own?"

Makri grins broadly and starts laying about her with her axe and sword. Her gladiator battle skills clear a space round us, which is just as well. When Gurd sees her he is so surprised he cracks his head on the raised front hoof of Saint Quatinius's horse and takes several seconds to recover.

"Makri," he cries, clutching his head. "You're alive!"

"Sure am," she yells back, planting her sword precisely in the chest of a red-clad monk unwise enough to try and hit her with a quarter staff. Captain Rallee, Gurd and I are inspired by Makri's return. We bring the advancing horde in front of us to a halt and start pushing them back. Monks, gangsters and Guards fall before Makri's axe as she scythes them down like a demon from hell let loose in the world for the purpose of slaughtering humans.

I get the impression that her brush with death has not soothed her anger over the way the monk kicked her a while back. She fights with a savage fury never before seen in Turai. No wonder they used to throw dragons, tigers and whole squadrons of Orcs into the arena against her.

Fighting is intense all over the room as the monks struggle with each other. The Venerable Tresius and Ixial the Seer, evenly matched, have stopped trading blows and now circle each other watchfully. Finally Tholius steps between them, raising his hands and bellowing at the top of his voice. The Prefect, who is something of a demagogue and has plenty of experience in talking to howling mobs, manages to attract the attention of the people around him.

"Stop this useless fighting," he roars. "We are just making it easy for them." He points to us. "Remove them and we can then discuss the distribution of the gold in a sensible manner."

The remaining monks disengage from each other and turn their heads to where we stand in front of the statue. The Brotherhood men look questioningly at Casax. He nods as if in agreement with Tholius. Everyone seems to think that the Prefect has the right idea. Now, rather than fighting one of many battles in the tavern, we are faced with the prospect of a concentrated attack from everybody.

The entire assembly fans out to encircle us and starts to advance. We don't have a chance. In the limited space even Makri's amazing skills cannot stand up against such a weight of numbers attacking from every direction. Some of the swiftest monks are already scaling the statue to attack us from behind. Others take the opportunity to fling small throwing stars at us before engaging with our swords. None of us is wearing armour and both myself and Makri find ourselves with painful wounds as stars strike and dig into our limbs.

It's time for some swift thinking. I can do that.

"The magic space," I roar. "Everybody in!"

I jump on the statue's plinth, knocking off a monk who's scrambling down from above. Gurd and Rallee look dubious, but as the great Human wave starts to break over us they leap up beside me. I take the edge of the purse in my hand and climb into the purple void.

"I don't like this at all," says Gurd, as I draw the purse over our heads.

"I wanted to see what it was like in here," says Makri.

And then we are fully enveloped in the magic space, a dimension quite different from our own, where odd things happen, strange creatures live and Humans are really not meant to visit.

We plummet down through the thick purple atmosphere. Wispy clouds laugh at us as we pass. We land gently on a green grassy plain. A huge blue sun burns high above. Beside us is the statue, in all its glory, undamaged by my blows with a sledgehammer. Sitting on the bronze horse next to Saint Quatinius is Hanama, Master Assassin.

"Welcome to the magic space," she says.

"Hello, Hanama," says Makri. "What are you doing here?"

"I heard you were dead," replies Hanama. "I came to pay my respects but you turned out to be alive. Good. As things in the tavern seemed confused I slipped in here till it quietened down. I was not expecting you to join me."

I glare at her suspiciously. It's a bit much, finding

Hanama here before me. For all I know she might have been sitting in the magic space for days. I could've been carrying her round in my pocket.

"Came to pay your respects to Makri, did you? More like came looking for Ixial the Seer. I know you have a contract on him."

"The Assassins Guild does not discuss its affairs with outsiders," replies Hanama coolly.

She's a calm woman, Hanama. Difficult to rile. She's small, and very pale. Assassins often are. The only pale people in Turai, in fact, apart from some of our aristocratic ladies who make a point of staying out of the sun for reasons of fashion. Sitting on the horse, with her thin body and black cloak, she looks like a child at play. She certainly doesn't look dangerous, though she is number three in the Assassins Guild. This is the woman who's reputed to have killed a Senator, a Sorcerer and an Orc Lord in the same day.

I'm not at all pleased to encounter her again. I detest all Assassins for the cold-blooded killers they are. The fact that they continually escape the consequences of their murderous actions due to the patronage of Turai's rich politicians doesn't make it any better.

It was rash of her to enter the magic space, though. I wonder if she realises it's not an easy place to get out of.

"How are you alive, Makri?" asks Gurd, a question I was meaning to ask myself before I got distracted.

She shrugs. She just woke up with a stone on her chest and a crossbow bolt lying beside her. There isn't so much as a scar on her body. I remember I left the stone on her, which was just as well. It must have taken longer to work on her than it did on Ixial, which is not surprising I suppose, seeing as she was so far gone she didn't even register on Astrath's lifestone. Quite something, this mixture of blood, I muse. I'll never believe Makri's dead again unless I see her lowered into her grave, and maybe not even then.

"An amazing artefact, the dolphins' healing stone. I wonder if I have to give it back?"

"Of course you have to give it back. The dolphins hired you to work for them."

"No fee was agreed. If they offer me fish I'm turning it down."

Captain Rallee suggests that they might have some sunken treasure to pay me with although the general consensus is that the dolphins are lucky for Turai so I shouldn't even be thinking about trying to make money off them.

"And they healed me," Makri points out. "I feel great."

"You'd probably have recovered anyway, with a good night's sleep."

Makri inclines her head towards the heavens. "Nice blue sun up there. Hey, it just went green. So what else happens in the magic space?"

The marble figure of Saint Quatinius suddenly swivels towards Hanama.

"Get off my horse," he says.

"All sorts of thing happen," I sigh. "It's really not a good place to be."

Even Hanama, trained in every form of concealment, both physical and mental, can't hide her surprise at being ordered about by a statue. She leaps down nimbly from the marble horse and gazes up suspiciously at the saint. He's now gone quiet.

"Did he *really* speak?" demands Gurd, who's raised his axe nervously. As a Barbarian he has never been comfortable with any form of magic, and this is all very strange to him.

"Yes. All sorts of things speak here."

We look around at the continually changing colours of the landscape.

"Is this where you go when you eat the mushrooms Palax collects in the woods?" asks Makri.

This passes me by completely. I don't know anything about the mushrooms Palax collects in the woods.

"Well, now we're here, what's the next move?" wonders Captain Rallee, a practical man and not one to stand around admiring the view.

"Incidentally, is the purse still visible in the outside world?"

"Yes."

"And we're inside it?"

"Yes."

"Then what if someone picks it up and throws it in the fire?"

"Who'd do that? It has a golden statue inside it."

"Prefect Tholius might decide to forgo the golden statue if he can get rid of all the witnesses to his crimes."

I admit this is a troubling thought.

"Can you get us out of here in a hurry?"

Before I can reply a large pig walks by on two legs. It greets us politely. Gurd grips his axe and the pig notices this with displeasure.

"Oh! Going to chop me up, eh? That's a Human for you, chop up a pig without giving it a second thought. How would you like it if you were just going about your daily business and someone came along and chopped you up and ate you?"

"The Human race has been given dominion over the beasts of the field," says Saint Quatinius, from his horse.

"Well, not by me," replies the pig, and they start arguing.

I'm still on a high at finding Makri is alive but when

I reflect that I intended to spend the summer quietly sipping ale and resting in the shade, and instead I now find myself inside the magic space listening to a theological debate between a saint and a talking pig while outside half of Turai's killers are waiting for me with swords in their hands, I get a little depressed.

The pig disappears without warning as bodies start raining down from the sky. At first I think it's more magical creatures. As the crowd of bodies floats to the grass—now a bright shade of orange—I realise that Tholius, Casax and the monks have followed us into the magic space. The lust for gold has no boundaries. We raise our weapons wearily to do battle again.

Our adversaries come to ground looking confused and disorientated but it doesn't take long to get their bearings as Tresius, Ixial, Casax and Tholius marshal them into order.

"Kill them!" roars Tholius again.

At that moment the ground cracks open at our feet and a river emerges in a torrent, separating us from our pursuers. By the time they collect their wits they're looking at us across fifty feet of swiftly flowing water. I laugh. A very satisfying turn of events. I saunter down to the water's edge.

"Hi, Tholius," I call. "Fancy a swim?"

Tholius is nonplussed. Ixial the Seer is untroubled.

"The river will not remain for long."

"I wouldn't count on your powers of farseeing working in here, Ixial. The magic space is very distorting, even for a man like yourself. Congratulations on your recovery. Now your legs are better you'll be able to walk up to the scaffold. Incidentally, it was rash of you to follow us. Just shows you're far too keen on gold for your own good. Do any of you have any idea how to get out of the magic space?"

From the looks of uncertainty that flit over the

various faces on the other side of the river I can tell that is something they haven't considered. Our conversation is interrupted by a brief but heavy downpour of frogs.

"So, Tholius," I shout, as the last frog hops merrily away. "What's the plan?"

"Kill you," he roars back.

"Not such a bad plan, perhaps. Depends on your point of view. Another alternative would be to turn yourselves over to Captain Rallee here, and face the consequences of your illegal actions."

Tholius isn't so keen on this. He likes his own plan better. Despite their losses in the tavern, the Prefect and Casax still have plenty of armed men with them. So do Ixial the Seer and the Venerable Tresius, so they'll probably be able to carry out his wish if this river suddenly disappears. I maintain a confident front and continue to torment Tholius from the safety of our present position.

Captain Rallee scratches his head. It annoys me the way he doesn't have any grey in his hair. Mine is just as long but it is starting to look streaky. I still contend that my moustache is better than his and it always has been.

"Thraxas. Just in case we ever get out of this place alive. And just in case I don't throw you right in the slammer for having the King's gold in your possession, how about filling me in on some details? I only came to commiserate at the death of your friend. I wasn't prepared to meet half of the city's low-life and a bunch of mad monks fighting over stolen treasure else I'd have brought some men with me. I take it this is all connected to Drantaax's murder?"

"It sure is. It's a complicated affair. I'll simplify it for you. These two groups of monks are rivals. Ixial the Seer is head of the Star Temple and Tresius is head of the Cloud Temple. They fought, partly about religion but mainly about who was to be number one chariot. Living up in the mountains drives them mad, I reckon. You remember how hot it was when we held off the Niojans at the pass?"

"Never mind the Niojans at the pass. What happened with the monks?"

"They fought, mainly. And then they split in two. Both temples found themselves missing a statue. Which gave Ixial the Seer a very good idea. He'd steal the new statue Drantaax was making for Turai to put him one up on Tresius and probably make the Cloud Temple monks return to the Star Temple. And then Sarin the Merciless, who used to be Ixial's student in the martial arts, came to Ixial with an even better idea. She knew Prefect Tholius back when she was bringing dwa into the city. He was taking a pay-off to look the other way, which is standard behaviour for officials in this city, yourself excepted of course. Whether the idea was Tholius's or Sarin's I don't know, but it occurred to one of them that the gold shipments from the King's mines passed by not too far from Ixial's monastery.

"These shipments are a well-kept secret. The routes and timings are only ever discussed in magic-proof rooms lined with Red Elvish Cloth, but Prefect Tholius obviously has connections at the Palace and learned when the next one was due. He gave the details to Sarin, who passed them on to Ixial. So the Star Temple robbed the convoy, slaughtering the guards in the process.

"Then came their very good idea. Instead of disappearing into the hills with the gold where they'd have been tracked soon enough by Palace Sorcerers, they brought the gold straight to Turai and hid it inside the new statue. You realise how safe that was?"

"Yes," says the Captain, who is a smart guy. "No Sorcerer would check inside a statue of Saint Quatinius. It would be blasphemous."

"Right. The plan was to leave it there till the statue

was taken out to the shrine. When the heat died down Ixial would steal it from the shrine, cut it open and take out the loot. Once he put it back together he'd have a nice pile of gold as well as a new statue. I guess he wasn't too worried about blasphemy.

"Which is where things went wrong. The Venerable Tresius had a spy in the Star Temple and he discovered what was going on and ever since then he's been after the gold and the statue for himself. The Cloud Temple made a full-scale attack on the Star Temple during which Ixial was nearly killed. He had to come to the city to get healed. By now Tresius had learned the gold was in Turai and probably in Drantaax's statue. He arrived too late to intercept it so he hired me to find it. I didn't realise that Saint Quatinius was full of gold though I knew something strange was going on."

I gaze over the river. The monks are looking back at us. Do they believe they are furthering their religion with this behaviour? Probably, if Ixial and Tresius tell them they are. A flock of silver birds flies overhead, turning gold and then white in front of our eyes. Heavenly music floats down from the sky. Fluffy rabbits emerge to play around our feet. It's cutesy time in the magic space.

"What really went wrong for Ixial and Tholius was getting involved with Sarin the Merciless. As soon as the gold was inside the statue and Ixial was lying crippled in the mountains she decided that it would be much better if she didn't have to share it around too much.

"She's a clever woman, Sarin the Merciless. Totally heartless, but sharp as an Elf's ear nonetheless. She knew that Sorcerers from the Palace and the Abode of Justice were looking for the gold. Old Hasius the Brilliant himself had been down to Drantaax's house. She couldn't load the statue on a wagon and ride out of town. She'd have been spotted right away. So she hunted around for some way of getting the gold safely away. And she hit on the notion of a magic purse. Rare items indeed, but she knew where to find one, thanks to her dwa-dealing days. She remembered that old Thalius Green Eye, who wasn't much use for Sorcery any more, was taking dwa up to the Palace in a magic purse. So she went and killed him, and stole it. And then, I think, she stole the statue, leaving some yellow flower petals to put Investigators off the scent. The Cloud Temple wear yellow flowers for ceremonial reasons. I guess that was her idea of a joke.

"And then something unusual happened. Sarin must have some shred of humanity in her miserable being because when she heard Ixial was being brought to the city to die she went back to see him. Being his student for four years might have stirred some emotion in her breast. I saw her try to kill Tresius, so she must feel something for Ixial. Sarin doesn't normally kill for anyone else's benefit. So I figure she felt something for her old teacher. Not enough to prevent her robbing him though."

"I suppose if Ixial was going to die she wasn't really robbing him, to be fair," says Makri, interrupting.

I frown at her.

"All these logic and rhetoric classes are bad for you, Makri. You should stick to being savage. Sarin practically killed you a few hours ago. Anyway, she was too smart to carry the statue in the purse when she went to see Ixial. He is a seer and might have perceived she had the gold. So she left the purse with the two men she'd hired to help her get the statue into the purse, a job she couldn't manage on her own. You could pull the purse right down over it, but you'd still need help to tip the base up. She probably told her two accomplices to disappear for a day or two and then meet her.

"Unfortunately they washed up in the Avenging Axe, which wouldn't have been a bad place to lie low if one of them hadn't happened to be a man I put in prison a few years back who was still looking for revenge. They were killed in the fight, which only brought their deaths forward a few days, because Sarin would certainly have disposed of them when she was done with them.

"That put me right in the centre of things. Once Sarin learned where the men had been killed she knew I was involved and figured I'd probably ended up with the purse. She's been after me ever since. So have the Star Temple. Whether Sarin told Ixial some tale to explain why I had the statue, or whether his powers led him to it, I don't know. Which brought the yellow monks down on my tail as well, when their spies told them what was going on."

I look down at the rabbit nestling on my toes, then up at the great comet that is now shining in the sky.

"Yes, Captain, while the Civil Guard has floundered around helplessly with no idea where the gold was, and these people have been chasing around after it, I've recovered it for the King. So don't give me the outraged bit about withholding evidence. I've solved a case that was quite likely to get you busted down to Private when you made no progress with it."

I notice Tholius from the corner of my eye. He seems to be getting closer. Much closer.

"Damn it. Why did no one tell me the river was drying up?"

"We were all fascinated by your explanation," says Makri.

"This is no time for sarcasm."

"No, I mean it, really. I love it when you work these things out."

The river is now down to about ten feet wide and the monks are starting to wade over.

"Run," says the Captain.

We run. The sun might be green but it doesn't

prevent it from being as hot as Orcish hell in here. I'm soon sweating badly and panting for breath. If we can reach a forest of yellow trees we'll have some cover. I struggle to keep up with the pace. Abruptly the forest disappears. Just vanishes into thin air. Damn this magic space. I halt at the statue of Saint Quatinius.

"Attack the heretics!" I demand, pointing at the pursuing horde. The statue doesn't move. So much for that idea I reflect grimly, and carry on running.

A giant castle hoves into view in the distance.

"Make for the castle!" yells Captain Rallee.

We make for the castle. As we approach, it disappears.

"To hell with this," says Makri, unsheathing her sword and turning to face her opponents. "I'm not running any more."

"Please, Makri, not now."

Makri plants her feet firmly on the ground, her sword and her axe in her hands, waiting for our pursuers to reach us.

"Why can't you just run away like a normal person?" I demand

"It's dishonourable."

"Well how much honour was there in the Orc slave pits, for God's sake?"

"Not much. But I'm not running any more. That's that."

I sigh, and draw my sword. "Well, I'm too beat to run any further anyway. I never figured I'd be making my death stand under a green sun."

"It's turned purple."

"Or a purple one."

Unwilling to leave us to be hacked down alone, Captain Rallee and Gurd stop running and stand at our side.

"Getting too old to run," says Gurd, with a grin,

which makes me remember what a good, cheerful companion he was when we were mercenaries together.

"Me too," I tell him. "And too fat. Well, we've got out of worse scrapes than this."

"Sure we have. Remember the Niojan riverboat that thought we were crocodiles?"

We bellow with laughter at the memory. I doubt we're fooling anyone. Tholius and the rest are now very close. Having combined forces and concentrated their attack I wouldn't think it'll take them too long to dispatch us. We have no cover at all and even Makri's remarkable fighting skills can't prevent the monks from encircling us and sticking us full of throwing stars. Makri is wearing only her chainmail bikini. None of us are wearing armour. We'll take plenty of them with us, but they'll win in the end.

The talking pig makes another appearance at our side. "Attack the heretics," I suggest, without much hope.

"Sorry, I'm on holiday," says the pig, and vanishes.

"What a waste of time this place is," I say, angrily. "You think we might get a dragon flying down to protect us or something like that. But no, all we get is a pig that talks about theology and then goes on holiday."

I stop speaking rubbish for a second. Something has just occurred to me.

"Makri, I just realised who really killed Drantaax."

At that moment the Venerable Tresius lands in front of me, somehow deflects my sword with the flat of his hand, and kicks me several feet in the air. It hurts. I'm bracing myself for it to hurt more on the way down when a terrific gale whips me up and blows me into a tree that has appeared from nowhere. Trees sprout up everywhere and suddenly a storm of random acts of magic makes it impossible for anyone to come to blows with anyone else. Ferocious insects of weird colours appear to torment us while the wind blows great gusts of purple hailstones about our heads. I notice Hanama in an adjoining tree, calmly waiting. I wonder if Ixial knows there's a contract out on him.

Combat is reduced to farce by the intervening magical forces. The trees disappear but before anyone can think about fighting again a volcano begins to sprout from the ground.

Everyone starts to look nervous as we wonder whether the angry-looking volcano will vanish before it erupts. Smoke pours from the apex and lava is starting to trickle down its sides. The earth begins to shake.

Captain Rallee looks at the growing volcano, then at me.

"How do we get out of here?" he asks, a demand echoed by Prefect Tholius as the ground shakes and groans and lava begins to pour in torrents towards us. Casax is a fearless man and stands his ground, but his Brotherhood enforcers are starting to look nervous.

"A good question. And one which Prefect Tholius should have thought of before following us in here. Escaping from the magic space is no easy matter. How about you?" I call over to Ixial the Seer. "Any suggestions?"

The volcano starts to erupt.

"Get us out of here!" roars Tholius.

"Why should I? You'll only kill us when we're back in the tavern."

I turn to Casax.

"Not much point taking us all back to Twelve Seas if the Brotherhood starts coming round giving me a hard time, is there?"

Casax, still without fear, ponders for a second or two, then shrugs his shoulders.

"Probably not, Investigator. But I'm not too mad at you for this. We want the gold and I'm not giving up on it, but if you get us out of here I'll forget that you've been holding out on us."

Molten lava is now pouring from the volcano and rocks are starting to crash around our heads. Any second now there's going to be one almighty explosion and Thraxas, Private Investigator, will never be seen again in the state of Turai.

I call over to Tholius.

"How about you, Prefect? You willing to walk away from the Avenging Axe if I get us back?"

Tholius doesn't have as much backbone as Casax.

"Yes," he screams. "Get us out!"

"And as for you, Ixial and Tresius. You better just promise in the name of Saint Quatinius not to harm us when we return."

Ixial and Tresius nod. I catch a look in Rallee's eyes showing that he doesn't think much of all these vows. Neither do I, but I'll have to hope for the best. The volcano shows no sign of disappearing and you can die here the same as anywhere else. If I get us out of the magic space I'll have to take them all with me, though I'd be tempted to leave them if I could.

I turn to Makri.

"Where's Hanama?"

She doesn't know. The Assassin has slipped off somewhere. There is a deafening explosion as the top of the volcano blows off and rocks the size of houses start tumbling around us. Ash rains down from the sky. It's difficult to breathe.

"Get us out," scream a dozen voices.

"Okay. Just let me get a sandwich."

I dig around in my bag and bring out one of the sandwiches Tanrose made me for my day's investigation. After all the running around and fighting it's looking somewhat the worse for wear, but it would do for lunch if I was hungry.

Everyone stares at me incredulously.

"Thraxas, this is no time to be thinking about your stomach!" cries Captain Rallee furiously as the molten lava starts to singe our toes.

"He's mocking us!" snarls Tholius. "I'll kill him before the volcano gets me!"

Remaining calm I remove the top layer from the sandwich, revealing some or Tanrose's home-cured meat. I scrape a few grains of salt off the meat. The volcano erupts even more violently than before. A six-foot wall of lava surges over the rim and races towards us. Young monks scream and fall to their knees in prayer.

I drop the salt on the ground. There's an even louder bang and the whole world shakes itself apart in a fantastic earthquake. Abruptly the earthquake halts, the air shimmers, and the magic space starts to melt away. We find ourselves deafened but otherwise healthy, back in the Avenging Axe. The volcano is gone. No pigs lecture us. Gurd looks at me wonderingly.

"How—?"

"Salt. Complete anathema to the magic space. Destroys it. A little trick I learned on my travels abroad. The magic purse is no more. Only foreign bodies like us and the statue could survive. Everybody all right?"

The monks start picking themselves off the ground, dazed from their experiences but relieved to be alive. No one is looking too comfortable. When you are one second away from death at the hands of a massive volcanic explosion and then the next second back in a tavern in Twelve Seas, it takes a little time to adjust.

Prefect Tholius is one of the first to get his wits back. He checks that his ally Casax is still in one piece. Then, seeing that he still has a number of men in good health, he turns and points at me.

"Kill that man," he orders.

I'm getting sick of hearing that.

The monks hold back, unsure of whether to join in. And at that moment, as Gurd, Makri, Rallee and myself are wearily raising our weapons and thinking that really there must be some easier way to make a living, almost everyone in the tavern collapses to the ground and lies unconscious on the floor.

Makri and I find ourselves staring stupidly at a mass of assorted monks and gangsters apparently all having an afternoon sleep. The only other person still standing is Casax.

"What happened?"

"Are we still in the magic space?" demands Makri.

"You are back in the Avenging Axe," says Astrath Triple Moon, appearing from the top of the stairs. I notice he's helped himself to a flagon of ale.

"Well done, Thraxas. I was a bit worried when you all disappeared into the magic space. That's really not a place you should go. But I thought you'd probably emerge all right. Salt?"

I nod.

"I've been looking at your grimoire," continues the Sorcerer. "Rather out-of-date, but functional enough. I thought you might need a little help when you got back so I had the sleep spell in readiness."

He looks at Makri. "I see your spell protection charms are working well."

Makri and I both wear spell protection charms round our necks. They're made out of Red Elvish Cloth, which is immensely powerful, woven in with copper beads and wires and treated by Astrath. We acquired them a couple of months ago, fortunately, because a spell protection charm is vital to a man in my line of work. After I pawned my last one I was left an easy target for any malicious Sorcerer who came my way. Spell protections are rare items, and very expensive, and only the city's most important officials such as the

Consul are issued with them as a matter of right, which is why Captain Rallee now lies sleeping at my feet, along with Gurd and everyone else struck down by Astrath's spell.

"Poor Rallee. They ought to pay him better. Good thinking, Astrath."

Casax, an important man in the underworld, also has a spell protection charm so he's still awake, but I can tell he's at a loss for what to do next. I suggest to him he should leave before I summon the Guards and they start rounding up everyone connected with the King's gold. The gangster's face remains impassive but for once he has to admit defeat. Faced with myself, Makri and Astrath Triple Moon, he can't get to the statue, and even though he has influence in this city he won't want to be connected with the gold theft. That would have repercussions too strong even for the Brotherhood to escape.

He turns and leaves without saying a word. Now we just have to decide what to do with everyone before they start waking up. Makri suggests killing the ring-leaders while they're still sleeping. I admit it as a possibility but wonder if there is some less drastic way to make ourselves safe.

There is the slightest of sounds behind us as Hanama emerges from behind the statue. She wears a plain black necklace, the standard spell protection charm of the important Assassin. This Assassin has a great capacity for disappearing and reappearing when you don't expect it.

"I'm glad you're still alive," she says to Makri, calmly, and walks towards the door.

"Don't bother thanking me," I call to her.

"What for? I knew how to get out of the magic space. I took the precaution of taking salt with me."

Hanama appears to have been untroubled by the

whole affair. She's cool in a crisis, I have to grant her
that.

"Is that really the King's gold?" she says, pointing
to the statue.

I look at the statue and nod.

"It is."

"Well done," says Hanama. "Another crime solved
by your powers of investigation."

She disappears through the front door. I stare after
her suspiciously.

"That was odd."

"She paid you a compliment," says Makri.

"That's what's odd. Why? The Assassins Guild doesn't
waste its time on compliments. Well, never mind. What
are we going to do now? We have about ten minutes
until everyone wakes up. I really can't stand any more
running around getting chased by everyone. I'm sick
of it."

I am heartily sick of the whole affair. I started off
just wanting to clear poor Grosex. Look where it got
me. Next time a Prefect insults me I should think twice
about losing my temper. But I probably won't.

I have to do something quickly. Tholius will be down
on me like a bad spell when he wakes up. We could
be back where we started and now I've destroyed the
magic space there's nowhere to hide.

"You could leave the tavern before they wake,"
suggests Astrath Triple Moon. "I could shelter you."

I'm not so fond of this idea. I don't feel like hiding.

"I could put the sleep spell back in my mind and
send them to sleep again when they wake."

"True. But we'd be here all day. The Guards would
probably like a long talk with some of these people.
It's no use going to the harbour station though. Tholius
is in charge there and they'd just throw us in the
slammer and I doubt we'd ever get out. But we could

try Captain Rallee's station. Once his men hear he's in trouble they'll come."

"What about the statue?"

"Without the magic purse no one's going to be able to move it in a hurry."

It means leaving the sleeping Gurd behind, but he'll be safe enough with Astrath watching over things. They're not after Gurd anyway. Makri and I make to leave. I get a strange feeling as I walk past the slumbering figure of Ixial the Seer. A very strange feeling. I bend down to examine him.

"He's dead."

"Dead?"

A slim dart is buried in his chest, just deep enough to reach his heart. An Assassin's weapon. I shake my head.

"That's why Hanama asked us to look at the statue."

You have to admire the woman's skill. In the brief seconds I was distracted she threw a dart into Ixial's chest, killing him casually in passing. And no one could say they witnessed the event.

"No one escapes the Assassins Guild," I sigh. "Come on, let's get the Guards."

I know most of the Guards at the Captain's station though that doesn't mean I'm a frequent or welcome visitor. Captain Rallee bans them from giving me information. But when I march in and tell them that their Captain is at present lying asleep in the Avenging Axe, with the Brotherhood, Tholius and two temples' worth of warrior monks waiting to attack him, and, furthermore, the King's missing gold secreted nearby, the station empties quickly enough. I stop off on the way to send a message to Praetor Cicerius. If there's a reward paid out for the recovery of the gold I don't want my share shuffled aside for some grasping Civil Guard.

It takes twenty minutes to make the round trip.

When we get back the tavern has emptied entirely of opponents.

Astrath looks abashed. "Sorry, I didn't have another spell to stop them escaping."

Captain Rallee is still yawning. He glares angrily at Astrath Triple Moon for sending him to sleep though he admits there was nothing else he could do in the circumstances.

"You ought to get a spell protection charm, Captain."

"On my salary?"

He starts barking out orders, sending men to the Abode of Justice and the Palace with news of what's been going on.

"You think Prefect Tholius will stay and try and bluff it out with his connections?"

"Doubt it. He's blown it this time. His connections will never smooth over his stealing from the King. I expect he's packed a bag and fled the city by now. Same with the monks. Was the Brotherhood in on the theft?"

I shake my head. They were just trying to pick up whatever they could. There's probably no way of making anything stick to Casax, not with the amount of bribe money the Brotherhood can feed to a jury when it needs to. Anyway, I can't see any jury convicting him of pursuing an Investigator and a Guard Captain through the magic space with murderous intent. It was established long ago in Turanian legal circles that the city statutes do not apply to events in the magic space.

A couple of Guards are wrapping up Ixial's body prior to carting it away to the morgue. When he saw the dart in Ixial's heart Captain Rallee didn't have to be told what happened.

"Hanama? You see her do it?"

I shake my head. "She's too smart for that."

"I hate these killers," mutters the Captain. "I'd be happy to see them all swinging on the gallows."

He knows there's no chance of that. The Assassins Guild has too much protection because the Senate finds them very useful at times. So, it's rumoured, does the King. Besides which, they rarely leave any evidence of their acts behind them. If the Guards ask a Sorcerer to examine the dart it'll turn out to have been painted with fragments of Red Elvish Cloth, or spell protected, or manipulated in some other way known only to the Assassins to make it untraceable. Trying to convict Hanama of killing Ixial would be like trying to catch the breeze.

Rallee accepts a beer from Gurd. It's against the rules for Guards to drink on duty, but they don't pay too much notice to this sort of rule. The Captain is very pleased to have recovered the gold, but I can tell he's not happy.

"I expect you'll be wasting no time in going to the courts and presenting evidence to get Grosex cleared of the murder?"

The captain hates it when I put one over on the Guard.

I finish off my own beer. "I'm going up to see him right now."

Soolanis and Dandelion appear with Palax and Kaby. They've been hiding in the caravan out the back. Captain Rallee stares at them perceptively.

"Keep taking dwa and it'll kill you," he grunts.

"Or I will," I add.

Soolanis was bad enough as a drunk. If she gets into dwa she might as well sell her father's villa and move on to the street right away. It'll save time. And it takes Palax and Kaby enough time and effort to earn money busking, so I don't understand why they then want to spend it on some useless drug. Nothing would surprise me about Dandelion. I take the healing stone and hand it to her, but even this brings little expression into her vacant eyes.

"Take this to the dolphins when you get your energy back."

I ask Makri to come to the law courts with me.

"You think Sarin might still be around?"

I shake my head. Sarin will have learned by now that the gold statue is beyond her reach. She won't trouble us again.

"She might be looking for revenge now Ixial's been killed."

"I doubt it. I don't think her loyalty to her old teacher would go that far. Sarin is focused on her own needs. Anyway, it wasn't our fault Ixial handed in his toga. It was Tresius who hired the Assassins Guild. You know, I'm not sure if Sarin enjoys anything except killing. Makes me wonder what she wants gold for anyway. Probably wouldn't know how to enjoy it if she got it. I'll still kill her the next time we meet."

Makri intimates that Sarin won't need me to kill her if she meets her first. She goes upstairs to put on her tunic before hitting the streets.

"Nice shape," says Captain Rallee when she's gone.

"I guess."

"You guess? Twenty years ago you'd have been baying at the moon if she walked by in that bikini, Orc blood or not."

"Twenty years ago I wasn't old, overweight and full of beer."

I'm completely drained. Captain Rallee takes us up to the law courts in a Guard landus. It's a silent journey in the early-morning light. I guess I should be happy as a drunken mercenary after coming out on top against formidable odds, but all I really want to do is sleep.

We arrive at the law courts with an hour or so to spare before the final day of the case begins. The sun beats down. There hasn't been a breath of wind in the city for weeks. Stals flop lifelessly on the statues in the forum. Sweat runs down the inside of my tunic. I'm fed up with the heat. I'm fed up with being fed up with the heat. In his black uniform tunic, Rallee suffers as much as I do. I notice that the Guards and officials of the courts still treat him with respect. He might have been bounced out of the Palace by Rittius but they know the Captain is worth ten of him any day.

In the forum outside the courts people gather for the business of the day; everything from petty criminals heading for spells behind an oar to wealthy merchants from the Honourable Association of Merchants involved in complicated commercial law suits. There are even a couple of golden-haired and green-clad Elves, sitting beside the fountain with an advocate and his legal advisers, poring over some old scrolls.

"Got fleeced on a deal to ship a load of silver," the Captain informs us. "Why these Elves still expect Turanian merchants to be honest is beyond me."

Makri hails them in the royal language as she passes.

The Elves leap to their feet in alarm, assuming that some important Elf Lord has arrived unexpectedly in the city. When they realise who has greeted them they practically fall over in their confusion. Makri grins and strolls on.

"I really thought Grosex killed Drantaax," says Captain Rallee as he leads us down to the cells below the courts. "He's such a sad little guy I couldn't help feeling sorry for him, though not sorry enough to stop him from hanging. I have to hand it to you on this one, Thraxas."

A sad little guy is a fair description of Grosex when we reach him. It's the last day of his trial and he knows he's going to be found guilty and hanged in short order. When we walk into his cell he's slumped on his bunk. His face lights up with hope when he sees me.

"Thraxas! I thought you'd given up on me."

"I never give up on a client," I tell him. "And I don't often lose one either."

I pause, looking awkwardly around the cell. It's completely bare. There's nothing to focus my eyes on except Grosex.

"Although technically speaking, you're not my client. Prefect Tholius dragged you off before you could pay me my retainer and we never did get round to formalising the deal. Which is unfortunate."

"What do you mean?"

"If you were my client I might have to think some more about it. Because I'm pretty unlikely to turn over any client of mine to the courts. Goes against the grain. Even if my client turns out to be guilty, I'd rather send him out of the city on a fast horse than hand him over. But as you're not really my client, and you did in fact kill Drantaax . . ."

I hold out my hands, palm upwards.

A look of terror crosses Grosex's face. "I didn't!"

I'm tired. I feel bad doing this. I want to get it over with quickly.

"Sorry, Grosex. I've been everywhere with this one. I've involved myself with killers, monks, the Brotherhood and Lord knows who else. Makri nearly got killed and plenty of others were. When you start playing around with so much illegal gold it spirals out of control. You should have stayed out of it. You were always going to end up way over your head."

"Are you saying Grosex is guilty?" demands Captain Rallee.

"Yes, unfortunately. Drantaax knew nothing about the theft of the gold. There was no reason for him to. His business was doing well. He had no gambling debts or drink problems. That was just a story made up by Grosex to give the sculptor some motive for being involved. But it wasn't Drantaax who Ixial approached with the proposition for hiding the gold in the statue. It was Grosex."

I stare at the apprentice. He stares back helplessly, like a rabbit.

"Why did you do it?"

Poor Grosex seems unable to speak. Makri and Captain Rallee look on with interest.

"I don't really care why you did it. Maybe you just wanted money. Drantaax didn't pay you much. I've seen the room in Twelve Seas where you lived. Maybe Calia encouraged you. You wouldn't be the first apprentice led down the garden path by the mistress of the house eager to get her husband out of the way. But if she was involved I doubt she wanted you to kill Drantaax."

I turn to the Captain. "She went on holiday with Drantaax."

"What?"

"On holiday. When the gold was stolen. They were having a break from the heat in Ferias. But when

Grosex arrived in my office he told me he and Drantaax had been working on the statue round the clock for days. While Drantaax was away Grosex did the business with the gold. I didn't add it up properly till we were in the magic space and something reminded me."

I don't mention that it was the talking pig that reminded me.

"Like I say, Drantaax knew nothing about the gold. Grosex loaded it inside the statue when Drantaax was away. Ixial arranged it all with him. And when Sarin's men came to the workshop looking for it, Drantaax learned what was going on. He returned from an appointment early and interrupted them in the process of removing the statue. So Grosex killed him. Stuck his knife in him. Simple as that. Unluckily for Grosex, Calia arrived back and started screaming for the Guards before he could remove his knife. And then he realised that leaving a knife with his aura in it sticking in the body wasn't the brightest thing he could've done, so he fled. He didn't have the nerve to try and make it out the city gates, so he ended up at my office.

"Which is the only smart thing he did," I add, glumly. "I have a reputation in certain circles for getting men off in dubious circumstances."

And that's about as much explaining as I want to do. I turn to go, but Captain Rallee grabs my tunic.

"You mean you started all this for no reason, Thraxas? Grosex stuck a knife in Drantaax? That's what the Guards have been saying all along."

"Well, you've got to get one right sometime."

"So thanks for dragging us all through the magic space and damn near getting us killed."

"I recovered the gold, didn't I?"

Captain Rallee isn't too pleased at all this. "I'll remember your words about sending your guilty clients on a fast horse out of town," he says acidly. "Try doing that again and I'll be down on you like a bad spell."

I walk out quickly, not wanting to catch Grosex's eye. I'm so keen to get out of the building I'm practically running when I get to the exit. By the time Makri catches up I'm well on my way to the nearest tavern.

"Don't feel bad," she says, and takes a beer to keep me company. "It's not your fault your client turned out to be guilty."

"It still makes me feel bad."

"If he'd paid you a retainer, would you really have got him out the city?"

"Maybe. I never like turning a client in. Bad for business. But Grosex deserves it. It was pretty cold-blooded of him to murder Drantaax. The sculptor might not have paid him too well, but he didn't do anything to deserve being killed."

I down my beer and order another. With the heat and the exhaustion and all my exertions leading to this sad denouement, I'm not in the best of moods. I'm annoyed at Grosex and I'm furious at myself for being taken in by his sad demeanour. I'm humiliated at the thought of Captain Rallee telling his cronies in the Guards that they were right all along and that old Thraxas must be losing his grip.

Furthermore Captain Rallee is now annoyed at me and he's in a position to make my life awkward. The Brotherhood are none too pleased with me either. They certainly suckered me with Quen. It was a smart move for Casax to put a spy on me. I imagine the Boar's Head just burned down by accident and Casax immediately saw his chance to get someone into the Avenging Axe. Quick thinking on his part. I could take it as a compliment that the moment he heard about the gold and the monks he reckoned that I might well be the man to find it. What I mainly feel is stupid for not suspecting anything. All that time the Brotherhood and their tame Sorcerer were wandering around pretending to be looking for Quen, they were really looking for the gold. Only the fact that Astrath had put a bafflement spell on the place kept them at bay, I suppose, till I took it into my head to expose the gold right under Quen's nose. That makes me feel annoyed at Makri. She offered Quen shelter when she pretended to be on the run. I'm about to vent some of my anger on her, when I remember I'm pleased she isn't dead. I probably should mention that.

"I'm pleased you're not dead," I tell her.

"Thanks. You don't sound too pleased."

"I am. But it was pretty dumb of you to bring a Brotherhood spy into the house."

"I didn't know Quen was a spy."

I inform Makri shortly that she's bound to get us into trouble if she insists on bringing in every waif who's looking for sanctuary.

"Not as much trouble as you taking on clients who are guilty of murder," retorts Makri angrily. "You didn't even have to take him on. You just got annoyed because Tholius offended your precious dignity."

"My precious dignity? I'm fed up with your stupid fixation with your own honour. You could have got us killed in the magic space just because you refused to run away from overwhelming odds. Good fighters know when to retreat."

"You don't have to tell me anything about good fighting," says Makri. "If I didn't spend half my life doing some good fighting at your side you'd be dead and buried by now."

"Is that right?" I demand, banging my fist on the bar. "You think just because you could beat a few Orc gladiators you're number one chariot? I was street fighting before you were born."

Makri is now irate. The heat has affected her as well. Customers edge away from us, wondering if swords are going to be drawn.

"Then maybe at your age you should be thinking about retiring," says Makri. "Concentrate on your drinking."

"Well, I like that. Next time someone fires a crossbow bolt into you don't expect me to save your life."

"If you hadn't bundled into me in the first place I'd have avoided it and there wouldn't have been any lifesaving to do."

Makri and I are now standing toe to toe, glaring into each other's eyes.

"Oh yes?" I roar. "It wasn't me bundling into you that made you get hit. It was taking dwa that slowed down your reactions!"

"I have not been taking dwa!" shouts Makri.

"Oh no? I saw you stumble when we met in Quintessence Street. How much time did you spend in Kaby's caravan with Dandelion and Soolanis?"

Makri is livid. The drinkers who had edged away now clear a wide circle around us.

"You fat drunk!" she yells.

"Don't call me fat, you pointy-eared dwa addict!" I yell back.

"How dare you say that!"

"Did I hurt your feelings? Why don't you go and tell your friend Hanama about it? She's always looking for some information."

For a second Makri looks as if she really is about to draw her sword. Instead she slams her leather tankard down on the bar so hard the handle snaps off, then storms out the tavern.

I yell some more abuse after her.

"Another beer," I say to the barman. For an instant he looks like he's about to ask me to leave the tavern but on seeing my face he thinks better of it and brings me a drink.

I'm about as angry as a wounded dragon. I can't stand it that Grosex turned out to be guilty after I decided he wasn't. I feel a little better for having someone to yell at. I finish my beer and get another. After that I get another. Then I get bored with the company I'm in so I make with a few insults about lawyers and head east to the Kushni quarter where I get spectacularly drunk with three mercenaries from Misan and a professional dice player from the far west and manage to forget what it is I'm so mad about.

I wake up under a bush. Some time during the night I've crawled into a small park and fallen asleep. At least I kept enough wits about me not to lie down in the gutter.

I stink of beer, sweat and various nameless things picked up from the streets. While I've been chasing monks around the city I've forgotten to wash. If I don't visit the Twelve Seas baths soon they'll be dragging me away as a health risk. A few beggars look at me vacantly as I haul myself to my feet. I quickly check my purse. It's still there. I bid them a cheery good morning and start walking back to Twelve Seas.

I'm feeling in reasonably good form, all things considered. No hangover. I've noticed before that a lesada leaf seems to keep them away for a few days. I ought to sail down south and bring back a shipload. Make my fortune with them in this city. I'm less unhappy with life. So Grosex is going to hang. Hardly my fault. And if the Guards and the Brotherhood are on my tail, then so be it. I've managed this far with precious few allies in Turai. I guess I can struggle on now.

So it's in fairly optimistic mood that I head back towards the Avenging Axe. Nothing like a night getting disgustingly drunk with some mercenaries to clear the system. Their leader was the size of an ox and dumb as an Orc but he was liberal with his money and very willing to buy a man a beer once he learned I was an old soldier with plenty of fighting experience. I remember a joke one of the others told about two Niojan whores and an Elf Lord and laugh out loud.

I find myself passing through Pashish. When I turn into the Road of Angels, a narrow street with tall tenements on either side, I remember that this was the address where Tresius told me he was staying while in Turai. Hardly salubrious, but good enough for a monk I suppose. Up in the mountains they're used to worse.

I wonder if Tresius is still in the city, and whether or not I should call in. He does owe me money, now I think about it. I found the statue. Things didn't go the way he planned, but that's not my fault. I realise there's little chance of him actually paying me anything but it will give me the opportunity to let him know what I think of people who come and tell me lies. And then hire Assassins to mop up the mess.

The tenement is not as bad as many in Turai but, with its crumbling grey stone and shaky timbers bleached by the sun, it's not the sort of place I'd like to live. Children have scratched their names into the stone and the front door hangs loose. Like every other front door in Turai, it's painted white but from the look of the building I doubt it's brought the tenants much luck. I push it open. Inside the torches are out and the staircase is dark. I walk up. Tresius told me he was living at the top. When I get to the topmost landing, it's so dark I can't see a thing. I'm fumbling around for a door when I walk right into it. There's a curse as it swings open into someone inside, then the noise of a person falling heavily to the ground. I'm in through the door in an instant, my sword drawn. I recognised that curse.

Just inside, struggling to her feet, is Sarin the Merciless. I place my sword point at her throat as an encouragement for her to stay where she is. Light from the room beyond filters into the corridor, and I glare down at Sarin. She glowers back up at me. Out of the corner of my eye I see something yellow. I risk a glance. Looks like a bundle of cloth, half in and half out of the room.

"The Venerable Tresius, I presume?"

Sarin doesn't reply. I warn her not to move.

"I'll be pleased of the chance to stick this through your neck."

"So why don't you?"

I don't know, really. I take another look at the yellow-clad body. "The gold's long gone. Why did you kill him?"

"He hired the Assassins to kill Ixial."

"So? What do you care?"

Sarin doesn't reply. If it was anyone else I'd understand readily enough. You can't let your teacher be killed and do nothing about it, not if you've spent years in the mountains under his tuition. I just never figured Sarin to have any emotion. Then again, she did go back to visit him when he was dying.

"So you've avenged Ixial. And yet you were quite prepared to cut him out of the deal with the gold. You were heading out of the city with it yourself."

"Of course."

"You really are as cold as an Orc's heart, Sarin."

I wonder what to do. Good fortune has arranged things so that the woman I swore to kill only yesterday is at my mercy. I just blundered in and knocked her over. And she has apparently just murdered Tresius, my client. Not much of a client though. I don't feel

too much like avenging Tresius. But there is the matter
of Soolanis. I told her I'd track down the killer of her
father.

"And here you are. I might not be able to prove to
the Guards you killed Thalius but his daughter will
probably be satisfied when I tell her the murderer is
dead."

I press the tip of my sword a little closer to her
throat. Sarin gazes up at me with contempt. She seems
incapable of showing fear. Maybe she's incapable of
feeling it. It would seem so, for even though she's lying
helpless on the ground, a fraction of an inch from
death, she has no qualms about insulting me.

"Thraxas, you are a bungling fool. Why anyone
would want you to investigate anything is beyond me.
I didn't kill Thalius. Not that I wouldn't have had it
been necessary. No one would miss him apart from
that drink-sodden daughter of his. But there was no
need to kill him. I merely stole his magic purse when
he was unconscious with dwa. I knew where he kept
it hidden and it was a simple matter. But since learning about the plans of the Star Temple, the Cloud
Temple followed me around the city. I imagine that
the Venerable Tresius killed Thalius Green Eye later
the same night."

"You expect me to believe that?"

"I don't care if you believe it or not. But if you take
a look in his robe you'll find something interesting."

I keep my sword at Sarin's throat. Again I wonder why this killer, in her plain man's tunic and
cropped hair, wears so many earrings. It seems
inappropriate somehow. I use my toe to prise the
yellow robe away from Tresius's chest. A bag tumbles
out, flat but long and curved to the shape of the
monk's chest. I stretch down carefully and examine
it. It's full of white powder.

"Dwa?"

"That's right. Didn't you notice your client was a dwa addict?"

"Not with the way he was leaping round and fighting, no."

"Well, he was. Which is why Ixial took over the monastery and threw Tresius out. And why Tresius couldn't resist robbing old Thalius of his supply when he followed me there, killing him in the process."

I stare down at Sarin. She's such a ruthless killer with such a total lack of remorse for her actions that it seems unlikely to me that she'd bother lying about them. But I don't like the ramifications of this at all. Yesterday I had three clients. Today one of them is going to be hanged and another of them turns out to have killed the third one's father. The curse of Thraxas. If word gets out, my business will suffer a hell of a slump. At least it throws some light on Sarin's actions.

"You knew Tresius had a load of dwa. Easy to sell. Make up for missing out on the gold. No doubt that's why you killed him, rather than to avenge Ixial."

"The two things happily coincided."

What a mess. Dwa, gold, warrior monks and Sarin the Merciless. I'll probably never sort it out entirely. Sarin is waiting for an opportunity to get out from under my sword but I'm careful not to give her one.

"You almost killed Makri."

"The bolt was meant for you. It would have killed you if your personal protection charm hadn't deflected it."

I don't tell her that I don't carry a personal protection charm and only avoided the bolt by luck. Sarin stares up from the ground at me defiantly. I think I catch a slight trace of mockery in her eyes. She knows I'm not going to kill her in cold blood. I can't. I'm sick of it all. I sheath my sword. Sarin springs nimbly to her feet.

"You are a fool," she says.

"So I'm told."

"If you get in my way again I'll kill you."

"People often tell me that as well."

"Is Makri dead?" asks Sarin.

"No."

She might even be pleased to hear this. It's hard to tell. She picks up her crossbow. Then she picks up the dwa.

"Thanks to you, Investigator, I'm not going to be rich on the King's gold. This'll do for now."

I make no attempt to prevent her. She slips through the door and disappears.

I glance at Tresius's body. "Did you really kill Thalius?" I demand, but there is of course no reply. "It was a bad idea to hire the Assassins to kill Ixial," I continue, talking to the corpse. "It's always a bad idea to hire the Assassins. They kill your enemy but it never stops there. Someone is always left wanting revenge."

A crossbow bolt is buried deep in his chest. Despite this his aged face is serene in death. I wonder if I should search the place. I decide not to. Let someone else sort it out.

My optimism has vanished. Dead Body Thraxas strikes again. It seems I can't move in this city without finding a corpse. It wouldn't be so bad if they weren't all people I was involved with in one way or another. Grosex will hang soon. Ixial and Tresius are dead. Tresius killed Soolanis's father, more likely than not. I sigh, and head on home. It's hot as Orcish hell. Why did anyone ever build a city here anyway? A beggar holds out a withered arm. I drop a small coin in it. I send an anonymous note at a Messengers Guild post, informing Captain Rallee about the whereabouts of Tresius's corpse

I probably should've killed Sarin when I had the

chance. Now I'll run up against her in some other case and in all probability she'll put a crossbow bolt into my belly. I grin wryly. At least she still thinks I carry a personal protection charm. Everybody thinks that. After all, I am a sorcerous Investigator, or meant to be. But I don't have the energy to carry that spell around in my mind all day any more.

I couldn't just kill her though. Not in cold blood, just sticking my sword through her throat. I've seen enough corpses these past few days.

I call in at the baths and clean myself up, then struggle past the building works in Quintessence Street. Stonemasons curse their apprentices as they strain to winch the heavy blocks up the scaffolding, and foremen yell angrily at carpenters and plumbers as they struggle with their work in the heat. It's a relief to get home.

Makri is cleaning the tables.

"Hey, Makri, did you hear the one about the Elf Lord and the two Niojan whores?"

Makri glares at me with loathing and stalks off angrily.

Damn. I'd forgotten about the argument. It comes back in a sudden rush. Did I really call her a pointy-eared dwa addict? I sigh. Now I won't even be able to have a beer in peace to get me over my woes.

Dandelion appears. The one person I don't want to see.

She smiles at me very sweetly and hands me a small purse made of cheap cloth. She's embroidered my name on it.

"It's from the dolphins," she explains. "Well, the purse is from me, but what's inside is from the dolphins. It's to say thank you for recovering their healing stone."

I open the purse. Inside are five antique gold coins tarnished from a long spell under water and a small green jewel. I remove one of the coins. It's a King Ferzius. You don't see many of them round these days, particularly in Twelve Seas. It's worth about fifty gurans. Five of them. Two hundred and fifty gurans. That's a good rate of pay in my line of work. My standard retainer is only thirty. A jewel as well. I'll get it valued by Priso at the pawnbroker's.

"Thank the dolphins for me," I tell Dandelion. "Tell them it's a generous payment."

"I knew you were the right man to help them," says Dandelion. She witters on about how I have some star lines in sympathetic alignment with the dolphins. I'm too drained to insult her so I just take my leave politely and head upstairs to my room, where I sit at my desk and stare into space. I realise I'm hungry. I need some of Tanrose's stew. If I go downstairs Makri will probably skewer me with her mop. I think it's time for her rhetoric class. I decide to risk it.

Tanrose ladles me a goodly portion of stew and a plate of pancakes to mop it up, but she gives me a funny look when I'm picking out four or five pastries to finish the meal.

"Makri is upset."

"I noticed."

"Why did you accuse her of being a dwa addict?"

"I was in a bad mood."

This seems to me like an entirely adequate explanation but Tanrose doesn't think so.

"No wonder she was insulted. And as for accusing her of passing information to the Assassins Guild! You know how loyal Makri is."

I raise my hands helplessly. "I didn't accuse her of passing on information. I merely insinuated it. It was in the heat of the moment. I'd just sent a client off to the gallows. What did she expect me to do—stand around cheering? Anyway, she insulted me plenty."

"Well, you're all grown-up, Thraxas," says Tanrose. "And you know half the people in Turai. There's plenty of places you can go to forget your troubles. I figure you can stand a few insults. Makri's young and she's still a stranger and she has plenty of aggravation about her Orc blood. She probably relies on you."

"Relies on me? What about all those rich ladies in the Association of Gentlewomen."

"I doubt she could count them as friends."

"Fine. So now I'm feeling guilty as well. What do you suggest I do?"

"Take her some flowers," says Tanrose immediately.

I scoff at this. "Tanrose, you place far too much belief in the healing power of a bunch of flowers. I admit that the last time Makri was upset it worked like a charm but that was strictly a one-off."

I had accidentally put her to sleep with a spell causing her to collapse in front of an opponent and naturally a woman as keen on fighting as Makri was enormously upset by this. So I followed Tanrose's suggestion and, to my amazement, Makri, on receipt of one not very large bunch of flowers, threw her arms round me, burst into tears and ran out of the room, actions which Tanrose later interpreted as meaning everything was okay. But that was only because no one had ever given her flowers before. She's not dumb enough to fall for it twice.

"Try it," says Tanrose.

I sigh. If Tanrose can't come up with anything better than that then the situation is probably hopeless.

Makri bursts through the front door.

"Great rhetoric class," she exclaims to the cook, then sees me at the bar. She walks past muttering about needing to air the place to get rid of the bad smell.

"To hell with this," I grunt, and storm out the front entrance, none too pleased at the task in front of me.

Baxos the flower seller has plied his trade on the corner of Quintessence Street for thirty years without benefit of custom from me. When I rolled up a few months ago looking for flowers for Makri, it practically caused a riot. This time it's just as bad.

"Hey, Rox," he calls over to the fish vendor. "Thraxas is buying flowers again."

"Still got his lady friend, has he?" yells back Rox, loud enough for the entire street to hear.

"That's the way to do it, Thraxas!" screams Birix, one of Twelve Seas' busiest prostitutes.

"He's a real gentleman!" screams her companion, to the amusement of the workers atop the nearest building, who start adding a few ripe comments of their own.

I hurry home. I know this isn't going to work again. I will have some harsh words for Tanrose when Makri tries to stuff the flowers down my throat. I storm into the Avenging Axe where Makri is telling Tanrose about her class. I ram the flowers into her hand without saying anything and march around the bar where I bang my fist on the counter and shout for a beer and a large glass of klee. As an apology I admit it lacks a certain grace.

Almost immediately I am tapped on the shoulder. It's Makri. She embraces me, bursts into tears, then runs out of the room. Remembering events last time I'm fairly sure this is a good sign, but I check with Tanrose just in case.

"Does that mean it's all right now?"

"Of course."

It all seems very strange to me.

"You know, Tanrose, I find this very peculiar. What the hell is so great about a bunch of flowers?"

"Lots of things, if you spent a large chunk of your life in an Orcish gladiator slave pit. Not many flowers there, I imagine. Makri's probably never been given a present before."

I suppose not.

"You think it would've worked with my wife?"

"It certainly wouldn't have hurt. Didn't you ever give her flowers?"

"Of course not. I didn't know I was supposed to. I wish I'd known you when I was younger, Tanrose. Might have made everything a lot easier."

I take my beer and a fresh portion of stew and slump at my favourite table, wondering about the mysterious ways of women. I reckon it's not really my fault I was never any good with them. They never taught us anything about the subject at Sorcerer's school.

Things return to normal, which is to say it carries on being hot. The street outside is full of building workers and I abandon all thoughts of work for the rest of the summer. *The Renowned and Truthful Chronicle of All the World's Events* carries story after story about the affair of the gold-filled statue and I get treated generously enough in the coverage, which is always good for business.

I manage to grab a piece of the reward for the recovery of the King's gold, though it's far from my fair share. By the time the Guards, lawyers, Praetor's clerks and sundry other city officials have taken their cut, there's not much left for the man who actually located it. I have to make a strong plea to Deputy Consul Cicerius to get even that.

We're sitting in the back yard where Palax and Kaby are playing a flute and a mandolin. The tavern has now emptied of visitors. Dandelion has gone back to live on the beach and Soolanis has returned to Thamlin, drinking less and organising a rich persons' branch of the Association of Gentlewomen, according to Makri.

"Was it Ixial or Tresius who started the whole thing off?"

"I don't really know. Once it was all over it was hard to say. Hard to say who did what, or who was worse. When I started off as an Investigator I thought every case would have a crime at the beginning and a solution at the end, but often it doesn't seem to be like that. Just a bunch of people going around, all behaving worse than each other, so in the end even they don't know exactly who did what. Still, I'd say they all got what was coming to them, especially Grosex."

He was hanged last week. I didn't bother attending. Calia is back in Pashish, missing Ixial more than Drantaax, I expect. At least she has Drantaax's valuable statues to see her through her old age.

"You know, I didn't even get paid by any of these people? Apart from the dolphins, of course. All that chasing round in the magic space and risking death at the hands of Sarin the Merciless for no remuneration. I must be slipping. I'll never get out of Twelve Seas at this rate."

"This'll help," says Makri, taking something out of the purse round her neck. It's a golden finger. "I broke it off the statue when we came back from the magic space," she explains. "I thought we were due some sort of reward. I'll halve it with you."

"Smart thinking."

I look at the golden finger. Half of that will make a nice packet of gurans. I'm not doing so badly really. A few nice cases over the winter, maybe some lucrative work from the Transport Guild or even the Honourable Association of Merchants, and I might yet make it out of Twelve Seas. If summer here is hell, winter's not much better. And in the Hot Rainy Season, which comes up in about a month, the streets turn to rivers and beggars drown in front of your e͟͟ can hardly bear to think about it.

I don't have to think about it right now. I pick up a "Happy Guildsman" jumbo-sized tankard of ale from the bar and lie back in the shade. Listening to Palax and Kaby playing music, I forget all about monks, killers and gangsters, and go to sleep.